RENDEZVOUS – SOUTH ATLANTIC

Douglas Reeman's reputation as a front-rank writer of sea stories is now secure. He has been hailed as 'a born storyteller' (*Sunday Telegraph*) and as 'a master in whose hands British naval fiction is safe' (*Chicago Tribune*). *Rendezvous – South Atlantic* has all the qualities that have won him acclaim: forceful narrative, convincing characters, and strongly drawn backgrounds.

Also in Arrow by Douglas Reeman

Douglas Reeman

RENDEZVOUS –
SOUTH ATLANTIC

ARROW BOOKS

Arrow Books Limited
3 Fitzroy Square, London W1

An imprint of the Hutchinson Publishing Group

London Melbourne Sydney Auckland
Wellington Johannesburg and agencies
throughout the world

First published by Hutchinson & Co (*Publishers*) Ltd
Arrow edition 1974
Second impression September 1974
This edition 1976
© Douglas Reeman 1972

Made and printed in Great Britain
by The Anchor Press Ltd
Tiptree, Essex

ISBN 0 09 907820 1

To the armed merchant cruisers Rawalpindi, Jervis Bay, Laurentic, Dunvegan Castle *and to all those other proud ships which sailed in peace but went to war when they were most needed*

*I am the tomb of one shipwrecked;
but sail thou: for even while we
perished, the other ships sailed
on across the sea.*
From The Greek Anthology

Contents

1 Scapa

The camouflaged Humber staff car ground to a halt, its front bumper within feet of the jetty's edge, and stood vibrating noisily as if eager to be off again.

The small Wren driver, muffled to the ears against the intense cold, made to switch off the windscreen wipers, saying, 'Well, here you are, sir. There'll be a boat across at any minute.'

She turned slightly as the car's only passenger said, 'Don't switch them off. Not yet.'

Oblivious to her curious stare, Commander Andrew Lindsay leaned forward to peer through the rain-slashed glass, his face outwardly devoid of expression.

Grey. Everything was grey. The misty outline of the islands, the sky, and the varied shapes of the ships as they tugged at their cables in the wind and rain. The waters of the great natural anchorage of Scapa Flow were the deeper colour of lead, the only life being that of swirling tide-race and the turbulent undertow.

Scapa. That one word was enough. To thousands of sailors in two world wars it spoke volumes. Damp and cold. Raging gales and seas so fierce as to need every ounce of skill to fight clear of rocks and surrounding islets.

As his eyes moved slowly across the anchored ships he wondered what his new command would be like. You could never tell, in spite of your orders, your searching through manuals and intelligence reports. Even at the naval headquarters in Kirkwall they had been unhelpful.

H.M.S. *Benbecula*, an armed merchant cruiser, had been fitting out for six months, and now lay awaiting her new captain. On the stormy crossing by way of the Pentland Firth from the Scottish mainland he had seen about a dozen young seamen watching him, their inexperienced eyes filled with what—curiosity, hope or, like himself, resignation? One thing was certain, they had all been as green as grass. In more ways than one, for within minutes of casting off most of them had been violently seasick.

And this was only September. The second September of the war.

The Wren driver studied his profile and wondered. Her passenger was about thirty-three or four. When she had picked him up by the H.Q. building she had seen him staring moodily at the glistening street and had sensed a sudden throb of interest. And that was unusual in Scapa. The Wrens were vastly outnumbered by the male services, and it had become hard to raise much excitement over one more newcomer. Yet there was something different about this one, she decided. He had fair hair, longer than usual for a regular officer, and his blue eyes were level and extremely grave. As if he were grappling with some constant problem. Trying to come to a decision. As he was at the moment as he stared over this hateful view. He had that latent touch of recklessness about him which was appealing to her, but at the same time seemed withdrawn. Even lost.

He said quietly, 'You can switch them off now. Thank you.'

Lindsay settled down in the seat, pulling his greatcoat collar about his ears. Grey and cold. Greedy and impatient to test him again.

He knew the girl was watching him and wondered idly what she was like under all those shapeless clothes and scarves. In her twenties probably, like most of the Wrens he had seen in the warm rooms of the H.Q. building. He smiled grimly. In her twenties. He had entered the navy as a twelve-year-old cadet in 1920. Twenty-one years ago. All that time without a break. Working and studying. Travelling and learning his trade. His smile vanished. Just for this. Command of some clapped-out merchant ship, which because of a few guns and a naval crew was classed as a warship. An armed merchant cruiser. Even the title sounded crazy.

'I think I can see a motor boat coming, sir.'

He started. Caught off guard. All at once he felt the returning anxiety and uncertainty. If only he was going back to sea in a destroyer again. Any destroyer would do, even one like the old *Vengeur*. But he must stop thinking like that. *Vengeur* was gone. Lying on the sea-bed in mid-Atlantic.

He saw the distant shape of the motor boat, her blurred outline scurrying above the white moustache of her bow wave. Soon now.

Warily he let his mind return to his last command, like a man touching a newly healed wound. He had been given her just two days after the outbreak of war. She had been old, a veteran V & W class destroyer built in the First World War, and yet he had come to love and respect her quaint ways and whims.

As the first nervous thrusts by friend and foe alike gave way to swift savagery, Lindsay, like most of his contemporaries, had had to start learning all over again. Theories on tactics became myths overnight. The firm belief that nothing could break the Navy's control of the seas was stretched to and beyond the limit of even the most optimistic. Around them the world went mad. Dunkirk, the collapse of Norway and the Low Countries, the French surrender with the subsequent loss of their fleet's support, piled one burden upon another. In the Navy the nearness of disaster and loss was more personal. Right here, within sighting distance of this quivering car, the battleship *Royal Oak* had been sunk at anchor by a

U-boat. The defences were supposed to be impregnable. That was what they always said.

And just six months ago, while he had been in hospital, the battle-cruiser *Hood* had been destroyed by the mighty German *Bismarck.* The Navy had been stunned. It was not just because a powerful unit had been sunk. In war you had to accept losses. But the *Hood* had been different. She had been more than just a ship. She had been a symbol. Huge, beautiful and arrogant, she had cruised the world between the wars, showed the flag in dozens of foreign ports, lain at anchor at reviews ablaze in coloured lights and bedecked with bunting to the delight of old and young alike. To the public at large she *was* the Royal Navy. Unreachable, a sure shield. Everything.

In a blizzard, just one shell had been enough to blast her to oblivion. From the hundreds of men who served her, only three had been found alive.

Perhaps his own *Vengeur* had been closer to reality, he thought vaguely. Old but well-tried and strongly built. She had served her company well, even at the last.

He could remember the moment exactly. As if it were yesterday. Or now.

His had been the senior ship of the escort to a west-bound convoy for the United States. Twenty ships, desperately needed to bring back the stores and needs of a nation alone and at war.

Two merchantmen had been torpedoed and sunk in the first three days, but after that it seemed as if the Atlantic was going to favour them. A great gale had got up, and for day after day the battered convoy had driven steadily westward, with *Vengeur* always hurrying up and down the straggling lines of ships, urging and pleading, threatening and encouraging. The rest of the escort had consisted of two converted trawlers and a patrol vessel which had been laid down in 1915.

It was all that the greatest navy in the world had to spare, so they had made the best of it.

Perhaps the invisible U-boats ran deep to avoid the storm and so lost the convoy, or maybe they went searching for easier targets. They would have had little difficulty.

But one U-boat commander had been more persistent and had managed to keep up with the ragged lines of merchantmen. He must have been trying for the most valuable ship in the convoy, a big, modern tanker which with luck would bring back enough fuel to carry the bombers across Germany and show *them* what it was like.

The wind had eased, and the sky had been clearer than for many days. It had almost been time to rendezvous with the American patrol vessels, an arrangement which made a lie to their neutrality, but one which was more than welcome to merchantmen and escorts alike.

There were three torpedoes, all of which missed the tanker by a narrow margin. But one hit the elderly *Vengeur* on the port side of her forecastle, shearing off her bows like a giant axe.

The ship's company had mercifully been at action stations at the time of the explosion, otherwise the watch below would have died or been drowned later when the forepart tore adrift.

As it was, the ship went down in fifteen minutes, with dignity. Or as the coxswain had said later, 'Like the bleedin' lady she was.'

Only five men had been lost, and all the remainder had been picked up from the boats and rafts by a Swedish freighter which had been an unwilling spectator to the sinking.

Lindsay dug his hands into his greatcoat pockets and clenched them into fists. Just one more sinking. It happened all the time, and the powers that be would be glad the *Vengeur* and not the big tanker had caught the torpedo.

It was later. Later. He gritted his teeth together to stop himself from speaking aloud.

The girl asked, 'Are you all right, sir?'

He turned on her. 'What the hell do you mean by that?'

She looked away. 'I'm sorry.'

'No.' He removed his cap and ran his fingers through his hair. It felt damp with sweat. Fear. 'No, I'm the one to apologise.'

She looked at him again, her eyes searching. 'Was it bad, sir?'

He shrugged. 'Enough.' Abruptly he asked, 'Are you engaged to be married or anything?'

She eyed him steadily. 'No, sir. I was. He bought it over Hamburg last year.'

'I see.' Bought it. So coolly said. The resilience of youth at war. 'Well, I'd better get out now. Otherwise the boat will go away without me.'

'Here, sir. I'll give you a hand with your bags.' She ignored his protests and climbed out of the car on to the wet stones of the jetty.

The wind slammed the door back against the car, and Lindsay felt the wind lashing his face like wire. Below the steps he could see the tossing motor boat, the oilskinned figures of coxswain and bowman.

He said, 'Maybe I'll see you again.' He tried to smile but his face felt like a mask.

She squinted up at him, the rain making her forehead and jaunty cap shine in the grey light. 'Maybe.'

'What name is it?'

She tugged down the sodden scarf from her mouth and smiled. 'Collins, sir.' She wrinkled her nose. 'Eve Collins. Daft, isn't it?'

She had a nice mouth. Lindsay realised one of the seamen was picking up his bags, his eyes on the girl's legs.

He said, 'Take care then.'

He walked to the steps and hurried down into the waiting boat.

The girl returned to the car and slid behind the wheel, her wet duffel coat making a smear across the worn leather. As she backed the car away from the jetty's edge she saw the boat turning fussily towards the anchorage. Nice bloke, she thought. She frowned, letting in the gear with a violent jerk, nice, but scared of something. Why did I give him my name? He'll not be back. She looked at herself in the mirror. Poor bastard. Like all the rest of us in this bloody place.

———————

Lindsay remained standing as the boat dipped and curtsied across the wind-ruffled water, gripping the canopy with both hands as he watched the anchored ships. Battleships and heavy cruisers, fleet destroyers and supply vessels, the grey metal gleamed dully as the little boat surged past. The only colour was made by the ships' streaming ensigns or an occasional splash of dazzle paint on some sheltering Atlantic escort. His experienced eye told him about most of the ships. Their names and classes, where they had met before. Faces and voices, the Navy was like a family. A religion. And all these ships, perhaps the best in the fleet, were tied here at Scapa, swinging round their buoys and anchors, waiting. Just in case the German heavy units broke out again to try and destroy the convoys, scatter the defences and shorten the odds against England even more.

Bismarck had been caught and sunk after destroying the *Hood*. But it had been a close run thing and had taken damn near the whole Home Fleet to do it. *Graf Spee* had been destroyed by her own people in Montevideo rather than accept defeat by a victorious but inferior British force. But again, she had done well to get that far, had sunk many valuable ships before she was run to earth. And even now the mighty *Tirpitz* and several other powerful modern capital ships were said to be lurking in Norwegian fjords or in captured French ports along the Bay of Biscay. Just gauging the right moment. And until that moment, these ships had to lie here, fretting, cursing and wasting.

He glanced at the boat's coxswain. Probably wondering what sort of a skipper they were getting. Was he any good? Could he keep them all in one piece?

The seaman said gruffly, 'There she is, sir. Fine on the starboard bow.'

Lindsay held his breath. For a moment she was just one more shadow in the steady downpour, and then she was right there, looming above him like a dripping steel cliff. Lindsay knew her history, had studied her picture and layout more than once, but after a low-lying destroyer, or any other warship for that matter, a merchantman always appeared huge and vulnerable. It took more than drab grey paint, a naval ensign and a few guns to change that.

Five hundred feet long from her unfashionable straight stem to her overhanging stern, and twelve-and-a-half thousand tons, she had steamed many thousands of miles since she had first slid into the Clyde in 1919. Born at a time of dashed hopes and unemployment, of world depression and post-war apathy, she had represented jobs to the shipyard workers rather than some source of a new hope. But she had done well for herself and her owners. Described in the old shipping lists as an intermediate liner, she had been almost constantly on the London to Brisbane run. Port Said, Aden, Colombo, Fremantle, Adelaide, Melbourne and Sydney. Her ports of call were like a record of the merchant navy itself, which in spite of everything had been the envy of the world.

Cargo, mail and passengers, she had pounded her way over the years, earning money, giving pleasure, making jobs.

After Dunkirk, when Britain had at last realised the war was not going to be won by stalemate, if at all, she had waited for a new role. The stately ocean liners had become hospital ships and troopers, and every other freighter, tanker or aged tramp steamer was thrown into the battle for survival on the convoy routes. *Benbecula* had done some trooping, but she was of an awkward size. Not suitable for big cargoes, too small for large numbers of servicemen on passage, she had been moved like a clumsy pawn from one war theatre to the next.

With the Navy stretched beyond safety limits she had been earmarked at last as an armed merchant cruiser. She could endure the heaviest weather and stay away from base far longer than the average warship. To patrol the great wastes of the North Atlantic off Iceland, or the barren sea areas of the Denmark Strait. Watch for blockade runners, report anything suspicious, but stay out of real danger. Any heavy naval unit could make scrap of an unarmoured hull like hers. *Rawalpindi* had found that out. And only some nine months ago the *Jervis Bay* had been sunk defending a fully loaded convoy a thousand miles outward bound from the American coast. The convoy had scattered in safety while the *Jervis Bay*, outgunned and ablaze, had matched shot for shot with a German battleship. Her destruction, her sacrifice, had brought pride as well as shame to those who had left the country so weak and so blind to its danger.

The motor boat cut across the tall bows and Lindsay saw the overhanging bridge wing, the solitary funnel and the alien muzzle of a six-inch gun below her foremast.

He said, 'She seems to have a list to starboard.'

The coxswain grinned. "S'right, sir. I'm told she nearly always has had. One of the old hands said she got a biff in some typhoon afore the war an' never got over it like.'

Lindsay frowned. He had not realised he had spoken his thoughts aloud. A slight list to starboard. And he was not even aboard her yet.

Again he sensed the chill of anxiety. He forced himself to go over the facts in his mind. Six six-inch guns, two hundred and fifty officers and ratings, most of whom were straight from the training depots.

The first lieutenant's name was Goss. John Goss.

The hull towered right over him now, and he saw the accommodation ladder stretching away endlessly towards several peering faces at the guardrail. How many passengers had swarmed up and down this ladder? Souvenirs, dirty postcards from Aden, a brass bowl for an aunt in Eastbourne.

Stop. Must stop right now.

He stood upright in the pitching boat as the bowman hooked on with studied ease.

As Lindsay jumped on to the grating the boat's mechanic hissed, 'Wot's 'e like, Bob?'

The coxswain watched Lindsay's slim figure hurrying up the side and replied through his teeth, 'Straight-ringer. A regular. Not like the last skipper.'

The mechanic groaned. 'Either 'e's blotted 'is copybook an' is no bleedin' good for nuthin' else, or we're bein' given some special, bloody-awful job! Either way it's no bloody use, is it?'

The coxswain listened to the squeal of pipes from the top of the ladder and said unfeelingly, 'Looks that way, so grab them bags and jump about.'

The other man muttered, 'Roll on my bleedin' twelve, and bugger all cox'ns!'

The coxswain tried to recall if there was a film on in the fleet canteen tonight. Probably full before he got ashore anyway. He glared at the dull sky and the rain. Bloody Scapa, he thought.

Lindsay looked at the assembled side party, anony-mous in their glistening oilskins. After the jetty and the boat, it seemed strangely sheltered here. The entry port was situated beneath the promenade and boat decks, and with the wind blowing across the opposite bow it was suddenly quiet.

'Welcome aboard, sir.' A tall, heavily built officer stepped forward and saluted. 'I'm Goss.'

Lindsay knew that Goss was forty-five, but he looked fifteen years older. He had a heavy jowled, unsmiling face, and in his oilskin he seemed to tower head and shoulders over everyone else.

Lindsay held out his hand. 'Thank you, Number One.'

Goss had not blinked or dropped his eyes. 'I've got one watch and the second part of port watch ashore on store parties, sir. We ammunitioned at Leith before we came here.' He moved his eyes for the first time and said almost fiercely, 'You'll not need to worry about this ship, sir.'

Something in his tone, the hint of challenge or aggressiveness, made Lindsay reply coldly, 'We shall have to see, eh?'

Goss turned away, his mouth hardening slightly. 'This is Lieutenant Barker, sir. Paymaster and supply officer. He's got the books ready for your inspection.'

Lindsay got a brief impression of a toothy smile, pale eyes behind hornrimmed glasses, and nodded. 'Good.'

Goss seemed very ill at ease. Angry, resentful, even hostile.

It had been a bad beginning. What the hell was the matter? Lindsay blamed himself. They were all probably more worried about their new captain than he had properly realised.

He tried again. 'Sailing orders will be coming aboard in the first dog watch.' He paused. 'So there'll be no libertymen, I'm afraid, until I know what's happening.'

Surprisingly, Goss smiled. It was more like a grimace. He said harshly, 'Good. Most of the hands are more intent on *looking* like sailors than doing anything useful. Bloody shower of civvies and layabouts!'

Lindsay glanced at his watch. It had stopped, and he remembered angrily that he had been looking at the clock on St. Magnus cathedral in Kirkwall to set the correct time when the Wren had arrived with her car.

Goss saw the quick frown. 'I'm afraid lunch has been cleared away, sir.' He hesitated. 'Of course I *could* call the cook and ——.'

Lindsay looked away. 'No. A sandwich will do.'

He could not even recall when he had last eaten properly. He had to break this contact. Find some privacy to reassemble himself and his mind.

'Then if you'll follow me, sir.' Goss gestured towards a ladder. 'The captain's quarters are below the bridge deck. Nothing's changed there yet.'

Lindsay followed him in silence. Changed? What did he mean? He saw several seamen working about the decks but avoided their eyes. It was too soon for quick judgements. Unlike Goss, who apparently despised men because they were 'civvies'. The Navy would be in a damn poor way without them. What did he expect for a worn old ship like this?

Aloud he asked, 'What about this list to starboard?'

Goss was already climbing the ladder. He did not turn round. 'Always had it'—— pause—— 'Sir,' was all he said.

The captain's quarters were certainly spacious and ran the whole breadth of the bridge. There was a ladder which led directly above to the chart room and W/T office, the navigation bridge and compass platform, and from it the occupant could see most of the boat deck and forward to the bows as well.

Goss opened the door, his eyes watchful as Lindsay walked into the day cabin.

After the *Vengeur* it was another world. A green fitted carpet and wood panelling. Good furniture, and some chintz curtains at each brightly polished scuttle. Above an oak sideboard was a coloured photograph of the *Benbecula* as she had once been. Shining green hull and pale buff funnel. Her old line, the Aberdeen and Pacific Steam Navigation Company, was also present in the shape of the company's crest and a small glass box containing the launching mallet used at her birth.

Goss said quietly, 'There are, *were* five ships in the company, sir.' He took off his oilskin and folded it carefully on his arm. He had the interwoven gold lace of a lieutenant-commander in the Royal Naval Reserve on his reefer. 'Good ships, and I've served in all but one of them.'

Lindsay looked at him gravely. 'Always with the one company?'

'Aye. Since I was fourteen. Would have been Master by now, but for the war.'

'I see.'

Lindsay walked to the nearest scuttle and looked at the swirling water far below. Goss's comment was part of the reason for his attitude, he thought. *Would* have been Master. Of this ship perhaps?

He turned and saw the books lined along a polished desk awaiting his scrutiny and signature. Neat and tidy like the oilskin on Goss's beefy arm.

He asked, 'Was this your last ship, Number One?'

Goss nodded curtly. 'I was Chief Officer. But when we stopped trooping and the Admiralty took over I stayed on with her. Being a reservist, they couldn't very well object.'

'Why should they *object*?'

Goss flushed. 'Not happy unless they're moving everyone about.'

'You may be right.' He turned away. 'Now if you'll arrange a sandwich I'll settle in while I'm reading these books.'

Goss hesitated. 'I hear you were in hospital, sir.' His eyes flickered. 'Lost your ship, I believe.'

'Yes.'

Goss seemed satisfied. 'I'll leave you then. Anything you want you can ring on those handsets or press the steward's bell, sir.'

The door closed silently and Lindsay sat down behind the desk. Not good, but it might have been a worse

beginning. A whole lot worse. He leafed through the neat
pages. Apart from Goss and himself there were seventeen officers aboard, including a doctor, and for some
obscure reason, a lieutenant of marines. Most of the
officers were hostilities-only. He smiled in spite of his taut
nerves. *Civvies,* as Goss would have described them. A
few, like Goss, including the engineer officers, Lieutenant Barker whom he had briefly met, and a Mr. Tobey,
the boatswain, were Royal Naval Reserve. Professional
seamen and well used to ships like *Benbecula.* That was
something. The only regulars appeared to be the gunnery officer, a Lieutenant Maxwell, and two pensioners
called back from retirement, Baldock, the gunner, and
Emerson, a warrant-engineer. He paused at the foot of
the page. And one solitary midshipman named Kemp.
What an appointment for a midshipman, he thought
bitterly. He saw himself in the bulkhead mirror and
shuddered. Or Commander Andrew Lindsay for that
matter.

The wind sighed against the bridge, and he was conscious of the lack of movement. A destroyer would be
pitching to her moorings even here in Scapa Flow. He
would have to meet his officers, explore the hull from
bridge to keel. Get the *feel* of her.

He lowered his face into his hands. Must do it soon.
Waste no time in remembering or trying not to
remember. But he had got over the *Vengeur,* as much as
anyone could who had seen a ship, his ship, die. But the
rest. He hesitated, remembering the doctor's calm voice
at the hospital. That might take longer. Avoid it, the
doctor had said.

Lindsay stood up violently. Avoid it. How the hell
could you? The man was a bloody fool even to suggest it.

He stared at a tall, mournful looking man in a white
jacket and carrying a silver tray covered in a crisp napkin.

The man said, 'I'm Jupp, sir. Chief steward.'

Lindsay swallowed hard. The steward must think him

mad. 'Put the tray down there, and thank you, er, Jupp.'

The steward laid the tray down and said dolefully, 'I made 'em meself, sir. Bit of tinned salmon I'd been savin'. Some spam, and a few olives which I obtained from a Greek freighter in Freetown.' He looked at Lindsay, adding, 'Nice to have you aboard, if I may make so bold.'

Lindsay studied him. 'I take it you were with the company, too?'

Jupp smiled gently. 'Twenty-three years, sir. We've 'ad some very nice people to deal with.' The smile became doleful again. 'You'll soon settle in, sir, so don't fret about it so.'

Lindsay felt the anger rising uncontrollably like a flood.

'I'm really glad you've come to us, sir.' Jupp made towards the door.

'Yes, thank you.'

Lindsay stared at the closed door, his anger gone and leaving him empty. Jupp seemed to think he was joining the company rather than assuming command. Yet in spite of his jarring nerves and earlier despair he took a sandwich from the plate. It was thin and beautifully cut.

There was a small card under the plate which read, 'On behalf of the Aberdeen and Pacific Steam Navigation Company may we welcome you aboard the S.S. Benbecula.' Jupp had crossed out the ship's title and inserted H.M.S. with a pencil.

Lindsay sank back into a chair and stared around the silent cabin. Jupp was at least trying to help. He reached for another sandwich, suddenly conscious of a consuming hunger.

So then, would he, he decided grimly, if only to hold on to his sanity.

———————

Jupp walked around the captain's day cabin, flicking a curtain into place here, examining an ashtray there, and generally checking that things were as they should be. It was early evening, but the pipe to darken ship had sounded long since as it seemed to get dark quickly in Scapa Flow. Not that it had been very light throughout Lindsay's first day aboard.

He sat at his desk, his jacket open as he pushed the last file of papers to one side. He felt tired, even spent, and was surprised to see that he had been working steadily for a full hour since his methodical tour around the ship.

The dockyard people at Leith had been very ruthless with their surgery, he thought. For once below 'A' Deck there appeared little left of the original internal hull. There was a well deck both forward and aft, but where the main holds had once been were now shored up with massive steel frames to support the main armament on the upper decks. There were four six-inch guns on the foredeck, two on either beam, and the remaining two had been mounted aft, again one on either side. There was not much alternative in a ship constructed for peaceful purposes, but it was obvious that at no time could *Benbecula* use more than half her main armament to fire at one target. There was an elderly twelve-pounder situated right aft on the poop, a relic of the ship's short service as a trooper, and on the boat deck itself he had discovered four modern Oerlikons. Altogether they represented *Benbecula*'s sole defence or means of attack.

Most of the original lifeboats had gone, and had been replaced by naval whalers, two motor boats and a number of Carley floats and wooden rafts. The latter were the only things which really counted if a ship went down fast.

She had a modern refrigeration space where he had found Paymaster-Lieutenant Barker and his assistants busily checking the last of the incoming stores. Barker had been a ship's purser before the war, some of that time in the *Benbecula,* and had spoken with obvious nostalgia of 'better days', as he had described them.

Many of the passenger cabins had been transferred into quarters for the ship's company, a rare luxury for naval ratings, even though the dockyard had seen fit to cram them in four or five to each space.

Accompanied by Goss, Lindsay had tried to miss nothing, had kept his thoughts to himself until he had completed his inspection.

Magazines for the six-inch guns had been constructed on the orlop deck below the waterline, with lifts to carry the shells and charges the seemingly great distance to the mountings above. The guns were very old. First World War vintage, they were hand-operated and almost independent of any sort of central fire control.

He had met Lieutenant Maxwell, the gunnery officer, although he had the vague impression the man had been waiting for him. Gauging the right moment to appear as if by accident.

Maxwell was a regular officer, but about the same age as himself. Thin featured, bony, and very rigid in his carriage, he never seemed to relax throughout the meeting. His knuckles remained firmly bunched at his sides, the thumbs in line with his trouser seams, as if on parade at Whale Island.

While they were speaking, Goss was called away by the duty quartermaster, and Maxwell said quickly, 'Pretty rough lot, I'm afraid, sir. But still, with a proper captain we'll soon whip 'em into shape.'

Lindsay had discovered that, unlike Goss, the gunnery officer had been referring to the R.N.R. officers and ratings of the ship's company. He had also gathered that Goss and Maxwell rarely spoke to one another.

Later, on the way to the boiler room, Goss had remarked sourly, 'Did you know, sir, Maxwell was on the beach for five years until the war? Made some bloody cockup, I expect. Damned unfair to have him put aboard *us!*'

Lindsay leaned back in the chair and interlaced his fingers behind his head. Goss probably thought the same about his new captain.

Jupp paused by the desk, his eyes glinting in the lamplight. 'I expect you'd like a drink, sir?'

'Thank you. A whisky, if you have it.'

Jupp regarded him gravely. 'I always manage to keep some for my captains, sir.' He sounded surprised that Lindsay should have doubted his ability to obtain something which was such a rarity almost everywhere.

Lindsay watched Jupp as he busied himself at the sideboard. *There* is a man who is happy in his work, he thought wearily.

Then he remembered Fraser, the chief engineer. Lieutenant-Commander (E) Donald Fraser had taken him on a tour around the boiler and engine rooms. He was a small, almost delicate looking man with iron grey hair, a sardonic smile, and a very dry sense of humour. Lindsay had liked him immediately.

Goss must be a good seaman, and Maxwell had sounded competent on matters of gunnery. Even Barker seemed shrewd and active in the affairs of his vital department. But Lindsay, even after much heart-searching, could not find much to like about any of them. Most ships' engineer officers were men apart, from his experience, defending their private worlds of roaring machinery from all comers, including captains, to the death. Fraser, on the other hand, was almost insulting about his trade and about the ships he had served. He had been at sea since he was seventeen. He was now fifty.

He had only been chief in the *Benbecula* for eight months, but had served before that in her sister ship, the *Eriskay*.

'Alike as two peas in a pod,' he had said without enthusiasm. 'Sometimes when I'm doing my rounds I almost forget I've changed bloody ships!'

When Lindsay had asked him about his previous service Fraser had said, 'I was with Cunard for ten years, y'know. Now there was a company!'

'Why did you leave?'

Fraser had run his wintry eye around the mass of glittering dials and throbbing generators before replying slowly, 'Got fed up with the wife. Longer voyages in this crabby company was the only peace I could get!'

As Lindsay had made to leave the engine room's humid air Fraser had said simply, 'You and I'll not fight, sir. I can give you fifteen, maybe sixteen knots. But if you want more I'll do what I can.' He had grinned, showing his small, uneven teeth like a knowing fox. 'If I have to blow the guts out of this old bucket!'

The whisky glass was empty, and he licked his lips as Jupp refilled it soundlessly from a decanter. He had hardly noticed it going down, and that was a bad sign. The doctor had said . . . he shut his mind to the memory like a steel trap.

Instead he turned over the rain-dampened envelope which the guardboat had dropped aboard during the first dog watch. Orders. But nothing fresh or even informative. The ship would remain at her present moorings and notice for steam until further notice.

Muffled by the thick glass scuttles he heard the plaintive note of a bugle. Probably one of the battleships. He felt suddenly tired and strangely cut off. Lonely. In a small ship you were always in each others' pockets. You knew everyone, whereas here. . . . He sipped the second drink, listening to the muted wind, the muffled footsteps of a signalman on the bridge above.

Jupp asked discreetly, 'Will you be dining aboard, sir?'

He thought suddenly of the small Wren with the wind-reddened face. He could go ashore and give her a call. Take her somewhere for a drink. But where? Anyway, she would probably laugh at him.

He replied, 'Yes.' He thought Jupp seemed pleased by his answer.

'I will try and arrange something special for you, sir.' Jupp glanced at the bulkhead clock as if troubled and then hurried purposefully away.

Lindsay switched on the radio repeater above the sideboard, half listening to the smooth, tired voice of the announcer. Air raids, and another setback in the Western desert. Last night our light coastal forces engaged enemy E-boats in the Channel. Losses were inflicted. The Secretary of the Admiralty regrets to announce the loss of H.M. trawler *Milford Queen*. Next of kin have been informed. He switched it off angrily without knowing why. Words, words. What did they mean to those who were crouching in the cellars and shelters, listening to the drone of bombers, waiting for their world to cave in on them?

There was a tap on the door. It was Fraser.

'Yes, Chief?' He thrust his hands behind him, knowing they were shaking violently.

The engineer officer held out a bottle of gin. 'I thought you might care to take a dram with me, sir?' His eye fell on the decanter. 'But of course if you were to offer something else, well now———.'

Lindsay smiled and waved Fraser to a chair, thankful he had come. Glad not to be alone on this first evening aboard. Knowing too why Jupp had been so concerned. Goss was first lieutenant and senior officer in the wardroom. He should have invited the new captain down to meet the other officers. Break the ice. Jupp would have been expecting it.

He looked at Fraser and realised he was studying him with fixed attention.

'Your health, Chief.'

Fraser held the glass to the light and said quietly, 'Ah well, we're both Scots, so there's some hope for this bloody ship!'

Beyond the tall sides of the hull the wind eased slightly, but the rain mounted in intensity, beating the black water like bullets.

Ashore, sitting in her cramped billet and darning a stocking, Wren Collins cocked her head to listen to it.

Aloud she said vehemently, 'Bloody Scapa!'

2 The nightmare

Andrew Lindsay awoke from his nightmare, struggling and tearing at the sheet and blankets, gasping for air, and knowing from the soreness in his throat he had been shouting aloud. Shouting to break the torment. Hold it at bay.

Stumbling and sobbing in the pitch darkness he groped his way across the cabin, crashing into unfamiliar furniture, almost falling, until he had found a scuttle. He could hear himself cursing as he fought to raise the heavy deadlight and then to unscrew the clips around the glass scuttle.

As he heaved it open he had the breath knocked from him as with savage eagerness the rain sluiced across his face and chest, soaking his hair and pyjamas until he was shivering both from chill and sheer panic. He thrust his head through the open scuttle, letting the rain drench over him, feeling the cold brass rim against his shoulders. The scuttle was large. Big enough to wriggle through if you tried hard enough.

Breathing unsteadily he peered through the rain. The sky was lighter, and he thought he saw the outline of another ship anchored nearby. It was impossible to tell what time it was, or how long the dream had lasted, or when it had begun. He had never been able to tell. Just that it was always the same.

Wearily he slammed down the deadlight and groped back to the bunk where he switched on the overhead reading lamp.

The sheet was damp, but not only from his rain-soaked body. He had been sweating as he had relived it. Sweating and fighting to free its grip on him.

He felt his breath slowing down and pulled his dressing gown from a hook. He was ice cold and shivering badly.

Around him the ship was like a tomb, as if she were listening to him. Not a footfall or even a creak broke the stillness.

Be logical. Face up to it. He went painstakingly through the motions, even filling his pipe unseeingly to steady himself. Suppose it would never loosen its grip? That the doctors had been wrong. After all, naval hospitals were overworked, too glutted with an unending stream of burned, scalded, savaged wrecks to care much about one more casualty.

He lit the pipe carefully, tasting the raw whisky from the previous night's drinking, and knowing he had been close to vomiting.

Across the cabin he saw his face in a mirror, picked out in the match flame as if floating. He shuddered. Drowning. The face was too young for the way he felt. Tousled hair, wide, staring eyes. Like a stranger's.

The tobacco smoke swirled around him as he stood up and walked vaguely back and forth on the carpet.

Perhaps if it had not happened right after the *Vengeur's* sinking he would have been able to cope. Or maybe unknowingly he had already seen and done too much. Used up his resistance.

Feet clattered on a ladder overhead. The morning watchmen getting their cocoa carried to them while they tried to stay awake on the bridge.

It was strange to realise that throughout his life in the Navy he had been content with almost everything. Perhaps because it *was* everything to him. His father he could hardly remember. He had been wounded in that other war at Jutland and had never really recovered. His mother, worn out with worry for her husband, nursing him, and hating the Service which had turned him into a remote, broken man, had remarried almost immediately after his death. Staying only long enough to carry out her dead husband's wish, that Andrew should be entered into the R.N. College at Dartmouth. She had married a Canadian, a much older man with a thriving business in Alberta, and had never returned. In her own way she was getting as far as possible from the sea which had taken her husband and separated her from her only son.

Denied a normal home life, Lindsay had given everything to the Navy. In his heart he wondered if that driving force, his inbuilt trust, had been the main cause of his breakdown. For war was not a matter of weapons and strategy alone. Above all it was endurance. To survive you had to endure, no matter what you saw or felt. The Atlantic had proved that well enough. Endurance, and the grim patience of one vast slaughterhouse.

Could any one thing break a man? How many times did he ask himself this same unanswerable question?

He sat down and stared at the glowing bowl of his pipe.

The Swedish ship had taken *Vengeur*'s survivors into New York. Had it been a British port things might have been different. But to men starved of bright lights, kindness and a genuine desire to make up for their suffering, it was another, unreal world. The cloak to hide, or at least delay the shock of war.

After one week Lindsay and his men, some other survivors and a large number of civilian passengers had been put aboard a Dutch ship for passage to England. It had an almost holiday atmosphere. The British seamen loaded with gifts and food parcels, the friendly Dutch crew, everything.

Lindsay had felt the loss of his ship much more once the Dutch vessel had sailed to join an eastbound convoy. Perhaps because for the first time he had nothing to do. A passenger. A number in a lifeboat, or for a sitting in the dining room.

He had shied away from the others, even his own officers, and had found himself mixing more and more with some of the civilian passengers. He had known it was to help him as well as them. He needed to do something, to occupy his mind, just as they required someone to explain and to ease the anxieties once the land had vanished astern.

There had been one family in particular. Dutch Jews, they had been in Italy when war had begun, and unable to reach home had started, as best they could, to escape. They needed no telling as to what would happen if the Germans got to them first. A nondescript Dutch Jew. Plump, balding and bespectacled, with a chubby wife who laughed a good deal. A quick, nervous laugh. And two children, who were completely unaware of their parents' sacrifices and strange courage on their behalf.

The family had got aboard a Greek freighter to Alexandria. Then in another ship via Suez to Durban, with the little man using his meagre resources and his wife's jewellery to oil the wheels, to bribe if necessary those who were too busy or indifferent to care about them.

Finally they reached America, and after more delays, examination of papers, and with money almost gone, they got aboard the Dutch ship.

Lindsay had asked why they had not remained in America. They would have been safe there. Well looked after. It made more sense. The little man had shaken his head. He was a Jew, but foremost he was Dutch. In England he would soon find work, he was after all a professional radio mechanic and highly skilled. He would seek work to help those who had not given in. Who were fighting and would win against the Nazis.

Almost shyly he had said, 'And I will know Holland is not so far away. My wife and children will know it, too.'

The pipe had gone out, and Lindsay found he was

staring fixedly at the closed scuttle. Holding his breath.

It had been a fine bright morning and warmer than usual. He had been sitting in his cabin watching the horizon line mounting the glass scuttle, hanging motionless for a few seconds before retreating again as the ship rolled gently in the Atlantic swell. The previous evening he had been on the bridge with the Dutch master, who had told him that six U-boats thought earlier to have been near-by had moved away towards another convoy further south. This convoy was fast, and with luck should reach Liverpool in two more days.

The Dutch family had been getting visibly anxious with each long day, and Lindsay had called into their cabin before turning into his bunk to tell them the news. He could see them now. The two children grinning at him from a bunk, their parents sitting amidst a litter of shabby suitcases. They had thanked him, and the children had thrown him salutes as they had seen his men do.

That following morning he had wondered how he would pass the day. He had known that the Dutch family would be awake in their cabin, which was directly below his own. They had often joked about it.

At first he had thought it to be far off thunder, or a ship being torpedoed many miles away.

Even as he had walked to the scuttle there had been a tremendous explosion which had flung him on his back, deafening him with its intensity. When he had scrambled to his feet he had seen with shock that the sea beyond the scuttle was hidden in smoke, and as his hearing had returned he had heard screams and running feet, shrill whistles and the clamour of alarm bells.

Another explosion and one more almost immediately shook the ship as if she had rammed full-tilt into a berg. When he had regained his feet again he had found he could hardly stand, that the deck was already tilting steeply towards the sea.

When he had wrenched open the scuttle and peered into the smoke he had realised that the ship was already settling down, and when he had looked towards the water he had seen one of the sights uppermost in his nightmare.

The sea had almost reached the next line of scuttles below him. And at most of them there were arms and hands waving and clutching, like souls in torment. It was then he had realised that his own scuttle was just too small to climb through.

More violent crashes, the sounds of machinery tearing adrift and thundering through the hull. Escaping steam, and the banshee wail of the siren. It had taken all his strength to stagger up the deck to the door. The passageway had been full of reeling figures, forgotten lifebelts and scattered trays of tea which the stewards had been preparing at each cabin door.

Lindsay was on his feet again, pacing up and down as he relived each terrible minute. Fighting his way down companion ladders, looming faces and wild eyes, screams and desperate pleas for help, and with the ship dipping steadily on to her side.

Their cabin door had been open just a few inches, and he had heard the woman sobbing, the children whimpering like sick animals. In a shaky voice the little Dutchman had explained that the whole cabin bulkhead had collapsed, had sealed the door. They were trapped, with the sea already just a few feet below the scuttle.

Lindsay could hear himself saying, 'You must put the children through the scuttle.' It had been like hearing someone else. So calm and detached, even though every fibre was screaming inside him to run before the ship took the last plunge.

The other voice had asked quietly, 'Will *you* look after them?'

Lindsay could not remember much more. The next scene had been on the ravaged boat deck. Shattered lifeboats and dangling falls. Two dead seamen by a ventilator, and an officer falling like a puppet from the upper bridge.

Down on the water, littered with rafts and charred wood, with bodies and yelling survivors, he had seen the children float clear of the hull. Very small in their bright orange lifebelts. He had jumped into the water after them, but when he had looked back he had seen that the whole line of scuttles had dipped beneath the surface. But here and there he had seen pale arms waving like human weed until with a jubilant roar the pressure had forced them back out of sight.

Lindsay had swam with the children to a half-empty lifeboat, deaf to their terrified cries, and still only half aware what had happened.

The small convoy had scattered, and when he had stood up he had seen the nearest ship, a freighter, being bracketed by tall waterspouts, until she too reeled to explosions and was ablaze from bow to stern. Then and only then had he seen the enemy. Lying across the horizon like a low, grey islet, lit every so often by rippling orange flashes from her massive armament. The enemy never got nearer than about seven miles, and methodically, mercilessly she had continued to drop her great shells on the sinking ships, on the boats and amongst the helpless victims in the water. To the men behind those powerful rangefinders and gunsights the targets would have seemed very near. Close enough to watch as they died in agony under that clear sky.

Eventually, satisfied her work was done, the German raider had disappeared below the hard horizon line. Later it was said she was a pocket-battleship or perhaps a heavy cruiser. Nobody knew for sure. All Lindsay knew was that he had to stay five days in the boat with seven others who had somehow survived the bombardment. Five men and the two Dutch children.

A corvette had found them eventually, and the

children were buried at sea the next morning along with some victims from a previous attack. Lindsay had held them against himself for warmth and comfort long after they must have died from exposure, terror and exhaustion.

War was not for little children, as some smug journalist had written later.

Lindsay sat on the edge of the bunk and stared at the carpet. He had actually allowed himself to think about it. Just this once. What did he feel now? Despair, fear of what might happen next time? He rubbed his eyes with his knuckles, hearing a bugle bleating out reveille across the Flow. *Wakey, wakey! Lash up and stow!*

If he felt anything, anything at all, it was hatred.

The door opened an inch and lamplight cut a path across the carpet to his bare feet.

Jupp asked, 'Are you ready for some tea, sir?'

Lindsay shook himself. 'Thanks.'

Jupp padded to the table. 'I heard you about, sir, so I thought to meself, ah, the captain'll like a nice hot strong cup of char, that's what I thought.'

'Heard me?' Caution again, like an animal at bay.

'Thought you was on the telephone, sir.' Jupp's face was in shadow. 'I was already in me pantry, an' the old *Becky*'s a quiet ship, sir.'

He peered at the disordered bunk and pursed his lips. 'Dear me, sir, you've 'ad some bad dreams, and we can't 'ave that.' He grinned. 'I'll fix you some coffee an' scrambled eggs.' Disdainfully, 'Powdered eggs, I'm afraid, but there's a war on they tell me.'

Lindsay stopped him by the door. 'So I believe.' He saw the man turn. 'And thanks.'

'Sir?' Jupp's features were inscrutable.

'Just thanks.'

Somewhere above a man laughed, and the deck gave a small tremble as some piece of machinery came alive.

Lindsay walked to the scuttle, the hot cup in his hand. A new day. For him and the ship. The old *Becky*. Perhaps it might be good to both of them.

———————

Lieutenant-Commander John Goss stepped over the coaming of Lindsay's cabin and removed his cap. 'You wanted me, sir?' His heavy face was expressionless.

'Take a seat.'

Lindsay stood by a scuttle watching the rain sheeting across the forecastle where a party of oilskinned seamen were working half-heartedly between the anchor cables. It was the forenoon, but the sky was so dull it could have been dusk. In spite of his bad night he was feeling slightly better. A good bath and Jupp's breakfast had helped considerably.

'I have sent round my standing orders, Number One, and I'd be obliged if you made sure that all heads of departments have read them.' He paused, knowing what was coming.

Goss said abruptly, '*I've* read them, sir. It's not that.'

'Well?' In the salt-smeared glass he saw Goss shifting his heavy bulk from one foot to the other. 'What's bothering you?'

'The watch bill. Action stations and the rest. You've changed my original arrangements.' In a harder tone, 'May I ask why?'

Lindsay turned and studied him calmly. 'Whether any of us likes it or not, Number One, this is a naval ship. As such she will have to work and, if necessary, fight as a single unit.'

Goss said stubbornly, 'I still don't see why——'

Lindsay interrupted, 'I studied your arrangements. You had put all the reserve people into one watch. The other watch was comprised almost entirely of hostilities only, new intakes, many of whom have never been to sea before. Likewise the allocation of officers.' He added slowly, 'Just what do you think might happen if the ship is caught napping and with two R.N.V.R. officers on the bridge, neither of whom has had the slightest experience?'

Goss dropped his eyes. 'They'll have to learn, sir. As I did.'

'Given time they might. But they'll have to be taught, like the rest of us. So I've allowed for it in my planning. A sprinkling in each part of both watches.'

'Yes, sir.' Goss looked up angrily. 'There's this other order. About the accommodation.'

Lindsay glanced at the ship's picture on the bulkhead. The *Benbecula* as she had once been. He could understand Goss's feelings, but like the ship's role they had to be overcome.

'Yes. Tell the chief bosun's mate to get his people to work right away. I want all the old titles removed or painted out, understood?' He saw Goss's eyes cloud over and added quietly, 'To the ship's company as a whole, as a *whole,* do you understand, *Benbecula* must represent part of the Navy. It is a wardroom, not a *restaurant* as the sign says. A chief and petty officers' mess, and no longer the cocktail lounge. Things like that can affect a man's attitude, especially a new, green recruit.'

'I don't need to be told about war, sir.'

Lindsay heard himself retort angrily, 'And neither do *I*, Number One, so do as I damn well say!'

When Goss remained stockstill, his cap crushed under his arm, he added, 'Whatever role we are given, wherever we are sent, things are going to be hard. If I am called to action I want a ship's company working as a team, one unit, do you understand? Not some collection of trained and untrained men, ex-merchant seamen and others brought back from retirement.' He was hoarse, and could feel his heart pumping against his ribs. The earlier sensation of control was slipping away, yet he had to make Goss understand. 'A ship of war is only as strong as her people, d'you see that? *People!'*

'If you say so, sir.'

'Good.'

He walked to a chair and slumped into it. 'You have been at sea long enough to know what can happen. The Atlantic is a killing-ground and no place for unwary idealists. I know how you feel about this ship, at least I think I do. You may believe that by keeping up the old appearances you'll make them survive. Believe me, you won't, quite the opposite. Many of the new hands come from training depots. Depots which up to a year or so back were holiday camps for factory workers and mill girls in the north of England. But after a while the trainees *believed* they were in naval establishments and progressed accordingly. Likewise this ship, so see that my orders are executed as of today.'

'Aye, aye, sir.' Goss sounded hoarse.

'I want to meet my officers today, too.' He glanced up quickly, seeing the shot go home. Goss looked suddenly uneasy. 'I've read all I can about them, but that is as far as it goes.'

'I'll arrange it, sir.' Goss sounded in control again. 'Eight bells?'

'Good.'

More calmly he continued, 'If the war gets no worse things are going to be bad. If it does,' he shrugged, 'then we'll be hard put to keep the sea lanes open. It's as simple as that.' Almost to himself he said, 'Once I thought otherwise. Now I know better. War isn't a game, and it's time we started breaking a few rules, right?'

Goss eyed him unblinkingly. 'Right.'

A telephone buzzed on the bulkhead and Lindsay seized it from its hook without leaving the chair.

'Captain.'

The voice said, 'Signal from shore, sir. Guardboat arriving with sealed orders forthwith.'

Lindsay looked at Goss's heavy face and thought about the voice on the telephone. What did he look like? What was his name? There was so much to discover. So little time.

'Thank you. Inform the O.O.D. please.' The phone went dead.

To Goss he said, 'Perhaps we shall know now.'

Goss looked around the cabin, his face suddenly desperate. 'They'll not be sending us to fight surface ships. Not after all that's happened, surely?' When Lindsay remained silent he said, 'One of our sister ships, the *Barra,* has got a nice billet at Singapore. She's an A.M.C. too, like us, but out there she'll be safe enough from these bloody U-boats.'

Almost gently Lindsay replied, 'Maybe you're right. But it's best to face the worst thing which can happen and plan from there.'

He turned away to hide his eyes, as the mental picture rose in his mind like some hideous spectre. The pale arms waving under the water. The soft, limp bodies pressed against his chest.

Goss opened the door. 'I——I'll carry on, sir.' Then he was gone.

Jupp entered the cabin by the other door and said, 'Guardboat's shoved off from the jetty, sir. I'd better start packin' up some of the glasses. They're hard to replace nowadays, and we don't want none of that issue stuff from naval stores.'

Lindsay relaxed slightly and smiled at Jupp's doleful face.

'What are you expecting?'

Jupp pouted. 'Sailin' orders they'll be, sir. We're off very soon now.'

Lindsay stood up. He was well used to lower deck telegraph and false *buzzes,* but the steward's tone made him ask, 'Have you heard something?' He smiled. 'You've a relative at H.Q. maybe?'

Jupp moved to another scuttle, his face grave. 'Look 'ere, sir.'

Through the steady downpour Lindsay saw a small boat chugging across the anchorage, several oilskinned figures crammed together for comfort like wet seals on a half-submerged rock.

Jupp said, 'That's the 'arbour-master's mob, sir. Earlier on I seen 'em checkin' our buoy and measurin' the distance to the next astern.' He glanced at Lindsay, his voice matter-of-fact. 'They'll be needin' it for another, bigger ship, I reckon. Stands to reason, don't it, sir?'

Lindsay nodded. 'Yes.'

Jupp asked, 'Will you be wantin' any letters taken ashore? If I'm right, that is.'

He shook his head. 'No. No letters.'

He walked towards his sleeping cabin and did not see the sadness in Jupp's deepset eyes.

———————

The *Benbecula*'s wardroom, which was situated forward of the promenade deck, had once been the main restaurant for the passengers, and had been her pride and joy. It ran the whole breadth of the hull, and was panelled in dark oak. Most of the furnishings were drawn from the original fittings, and the chairs around the long polished table all bore the company's crest, as did the deep leather ones grouped by the stately coal stove at the after bulkhead. A few additional concessions had, however, been made. Officers' letter rack, a picture of the King, and a stand containing pistols which did little to alter the general appearance of wellbeing and comfort.

Sharp at noon Goss had arrived to accompany Lindsay to the wardroom and had said nothing as they passed two seamen who were busily removing the glass sign which proclaimed it to be a *Restaurant — First Class Only*. Lindsay doubted if the sign had ever been needed, for he had learned that *Benbecula* had never carried anyone but first class passengers. Except, that is, for emigrants to Australia, and it was hardly likely they would have misunderstood the rules.

As they entered all the officers rose to their feet, their expressions a mixture of curiosity, apprehension and expectancy. It was plain that Goss had already arranged them in some sort of order, while in the background two white-coated stewards hovered in readiness to serve drinks once the formalities were over.

Lindsay knew better than to expect a complete analysis at so brief a meeting. Some faces stood out more than others, however. There was a Lieutenant Stannard, the navigation officer, a lean, beanpole of a man with a skin like leather. A reservist, he was also an Australian who had served with the company before the war.

As Lindsay shook his hand he drawled, 'I sure hope we're going back on the Far East run, sir. The old ship can find her own way there by now.' He shrugged. 'Otherwise I'm not too optimistic!'

Maxwell was present of course, rigid as ever, and slightly apart from the professional seamen and the amateurs, like a disapproving referee at some obscure contest.

The ship's doctor, Surgeon-Lieutenant David Boase, returned Lindsay's handshake, and in answer to a question said, 'First ship, sir. I was at Guy's.'

Despite the red marking between his wavy gold stripes, Lindsay guessed that like so many of his contemporaries Boase was little more than a glorified medical student. But better than no doctor at all.

There were four sub-lieutenants, very new, and all but one of whom had never been to sea before except as ordinary seamen doing their obligatory service prior to going to *King Alfred*, the officers training establishment. The exception was named Dancy, a serious faced young man who said quickly, 'Actually, sir, I *have* done three months watchkeeping before joining this ship.'

Lindsay eyed him curiously. 'What ship?'

'The *Valiant*, sir.'

Lindsay was surprised. 'I'd have thought this is a bit of a change from a big battleship, Dancy.'

Dancy flushed. 'Oh no, sir. Not *that Valiant*. Actually she was an armed yacht at Bristol.'

The laughter helped to break the ice, and Goss said ponderously, 'Shall I call the stewards over now, sir?'

Lindsay nodded and let his eyes move round the faces which would become so familiar, given luck and time.

As Goss bustled away he saw Tobey, the big boatswain, talking with the two elderly warrant officers, Emerson and Baldock, and wondered what they thought about this appointment after their peaceful retirement.

Lieutenant Mark de Chair of the Royal Marines, a slim, elegant figure with a neat clipped moustache said suddenly, 'I expect you're wondering why I'm aboard, sir?'

Lindsay smiled. 'Tell me.'

'I was put here with my sergeant and thirty marines to man the ship's armament when we were trooping, sir.' He shrugged. 'The troops have gone, but their lordships in all their wisdom thought fit to forget us.'

'I've arranged for you to continue manning the after guns.'

Lindsay took a glass from a steward and waited until they were all silent again. A mixed wardroom, he thought. Like most ships these days, and yet. . . .

He said quietly, 'Well, gentlemen, I am sorry this has to be brief. I will have to get to know you better,' he paused, 'when we are at sea.' He felt the sudden expectancy move around him like a small wind. 'Our sailing orders have arrived.' He thought of Jupp by the scuttle. How right he was. 'We will slip from our buoy at 0800 tomorrow and proceed on independent patrol.'

He could see his words hitting home, affecting each and every one present in the way it would touch him. Fraser's relaxed indifference, his second engineer, Lieutenant (E) Dyke, frowning slightly as if going over his own watch-bill of stokers and mechanics. Barker biting his lip, squinting behind his glasses, seeing each sea mile steamed as so many sausages and tins of corned beef, rum and gallons of tea. Stannard, the navigation officer, balanced on his toes, thinking of his charts perhaps, or returning to his far off homeland. Maxwell, stiff and sphinxlike. And some of the rest, so young, so unsure that it made you feel sorry for them.

Lindsay continued, 'We will patrol the south-western approaches to Iceland, to extend when required into the Denmark Strait.' He had to steel himself to say the words. In his mind's eye he could see the raging desert of tossing whitecaps and dark-sided rollers, of shrieking gales, and ice. The Denmark Strait.

Stannard was the first to break the stunned silence. 'Jesus, sir, they sure believe in pitching us into the deep end!'

Goss muttered, 'We've had no time. No time to get things ready——' His voice trailed away.

Lindsay looked round their faces again, knowing it would be like this. He lifted his glass. 'To the ship, gentlemen.' As they drained their glasses without a word he added, 'And remember this. Our people will be looking to you after today. As I will. So let's not have too much despondency about, eh?'

He let his eye fall on Fraser. 'I'd suggest a party tonight——'

He turned as a figure stepped into the wardroom. It was Kemp, the midshipman, the only officer he had not met. Kemp had been acting O.O.D. during the meeting, and his face was pink with cold from the upper deck.

Kemp said, 'Signal from H.Q., sir.' He proffered a soggy sheet of pad. 'Would you report there at 1600, sir.'

Lindsay glanced at the signal, aware of all the eyes watching his face.

'Affirmative.' As the boy turned to go he added, 'You'll be allocated to dealing with ship's correspondence on top of your other duties.'

Kemp stared around the other officers and nodded. 'Yes, sir.'

Lindsay said, 'We're sailing at 0800 tomorrow. Iceland patrol, if you're interested.'

As the boy hurried away Lindsay noticed that one of the stewards had also gone. The news would be all over the ship by now, and perhaps it was better so. It would help prepare them for the formalities of getting under way.

He put down his glass. It was time to leave them to sort themselves out.

He said, 'There will be no shore leave, so inform your departments accordingly. Arrange for mail to be dropped tonight. After that,' he forced a smile, 'we are in business.' He nodded to Goss. 'Thank you. Carry on, please.'

Despite the rain and chill wind he made himself walk around the boat deck, his hands in his pockets, his head bowed against the weather. Part of the deck still bore the faded marks where handball had once been played in the Pacific sunlight. He walked past the hooded Oerlikons and climbed slowly up to the bridge. It would be strange to con a ship with the helmsman right there with you, he thought vaguely. It was a spacious bridge, the brass telegraphs and binnacle, the polished wheel deserted, as if waiting for the place to come alive again. Once the time came it would never be quiet, nor empty.

On either side of the wheelhouse the open bridge wings stretched out over the side, and he walked to the port gratings, his shoes squelching in rain puddles as he peered across at the murky shoreline.

A petty officer was leaning over the wing, the rain

bouncing off his oilskin and cap like hail as he stared at the water far below.

He swung round and saluted as Lindsay crossed to his side and said, 'Ritchie, sir. Yeoman of signals.'

He had a round, homely face, and Lindsay knew from experience that a yeoman of signals was just about one of the most important members of any bridge, no matter what ship.

'You've heard the news, Yeo?'

He nodded. 'Aye, sir.' Ritchie seemed oblivious of the rain. 'I'm not bothered.'

There was something strange about him. Remote.

Lindsay asked quietly, 'Had any leave lately?'

Ritchie looked away. 'Last month, sir.' When he faced Lindsay again there were tears running unheeded with the rain. 'Bloody street was gone, sir!' The words were torn from him. 'Nothing left.'

Lindsay stared at him. Helpless. 'Did you have——'

'Wife an' two kids, sir.' He brushed his face with his sleeve. 'All gone.' He recovered himself and said, 'Sorry about that, sir.'

'Yes.'

He remembered one of the children stirring in the lifeboat on the last night before the corvette found them. Dreaming perhaps. Like Ritchie's kids when the bomb had come down.

Ritchie said suddenly, 'You'd better get under cover, sir.' A smile creased his face. 'You'll be wanted on the bridge, not in the sickbay.'

Lindsay touched his arm. 'Yes.' As he turned to go he added, 'If you want leave I'll see if I can arrange it.'

Ritchie was looking skyward towards a slow-moving Walrus flying boat, his face like a mask.

'Thank you, sir, but no. You'll need a good signals department, I'm thinkin'.' He hesitated. ' 'Sides, I'd like the chance to get back at those bastards!'

Later when Lindsay went ashore to see the Chief of

Staff and to receive his patrol intelligence he remembered Ritchie's words and wondered if he too might be influenced by what had happened.

The Chief of Staff, a serious faced, urbane captain, was brief and to the point.

'Things are bad, Lindsay, very bad. There is talk of more German raiders breaking out, probably from French ports. However,' he glanced up at the great wall chart with all its coloured ribbons and flags, 'it is not unlikely they might try the longer way round.'

'The Denmark Strait.'

'Correct.' The captain eyed him distantly. 'I want no heroics. Any sighting report can be used right here in Scapa.'

Again he looked at the chart, and Lindsay saw the great clusters of crosses, each mark representing a ship sunk by enemy action. There must be hundreds, he thought.

The captain said, 'I know something of your experiences, and I'm sorry you've not been offered a command more fitting to your rank and knowledge. However,' there was that word again, 'in war we accept orders without question.'

A quick handshake, a fat envelope from a tired looking lieutenant, and it was over.

The staff car was waiting to take him back to the jetty, but there was a different Wren behind the wheel. She was pale and thin, and spent most of the journey sneezing into a handkerchief. When he asked her, she had never even heard of Wren Collins.

Between sniffs she complained, 'I've only just arrived at the base, sir. It's not fair really. Most of my friends have got draft chits to Ceylon.'

Lindsay thought of Ritchie and all those others like him. 'Yes,' he replied coldly. 'It really is too bad.'

On the way to the ship in the motor boat he thought of the next day and the days after that. How they would manage.

A motor fishing boat packed with libertymen on her way to Lyness wallowed past in the gloom and he heard the sailors singing above the din of rain and wind.

'Roll on the *Nelson,* the *Rodney, Renown,* this one-funnelled bastard is getting me down.'

He watched them in the rain and recalled the Chief of Staff's warning. *No heroics.*

But if these men could sing like that, there was still some spark of hope. For all of them.

3 Raider

Lindsay sat in his cabin, his legs thrust out in front of him, and peered at his watch. Half an hour to go. He made himself reach out for another cup of black coffee, sipping it slowly to clear his thoughts.

The ship around and below him was not so quiet as before. From the moment the hands had been called until the muffled pipe over the tannoy system, 'Special sea-dutymen to your stations!', there had been a feeling of nervous expectancy. As there always seemed to be when about to leave harbour. You never got used to it.

The cabin was dark, for the deadlights were still tightly shut, as they probably would be for most of the time. He glanced at his leather sea-boots and at the duffel coat and binoculars waiting on another chair. How often had he waited like this? he wondered. It would be strange to take *Benbecula* out of the Flow for the first time. Not that Lindsay was unused to handling big ships. He had served as navigation officer in a cumbersome submarine depot ship in Malta for two years, even though at heart he was still a destroyer-man. No, it was not that. It was going back. To the Atlantic and all it had come to mean to him.

The deck gave a nervous tremble, and he pictured Fraser far below in his inhuman world of noise and greased movement. Mouthing to his men in that strange engine room lip language, his eyes on the great dials above his footplate. It was lucky *Benbecula* was twin-screwed. Many ships built between the wars had only one propeller. Sufficient in peacetime perhaps, with tugs always on hand when entering and leaving harbour. He smiled grimly in spite of his tense nerves. It would put a swift end to everything if he lost control in the Flow's perverse tide-races before he had even got her clear.

More sounds now. Wires scraping along the forecastle, the distant bark of orders. That would be Maxwell preparing to slip the final wire from the ring of their buoy. The last boat had been hoisted inboard, the shivering seamen picked up from the buoy where they had fumbled to unshackle the massive cable while the spray had tried to pluck them into the Flow.

Bells clanged overhead, and he guessed Goss was testing the telegraphs, watching every move to make sure the captain would find no fault with his precious ship.

He replaced the cup and stood up, patting his pockets automatically to make sure he had all he required. Pipe and pouch. And a small silver compass. He turned it over in his hands under the deckhead light. Inscribed on the back was, *'Commander Michael Lindsay. H.M.S. Minden—1914.'* It was just about all he had to remind him of his father now. He thrust it into his pocket, feeling the newness of the jacket. Like everything else, his old clothes were on the sea-bed in *Vengeur.*

There was a tap at the door and Goss looked in at him. 'Ready to proceed, sir.'

'I'll come up.'

He slipped into the duffel coat and slung his glasses around his neck. As he picked up his cap he took a last glance round the quiet cabin. It was time.

Goss followed him up the bridge ladder, between the W/T office with its constant stammer of morse and crackling static and the austere chart room, the deckhead lights trained unwinkingly on the table and instruments.

He strode out to the bridge and crossed to the clearview screens on the windows. Figures moved busily on the forecastle, and a solitary signalman stood shivering right in the bows, ready to lower the Jack when the slipwire came free.

He turned and looked at the bridge party. Chief Petty Officer Jolliffe, the coxswain, whom he had already met briefly on his inspection, was standing loosely at the wheel, his eyes gleaming in the compass light as he idly watched the gyro repeater. He was a barrel of a man, but on the short side, so that his legs appeared too frail for his massive body and paunch. No trouble there. Jolliffe had been coxswain of a battle-cruiser and was used to the whims of big ships. At each brass telegraph the quartermasters lounged with their hands ready on the levers. On either bridge wing the signalmen stood by their shuttered lights and flags, the yeoman, Ritchie, with his long telescope trained towards the shore.

Lieutenant Stannard saluted formally and said, 'Wind's nor'westerly, sir. A bit fresh for my liking.' In the dull grey light he looked even more leathery, his eyes very bright below his cap.

Hovering in the background, two of the sub-lieutenants, Escott and Smythe, were trying not to be seen, their single gold stripes shining with newness.

Goss paced from side to side, his head thrust forward as if to discover some last fault. He glared at the two sub-lieutenants and barked, 'Get out on either wing, for God's sake! You might *learn* something!'

Seizing oilskins they fled away, and Lindsay saw one of the quartermasters wink at his mate.

Goss did no good at all by bellowing at them in front of the ratings, he thought. But there was not time for another confrontation now.

Ritchie yelled, 'Signal, sir!' A light winked impatiently through the rain. Like a bright blue eye.

'Proceed when ready!'

Lindsay tried not to lick his lips. 'Ring down standby.'

The bells were very loud, and he walked to the port door of the wheelhouse and peered over the screen towards the forecastle party. Maxwell was squinting at the bridge, his sodden cap tugged over his eyes as he awaited the order.

Lindsay relaxed slightly, tasting the blown salt on his lips, feeling his cheeks tingling in the crisp air.

'Very well, Yeoman. Make the affirmative.'

Seconds later a red flare burst against the leaden clouds and drifted seaward on the wind.

Stannard called, 'That was the signal from the boom vessel, sir. Hoxa gate is open for us.'

He sounded cheerful enough. Lindsay had heard him bawling some Australian song at the wardroom party when he had turned into his bunk. Every other word had been obscene. But he appeared to have avoided any sort of hangover. Which was more than could be said for Dancy, the sub-lieutenant *with* experience. His face was the colour of pea soup as he staggered aft along the boat deck where the marines and some of the hands had fallen in for leaving harbour.

Feet thumped above the wheelhouse where Chief Petty Officer Archer and his boatswain's mates were assembled to pipe as and when they passed any other ship. The Navy never changed. No matter what.

Lindsay lifted his hand and watched Maxwell point with his arm to indicate that the buoy was close up under the starboard side of the stem.

Once free, the wind would carry the ship abeam like a drifting pier, Lindsay thought. But there was plenty of room. Had wind and tide been against them, he would have had to contend with the nearby battleship and three anchored cruisers. He could see several tiny figures watching him from the battleship's quarterdeck and her name gleaming dully in the morning light. *Prince of Wales.* The ship which had been in company with *Hood* when she had been blown to oblivion. She had been too new, too untried to be much help, and Lindsay wondered briefly how he would have felt, had he been in her at the time.

'Slow ahead together.'

He saw the telegraphsmen swinging their brass handles and turned away to make a chopping motion with his hand towards Maxwell in the eyes of the ship. He saw a petty officer swing his hammer, heard the clang of steel as the slip was knocked away, and the instant rush of activity as the oilskinned seamen tumbled aft, dragging the mooring wire with them. The buoy appeared immediately, as if it and not the ship had taken wings.

Jolliffe intoned, 'Both engines slow ahead, sir. Wheel's amidships.'

'Port ten.'

He raised his glasses and watched the low humps of land beginning to drift across the bows. It was strange to have the great foremast right in front of the bridge with all its tangle of rigging and derricks. Standing at one side of the bridge it made the ship feel lopsided, Lindsay thought. The list to starboard did not help either.

He heard Goss say in a fierce whisper, 'She's making too slow a turn.'

He glanced at him. Goss seemed to be thinking aloud. All the same, he was right.

'Increase to fifteen. Starboard engine half ahead.'

That was better. A noticeable crust of white spray was frothing back from the stem now, and he could feel the bridge vibrating steadily to the additional thrust of screws and rudder.

Two incoming trawlers pounded past the port side, their spindly funnels belching smoke, their ensigns little more than scraps of white rag, after another anti-submarine patrol.

'Midships. Slow ahead starboard.'

Lindsay watched the nearest trawler as it rolled dizzily in the cross-current, showing its bilge. God knows what they're like in open water, he wondered.

Faintly across the water he heard the shrill of a pipe. Somebody, somehow was trying to pay respects to the *Benbecula* as she towered past on her way to the gate.

Overhead he heard Archer bellow *'Pipe!'* And the answering squeal from his line of boatswain's mates.

From aft another shout, that would be Mr Baldock, the elderly gunner. 'Attention on the upper deck there! Face to port an' salute!'

On the forecastle the seamen were still fighting with the seemingly endless mass of uncoiled wire, like people caught by some deadly serpent.

Lindsay steadied his glasses and watched the land closing in on either bow where the humps of Flotta and South Ronaldsay crouched on guard of the Sound. He could just make out the hazy shape of the boom-defence vessel, and beyond her another A/S trawler, sweeping to make sure no U-boat would slip inside while the gate was open.

'Take her out, Cox'n.'

There was no point in confusing the helmsman with unnecessary orders now. Jolliffe could see as well as anyone what was required. He was easing the spokes back and forth in his great red fingers, his eyes fixed on the channel.

A signalman said, 'I think someone's calling us up, Yeo!'

Ritchie was through the door and across to the opposite bridge wing in seconds.

'Where, lad?' His telescope was swinging round like a small cannon. Then, 'Gawd, you need yer eyes testin', it's a bloody car flashin' its lights!'

Lindsay walked to the open door as the yeoman exclaimed, 'You're right, lad, it *is* callin' us.' He looked at Lindsay. 'He'll cop it if the officer of th' guard spots 'im!'

Lindsay raised his glasses as the signalman, mollified, reported, 'He says *Good Luck*, sir.'

A hump of land was cutting Lindsay's vision away even as he steadied his glasses on the distant lights. The battered staff car was parked dangerously close to the sea's edge, and he could picture her as she sat muffled to her ears. Watching the old ship edge towards the boom gate.

He said, 'Acknowledge.' He knew they were staring at him. 'And say *Thank You*.' The lamp started to clatter, and then the car was lost from sight.

He saw one of the sub-lieutenants put out his hand to the screen as the deck lifted to the first low roller. On the bow the boom vessel was puffing out dense smoke as she started to set her machinery in motion again. A man waved from her bridge and then scuttled back from the rain.

Lindsay stooped behind a gyro repeater and said, 'Starboard ten.' The dial ticked gently in front of his eyes. 'Midships. Steady.'

'Steady, sir. Course two-two-zero.'

Stannard said quietly, 'New course in fifteen minutes, sir. Two-five-zero.'

'Very good.'

Lindsay walked out to the wing and rested his gloved hands on the screen. Already the land had fallen away to port, and he could see the whitecaps cruising diagonally towards the ship in an endless array. He felt for his reactions, then banged his gloved hands together, making a signalman start violently. He felt all right. It was amazing.

He thought suddenly of the girl in the car. She must have got up specially and wangled her work-sheet to get to that point in time to see them sail. He was being stupid, but could not help himself.

A telephone buzzed and Stannard called, 'From masthead, sir. Ship closing port bow.'

Lindsay glanced up at the fat pod on the foremast. It was hard to get used to after the congested layout of a warship's bridge and superstructure.

Goss asked, 'Fall out harbour stations, sir?'

But Lindsay was watching the approaching ship through his glasses. She would pass down the port side with a good half cable to spare. It was not that. He felt the tightness in his throat as she loomed slowly and painfully out of the rain and spray.

A cruiser, she was so low in the water aft that her quarterdeck was awash. Her mainmast had gone, and her after turret was buckled into so much scrap. She had received a torpedo which had all but broken her back, but she was fighting to get back. To get her people home.

A destroyer was cruising watchfully to seaward, and two tugs followed close astern of the listing ship. Like undertakers men, Lindsay thought with sudden anger.

He snapped, 'No, Number One! Have the hands fall in fore and aft! And tell the buffer I want the best salute he's ever done!' He saw Goss's face working with confusion and doubt. Probably thinks I'm mad.

As seamen and marines ran to fall in on the *Benbecula*'s decks, Lindsay walked to the end of the wing and raised his hand to his cap as the cruiser moved slowly past.

The pipes shrilled and died in salute, and then Lindsay saw a solitary marine, his head white with bandages, walk to the cruiser's signal platform and raise a bugle to his lips. The *Still* floated across the strip of tossing grey water, and above the neat lines of sewn up bodies on the cruiser's deck. Along the *Benbecula*'s side the lines of new, untried faces stared at the other ship in silence, until the bugle sounded again and Archer yelled, 'Carry on!'

Stannard said quietly, 'That was quite a scene, sir.'

Lindsay looked past him at the young signalman who had seen the car's lights. He was biting the fingers of his gloves and staring astern at the listing cruiser.

'It will do them good!'

He had not meant to speak so harshly, nor were they the words he had intended. So nothing had changed after all. Not the bitterness or the shock of seeing what the Atlantic could do.

Stannard said, 'Time to alter course again, sir.'

Lindsay looked at him, seeing the hurt in his eyes. 'Very well, take the con.' To Goss, 'Fall out harbour stations, if you please. We will exercise action stations in ten minutes, right?'

Goss nodded. 'Yes, sir.'

The *Benbecula*'s straight stem lifted and then ploughed sedately into a low bank of broken rollers. Spray dappled the bridge windows and made the anchor cables look like black glass.

Later, as she came around the south-western approaches to the Orkneys, past the frozen shape of the Old Man of Hoy, she rolled more steeply, her forward well deck catching the incoming sea and letting it sweep lazily to the opposite side before gurgling away through the scuppers.

Then at last she turned her stern towards the land and headed west-northwest, and by noon, as the watch below prepared to eat their meal and the other half of the ship's company closed up at defence stations, she had the sea to herself.

Lindsay remained on the open wing, his unlit pipe in his teeth, his eyes fixed on the tossing wilderness of waves and blown spume.

He was in the North Atlantic. He had come back.

'Char, sir?'

Lindsay turned in his tall chair and took a cup from the bosun's mate of the watch. As he held the hot metal against his lips he stared through the streaming windows and watched the solid arrowhead of the bows etched against the oncoming seas.

For eight days since leaving the buoy the scene had hardly changed. The weather had got colder, but that was to be expected as hour after hour the ship had ploughed her way to the north-west. And apart from some armed trawlers and a solitary corvette, they had sighted nothing. Just the sea, with its endless panorama of wavecrests and steep rollers.

He felt the deck vibrate as the stem smashed through one more bank of cascading water, and saw the feathers of spray spurting up through the hawsepipes as if from powerful hoses.

Stannard walked across the bridge, his lean body angled to the uneven motion.

'First dog watchmen closed up at defence stations, sir. Able Seaman McNiven on the wheel.' He looked through a clearview screen. 'I guess we've arrived.'

Lindsay nodded. 'Yes.'

An invisible dot on the ocean. The starting leg of the patrol area. Area Uncle Item Victor. A sprawling parallelogram which measured five hundred by three hundred miles. As far north as the Arctic Circle between Iceland and Greenland. It had been impossible to get an accurate fix, and their position was obtained by the usual method, described by navigators as 'by Guess and God'. Dead reckoning. Except that in this case you could not afford to be too casual, or you might end up dead in another sense.

'Very well, Pilot. Bring her round to three-five-zero. Revs for ten knots.'

He heard Stannard passing his orders, the instant reply from the engine room bells to show that Fraser's people were wide awake.

When the ship turned slightly to port the motion became more unsteady and violent, the waves piling up against the starboard bow before exploding high over the rails and hissing viciously across each open deck. Below there would be more wretched sufferers retching and groaning at this added onslaught, he thought.

He watched a tall greybeard of a wave surging down the starboard side, taking its time, as if to find the best place to attack. Just level with the bridge its jagged crest crumbled and broke inboard, the shock transmitting itself through the whole superstructure like something solid. It was almost pitch dark beyond the bows, with only the wave-crests to determine sea from sky.

Lindsay ran his fingers over the arms of the chair and recalled Goss's face when he had told him what he required. Goss did not seem to understand that it was no good trying to act as if everything was normal and routine.

The watches changed, the relieved men scampering thankfully below to cabins and messdecks for some brief respite, but Lindsay had been on the bridge almost continuously since leaving the Flow. 'I want a good strong chair, Number One.' That had been the first day out, and the shipwrights had built it during one watch from solid oak which had lain hitherto unnoticed, in a storeroom. Bolted to the deck it gave Lindsay good vision above the screen and was within reach of the bridge telephones. But Goss had stared at it with something like horror.

'But, sir, that timber was being saved! You just can't get it any more.' Like Jupp and his damn glassware.

But if he was to keep going, to hold on to the vital reserve which might be demanded in the next hour or minute, he *needed* a good chair.

It was strange how Goss avoided facing the truth about the ship and her new purpose. Or maybe he wanted the captain to crack under the strain so that he, after all, could take command.

Lindsay thought too of the practice drills he had carried out on passage to the patrol area. In spite of the severe weather he had put almost every part of the ship through its paces. Gun and fire drill. Damage control and anti-aircraft exercises, until he had seen the despair, even hatred on the faces around him.

Maybe Goss had some justification for expecting him to crack, he thought bitterly. Once or twice he had heard himself shouting into a telephone or across the open wing to some unfortunate man on the deck below.

The gun drill had been the worst part. Pathetic, he had called it, and had seen Maxwell's rigid face working for once with something akin to shame. While mythical targets had been passed down from the so-called control position above the bridge, the crews of the six guns had endeavoured to locate and cover them with minimum delay. But each gun was hand-operated, and valuable time was lost again and again while Maxwell and the assistant gunnery officer, Lieutenant Hunter, had shouted themselves almost hoarse with frustration and despair. In most warships, and certainly all modern ones, it was possible to train all major guns, even fire them, direct from the control and rangefinder above the bridge. One eye and brain, like that of a submarine commander at a periscope. But *Benbecula*'s firing arrangements had not even begun to reach a stage where some hope was justified. The six-inch gun crews had no protection from the weather, and had to crouch behind the shields, shivering and cursing as ranges and deflections were passed by telephone and then yelled to them above the din of sea and wind. And having no power at each mounting it also meant that the big shells and their charges had to be manhandled and rammed home with sheer bodily strength. If the deck chose to tilt the wrong way at the moment of loading it could mean disaster for an unwary seaman. The massive breech block of such a gun could swing shut, despite the normal precautions, and bite off a man's arm like a horse snapping at a carrot. It was hardly likely to encourage the gun crews to take risks, but on the other hand it reduced the speed of loading and firing to a dismal crawl.

A telephone buzzed at the rear of the bridge and the bosun's mate called, 'Number Three Carley float is comin' adrift, sir.'

Stannard opened his mouth and shut it. He crossed to the chair and said quietly, 'Can't very well send the lads out in this, sir. Shall I tell the buffer to scrub round it until daylight?'

Lindsay tried to answer calmly. 'Do it now. The boat deck is miles above the waterline. Pass the word for lifelines to be rigged. That should do it.'

Stannard remained beside the chair, his dark features stubborn. 'In my opinion, sir——'

Lindsay swung round, seeing in those brief seconds the pale faces in the background, watching and listening.

Sub-Lieutenant Dancy, Stannard's assistant for the watch, the signalman, the men at the telegraphs, all parts of the ship. Extensions of his own thoughts and interpretations.

'Just *do* it, Pilot!' He could not control it any longer. 'With the sort of results I've been getting since I took command, I think liferafts are about the most useful things we've got! By God, do you imagine *this* is bad?'

Stannard stood his ground, his face angry. 'I merely meant——' He shrugged. 'I'm sorry, sir.' He did not sound it.

'Well, listen to me, will you?' He kept his voice very low. 'The weather is going to get worse, much worse. Before long we will have both watches on deck with steam hoses to cut away the ice. We are up here to do a job as best we can. It does not mean being battened down below and weeping for mother every time it bloody well rains!'

Stannard turned and beckoned to Dancy. 'Go yourself, Sub. Tell the buffer to take all reasonable precautions.' He kept his back to Lindsay. 'No sense in killing anyone.'

Lindsay leaned back in the hard chair, feeling its arms pressing into his ribs on one side then on the other as the old ship rolled heavily in the troughs. He wanted to go out on the wing in spite of the weather and watch the men detailed to replace the lashings on the Carley float. At the same time he knew he must stay where he was. Let them get on with it. Allow them to hate his guts and so work better for it, if that was what they needed.

He peered at his watch. In fifteen hours they would officially relieve another armed merchant cruiser from this patrol. They would not see her, however, which was probably just as well. It would do no good for some of the ship's company to see what the other A.M.C. looked like at close range. How they would be looking themselves after a few weeks of this misery.

The telephone buzzed again. 'Float's secure, sir.'

'Very good.'

Lindsay rubbed his chin, feeling the bristles rasp against his glove. He felt strangely relieved, in spite of his forced calm.

Dancy entered the bridge, his figure streaming, his face glowing with cold. He sounded pleased with himself.

'Not too bad, sir.' He clung to the voicepipes as the deck tilted and shuddered sickeningly beneath him. 'But by God it's parky out there!'

Stannard said shortly, 'I'm going to the chart room, Sub. Take over.'

Dancy stood beside the chair and rested his hands below the screen. Lindsay glanced at him curiously. Like the others, he knew little about him. Young, serious looking, but little else to give a clue. Without his cap and duffel coat he might even be described as nondescript.

He asked, 'What were you before you joined, Sub?'

Dancy said vaguely, 'I—I wrote things.' He nodded. 'Yes, I was a writer, sir.'

Lindsay watched his profile. His own information described Dancy's previous calling as bank clerk. But if he wanted to see himself as something else, what did it matter? Nothing which had happened before the Germans marched into Poland made any sense now. All the same. . . .

'Tell me about it.'

Dancy frowned. 'Well, I've always had this terrific feeling about the sea, sir. My parents didn't really want me to go into the Navy, and after school I tried my hand at writing.'

'Books?'

Dancy sounded uncomfortable. 'Not books, sir.'

'What then?'

'Things, sir'. Dancy looked at him desperately. 'About the sea.'

Stannard came back suddenly. 'Sir? Sickbay has just called. The doc wants,' he hesitated, 'he *asked* if you could change course for about twenty minutes. A seaman's

fallen down a ladder and broken his hip. Doc says he can't
fix it with all this motion.'

Lindsay looked at him. He could see the man's resentment building up. Waiting for him to refuse the doctor's
request. *He must think me a right bastard.*

'Very well, Pilot. But work out the additional revs we will
need to make up time, and inform the chief.'

Stannard blinked. 'Yes, sir. Right away.'

As he vanished, Dancy said seriously, 'Of course, I had
to do other jobs as well. For a time, that is.'

Lindsay slid from the chair, wincing as the stiffness
brought pain to his legs.

'Well, there's a job for you now.' He waved around the
bridge. 'Take over. I'm going to my cabin for a shave.' He
saw Dancy's face paling. 'Just call pilot if you can't cope.'
He tapped the brass telephone by his chair. 'Call *me* if you
like.' He grinned at Dancy's alarm. 'Good experience later
on for your writing, eh?'

With a glance at the gyro he walked stiffly to the ladder
abaft the wheelhouse and did not look back.

Dancy remained staring fixedly at his own dim reflection in the spray-dappled glass. He felt riveted to the deck,
unable to move. Even his breathing had become difficult.

Very cautiously he looked over his shoulder. The quartermaster's eyes glittered like stones in the dim compass
light, the rest of the bridge party swayed with the ship, like
silent drunks.

Nothing had changed, and the realisation almost
unnerved him. *He* was in sole command of this ship and
some two hundred and fifty human beings.

The quartermaster, for instance. How did he see him?
he wondered. Authority, an officer in whose hands he was
quite willing to entrust his life?

He asked suddenly, 'How is she handling, Quartermaster?'

The seaman, McNiven, stiffened. He had been watching the ticking gyro, holding the staggering ship dead on

course, so what the hell was wrong with Dancy? His eyes flickered momentarily from the compass, sensing a trap of some sort.

'All right.' He waited. 'Sir.'

He had been thinking about his last leave in Chatham. The girl had seemed fair enough. But after a few pints under your belt you could get careless. He stirred uneasily, just as he had when the bloody Aussie navigator had spoken to the skipper about the sickbay. Suppose that bloody girl had given him a dose? What the hell should he do?

Dancy said, 'Oh, in that case,' he smiled through the gloom, 'carry on.'

McNiven glared at Dancy's back. Stupid sod, he thought. *Carry on.* That's all they can say.

Unaware of the quartermaster's unhappy dilemma, Dancy continued to stare straight ahead. It was true what he had told the captain. Partly. He had always loved the sea and ships, but his parents' means and open opposition had prevented his chances of trying for Dartmouth. At the bank he had often met a real naval officer. He used to come there when he was on leave to draw money, and Dancy had always tried to be the one to serve him. He had listened mesmerised to the man's casual comments about his ship, and the exotic places like Singapore and Bombay, Gibraltar and Mombasa. And later he had let his craving, his desperate imagination run riot.

He sometimes told himself that but for the war he would have gone raving mad at the bank. Mad, or turned to crime, robbing the vault, and making old Durnsford, the manager, beg on his knees for his life. He knew too that if the war had not come to save him he would have stayed on at the bank. No madness or crime, just the miserable day to day existence, made endurable only by his imagination.

At *King Alfred* when he had been training for his temporary commission he had met another cadet of about his own age. An Etonian, someone seemingly from another planet, he had transformed so much in Dancy's caution and suburban reserve. And it had been catching. When Dancy had gained the coveted gold stripe and had been sent to the little armed yacht at Bristol, the first lieutenant had asked him about his earlier profession. *Profession.* He could still remember that moment. Not job or work. Or business, as his mother would have described it. It had seemed quite natural to lie. 'I'm a writer,' he'd said. It had been easy. The officer had been impressed, just as Commander Lindsay had been. Writers were beyond the reach of Service minds. They were different and could not be challenged.

Stannard slammed back through the door and stared at him.

'Where's the cap'n, for Chrissake?'

'He left me in charge.' Dancy's eyes wavered under the Australian's incredulous gaze.

Stannard muttered, 'Must be off his bloody head!' He looked at McNiven. 'I'm going to alter course to zero-two-zero in half a sec. I'll just inform the sickbay.' He glanced at Dancy. 'In *charge*. Jesus!'

———————

Lindsay completed the shave and studied his face critically in the mirror. There were shadows beneath his eyes and his neck looked sore from wearing the towel under his duffel coat. But the shave, the hot water refreshed him, and he wondered how the surgery was going on the seaman's hip.

He glanced towards his other cabin and pictured the bunk beyond the door. The warm, enclosed world below the reading lamp. Perhaps later he might snatch some proper sleep.

Jupp padded into the cabin and laid a silver coffee pot carefully between the fiddles on a small table.

He said, 'The old girl's takin' it quite well, sir. Not too bad at all.'

Lindsay sat in a chair and stretched out his legs gratefully.

'At least the decks aren't awash all the time. That's something.'

The telephone rattled tinnily, and when he clapped it to his ear he heard Stannard say, 'The doc's reported that he's finished, sir. I'm about to alter course, if that's all right by you?'

'Good. Carry on, Pilot.'

He felt the deck tremble, a sudden tilt as the helm went over, and saw the curtains on the sealed scuttles standing out from the side as if on invisible wires. The sea boomed along the hull, angry and threatening, and then subsided with a slow hissing roar to prepare another attack.

The telephone buzzed again.

'Captain.' He raised the cup to his lips, watching Jupp as he stooped to pick a crumb from the carpet.

Stannard sounded terse. 'W/T office has picked up an S.O.S., sir. Plain language. It reads, *Am under attack by German raider.*' He paused, clearing his throat. 'Seems to be a Swedish ship, sir, probably a mistake on the Jerry's part——'

Lindsay snapped, 'Keep on to it!' He dropped the cup unheeded on the tray. 'I'm coming.'

He bounded up the ladder and found Stannard waiting outside the W/T office door. Two operators were crouched below their sets, and Petty Officer Telegraphist Hussey had also appeared to supervise them, his pyjamas clearly visible under his jacket.

He saw Lindsay and said awkwardly, 'Was just having a nap, sir. Had a feeling something like this might happen.' He was not bragging. Old hands often found themselves called to duty by instinct, and Lindsay had no intention of questioning it.

Lindsay asked, 'What do you make of it?'

From the door Stannard said, 'She gave a position, sir. I've got it plotted on the chart. She's about ninety miles due north of us.'

Hussey looked up from his steel chair. 'Someone's acknowledged, sir.'

Lindsay bit his lip. 'That'll be *Loch Glendhu,* the other A.M.C.'

Hussey added after a pause, 'Dead, sir. Not getting a peep now.'

Stannard said uneasily, 'That might mean anything.'

'Let me see your calculations.' Lindsay brushed past him into the chart room. In spite of the steam pipes it was damp and humid, the panelled sides bloomed with condensation.

'*Loch Glendhu* should be pretty near there, sir, according to our intelligence log.' Stannard seemed calm again, his voice detached and professional.

Lindsay stared at the neatly pencilled lines and bearings on the chart. *Loch Glendhu* was bigger than *Benbecula* and better armed. But no match for a warship. Perhaps she would haul off and report to base for instructions.

'Keep a permanent listening watch for her. Tell Hussey to monitor everything.'

What the hell was a Swedish ship doing up here anyway? Probably using the Denmark Strait as a matter of safety. Bad weather was better than being sunk by mistake in the calmer waters to the south.

'Lay off a course to intercept, Pilot.'

He recalled Fraser's words. *I can give you sixteen knots.* It would take over five hours to reach the neutral ship's position. Longer if he waited for instructions from some duty officer in the Admiralty operations' room. Five hours for men to die beyond reach or hope.

He realised that he was sweating badly in spite of the unmoving air, could feel it running down his spine like iced water. Without effort he could see the low grey shape on the horizon, feel the breath-stopping explosions as the

raider's shells had torn steel and flesh to fragments all
around him. He tried not to look at the nearest scuttle with
its sealed deadlight. Tried to shut it from memory.

Lindsay asked, 'Have you got it yet?'

Stannard put down his brass dividers and looked up
from the chart. 'Course would be zero-one-zero, sir.'

Lindsay nodded. 'Not would be, Pilot, *is*. Bring her
round and get the chief on the telephone.'

He realised that Goss was on the bridge, his heavy face
questioning and worried.

He said, 'The A.M.C. we're relieving is probably going
to assist another ship, Number One.'

Goss nodded jerkily. 'I know. I just heard. Neutral, isn't
she?' It sounded like an accusation.

'Nobody's neutral up here.'

Stannard called, 'The chief's on the phone, sir.'

Lindsay took it quickly. *'Loch Glendhu'*s in trouble,
Chief.'

Fraser sounded miles away. 'I'll give you all I've got.
When you're ready.'

Lindsay looked at the others. 'We'll see what we can do.'
To Stannard he added, 'Right. Full ahead together.'

The telegraphs clanged over, and far below,
enshrouded in rising steam on his footplate, Fraser
watched the big needles swing round the twin dials and
settle on FULL.

Slightly below him he saw his assistant, Lieutenant
Dyke, grimacing at him and shaking his head. His lips said,
'She'll knock herself to bits.'

Fraser's lips replied, 'Bloody good job.'

Then the noise began to mount with each thrashing
revolution, the machinery and fittings quivering to join in
with their own particular din, and Fraser forgot Dyke and
everything else but the job in hand.

4 A ship burns

'Still nothing from W/T office, sir.' Stannard sounded wary.

Lindsay nodded but kept his eyes fixed on the ship's labouring bows. *Benbecula* was no longer riding each wavecrest but smashing through the angry water like a massive steel battering ram. The spray rose in an almost unbroken curtain around the forecastle, crumbling in the wind to rain against the bridge screens like pebbles, and the motion was savage. Every strut and frame in the superstructure seemed to be rattling and protesting, and as the sea sluiced up and over the well deck Lindsay saw the foot of the foremast standing like an isolated pinnacle in the great frothing white flood. He wondered briefly what the lookout would feel in his snug pod, and if the mast was quivering to the onrushing water.

A quick glance at his watch told him that they should sight something soon, if something there was. The hours since that short, feeble burst of morse had felt like days, and all the while the ship had crashed and rolled, pitched and battered her way forward into the teeth of sea and wind alike.

There was a metallic scrape above the bridge and he imagined Maxwell in his control position testing the big rangefinder, cursing his spray-smeared lenses. It was a good rangefinder, but in a war where weapons had long since outstripped the minds of those who planned day-to-day survival, it was already out of date. Even the old

Vengeur had been allowed some of the better sophisti-
cated detection equipment, and newer ships were fitted
with the latest, and even more secret, gear. But *Benbecula*
was right down at the bottom of the list as far as that was
concerned. Convoy protection, anti-submarine tactics
and strikes on enemy coastal resources took all the prece-
dence, which on paper was only right. But as he stared
intently through the whirring clearview screen Lindsay
wondered what the planners would think if they were
here on the bridge instead of their comfortable nine-to-
five offices. It was almost unnerving to imagine the radio
operators at this very moment, at Scapa or down in the
cellars of the Admiralty. Information and calls for help
or advice. A convoy massacred, a U-boat sighted, or some
maddening signal about clothing issue and the need to
entertain a visiting politician. The telegraphists would be
hardened to all of it. Probably sitting there right now,
sipping tea and chatting about their girls, the next run
ashore.

He glanced quickly around the bridge. Tense and
expectant, a small, sheltered world surrounded by sea
noise and the creaking symphony of metal under strain.

It was all over the ship by now, and he made a mental
note to arrange for the tannoy system to be extended to
all decks and flats so that if necessary he could speak to
every available man himself.

He tried to remember the exact layout of his command, see it like some blueprint or open plan. They were
all down there listening and waiting. Hearing the sea and
feeling the hull staggering as if to fall apart under them.
Warm clothing and inflatable lifebelts. Those little red
lights which were supposed to show where a man was
drifting in the water.

Stannard said, 'Time, sir.' He sounded less weary now.
Alert, or maybe frightened like most of them.

Lindsay felt the sudden dryness in his throat. *As I am.*
'Very well, Pilot.'

He reached forward and held his thumb on the small red button. Just a while longer he hesitated. It was their first time together. As a ship's company. He cursed himself for his nagging anxiety and thrust hard on the button.

The alarm bells were muffled, but nevertheless he could hear them screaming away throughout the ship, and the instant clatter of feet on bridge ladders, the dull thuds of watertight doors slamming shut.

As messengers and bosun's mates hurried to voice-pipes and telephones the reports started to come in from every position.

'Number Six gun closed up!'

'Number Four gun closed up!'

'Damage control party closed up!'

The mingled voices and terse acknowledgements sounded unreal, tinny. Through the drifting spray he saw crouching figures hurrying towards the forward guns, and could almost feel the icy metal of shell hoists and breeches.

Stannard said, 'Ship closed up at action stations, sir.'

Lindsay eyed him searchingly. 'Good. Three minutes. Not at all bad.'

He swivelled in the chair and looked at the figures which had filled the bridge. His team for whatever would happen next.

Jolliffe on the wheel, wiping condensation off the gyro repeater with his sleeve. Quartermasters and messengers, signalmen, with Ritchie gripping a flag locker while he adjusted his night glasses. Stannard and young Dancy, and Lieutenant Aikman, listed as boarding officer, ready to fight, die, go mad, anything.

He turned back to the whirring screen. Goss was in damage control. All spare stokers and extra hands with him ready to shore up bulkheads, put out fires, hold the ship together with bare hands if necessary. And Goss was

far enough from the bridge to survive and assume command should Lindsay fall dead or wounded. It was
practical not to put all your eggs in one basket. Practical,
but hardly comforting.

He thought of the marine lieutenant, de Chair, down
aft with his two six-inch guns and the feeble twelve
pounder. If he was inwardly resentful at being quarters
officer of an ancient battery in an A.M.C. he gave no hint
of it. Elegant, deceptively casual, he would be more use
leading his marines in open combat, he thought.

Stannard replaced a handset. 'Nothing from masthead, sir.'

'Thank you.' Another glance at his watch. 'Reduce to
half speed.'

No sense now in shaking the machinery to pieces. He
felt the chair quiver with something like relief as the
telegraphs clanged their reply.

The Swedish ship might be sunk, or in the confusion
had given the wrong position. The enemy could have
realised his mistake and ceased fire and already be many
miles away, steaming for home like a guilty assassin.

And there had been no signal from *Loch Glendhu*
either. But up here in the Denmark Strait you could
never rely on anything. Only eyes, ears and bloody
instinct, as someone had once told him.

The screen was squeaking more loudly, and he realised
the glass was being scattered with larger, paler blobs than
mere spray.

Stannard muttered, 'Bloody snow. That's just about all
we need!'

It was more sleet than snow, but it could get worse, and
if it froze the gun crews would be hard put to do anything.

The wavecrests were less violent, the troughs wider
spaced, and he guessed the snow would be coming very
soon now. He shuddered inwardly and wondered if the
German invasion of Russia was facing this kind of

weather. In spite of everything he was suddenly thankful to be here, enclosed by the ship, and not slogging through frozen mud, waist-deep in slush. A ship was a home as much as a weapon. A soldier fought often without knowing where he was, or if he was alone and already considered expendable by the master-minds of war.

The telephone made him flinch in his seat.

Stannard snapped, 'Very well. Good. Keep reporting.' Then to Lindsay, 'Masthead reports a red glow, sir. Fine on the port bow.'

Before he could reply the speaker at the rear of the bridge intoned, 'Control . . . Bridge.' It was Maxwell's voice, unhurried and toneless. 'Red two-oh. Range one-double-oh. A ship on fire.'

Lindsay swung his glasses to the screen. Nothing. Maxwell's spotters had done well to see it in such bad visibility. He slid from the chair and lowered his eye to the glowing gyro repeater.

'Port ten.'

'Port ten, sir. Ten of port wheel on, sir.' Jolliffe's voice was heavy. Like the man.

'Midships. Steady. Steer three-four-zero.' To Stannard he added, 'I hope your people know their stuff. I'm going to need a good plotting team when we clear this lot.'

He picked up another telephone and heard Maxwell's voice right in his ear.

'Guns, this is the captain. I'll not take chances. A diagonal approach so that you can get all the starboard battery to bear, right?'

Maxwell understood. 'Starshell on One, sir?'

'Yes.'

He heard the distant voices of the control team already rapping out ranges and bearings to the crews below.

'And you did well to find her. *Loch Glendhu* must have misread the signal, or buzzed off in pursuit.'

He replaced the telephone.

Dancy reported, 'Number One has loaded with star-shell, sir.'

The gunnery speaker again. 'All guns load, load, load, semi-armour-piercing!'

Lindsay had taken out his pipe without realising it and gripped it in his teeth so hard that the pain helped to steady him.

'Now, Pilot. Bring her round to three-two-five.'

Even as the wheel went over the speaker said, 'Range now oh-eight-oh.'

Four miles. But in this driving sleet it could have been a hundred. Lindsay concentrated his mind on the voices which muttered and squeaked on every line and speaking tube. He recalled the brand-new sub-lieutenants, down there acting as quarters officers on the forward arma-ment. The seasoned gunlayers and trainers knew what to do if anyone did, and the young officers were there to learn rather than do much more.

But Lindsay knew from bitter experience that time was not always kind. In the *Vengeur* he had seen one of the four-inch guns manned by a midshipman, two stokers and a cook when its real crew had been ripped to bloody remnants under an air attack. You could never rely on time.

'There it is!' Stannard craned forward. 'Starboard bow, sir!'

Lindsay held up his glasses and saw the flickering glow for the first time. It was reflected more in the low clouds than on the water, and the thickening sleet made even that difficult.

Stannard added grimly, 'The starshell'll scare the hell out of the poor bastards.'

'Better that than make a bad approach. If the snow comes down we might lose her altogether.'

Maxwell's voice sounded muffled as he spoke into his array of handsets. 'Number *One* gun. Range oh-seven-five.' One of the sub-lieutenants must have interrupted him for he rasped savagely, '*Listen,* for God's sake. Bearing is still Green oh-five, now get on with it!'

The crash came almost before the speaker had gone dead again, the sound of the shot coming inboard on the wind like a double explosion. When the shell burst it was momentarily like some strange electric storm. Lindsay realised that the gunlayer had applied too much elevation so the flare had burst in or above the clouds. Their bellies shone through the sleet like silver, and then as the flare drifted into view the sea was bathed with the hard, searing glare of a glacier.

The ship was already well down in the water, her tilting hull shining in the harsh glare, the smoke from her blazing interior pouring downwind in one solid plume, black and impenetrable. The fires were very low now, although here and there along the hull fresh outbursts shot skyward, hurling sparks and glowing embers across the water like tracers.

The flare was almost gone. 'Another!' Lindsay could not take his eyes from the dying ship. Knowing he was right. Willing otherwise. Sweating.

A door banged open and Mr. Tobey, the boatswain, entered the wheelhouse, the icy air following him as he sought out Lindsay's figure.

'Beg pardon, sir. I was just wonderin'. If those poor devils which is still alive can't understand our lingo, 'ow will we make 'em understand what we're doin'?' He did not see Lindsay's frozen expression. 'I got my people ready at the rafts and lines——'

Stannard said quietly, 'The midshipr..an on my plotting team can speak Swedish, I believe, sir.'

Lindsay let the glasses fall on to his chest. He had to draw several deep breaths before he could find his voice again.

'They will understand, Mr. Tobey.' He walked to the open door. 'She's *Loch Glendhu.*' He seized the frame to steady himself. 'I've met her before. I know her.'

Stannard said softly, 'Oh, my God.'

Tobey was staring past Lindsay at the flickering pattern of flames. 'Sea's quietened a bit, sir. The whalers could be lowered.'

Lindsay did not turn. 'Starboard ten.' He waited, his nerves screaming soundlessly. 'Midships. Steady. Slow ahead together.' Then he looked at Tobey's shocked face. 'Yes. Whalers and rafts. Call for volunteers.'

He swung round as a sharp explosion threw an arrowhead of fire high into the sky. A magazine perhaps. Not long now.

Ritchie stepped aside as Tobey ran past. 'Shall I call 'er up, sir?'

Lindsay said flatly, 'Just tell her to hold on.' He heard Ritchie jerking the lamp shutter, but as he had expected, there was no reply. He said, 'Keep trying. There'll be some left alive. They'll need all the hope they can get in the next minutes.'

Another face emerged in the gloom. It was Boase, the doctor. He said to Stannard, 'How many left, d'you think?'

It was too much for Lindsay's reeling mind. 'Where the hell do you imagine you are?' He was shouting but could not hold it back. Boase was like those other doctors. Ignore it. Forget it. Don't worry. The stupid, heartless bastards!

Boase fell back. 'I'm sorry, sir, I didn't mean——'

Lindsay shouted, 'You never bloody well do mean anything! This isn't some teaching hospital put here for your benefit! Not a Saturday night punch-up with a few revellers at your out-patients department while you play God!' He swung round and gestured towards the sea. Framed in the door, with the sleet glittering redly in the flames, it looked as if the sky was raining blood. 'Take a good look! There are men dying out there. Cursing the blind, ignorant fools who let them go to war in ships like that one. Like our own!'

A bosun's mate said hoarsely, 'Boats ready for lowering, sir.'

Stannard spoke first. 'Very well. Tell them to watch out for burning oil——'

Lindsay said, 'Stop engines.'

He wiped his forehead with his hand. The skin was hot, burning, despite the cold air from the door. It was not the doctor's fault. It was unfair to take it out of him in front of the others. Unfair, and cruelly revealing about his failing strength and self-control.

The deck swayed very slowly as the ship idled forward, her screws stopped for the first time since leaving the Flow.

More sounds rumbled in the darkness, like a ship breaking up. Crying out in her own way against the fools who had let it be so. All the fires had gone but for one darting tongue which appeared to be burning right through the other ship's bilge plates as she started to roll on her side, the sea around her misty with steam and whipped spray.

Small lights glittered in a deep trough, and he saw one of the whalers pulling strongly towards the sinking ship. He gritted his teeth as another crash from the forward gun hurled a starshell high over the scene of misery and pain.

Along the *Benbecula*'s side the boatswain had lowered some of the rafts, to act as staging posts for the survivors before they were hauled bodily up her tall hull. He saw white jackets in the cold and wet, and hoped Boase was there too with his stretcher parties.

When he looked up at the funnel with its low plume of dark smoke he realised that one side of it was shining like ice in the glare. The snow had started. There was not much time left. In the whalers the volunteers would even now be watching the snow, fearing more perhaps for their own survival than those they had gone to save.

He thought too of the corvette's small quarterdeck on that morning. The line of corpses awaiting burial, like those aboard the listing cruiser at Scapa. And the two small ones at the end of the line. Like little parcels under the flag as they had gone over the rail. *Look after them.* Well, they had gone where there was no more hurt. No persecution.

Stannard said loudly, 'She's going!'

More frothing water, and the last flame extinguished with the suddenness of death. Then nothing.

It seemed like an age before Stannard reported, 'Boats returning, sir.'

He walked to the extent of the starboard wing and peered down through the snow flurries. The boats were crammed with bodies. Shining with oil. A familiar enough sight in the Atlantic. Others clung around the sides of the boats, treading water, their gasps audible even on the wing. Here and there a red lifelight shone on the water, others floated away unheeded, tiny scarlet pinpricks, each marking a corpse.

He tried to tear his eyes from the struggling figures below him. There was so much to do. A signal to be coded and despatched, to inform those who were concerned with what had happened. Start the wheels turning. The Secretary of the Admiralty regrets to announce the loss of H.M.S. *Loch Glendhu. Stop it.*

Lindsay thrust himself bodily from the wet steel and turned to see Lieutenant Aikman staring at him.

'Go and make sure that everything's all right! If they need more hands, take them from aft. I want those boats hoisted and secured without delay.' He watched the officer scurrying for the ladder. One more victim of his own despair and blind anger.

Dancy said hoarsely, 'If I have to die, I hope it's like that, sir.'

Lindsay looked at him for several seconds, feeling his anger giving way to a kind of madness, with wild,

uncontrollable laughter almost ready to burst out. Then
he reached out to pat Dancy's arm.

'Then we shall have to see what we can do. But before
you decide anything definite, go and visit the survivors in
the sickbay. Then tell me again.'

Stannard called, 'Ready to get under way, sir.'

Lindsay saw his own reflection in the glass screen, as if
he was indeed outside himself, assessing his resources.

'Very well. Slow ahead together. Bring her round on
course again.'

He saw Ritchie thumbing through a manual then holding his torch steady above one page.

He asked, 'How many, Yeo?'

Ritchie replied quietly, 'She 'ad a company of three
'undred, sir.'

Goss appeared through the rear door and said thickly,
'We've picked up thirty, sir.'

Lindsay seated himself carefully in the tall chair.
Strange how light his limbs felt. As in the dream.

Goss seemed to think he had not heard. 'Only *thirty,*
sir!'

'Thank you, Number One. We will remain at action
stations for another hour at least. Pass the word for a
good lookout while visibility holds.'

Not that they'll need telling now, he thought dully.

He heard Goss slamming out of the wheelhouse. Probably cursing me. The iron, cold captain that no pain, no
sentiment can reach. God, if he only knew.

One hour later the snow came down, and within no
time at all the ship was thrusting her way through a
swirling, white world, enclosed and excluded from all
else.

As the men left their action stations and ran or staggered below to warmth and an illusion of safety, Lindsay
heard a sailor laughing, the sound strangely sad in the
steady blizzard.

Horror from what they had witnessed was giving way

to relief at being spared. Later it would be different, but now it was good to hear that someone could laugh, he thought.

———————

Goss clumped into the wheelhouse, shaking snow from his oilskin and stamping it from his heavy sea boots. The bristles on his chin were grey, almost white, so that in the hard reflected glare he looked even older.

'Ready, sir.' He watched as Lindsay slid from his chair and walked towards the starboard door.

The motion was steadier, and overnight the sea had lost much of its anger, as if smoothed and eased by the growing power of the snow. Yet there was some wind, and every so often the snow would twist into strange patterns, swirling around the bridge superstructure, or driving like a desert storm, parallel with the deck.

Lindsay rested one hand on the clip. Apart from a few short snatches in his chair, he had not slept, and as he stood by the door he could feel the chill in his bones, the inability to think clearly.

Goss's eyes, red-rimmed with salt and fatigue, followed him as he tugged open the door and stepped on to the open wing. Watching him. Searching for something perhaps.

The snow squeaked under his leather sea boots, but there was no ice as yet. He felt it touching his face, pattering across his oilskin as he moved slowly to the extremity of the wing. There was hardly any visibility, and when he peered down he saw the sluggish bow wave sliding past as the only sign that the ship was still thrusting ahead.

He raised his head and stared fixedly abeam, the snow melting on his lashes, running down his cheeks like the tears on Ritchie's face that day at Scapa. The yeoman was here now, his features like stone.

In spite of the snow and dirty slush there were many

others from the watch below. Dark clusters of men against the glittering, descending backcloth.

He heard himself say, 'I'll be about ten minutes, Number One.'

Is that all it took? He did not wait for Goss's reply but turned and clattered down the ladder, his boots slipping on the slush, his hands cold on the rungs, for he had forgotten his gloves. Down more ladders to the promenade deck. As he strode aft, his legs straddled against the steady motion, he saw flecks of rust showing already through the new grey paint. He paused and looked abeam. Out there, some one hundred and fifty miles away, was the western extreme of Iceland. The nearest land. Up here, the only land.

He quickened his pace, and when he reached the after well deck he had to steel himself again before he could climb down the last ladder where Maxwell and Stannard were waiting to assist with the burials.

There were only eight of them. Five of those who had been picked up alive. The others had been hauled aboard the whalers by accident. Only eight, yet the line seemed endless, so that in his mind's eye Lindsay could picture all the others which *Benbecula* had left in her wake. There had been three hundred in *Loch Glendhu*'s company, Ritchie had said.

He strode to the side and returned Maxwell's salute. Beyond the gunnery officer he saw more watching figures and Lieutenant de Chair with some of his marines.

God, how could he do it? Just ten minutes, he had told Goss, but he was already cracking. He could feel his reserve stripping itself away like a protective skin. Leaving him naked to their serious faces.

He cleared his throat. 'Let's get on with it.'

As he pulled the little book from his pocket he looked up, caught off guard as de Chair said quietly, 'Very well, Sarn't. Off coats.'

He stared, almost dazed, as the marines obediently stripped off their shining oilskins and formed into a tight, swaying line behind the canvas-covered bodies. He realised they were all in their best blue uniforms, that somehow they were shaved. In spite of everything. *Oh God, what are they doing to me?*

Blindly he thumbed open the book, the print dancing before him, the snow falling softly on his hands.

'Now.'

He removed his cap and squinted up directly into the snow. It was so thick that he could not see if the ensign was at half-mast or not. What the hell did it matter to these dead men?

Maxwell shouted towards the bridge, and Lindsay heard the distant clang of telegraphs as the engines fell silent once more.

He stared hard at the open page and then, with sudden resolution, thrust the book back into his pocket. He did not need it any more. He had spoken the words too often. Heard them more than enough to forget even if he wanted to.

'We commend unto Thy hands of mercy, most merciful Father, the souls of these our brothers departed, and we commit their bodies to the deep. . . .'

He licked his lips as the marines edged forward, their faces like Ritchie's had been as they raised the neat bundles beneath the two large ensigns.

It was always a bad moment. When you did not know any of these quiet bundles. Strangers . . . not even that. Only the uniforms had been the same.

One of them was *Loch Glendhu*'s captain, who had died within thirty minutes of being carried aboard. By rights he should have died back there on his bridge. He had been hit by several shell splinters and had been savagely burned before an explosion had blasted him into the sea. Even then he had refused to die. Maybe he had seen Ritchie's signal lamp, or the whalers coming for his men.

Or perhaps he needed to stay alive just long enough to tell what he knew. To pass on his dying anger and hatred.

Lindsay had left the bridge for a moment to visit him in the sickbay, had watched the other captain's mouth through the bandages as he had gasped out his short, bitter story.

There had been no Swedish ship. No neutral under attack. Just the big German raider, lying there waiting for them like a tiger shark. True, she had looked Swedish, with her painted flag and neutral colouring, but as *Loch Glendhu* had turned to offer help, the enemy's guns had opened fire from a dozen concealed positions, smashing through the hull, blasting men to pulp who seconds before had been preparing to lower boats, to give aid.

As *Loch Glendhu* had become a raging inferno and had begun to settle down, the raider had gathered way, pausing only to fire a few more shells and rake the shattered vessel with automatic fire.

The dying captain had said, 'It was my fault. Should have been ready. Expecting it. But it was something different. New.' Then he had died.

Lindsay had been speaking the familiar words even though his mind had been reliving those last moments. When he looked again the flags were being folded, the bodies gone.

He nodded to Maxwell, and within seconds the big screws had started to churn the sea into a busy froth. He replaced his cap, the rim cold around his forehead, like ice-rime.

The marines were struggling into their wet coats, Stannard was staring over the rail, his eyebrows white with snow.

It was done. Finished.

Again he returned Maxwell's salute and said, 'Thank you, Guns.' He looked at the others. 'All of you.'

Stannard fell into step beside him as they walked forward along the promenade deck.

Lindsay heard himself say, 'I will make that signal now, Pilot. Can't tell them much——' He shrugged, knowing Stannard was looking at him. Thinks I don't care, or that I am past caring. Or searching for some explanation when there's none to offer.

As they started up the last ladder Lindsay heard voices. Low voices made harsh with anger. He climbed on to the open wing and saw Goss hunched in one corner, his massive figure towering above Fraser, who was glaring up at him, his white overalls coarse against the swirling snow.

Lindsay snapped, 'What the hell is going on?' Beyond the others he saw that the wheelhouse door was closed so that the anger would remain unheard.

Goss whirled round. 'Nothing, sir!'

Fraser exploded, 'Nothing, my bloody arse!' He hurried towards Lindsay. 'I came on deck. Just to watch quietly when——' He glanced briefly aft. 'But there were too many of the lads there, and I wanted to be on my own.' He held up a greasy hand as Goss made to interrupt. 'I was forrard, by Number Two gun when the engines stopped.'

For an instant longer Lindsay imagined that Fraser's keen ear had detected some flaw in the engines' familiar beat.

The little engineer added slowly, 'I heard something sir.'

Goss said harshly, 'You can't be sure, for God's sake!'

Fraser looked at Lindsay, his tone suddenly pleading. 'I've been too long in my trade not to recognise a winch, sir.' He swung round and pointed into the driving snow. It was thicker and the forecastle only just visible. Beyond the bows it was like a white wall. 'There was a ship out there, sir. I *know* it!'

Lindsay stood stockstill, his mind filling with words, faces, sounds. The burial service. The marines in their blue uniforms. The snow. Two dead children.

Goss said thickly, 'Suppose you were mistaken, Chief?' When nobody answered he added in a louder voice, 'Might have been anything!'

Stannard was still on top of the ladder, unable to get past Lindsay. He called, 'But surely no bloody raider would still *be* here?'

Lindsay moved slowly towards the forepart of the screen. 'Why not?' His voice was so quiet that the others drew closer. 'He's done pretty well for himself so far. Sunk an A.M.C. without any fuss at all.' How could he sound so calm? 'He's probably sitting out the snow and preparing for *Loch Glendhu*'s relief. Us, for instance.'

Goss stared at him incredulously. 'But we don't *know*, sir!'

Stannard said, 'Could be. He'd listen for any signals. Just make sure there were no other ships around to spread the alarm——' He fell back as Lindsay thrust him aside and wrenched open the wheelhouse door.

As he tore off the dripping oilskin and dropped it unheeded to the deck he snapped, 'Back to your engine room, Chief. I want *dead slow,* right?' He looked at Stannard. 'Pass the word quickly. I want the hands at action stations on the double. But no bells or pipes, not a bloody sound out of anyone.' He sounded wild. 'Send them in their bare feet if necessary!'

Midshipman Kemp had emerged from the chart room and Lindsay seized his arm saying, 'Get the gunnery officer yourself, lad, and be sharp about it!'

The boy hesitated, his face very pale. 'Where is he, sir?'

'Down aft. He's just helped to bury some of our friends.' He looked coldly at Goss by the door. 'Well, I intend to bury some of those bastards if I can!'

He ignored the startled glances and walked to the front of the bridge.

The deck was trembling very gently now. Fraser must have run like a madman to reach the engine room so quickly.

Five minutes later Stannard said, 'Ship at action stations, sir.'

Lindsay turned and ran his eye over the others. Jolliffe had certainly been fast enough. He was still wearing old felt slippers and there were crumbs on his portly stomach.

'I need three good hands up forrard.' It was like speaking his thoughts aloud. Describing a scene not yet enacted. 'Right in the eyes of the ship. Yeo, send some of your bunting-tossers. They'll have keen ears and eyes. If,' he checked himself, 'when we run this bastard to ground I want to see him first. So he'll know what it's like.'

Ritchie buttoned his oilskin collar. 'I'll go meself, sir.' He beckoned to two of his signalmen. 'It'll be a pleasure.'

Like a towering ghost the *Benbecula* glided forward into the snow, her decks and superstructure already inches deep from the blizzard.

Apart from the gentle beat of engines, the occasional creak of steel or the nervous movement of feet above the bridge, there was nothing to betray her.

Lindsay took out his pipe and put it between his teeth, his eyes on Ritchie's black figure as it hurried between the anchor cables. Perhaps Fraser had been wrong. There might be nothing out there in the snow.

He thought suddenly of the dying captain. *Something different*, he said, ashamed perhaps for not understanding the new rules.

He gripped the side of his chair and waited. At least we will have tried, he thought.

5 Learning

Petty Officer Ritchie tore off one glove with his teeth and fumbled with the clip on the small telephone locker. He was as far forward in the bows as he could reach, and was conscious of the muffled stillness, as if the ship were abandoned in the steady snowfall. He wrenched the door open and clapped the handset to his ear. As he glanced aft he noticed the bridge was almost hidden by snow, with only the wheelhouse windows showing distinctly, like square black eyes.

'Bridge.' It was the captain's voice, and Ritchie could imagine him standing beside his chair as he had last seen him, peering down towards the forecastle.

'Yeoman, sir.' He turned his back on the bridge and stared over the steel bulwark. 'In position now.'

'Good.' A pause. 'I will keep this line open.'

Ritchie touched the snow which lined the bulwark like cotton wool. It felt stiffer. Maybe a hint of ice, he thought, as he moved his eyes slowly from side to side. Occasionally the wind became more evident as it twisted the snow into nervous, darting patterns, and he saw the sea moving slowly towards him, dark, like lead. Despite all his layers of clothing he shivered. He had heard the officers talking, and his own experience told him the rest. You could not serve on a dozen bridges over the same number of years without learning.

He held his breath as a shadow lifted through the snow, and then relaxed slightly. The wind had cut a path just long enough to reveal an open patch of water. A small, dismal patch which for a few seconds had become a ship. If there was a ship out there, he knew she could just as easily be listening and waiting for them.

The hunter once again. Right now those bloody Germans might be adjusting their sights, hands tightening on triggers and shells while *Benbecula*'s outline nudged blindly into their crosswires. Even if the captain was right, and they got off the first salvos, both ships might pound one another to scrap, sink out here, one hundred and fifty miles from land.

To his left he heard Cummings, one of the young signalmen, sniffing in the cold air, and wondered briefly what he made of it all. Six months ago he had been a baker's roundsman in Birmingham, and now . . . he shook himself angrily. What the hell difference did it make? It was odd the way the snow made you drowsy, no matter how tensed up you were.

God, the deck was steady. Hardly an engine vibration reached him in the eyes of the ship, and in the handset earpiece he imagined he could hear Lindsay breathing. A good bloke, he thought. Not condescending like some of the arrogant bastards he had met. Genuine, maybe a bit too much so. Like someone nursing an old hurt. Something which was tearing him apart, so that when he heard of others' troubles he felt it all the more. Like the burial service, for instance. He started. Was that only moments ago?

He had seen it then as the captain had spoken the prayer over the corpses. The same expression he had witnessed in London at the mass burial. Almost the whole street. The whole bloody street. They had said the bombers had been making for the London docks, but they had hit his street just the same. The East End was never the most attractive of places. Terraced houses, every one the same as its neighbour, and each with its own backyard the size of a carpet. Madge had always insisted on calling it a garden. He felt his lips move in a small smile. A garden.

The burial had been worse because of the weather. Bright and sunny, as if the world wanted to ignore their little drama. Red buses passing the end of the street in regular procession, making for Bethnal Green Underground station. A barrage balloon, fat and shining in the sunlight like a contented whale. A workman whistling in the ruins of a church which had been blitzed the week before.

But the faces had been the same. Frozen. Like Lindsay's. He wondered if anyone else had noticed. Not Maxwell, he was sure of that. Stupid parade-ground basher. Should have been a bloody Nazi himself.

He stiffened. There it was again. His head swivelled round as he heard the faint but distinct clang of metal.

'Green four-five, sir. As far as I can tell. I 'eard metal.'

A small shudder ran through his boots and he guessed that the helm had gone over.

Then Lindsay said, 'Keep it up, Yeo.' Cool, unhurried, as if he was reporting on a cricket match.

Cummings whispered, 'What d'you think, Yeo?'

Ritchie shrugged. 'I dunno.'

He felt the sweater warm against his neck. Madge had made it for him from an old jumper she had unravelled to get the wool. He tried to control the sudden surge of emotion. He had to get used to it. Accept it. But how long would it take? Only yesterday he had heard Hussey, the PO telegraphist, describing his service in a China river gunboat before the war. He had said to himself, *I'll tell the kids about that, next leave.* It was small, unguarded moments like that which left him aching and lost.

The snow whipped against his cheek in a wet mould, as with sudden force the wind swept hard across the bulwark. He dashed it from his eyes, and when he looked again he saw the other ship.

It was incredible she could be so close, that she had been there all the while. She lay diagonally across *Benbecula*'s line of advance, the stern towards him, her tall upperworks and poop gleaming like icing on a giant cake.

He said hoarsely, 'Ship, sir! Fine on th' starboard bow! Range about two cables!'

As the endless seconds dragged past he kept his eyes fixed on the other vessel. She was big right enough, probably a liner, with two funnels and a large Swedish flag painted on her side. As he watched he saw part of her upper bridge move slightly, and realised it was being lifted bodily by one of her forward derricks. The chief had heard a winch. The Germans were changing their appearance already. Preparing for their next victim. There was a sudden flurry of foam beneath her high counter where seconds earlier the enemy's hull had rolled, drifting on the sluggish rollers.

He rasped, 'Down, lads! She's seen us!' He grabbed Cummings' sleeve and dragged him gasping to the deck. "Old yer 'eads down, and keep 'em there till I tells you different!'

Cummings lay beside him, his body only inches away, eyes filling his face as he gasped, 'I—I'm going to be sick!'

Ritchie opened his mouth to say something but heard the sudden tinkle of bells at the nearest gun and changed his mind.

Like the yeoman, Lindsay had seen the other ship's blurred outline with something like disbelief. Perhaps the snow was passing over, but it gave the deceptive impression of leaving one opening, an arena just large enough to contain the two ships, while beyond and all around the downpour was as thick as before.

'Port fifteen! Full ahead both engines!'

The sharpness of his voice seemed to break the shocked stillness in the wheelhouse, and the figures on either side of him started to move and react, as if propelled by invisible levers.

'Midships! *Steady!*'

Jolliffe muttered, 'Steady, sir. Course three-five-five.'

Voicepipes and handsets crackled on every side, and he heard Maxwell shouting, 'Commence, commence, commence!' And the instant reply from the fire gongs.

By turning slightly to port Lindsay had laid the enemy on an almost parallel course some four hundred yards away. He watched the sudden flurry from her twin screws, saw her poop tilt slightly to their urgent thrust, and knew that in spite of everything his small advantage could soon be lost.

Then, with bare seconds between, the three starboard side guns opened fire. Number Three which was furthest aft fired first, and he guessed the marines had been quicker to translate the shouted instructions into action. The six-inch shell screamed past the bridge, the shock-wave searing against the superstructure like an express train charging through a station. The other two guns followed almost together, the smoke pluming across the deck, the savage detonations shaking the gratings beneath Lindsay's feet and bringing several gasps of alarm.

'She's turning away!' Lieutenant Aikman almost fell as Number Three gun hurled itself inboard on its recoil springs and sent another shell screaming across the grey water.

Tonelessly the voice of a control rating said, 'Over. Down two hundred.'

The deck was quivering violently now as the revolutions mounted, and the bow wave ploughed away on either beam like a solid glass arrowhead.

'Starboard ten.' Lindsay dropped his eye to the gyro. 'Midships.' He saw droplets of his sweat falling on the protective cover. 'Steady.'

When he raised his head again the enemy was nearer, the bearing more acute.

A bosun's mate shouted, 'Number Three gun 'as ceased firin', sir. Unable to bear!'

Lindsay looked at Stannard. It could not be helped. If

he hauled off again to give the marines a clear view of the enemy the other ship would escape in the snow. She was big. About seventeen thousand tons. Big, modern and with all the power required to move her at speed.

The two forward guns, their view unimpeded by the superstructure, fired again. The long orange tongues leaping from their muzzles as the shells streaked away towards the enemy.

Through the snow flurries Lindsay saw a brief flash, like a round red eye, and heard Maxwell yell, 'A *hit!* We hit the bastard!'

She was pulling away with each second, her funnels already hidden by the snow.

Lindsay dashed his hand across his forehead and waited, counting seconds, until the guns fired once more. Longer intervals now. He pictured the shell hoists jerking up their shafts, cooks, stewards, writers and supply ratings cursing and struggling to feed the guns with those great, ungainly missiles while the hull shook around them. And in the engine and boiler rooms Fraser's men would be hearing the explosions above the din of their machinery, watching the tall sides and praying that no shell came their way. The inrush of water, the scalding steam. Oblivion.

The snow lifted and writhed above the enemy ship, and Lindsay saw the telltale orange flash. The other captain had at last got one of his after guns to bear.

The shell hit the *Benbecula*'s side like a thunderclap, the shock hurling men and equipment about the bridge, while above the starboard bulwark the smoke came billowing inboard in a solid brown fog.

Lindsay gripped the voicepipes and heard splinters ripping and ricocheting through the hull, and tasted the lyddite on the cold air.

But the guns were still firing, and above the din he heard layers and trainers yelling like madmen, the rasp of steel, the clang of breech blocks before the cry, *'Ready!'*

Aikman called, 'Damage control reports a fire on A deck, sir. Two casualties.'

'Very well.'

Lindsay raised his glasses and studied the enemy. Nearly gone now, her shortened outline was just a murky shadow in the snow.

He had to chance it. 'Port ten.' To Aikman he snapped, 'Tell the gunnery officer to bring Number Three to bear.'

He watched the ticking gyro. 'Midships.' He did not wait for Jolliffe's reply but strode to the starboard side, feeling the icy wind clawing his face through the open window.

de Chair's gun reopened fire even as the enemy settled on the *Benbecula*'s starboard bow, and the shell hit her directly abaft the bridge. This time the explosion was more dramatic, and Lindsay guessed the exploding shell had also ignited either a small-arms magazine or some signal flares.

The snow seemed to glow red and gold as the flames licked greedily around one of the tall funnels, starting more scattered explosions to litter the churned water alongside with falling fragments.

The enemy fired again, and as before her gunnery was perfect. The shell hit *Benbecula*'s side further aft, exploding deep inside the hull and sending white-hot splinters scything in every direction. Some burst upwards through the boat deck and cut a whaler in halves, leaving bow and stern dangling from the davits like dead fruit.

Stannard said hoarsely, 'Snow's getting heavier again.' He ducked involuntarily as a shell exploded alongside, the flash masked instantly by a towering white water-spout. Bridge and wing were buried under cascading water, and Lindsay heard Jolliffe cursing one of the quartermasters who had fallen against the wheel.

Lindsay rubbed his glasses and peered after the enemy in time to see her fading completely into another squall. Only the glare of her fires was still visible, and he heard several small explosions on the wind as de Chair's last shell continued to spread its havoc between decks.

Aikman reported, 'Damage control have A deck fire under control, sir. Second hit was also A deck. No fire, but four men wounded.'

Another telephone jarred the sudden stillness and Stannard said, 'It's the chief, sir. He asks if he can reduce revs. Starboard shaft is overheating. Nothing serious, he thinks, but——'

Lindsay realised the Australian was staring at him and then his reeling mind recalled what he had been asked.

'Thank you, Pilot. Reduce to slow ahead.'

No sense in tearing the engines to pieces for nothing. The enemy would not come back for another try. Not this time. It was too risky.

He added slowly, 'Get a signal coded up right away. To Admiralty. Advise on our position, course and approximate speed of enemy.' He rubbed his eyes, forcing his mind to respond. 'Tell them we have engaged enemy raider and obtained two hits. Extent of her damage not known.'

Stannard lowered his pad. 'Is that all, sir?'

Lindsay walked to the door and wrenched it open as thankfully the bridge messengers started to close the glass windows again.

'Mention that *Loch Glendhu* has been sunk, and check with the sickbay for a list of survivors.'

He heard Stannard leave the wheelhouse and leaned over the wing to watch some of the damage control team scurrying along the forward well deck, bowed against the wind. Or fearful perhaps the enemy could still see them.

He was shaking uncontrollably, yet when he looked at his hands they seemed quite steady. Perhaps it was in his mind.

There were clangs and shouts, more orders as seamen and stokers ran to deal with damage and plug up the gaping splinter holes.

Goss appeared suddenly in the wheelhouse door. 'Nobody dead, sir.' He sounded accusing. 'One man's lost a foot, but the doc says he'll live——' He swung round as Ritchie pushed his way to the door.

Ritchie said harshly, 'There was *one* killed, sir.' He paused, recalling the astonishment on the boy's face. The eyes glazing with drifting snow. He said, 'Ordinary Signalman Cummings, sir. Shell splinter got 'im in the spine.' *But for his body, I would have got it.* 'I didn't realise he'd bought it till I told 'im it was all over.'

Lindsay nodded. Bought it. What the Wren had said at Scapa.

'You did bloody well, Yeo.'

Ritchie shrugged. 'It's a start.'

Goss cleared his throat noisily. 'About the *damage*.'

'Yes?'

'It's a dockyard job, sir.'

Lindsay could feel his nerves dragging like hot wires. He wanted to shake Goss, hit him if necessary to make him understand.

Instead he said flatly, 'No, it isn't, Number One. It's *yours,* until we hear to the contrary.'

Goss spoke between his teeth. 'If the snow hadn't eased at that moment we might have run straight into that German!'

Lindsay swung on him. 'Well, at least we'd have sunk the bloody thing! Now, for God's sake get on with those repairs!'

He turned to watch some seamen carrying a limp body aft from the forecastle. Cummings. Was that the man's name?

Dancy poked his head through the door. 'The chief has said everything's all right, sir.'

Lindsay looked at him. He had forgotten all about Dancy. But he seemed steady enough for his first action.

'Thank him for me, Sub. And fall out action stations.'

He realised Dancy was still there, staring at him as if for the first time in his life. 'Well?'

Dancy flushed. 'I—I'm sorry, sir. It's just that I wouldn't have believed it possible.' He seemed quite oblivious of Lindsay's grave face or Ritchie's despairing glance. 'To handle a ship like this, to outmanoeuvre that German——'

Lindsay held up his hand. 'Write about it one day, Sub. Tell your mother if you like, but spare *me*, will you?'

Dancy withdrew, and seconds later the upper deck tannoy grated, 'Fall out action stations. Starboard watch to defence stations.' The merest pause, then 'Up spirits!'

Lindsay looked at Ritchie, feeling the grin spreading across his face, pushing the despair aside like the wind had laid bare the enemy.

'Good advice, Yeo.' He walked towards the wheelhouse again. 'I think we deserve it!'

Ritchie watched him and then shook his head. You'll do, he thought. For me, and this poor old ship. You'll do.

Sub-Lieutenant Michael Dancy pushed aside the heavy curtain and stepped into the wardroom. With only half the deckhead lights in use the wardroom looked cosy and pleased with itself, the oak panelling gleaming softly in welcome. Just over an hour to midnight, and as Dancy had the middle watch he saw no point in trying to sleep.

By the fat coal stove he saw Barker in conversation with Boase, the doctor, although the latter's face was so expressionless it seemed hardly likely he was doing more than listening.

Barker was saying, 'We had some very rich passengers, of course. None of those save-up-for-the-cruise-of-a-lifetime types. Real class.'

Boase eyed him wearily. 'Good.'

The ex-purser lowered his voice. 'Like this ship today. I'm not saying that some of these temporary chaps don't mean well.' He winked. 'But you know what they say about the sow's ear, eh?'

Boase yawned. 'Nobody's more temporary than I am.'

Barker shot him an ingratiating smile. 'Ah, but you're *professional,* it's quite different!'

Dancy turned away. Quite apart from disliking Barker, he could not bear to watch him and the doctor sipping their drinks by the fire. Normally Dancy did not drink much. Before the war he had been unable to afford it, except at Christmas time, and in any case his mother disapproved, hinting darkly at a nameless uncle who had *gone off the rails.* After being commissioned and sent to the armed yacht he had been involved in several minor drinking bouts, most of which had ended in dismal failure and agonising sickness.

But tonight he did feel like it. A celebration all of his own.

He sat in a deep chair with his back to the others and stared unseeingly at the swaying curtains which partitioned off the dining space, half listening to the wind sighing against the hull. It was difficult to accept that only this morning they had been in action. Had fired and been fired upon. Had buried a young signalman, their first real casualty, and *he* had lived through all of it.

Dancy felt as if his lungs were too large for his body, that he wanted to shout or laugh out loud. What did that old woman Barker know about it anyway? He was more concerned with corned beef and the issue of clothing than the business of fighting. While Barker had been hidden below, he, Michael Dancy, had been up there beside the captain, seeing it, feeling it, and not breaking as he had once thought he would.

He heard the bell go and knew the others were ringing for more drinks. But he must go on watch soon, and had been left in no doubt by the first lieutenant what would happen to a watchkeeping officer who drank.

He tried to assemble his memories into order, to capture each moment. He smiled. As a writer should. But it was still difficult. It had been so swift, with the din and

smells all mixed together in his mind. And all the while
this great ship, and she was enormous after the armed
yacht, had wheeled and pounded through the snow, guns
blazing and—— He turned his head angrily as Fraser
entered the wardroom and threw himself into a chair,
prodding the bell push in the same movement.

Barker said, 'Of course, Doc, that was *why* the company
was such a success. We only had the five ships, but there
was true devotion, a sense of service and loyalty so lacking
today.'

Fraser had his eyes closed. 'Crap,' he said.

Barker glared at him. 'How can you say such a thing?'

The engineer opened his eyes as a steward glided into
the lamplight. He said, 'I want a treble gin.' Then to
Barker he added slowly, 'The reason this company was a
success, and I'm not denying it, was the fact that the
owners were the meanest set of skinflints ever dropped
the wrong side of a blanket!'

Boase stirred uneasily and glanced from one to the
other.

Fraser continued calmly, 'See all this panelling, Doc?'
He waved one hand and displayed the black grease on his
fingers. 'All the pretty cabins? Well, it only went down as
far as B deck. The rest, the crew's quarters and the poor
emigrants section, was like the bloody Black Hole of
Calcutta!' He looked at Barker's outraged face. 'Man,
you're daft if you think loyalty played any part. Men
needed work, and had to lick boots to get it. But you
wouldn't know anything about that!'

The steward was just placing the brimming glass beside
him when the bulkhead telephone buzzed impatiently.
The steward said, 'For you, sir.'

Fraser seized the phone and jerked his head to the
other voice. 'Yes. Yes. Oh, Jesus, not that freshwater
pump again. This bloody ship'll be the death o' me!' He
dropped the phone and downed the gin in one long
swallow.

As he walked to the door he added, 'One thing. If I run short of hot air for the boilers, I'll know where to come!' The door slammed behind him.

Barker stood up, visibly shaken. 'I'll turn in now.' He looked round the wardroom. 'I might have to check some ledgers first, of course.'

As he hurried away Boase said softly, 'Of course.'

Then he smiled at Dancy. 'You look ready to do great deeds.'

Dancy replied coldly, 'I have the middle.'

'Ah.' Boase squinted at the clock. 'Think I'll go to bed, too.'

Dancy opened and then shut his mouth. *Go to bed.* Boase had not even learned the right terms. Funny chap. Very cool and distant, yet they said he had sawn off a man's foot and saved his life.

'Anything more, sir?' The steward yawned ominously.

'No. You can turn in.'

The steward's eye dropped very slightly to the single stripe on Dancy's sleeve. 'You doing Rounds then, sir?'

Dancy looked away. 'Well, no, not exactly.'

The steward slammed into his pantry muttering, 'Then I'll wait for someone who *is.*'

The door opened again and Dancy saw it was Kemp, the midshipman. Apart from the other sub-lieutenants, Kemp was the newest officer in the ship. In addition, he was the only one upon whom Dancy could exercise his scanty authority.

The boy said quietly, 'I—— I was just looking to see if——' his voice trailed away.

Dancy frowned. 'Sit here if you like.' He glanced at his watch for several seconds. 'I've got the middle.'

Kemp nodded. He was a slightly built youth, even slender, and his even features were extremely pale. But unknown to the young midshipman he possessed one tremendous gift, one glittering asset which Dancy could never hold or share. He was a regular and had been to

Dartmouth. Dancy had already discovered that he was
the son of a senior officer, one of a family of naval men.
He seemed to epitomise all Dancy's peacetime dreams,
but at the same time did not really fit the role.

He asked casually, 'Your old man, pretty senior, I
believe?' Old man sounded just right, he thought.
Assured. A man of the world.

Dancy had learned his etiquette the hard way. Once in
the armed yacht there had been a party and several
women had been invited as guests. He had asked one very
poised young lady about her father and she had replied,
'Oh, Daddy's a sailor.'

He had been horrified. 'Not an *officer*?'

She had stared at him as if he had spoken some terrible
obscenity. 'But of course, silly! What else?'

Yes, Dancy was learning.

Kemp replied, 'He's a captain. Shore job at Rosyth.' He
sighed. 'He was beached between the wars for several
years.'

Dancy nodded gravely. 'I'll bet he's glad to be back.'

Kemp looked at him, his eyes strangely sad. 'Glad?
That's an understatement.'

'Yes.' Dancy was getting irritated without knowing
why. It was like talking to a stone wall. 'You sound as if
you're unhappy about the ship or something.'

'I am.' He shrugged. 'Not the ship exactly. It's the
Service. I hate it.' Now that he had begun he seemed
unable to stop himself. 'I never wanted to enter the Navy.
Never. But he kept on at me. Kept on reminding me of
my obligations, my duty.'

Dancy said, 'I expect it was all for the best.' God, he
sounded like his own father. He tried again. 'But surely
he knew the Navy well enough to understand, eh?'

Kemp stood up violently, a lock of hair falling across
his eyes. 'My father understands nothing about me, and
cares less! He's a stupid, pompous bigot, so stop asking
about him will you, *please*?'

Dancy was aghast. 'There's no call to speak like that! By God, if I'd had half your chances in life——' He checked himself hastily. 'What I mean is, if I'd not taken another profession I'd have wanted to enter the Service.'

Kemp's hands were shaking at his sides. 'Well, you got there in the end, didn't you, *sir*!'

As he ran for the door he almost collided with Stannard who was carrying his cap and duffel coat and wearing his scarred sea boots. He watched the midshipman run past and said dryly, 'Hell, that young fella's keen to go somewhere.'

Dancy said angrily, 'Doesn't know when he's well off.' It was like a betrayal, a broken image. 'I'll be watching him in future.'

The Australian grinned lazily. 'You do that, Admiral, but in the meantime shift yourself to the bridge, chop, chop!' He gestured to the clock. '*Our* watch, I believe?'

Dancy's frown faded. Stannard was a bit coarse at times, but he was all right. He had been on the bridge with him. Never got in a flap.

Stannard paused by a screen door and looked at him searchingly. 'Ever had a woman, Sub?'

Dancy stared at him. 'Well, I——that is——'

Stannard pursed his lips. 'Have to do something about that then!'

Outside the night was black. No stars or snow. Just the wind and the drifting feathers of spray above the guard-rail.

Dancy buttoned his bridge coat and followed the lieutenant to the ladder. That was more like it. He was accepted.

———————

Jupp stopped beside Lindsay's littered desk and placed a large china mug carefully on a mat before removing its lid.

He watched Lindsay and said, "Ot soup, sir. Just th' job before you turn in.'

Lindsay leaned back in his chair and smiled wearily. 'Smells fine.'

Feet scraped on the ladder overhead and he heard muffled voices and more footsteps clattering hurriedly from the bridge. The watch was changing. Midnight.

The soup was very hot, and Lindsay realised he was ravenous, that he had hardly eaten since the brief action with the enemy. It had been a long day. Inspecting damage between decks, checking the progress of repairs, burying Cummings in another quick service at the rail. Poor Cummings, he had not even got used to living.

It was quite impossible to learn anything about the damaged raider. The Admiralty had merely acknowledged his signal. He felt vaguely bitter about it, yet knew it was because he was tired. Worn out. It was unlikely anything could be done about the other ship. It had been too stormy for flying off aircraft, and the sea was a big place. The German was probably steaming like hell for base, to some secluded Norwegian fjord where she could lie up and lick her scars.

He gripped the mug more tightly. At least she had not got completely away with it. Her captain might remember this day as he dropped his own men over the side with a prayer or some jolly Nazi song. He realised Jupp was still watching him, his hooded eyes worried.

The chief steward said, 'The lads took it right well, I thought, sir.'

Lindsay nodded. 'Yes.'

He recalled the great blackened areas on A deck where the shells had exploded. Buckled frames, and plates like wet cardboard. A ventilator so riddled with splinters it had looked like one huge pepper pot. The damage was bad, but had *Benbecula* been a destroyer those two big five-point-nine shells would have broken her back like a carrot. He had visited the sickbay, giving the usual words, seeing the grateful smiles from the wounded men who were not too drugged to understand him. Their immediate shock had given way to a kind of pride. They were probably dreaming of that first leave, the glances of admiration and pity for their wounds. Except the one without a foot. He had been a promising tennis player before the war.

The telephone buzzed. It was Stannard.

'Middle watch at defence stations, sir. Time to alter course in seven minutes.'

The next leg of the patrol. It would be a beam sea, uncomfortable, as they were cruising at a mere seven knots.

'I'll come up, Pilot.' He hesitated. 'No, you take her. Call me if you want anything.' He dropped the handset. Stannard was competent, and it did no good to have a captain breathing down their necks all the time. Let them learn while there was still time.

There was a tap at the door and Maxwell peered in at him. 'You wanted me, sir?'

The gunnery officer's face was red from the wind, but his uniform was impeccable. As usual he wore a bright whistle chain around his neck, the end of which vanished into the breast pocket of his reefer, and Lindsay was reminded of the leather-lunged instructors at the gunnery school.

'Yes, Guns. Sorry to keep you from your bunk after you've been on watch. Just a couple of points.'

Maxwell removed his cap. He had a very sharp, sleek head. Like a polished bullet.

He said, 'Would have been earlier, sir. Hate unpunctuality. But my relief was late.'

'Late?' That was not like Stannard.

Maxwell did not blink. 'One and a half minutes, sir.'

Jupp hid a grin and slid from the cabin.

Lindsay looked at the lieutenant thoughtfully. An odd bird even for his particular trade. Maxwell had made some error or other before the war and been allowed to leave the Navy without fuss. It would not have been difficult when the country was more concerned with cutting down the services than facing the reality of a new Germany.

He said, 'Whenever we return to base I want you to do something about the armour plate on the bridge. Lowering the windows in action prevents injuries from glass splinters, but it's not enough. The watchkeepers and gunnery team must have proper protection.'

A small notebook had appeared in Maxwell's hand as if by magic. He snapped, 'Right, sir.'

'The W/T office needs it also, but I'll get on to Number One about that.' It was amazing how little attention had been given to such matters, he thought. 'Then there are the bridge machine guns. Old Lewis guns from World War One by the look of them.' He watched the pencil scribbling briskly. 'See if you can wangle some Brownings from the B.G.O.'

Maxwell eyed him wearily. 'Wangle, sir?'

'Then I'll give you a chit, Guns, if it makes you happier.'

Maxwell showed his teeth. 'Go by the book, that's me, sir. Follow the book and they can't trample you down.'

'It's happened before then?'

Maxwell swallowed hard. 'It was nothing, sir. Bit of a mix-up back in thirty-seven. But it taught me a lesson. Get it on paper. Go by the book'

Lindsay smiled. 'And they can't trample you down, eh?'

'Sir.' Maxwell did not smile.

A man entirely devoid of humour, Lindsay decided. He said, 'The gunnery this morning was erratic. The marines got off two shots to every one from forrard. Not good enough.'

Maxwell said swiftly, 'My assistant, Lieutenant Hunter, is R.N.R., sir. Keen but without proper experience.' He let the words sink in. 'But I'll get on to him first thing tomorrow.'

The deck quivered, and Lindsay saw the curtains begin to sway inwards from the sealed scuttles. She was turning.

He said, 'You deal with it, Guns. It's your job.'

Maxwell's mouth tightened into a thin line. 'I did not mean to imply——' he stopped.

'Carry on then.'

As the door closed Lindsay stood up and walked slowly into the other cabin. The small reading light gleamed temptingly above his bunk, and Jupp had put a Thermos beside it, wedged carefully between two shoes, in case the motion got too bad. In spite of his dragging weariness Lindsay smiled at the little gesture. Jupp would make a damn good valet, he thought.

He lay down on the bunk fully clothed, and after a few seconds hesitation kicked off his sea boots.

It never stopped. Demands and questions, jobs needing attention, reports to be checked and signed. His eyelids drooped as he thought back over the day, the enemy ship's outline looming through the snow. The anguish of sudden fear, the cruel ecstasy at seeing the shell burst on her upperworks.

He listened to the sea booming against the side, the darting spray across the scuttles, and then fell into a deep sleep.

How long he slept he did not know. All he understood was that he was fighting with the blanket, kicking and gasping as the nightmare flooded around him more vividly than ever.

He rolled on to his side, half blinded by the reading light which was shining directly into his eyes, and as the madness retreated he heard a voice, remote but insistent, which seemed to be rising from the bunk itself.

'Officer of the watch.' It was Stannard, and Lindsay stared at the telephone as it swung back and forth on its flex, the voice repeating 'Officer of the watch' like some cracked record.

He must have knocked it off in his nightmare, in his terror to escape from the torture.

He seized it and said, 'Captain.'

Stannard said, 'I'm sorry, sir. I thought you were calling me.'

Lindsay fought to keep his tone even. 'It's all right, Pilot. What time is it?'

'0350, sir. I'm just calling the morning watch.' A pause. 'Visibility as before. Wind's still north by east.'

'Thank you.'

He lowered the phone and lay back again. God, how long had the line been open? What had he been saying? He rubbed his eyes, trying to clear his mind, remember.

Then he swung his legs from the bunk and groped for Jupp's Thermos. What would he do? *Bomb-happy,* some people called it. He might even have said it once about others. He shuddered violently, pulling at the Thermos cap. Not any more.

Up on the bridge Dancy was standing beside the voice pipes and turned as Stannard replaced the telephone.

Stannard did not look at him. 'Sure. Just the skipper asking about the time.'

When Dancy had turned away he bit his lip with sudden anxiety. He should not have listened. Should not have heard. It was like falling on a secret, laying bare something private or shameful.

Heavy boots thumped on the ladder as Goss mounted to take his watch. Stannard thought of that desperate, pleading voice on the telephone and thanked God he and not Goss had heard it. Things were bad enough without that. They needed Lindsay, whatever he was suffering. He was all they had.

He faced Goss's heavy outline and said, 'Morning, Number One.'

Goss grunted and waited until Stannard had made his

formal report. Then he moved to Lindsay's chair, and after a small hesitation climbed into it.

Stannard walked to the ladder. Goss's action was almost symbolic, he thought.

Throughout the ship the watch had changed, and in bunks and hammocks men slept or lay staring at the deckhead reliving the fight. Drowsy cooks tumbled cursing from their snug blankets and made their way to the waiting galley with its congealed grease and dirty cups left by the watchkeepers. Barker sprawled on his back snoring, a copy of *Lilliput,* and not a ledger, open on his chest to display a voluptuous nude. In the sickbay an attendant sat sleeping beside the man who had lost his foot, and in another white cot a wounded stoker was crying quietly on his pillow, even though he was asleep. In his cabin, Midshipman Kemp was wide awake, looking up into the darkness and thinking about his father. Further aft, in the chief and petty officers' mess, only a blue police light glowed across the tiered bunks. Ritchie slept soundlessly, while on a shelf beside his bunk the pictures of his dead family watched over him. Jolliffe, the coxswain, was having a bad dream, his mouth like a black hole in his heavy face. His teeth, like his slippers, were within easy reach should the alarm bells start again. In the stokers' messdeck, Stripey, the ship's cat, lay curled into a tight ball inside someone's metal cap box, his body trembling gently to the steady beat of the screws.

Indifferent to all of them, the *Benbecula* pushed slowly across a steep beam sea, her shape as black as the waters which were hers alone.

6 Officers and men

If the Icelandic patrol known as Uncle Item Victor had been created solely to test man's endurance it was hard to imagine a better choice. By the middle of October, a month after their clash with the German raider, *Benbecula*'s ship's company had reached what most of them imagined was the limit. To the men at the lookout and gun positions it appeared as if the ship was steaming on one endless voyage to eternity, doomed to end her time heading into worse and worse conditions. Only the bridge watchkeepers really saw the constant changes of course and speed as the old ship ploughed around her desolate piece of ocean.

During the whole of that time they had sighted just one ship, a battered little corvette which had been ordered to rendezvous with them to remove the wounded and the handful of survivors from *Loch Glendhu*. For two whole days the ships had stayed in company, hoping and praying for some easing of the weather so that the transfer could be made. Even some of *Benbecula*'s most dedicated grumblers had fallen silent as hour by hour they had watched the little corvette lifting her bows towards the low clouds, lurching and then reeling into troughs with all but her bridge and squat funnel submerged.

Then, during a brief respite, and with *Benbecula* providing some shelter from the wind, the transfer had taken place.

Even then, and in spite of Fraser's men pumping out gallons of oil to settle the waves, it had nearly ended the lives of some of them. Lindsay had ordered the remaining whaler to be lowered, as a breeches buoy or any sort of tackle was out of the question. The boat had made three trips, rising and vanishing into the troughs like a child's toy, reappearing again with oars flashing like silver in the hard light as they battled towards the corvette.

Then with a defiant toot on her siren the corvette had turned away, her signal lamp fading as she pushed into yet another squall which must have been waiting in the wings for the right moment.

Alone once more they settled down to their patrol, or tried to. But it was a bitter world, an existence and nothing more. The weather was getting much colder as winter tightened its grip, and each dawn found the superstructure and gun barrels gleaming with ice, the signal halliards thick and glittering like a frozen waterfall. If watchkeeping was bad, below decks was little better. Nothing ever seemed to get dry, and in spite of the steam pipes the men endured damp clothes and bedding while they waited their turn to go on deck again and face the sea.

Once they rode out a Force Eleven storm, their greatest threat so far. Winds of almost a hundred knots screamed down from Greenland, building the waves into towering, jagged crests, some of which swept as high as the promenade deck, buckling the guardrails before thundering back over the side. Patches of distorted foam flew above the bridge and froze instantly on guns and rigging, so that the watch below were called slipping and cursing to clear it before the weight of ice could become an additional hazard.

The ship seemed to have shrunk in size, and it was hard to find escape. Tempers became frayed, fights erupted without warning or real cause, and Lindsay saw several

resentful faces across the defaulters' table to show the
measure of their misery.

Much of the hatred was, of course, directed at him. He
had tried to keep them busy, if only to prevent the
despair from spreading over the whole ship.

Fraser had been a tower of strength. Like scavengers,
he and some of his artificers had explored the bowels of
the ship, even the lower orlop, and with blow torches had
cut away plates from unused store rooms. They had
skilfully reshaped them before welding them in the flats
and spaces damaged by the enemy shells. He had even
created his own 'blacksmith's shop' as he liked to call it,
where his men were able to cut and repair much of the
damaged plating and frames which otherwise would
have waited for the dockyard's attention. For to Fraser
the enforced isolation seemed to act as a test of his personal resources and ability, but when Lindsay thanked
him he had said offhandedly, 'Hell, sir, I'm only trying to
hold the old cow in one piece until I get a transfer!'

The outbreaks of anger and conflict were not confined
to the lower deck. In the wardroom Maxwell had a
standing shouting-match with Goss, while Fraser never
lost a chance to goad Barker whenever he began to
recount stories of his cruising days.

There had been one incident which lingered on long
after it had happened. Like the rest of the ship, the
wardroom was feeling particularly glum about the latest
news of their relief. Another A.M.C. should have
relieved them on the sixteenth of the month. Due to
unforeseen circumstances, later discovered to be the ship
had run into a pier, the relief was to be delayed a further
week. Another seven days after what they had already
endured was not much to those who arranged such
details. To most of the ship's company, however, it felt
like the final blow. Some had been counting the days,
ticking off the hours, willing the time to pass. As a stoker
had said, 'After this, even bleedin' Scapa'll suit me!'

In the wardroom it had been much the same. At dinner, as the table tilted sickeningly from side to side, the crockery rattling in the fiddles, the little spark had touched off a major and disturbing incident.

One of the sub-lieutenants, a pleasant faced youngster called Cordeaux, had been talking quietly to Dancy about gunnery. He was quarters officer of Number Two gun, which had still to be fired in anger, and because of the icy conditions had had little opportunity to watch its crew at drill. Dancy had turned to de Chair who was sitting beside him moodily staring at some greasy tinned sausages on his rattling plate.

'You're better at gunnery, Mark.' Dancy had nudged Cordeaux. 'The marines always are!'

de Chair had emerged from his brooding thoughts, and in his lazy drawl had begun to outline the very points which had baffled Cordeaux.

Maxwell had been sitting at the head of the table and had said sharply, 'By God, I'm just about sick of hearing how bloody marvellous the marines are at gunnery!' He had jabbed his fork towards the startled Cordeaux. 'And you, Mister, can shut up talking shop at the table! I know you're green, but I'd have thought good manners not too hard to imitate!'

Cordeaux had dropped his eyes, his face scarlet.

Then de Chair had turned slowly and said, 'He was speaking to me, Guns. As it happens, I do not believe that something concerning our job is a blight on the dinner table.' He had eyed him calmly. 'More useful than some of your topics, I'd have imagined. Your mind hardly ever seems to move beyond certain sexual activities, all of which put *me* off my dinner!'

Nobody spoke.

Then Maxwell had smiled. 'We are edgy tonight! Are you a bit peeved because the captain hasn't put you in for a medal because of your *superb* gunnery? Bloody luck is more like it!'

de Chair had stood up very slowly, his neat figure swaying easily with the deck. 'Perhaps. But at least I have so far confined *my* gunnery to killing Germans.'

Maxwell's face had been suddenly drained of colour. 'What the hell d'you mean?'

The marine had moved towards the door. 'Just stay off my back, Guns, or by God you'll regret it!' The words had hung in the air long after de Chair had left.

Maxwell had said haltingly, 'Can't imagine what the bloody man is talking about.'

But nobody had looked at him.

Barker had not been present on that occasion, but had received news of the flare-up within the hour. One of the stewards had served in the ship in peacetime and had been well trained by Barker in such matters. In fact, when he had been the ship's purser Barker had evolved an almost foolproof intelligence service. The ship's hairdresser had hoarded vital information about the rich female passengers, the senior stewards had hovered at tables and around the gaming room just long enough to catch a word here, a tip there. There were others too, and all the information went straight to Barker.

With the hopeless mixture of hostilities only ratings, regulars and ex-merchant seamen he had found it harder to rebuild his network, but he was starting. He disliked the regular naval officers, mainly because they made him feel inferior, or so he believed. For that reason he was glad to obtain the news of a clash between de Chair and Maxwell. Of Lindsay he knew nothing as yet. Very controlled, and from what he had heard, extremely competent. Nobody's fool, and with a sharp edge to his voice when he needed it. Midshipman Kemp, at the bottom of the scale, was the son of a senior officer. Kemp, in Barker's view, was worth watching. Any connection with a senior officer was always useful. The midshipman himself was not. Rather shy, not exactly effeminate, but you could never be sure. He had discarded Emerson, the warrant engineer. A pensioner, he was old, fat and dull. He dropped his aitches, referred to his far off wife as 'me old woman', and was generally distasteful.

But Maxwell now, here was something. Goss had hinted that the lieutenant had been under a cloud before the war, but Barker had always imagined it to be connected with some minor breach. Slight discrepancy in mess funds, or found in bed with his C.O.'s wife. Nothing too damning. But from what the steward had heard and seen it now appeared very likely that Maxwell had been involved in a serious accident.

He would, however, treat de Chair with an even greater respect from now on, even if he was a regular. de Chair was exactly like some of the passengers whom Barker had served in the better days of cruising. Outwardly easy-going, deceptively relaxed, but with all the toughness of arrogance and breeding just below the surface. Not a man to trifle with.

It was a pity about Jupp, he had thought on more than one occasion. As chief steward and a personal watchdog over the captain, Jupp should have been the mainspring of the whole network. Barker had served with him twice before, and knew better than to try and force the man to betray his trust. It could be dangerous to push him. You could never be entirely sure how much a senior steward knew about his purser. Barker owned a boarding house in Southampton and another in Liverpool. People might suggest it impossible to acquire such property on his pay alone. They would have been right, too.

The only officer in the ship with whom Barker shared some of his confidences was Goss. Not because he particularly liked him, in fact, he usually made him feel vaguely uneasy. Goss had somehow never bothered to rise with his rank, not, that is, in Barker's view. Beneath warm, star-filled skies in the Pacific, with all the magic of a ship's orchestra, the gay dresses and white dinner jackets,

Barker had always felt in his element. But once or twice at the chief officer's table in the dining room he had squirmed with embarrassment at Goss's obvious lack of refinement. Big, self-made, meticulous in matters of duty, Goss seemed unable to put on a show for the passengers at his table. Barker had seen the quick smiles exchanged between them as Goss had told some ponderous story about raising an anchor in a gale, or the time he had fought four drunken stokers in a Sydney bar and knocked them senseless. He was a difficult man to know, harder still to befriend.

But he *was* the first lieutenant, and in Barker's eyes still the senior chief officer in the company. Once the war was over, breeding or not, Goss would get a command. With his seniority plus war experience the company could hardly avoid it. When that happened, Barker would be ready for his own step up the ladder, if he had anything to say about it.

So without too much hesitation he had made a point of visiting Goss that same night. Goss, he knew, had the middle watch, and as was his normal practice stayed in his roomy cabin out of sight until a few minutes before the exact time due on the bridge.

It was not that Goss openly discouraged visitors to his private domain, it was just that his attitude was generally unwelcoming, like some trusted curator of a museum who resented visitors on principle.

If the rest of the ship had been altered and scarred by the Navy's ownership, Goss had somehow retained his old surroundings more or less as they had always been, so that his cabin was, in its own way, a museum, a record of his life and career.

There were many framed photographs of the ship and other company vessels in which he had served over the years. Pictures of groups, large and small, officers and owners, self-conscious passengers and various happenings in several ports of call. A blue and white house-flag of the company adorned one complete bulkhead, and the shelves and well-polished furniture were littered with models and mementos and more framed pictures. One of them showed Goss shaking hands with old Mr Cairns, the head of the company, who had died just a few weeks before the war.

Whenever Barker visited the cabin he always looked at that particular picture. It was the only place where he had seen Goss smile.

Goss had listened to Barker's casual excuse for the visit without emotion. Stores had to be raised from an after hold the following day and would the first lieutenant arrange some extra working parties for the task? It had all sounded innocent enough.

As he had gone through the motions Barker had studied Goss's heavy features with methodical interest. He had been sitting in one of his fat leather chairs, his jacket hanging neatly on a hook behind the door, his cap and binoculars within easy reach. But without a collar or tie, in his crumpled shirt and a pair of old plimsolls, he had looked like one of his own relics. Had Barker possessed an ounce of sensitivity he might have felt either concern or even pity, but instead he was merely curious. Goss, the great unbreakable seaman, looked old, tired and utterly alone.

Goss had said eventually, 'That all?'

'Of course.' Barker had walked round the chair, steadying himself against the table as the ship rolled wearily into one more trough. 'Oh, by the way, I *did* hear something about Maxwell. Seems he was in an accident of some sort.' A carefully measured pause. 'de Chair was saying a few words on the matter at dinner. Pity you weren't there yourself.'

'Accident?'

Barker had shrugged carelessly. 'Gunnery, I believe. Probably shot some poor sod by mistake.'

'Probably.'

Barker had been astounded at Goss's indifference. He had merely sat there staring into space, one foot tapping slowly on the company carpet, a sure sign he wished to be left alone. It had been altogether quite unnerving.

'Just thought you'd like to hear about it.'

Goss had said slowly, 'You know, Henry, I was thinking just now.' He nodded heavily towards the photograph. The one with the smile. 'Old Mr Cairns was a good owner. Hard, some said, and I daresay he remembered the value of every rivet down to the last halfpenny. But he had an eye for business, and knew every officer on his payroll. Every one, even the bloody apprentices. Now he's dead and gone. And it looks as if the company'll never survive either.'

Barker had gone cold. 'But after the war there'll be full compensation, surely? I——I mean, the government can't just take the ships, work the life out of them, and then give nothing back afterwards!'

Goss had heaved himself upright, so that his massive head had almost touched the steam pipes. 'Even if we win the war, and with some of the people I've seen aboard this ship I am more than doubtful on that score, things will never be the same. Mr Cairns' young nephew is in the chair now. Snooty little upstart with an office in London instead of down where the *ships* are. Had him aboard for our last peacetime trip.' His features had hardened. 'All gin and bloody shrimp cocktails, you know the type.'

Barker had swallowed hard. He knew. He liked to think of himself like that.

Goss had rambled on, as if to an empty cabin. 'I was promised the next command, but I 'spect you knew that. Promised. I'd have had the old *Becky* by now, but for the bloody war.'

There had been something like anguish in his voice which had made Barker stammer, 'Well, I'll be off then. Just thought I'd fix up about tomorrow——'. He had left the cabin with Goss still staring fixedly at the framed photograph.

As the door had closed Goss had taken a small key from his pocket, and after a further hesitation had opened a cupboard above his desk. Inside, gleaming from within a protective oilskin bag, was the cap. The company's badge and the captain's oak leaves around the peak were of the best pre-war gold wire, hand woven by a little Jewish tailor in Liverpool.

After locking the cupboard again he had slumped into the chair and lowered his face into his hands.

'I'd have had this ship by now. It was a *promise*.'

The words had hung in the sealed cabin like an epitaph.

A week later, as the *Benbecula* headed south-east away from the patrol area, those who were on deck in the bitter air saw the other armed merchant cruiser steaming past less than a mile distant. Even without binoculars it was possible to see the fresh paint around her stem, evidence of her collision with the pier, her guilt which had allowed an extra week in harbour while *Benbecula* endured the gales and the angry seas.

Lindsay sat in his tall chair and watched the other ship until she had passed out of his line of vision. The obvious excitement he had felt all around him as he had given orders to leave the patrol had momentarily given way to a kind of resentment as the relief ship had forged past. Not so much perhaps because she was late, but because she was heading into what appeared to many was calmer weather. The wind was fresh but no longer violent, so that the watch below was called less often to hack and blast away the clawing ice from decks and guns. To the men who imagined they had now seen and endured everything the Atlantic could offer, it seemed unfair their relief should get it so easy.

Lindsay sat back and looked at the hard, dark horizon line. With the ship so steady it made the list all the more apparent. The horizon seemed to be tilting across the bridge windows like an endless grey hill.

Behind him he could hear a signalman talking quietly with Ritchie, the occasional creak of the wheel and Maxwell's clipped voice from the chart room door. The afternoon watch was almost finished, and the sky above the horizon was already duller with a hint of more snow. It was natural for the new hands to complain about the other A.M.C.'s luck, he thought. The more seasoned men would know the real reason for the change. Ice. Before winter closed in completely there would be plenty about to the west and north, some perhaps as far down as this. He had already discussed it with Goss, but as usual it was hard to fathom the extent of his words.

Lindsay had been a first lieutenant himself to several commanding officers, and he could not get used to Goss's total lack of feeling for his new role. A first lieutenant in any naval vessel was the link between officers and captain, the one man who could and should weld the ship into one tight community. Goss was not a link. He was like a massive watertight door which kept his captain even more aloof and remote than usual.

There was no doubting his efficiency in seamanship and internal organisation. But there it ended, and unless he could bring himself to change his days were numbered afloat, Lindsay decided.

Maxwell crossed to his side and stood fidgeting with the chain around his neck. 'D'you think there's any chance of leave, sir?'

Lindsay watched the lieutenant's reflection in the salt-smeared windows.

'Unlikely, Guns. A lick of paint, a few bits of quick welding and we'll be off again, in my opinion.'

Strange about Maxwell, he thought. He had been very quiet lately. Too quiet.

Maxwell said, 'Oh, in that case——' He did not go on.

'You worried about something?'

'Me, sir?' Maxwell's fingers tugged more insistently at the chain. 'No, I was just thinking. I might put in for an advanced gunnery course. Not much scope in this ship.'

He spoke jerkily, but Lindsay thought the words sounded rehearsed. As if he had been planning the right moment.

'And you want me to recommend you?'

Maxwell shifted his feet. 'Well, in a manner of speaking, yes, sir.'

Lindsay took out his pipe. It couldn't be much fun for Maxwell. A gunnery officer of the old school, who because of time lost on the beach was watching men far more junior being appointed to brand-new warships just as fast as they were built. But there was more to it than that. Maybe it was his assistant, Lieutenant Hunter. Only a temporary officer perhaps, and in peacetime the owner of a small garage many miles from the sea, but Hunter had got to grips with the ancient armament as if born to it. Probably because he had not had many dealings with any other kind, or maybe, like Fraser, his natural mechanical bent made him accept the old guns like some sort of personal challenge rather than an obstacle.

'I'll think about it, Guns. But I need either you or a damn good replacement before I recommend anything, right?'

Maxwell nodded. 'Yes, sir.'

The duty bosun's mate said, 'Beg pardon, sir, but Number Six gun 'as just called up. They say one of the liferafts is workin' adrift again on th' poop.' He sounded disinterested. Ten more minutes and he would be in his mess. Hot sweet tea and then his head down until supper-time.

Maxwell glared. 'Right, tell Lieutenant Aikman to deal with it.'

The man continued to stare at him, the telephone in his first. 'But you sent 'im to the chart room, sir.'

Maxwell nodded jerkily. 'Oh, yes.' To Lindsay he added, 'He's fixing the plot.'

Lindsay turned slightly to study him. Maxwell was not usually rattled.

He asked, 'What about young Kemp?' He had appointed the midshipman to Maxwell's watch for the experience, as well as to keep him from being bored to death by the ship's correspondence duties.

Maxwell nodded. 'Yessir.' To the seaman he barked, 'Mr Kemp is up in control. Pass the word for him to lay aft, chop, chop. The buffer will let him have a couple of hands.' He added angrily, 'Bloody well get a move on!'

Lindsay faced forward again, troubled by Maxwell's sudden irritation. Perhaps it was his own example which had done it. Maybe his outward mask of self-control was not so strong as he believed.

He heard the bosun's mate passing the order on the handset, his voice sullen.

Maxwell returned to his side and said vehemently, 'Number Six gun, was it. Those marines are just trying to rile me.' He seemed to realise he had spoken aloud and swung away, adding sharply, 'Pipe the port watch to defence stations. And I'll see that rating who was smoking on duty in five minutes, got it?'

The bosun's mate faced him coldly. 'Got it, *sir.*'

Lindsay thought about Goss and came to a decision. Maxwell's attitude was dangerous and could not be tolerated. But it was the first lieutenant's job to deal with internal grievances, and deal with them he would.

———

By the time Midshipman Kemp had made his way aft to the poop the daylight was almost gone. As he groped along the guardrail he could feel the ice-rime under his glove and wished he had put something warmer than an oilskin over his other clothing. The sea looked very dark, with deep swells and troughs, through which the ship's wake made a frothing white track, fading eventually into the gathering gloom.

Beside the covered twelve-pounder he found Leading Seaman Swan waiting for him, one foot on the lower guardrail while he stared astern with weary resignation.

Kemp asked, 'Where are the others?'

Swan straightened his back and looked at him. He was a big man, his body made even larger by several layers of woollens beneath his duffel coat. He had already done several repair jobs about the upper deck in the freezing weather and was just about ready to go below. His neck and chin felt sore, mainly because he had started to grow a beard, and the cold, damp air was playing havoc with his patience. Kemp's arrival did nothing to help ease his irritation. Swan was a regular with seven years service to his credit and was normally quite tolerant of midshipmen in general. They were the *in-betweens.* Neither fish nor fowl, and were usually taken at face value by the lower deck. Hounded by their superiors, carried by petty officers and leading hands, midshipmen were more to be pitied than abused. But just this once Swan did not feel like carrying anyone, and Kemp's obvious uncertainty filled him with unreasoning resentment.

He replied offhandedly, 'They'll be here any second.' He waited for Kemp to pull him up for omitting the *sir.*

Kemp shivered and said, 'What's the trouble anyway?'

The leading seaman gestured with a massive, leather-gauntleted fist towards the nearest raft. It was poised almost vertically on two wooden skids, so that in a real emergency it could be released to drop straight down over the port quarter.

'Trouble with some of these bloody O.D.'s is that they paint everything. Some idiot has slopped paint all over the lines, and in this sort of climate it only makes 'em fray more easily.' He saw Kemp's eyes peering doubtfully at the heavy raft and added harshly, 'Not that it matters much. What with paint and the bloody ice, I doubt if the thing would move even if Chatham barracks fell on it!'

Two seamen loomed up the poop ladder and he barked, 'Where the hell have you been? I'm just about two-blocks waiting in the sodding cold!'

The first seaman said, 'The officer of the watch 'ad me on the rattle for smokin'.' He looked at Kemp. 'That's wot.'

Swan waited for Kemp to say something. Then he said angrily, 'Well, just you wait here. I'm going to get some new lines. You can start by checking how many of the old ones are frayed, right?'

As he stamped away one of the seamen muttered, 'What's up with Hookey then? Miserable bastard.'

Kemp gripped the guardrail with both hands, willing himself to concentrate on the raft. He knew the two seamen, like Swan, were testing him, that almost any other midshipman from his class would have snapped back at them. Won their obedience, if not actual respect. It was always the same. He seemed unable to face the fact he was here, that no amount of self-deception would change it. He could almost hear his father's resonant voice. 'I can't think where you get it. No moral fibre, that's you. No *guts!*'

He heard one of the seamen duck behind the twelve-pounder gunshield and the rasp of a match. If Kemp was unwilling or unable to act, they were quite happy to wait for Swan's return.

One of them was saying, 'Did you 'ear about that stoker in Scapa?' 'Ad a cushy shore job stokin' some admiral's boiler, an' they found 'im in 'is bunk with a bloody sheep!'

The other voice said, 'Never! You're 'avin me on!'

'S'truth.' He was enjoying the much-used yarn, especially as he knew the midshipman was listening. 'When the jaunty slapped 'im on a charge he told 'im that he didn't know it was a sheep. But that 'e'd been so long in Scapa 'e thought it was a Wren in a duffel coat!'

Kemp thrust himself away from the rail. 'That's enough, you two!'

They both stared at him in mild surprise.

'Start working on those lines!'

One of them said, 'Which lines, sir?'

The other added, 'Can't see much in this light, sir.'

Kemp felt the despair rising like nausea. It had been the same when Dancy had been questioning him about his father. It was always like that.

He seized the nearest seaman's sleeve and thrust him towards the raft. 'Get up there and *feel* them one at a time!' He swung on the second man. 'And you start freeing the ice from the metal slips. Swan will probably want to splice them on to the new lines.'

Behind his back the seaman on the raft made an obscene gesture and then looked away as Kemp returned to the rail.

Kemp was shivering uncontrollably beneath the oil-skin. He knew it was partly because of the cold, but also due to his inability to play out his part as he knew he must if he was to keep his sanity. Kemp was an only son and in the beginning had been prepared to try and see his father's point of view. From as far back as he could remember it had been like that. The tradition, the house full of naval portraits and memories, even now he could understand his father's desire to see him following the family's heritage. Perhaps if he had known what he had wanted to be, had found someone to help and advise him, then his father might have relented. But at eighteen Kemp was still unsure. All he did know for certain was he did not want or need the Service, and that his father had become more than an adversary. He was the very symbol of all he had come to hate.

When he had been appointed to this ship he had

known his father's hand was in it. *To knock some sense into him. Smooth the rough edges.* In some ways Kemp had almost believed it himself. The officers were so unusually mixed and totally different from those he had met before.

He was not so inexperienced that he could not recognise the antagonism and occasional enmity between the officers, but when it came down to it they all seemed to be the same. In the action, as he had crouched inside the chart room he had heard their voices. Flat, expressionless, moulded to discipline, no matter what the men really thought behind the words.

He looked up startled as Swan bounded up the ladder carrying a huge coil of line.

Swan shouted, 'What the *hell* are you doing up there, Biggs? Come down immediately and fix a lifeline, you stupid bugger!'

Even as he spoke the other seaman inadvertently cut through a lashing with his knife. Perhaps because his fingers were cold, or maybe the icy planking beneath his boots took him off balance, but the result was the same, and immediate. The end of the severed lashing, complete with a metal shackle, slashed upwards like a frozen whip, cutting the seaman Biggs full in the face as he made to scramble back to the deck. Kemp stared horrified as the man swayed drunkenly, his duffel coat pale against the black sea at his back. Then as Swan flung himself on to the raft Biggs fell outboard and down. One second he was there, the next nothing. He had not even had time to cry out.

Swan pushed Kemp aside and groped for the handset by the twelve-pounder. But the canvas cover was frozen iron-hard, and with a sob he ran for the ladder, yelling to the nearest marine gun crew as he went.

Kemp gripped the rail and peered down into the churning white wash. But he did not know where to look. Where would Biggs be? Below, staring up at his ship as she faded into the darkness? Or already far astern, choking and crying out in terror? He began to fumble with a lifebuoy and was still struggling with its lashing as Swan came aft again.

Swan said hoarsely, 'Forget it. He'll have been sucked into the port screw.'

The other seaman, who was still standing transfixed with the knife in one hand, said brokenly, 'We're turnin'! The wheel's gone over!'

Kemp stared at the ship's pale wake as it began to change into a wide sweeping curve. In a moment he would wake up. It was a mad dream. It had to be.

Right in his ear Swan said, 'They'll have to go through the motions. Even if he missed the screws he'll be a block of bloody ice in minutes!'

A marine corporal from Number Six gun clattered on to the poop and snapped, 'Captain's compliments, Mr Kemp, and he wants you on the bridge right away.' He looked at Swan. 'You, too.'

The man with the knife said in a small voice, 'Worn't my fault, Hookey!'

Swan looked at Kemp with savage contempt. 'I know. You were obeying orders!'

Kemp tried to speak, his mind reeling with shock. 'I——I'm sorry——I was only trying to. . . .'

Swan gestured astern. 'Tell *him*, sir! He'll be bloody glad to know you're sorry, I don't think!'

All the way along the upper deck Kemp was vaguely aware of silent, muffled figures watching him as he passed. No matter what had really happened, he was already condemned in their eyes. Their silence was like a shouted verdict.

As they reached the door at the rear of the bridge Kemp heard Lindsay's voice, very level, as if from far away.

'Another five minutes, Pilot. Then bring her back on course.'

Then Stannard's voice. 'If he'd had a lifejacket on, sir, with a safety lamp——'

Lindsay had turned away again. 'But he hadn't.'

Stannard saw Kemp's outline in the door and shrugged. There seemed to be nothing left to say.

7 A Wren called Eve

The Chief of Staff looked up from his desk as Lindsay entered the office, and then waved to a chair.

'Take the weight off your feet. I'll not keep you a minute.'

Lindsay sat. After the bitter air across the Flow as he had come ashore in the motor boat the office seemed almost tropical. It was evening, and with windows sealed and a great iron stove glowing pink with heat, he felt suddenly drowsy.

The grave-faced captain was saying into a telephone, 'Very well, Flags, if you say so. Another draft coming in tonight. Get on to stores and find out about kitting them up. Right.'

He put down the telephone and shot Lindsay a brief smile. 'Never lets up.' He groped in a drawer and took out two glasses and a bottle of Scotch. 'The sun, had it been out today, would be well over the yardarm by now, eh?'

Lindsay relaxed slightly, hearing the wind hissing against a window, the clatter of a typewriter in the next room.

Benbecula had picked up her buoy that morning, and while he had stood on the bridge wing to watch a fussy tug assisting the forecastle party with the business of mooring, he had allowed a grudging admiration for the Flow. The snow had held off, and it was not raining either. In the hard morning light there had even been a kind of primitive beauty. The cold, pewter water and hunched brown islands were as uncompromising as ever, but seemed to say, we were here first, so make the best of us.

The whisky was neat and very good.

The captain said, 'I didn't call you over until now because I thought you'd have enough to do. Anyway, it gave me time to study your report.' He smiled and some of his sternness faded. 'You did damn well to have a crack at that raider. Against all sane instructions, of course, but I'd have done the same.'

Lindsay replied, 'I wish I could have finished him.'

'I dare say. We had a couple of clear days recently and the R.A.F. got a reconnaissance flight going. Your raider is holed up in Norway, if you're interested. She's the *Nassau*, seventeen thousand tons, and fairly new. Used to run to the East African ports.' He refilled the glasses. 'Intelligence have reported she's completely converted as a raider.' He added wryly, 'Of course, they didn't tell us anything about her until a few days ago.'

Lindsay nodded. He had been expecting the captain— his name was Lovelace — to go for him, to attack him for taking independent action. But now he could understand. As *Benbecula* had entered the boom gate he had been watching and waiting for orders to moor on some vacant buoy, wherever was convenient to the harbour-master rather than the returning A.M.C. He need not have bothered, as the Flow had been almost deserted.

The officer who had come aboard from the guardboat to collect Lindsay's despatches and mail had said, 'Several of the battlewaggons have sailed for the Far East and others to the Med. The shop window's a bit bare at the moment.'

So even if *Benbecula* had complied to the letter of her orders, to stand off and await assistance, there would have been little available. No heroics, Lovelace had said at their other meeting. Now it looked as if heroics were just about all they had.

As if reading his mind the captain said, 'We're tightly

stretched. Things are getting bad in the Med. and we've had some heavy losses in Western Approaches. My operations staff will let you have all the backlog when you're ready for it.' He looked grave. 'We have not released the news of *Loch Glendhu*'s loss to the public as yet. The less the enemy knows about our meagre resources the better. Of course, the German radio has been playing it up. They claim they sank a heavy cruiser. Maybe they really believe it, but my guess is it's all part of the probing game. Testing our strength.'

Lindsay felt suddenly depressed. The endless strain, the continuous effort needed to pull his new command into a fighting unit were taking their toll.

He said, 'It all sounds pretty hopeless.'

Lovelace paused with the bottle in mid air above Lindsay's glass. 'Come on, man, I thought you Scots could drink!' With his eyes on the bottle he added slowly, 'Hard luck about losing that chap overboard. Still, you were damn lucky with your previous casualties. And with a partly trained company like yours I'd have expected ten times the number.'

'Yes.' He let the neat whisky burn across his tongue, recalling Kemp's pale face, his wretchedness as he had stammered out his story of Biggs' death. The leading hand, Swan, had been stiff, even angry. *'Mr Kemp's got no idea of things, sir.'*

Things, as Lindsay well knew, needed time to be mastered. Kemp had had very little. But he also lacked something else. Perhaps he did not care.

Lovelace asked, 'What have you done about the midshipman?'

'Nothing, sir. It was an accident due more to ignorance than carelessness. I doubt Kemp will ever forget it.'

He thought of Fraser's reaction. 'Just one of those things,' was all he had said.

Lovelace nodded, apparently satisfied. 'Fine. I should keep Kemp busy, Make him jump about. If I transferred

him elsewhere it would do him more harm than good.'
He shot Lindsay a searching glance. 'Unless, of course,
you want him shifted?'

'No. I'll see how it works out.'

'Good. Especially as I'll have to take some of your
people anyway. Tobey, your boatswain, and a few other
key ratings. I need them as replacements. You'll have to
fill the gaps from the next incoming draft.' He smiled
grimly. 'Straight from the training depot, naturally.'

The telephone buzzed and Lovelace snapped, 'I will
see the commanding officer of *Merlin* in three minutes.
Tell him to warm his backside on your fire until I'm
ready.'

Lindsay stood up. 'Any orders for me, sir?'

'Soon.' Lovelace looked distant again, already grappling with the endless complications of his office. 'I've
told the maintenance commander to do all he can. The
repair ship is standing by to help, but anything she or
your people can't manage will have to wait. I'm afraid a
week is about all you can expect, so work along those
lines. I hear you've completed refuelling, so you can allow
local leave whenever it suits you.'

Lindsay picked up his cap. The whisky was burning his
stomach like fire. All a question of priorities, and his old
ship was very far down that list. A week, and back to
patrol duty. Ice. Men being worn out by cold and endless
discomfort. They were the dangerous times, when small
personal needs blunted a man's vigilance. Maybe *Loch
Glendhu*'s people had been like that. Too tired, too beaten
down by the seemingly futile patrol to see their peril until
it was beyond their scope.

He said, 'Thank you for the drink, sir.'

Lovelace grinned. 'My pleasure. I hear so much gloom
that it's a real prize to meet somebody who's achieved
something at last!'

Lindsay left the office, and as he walked through the
adjoining room he saw the officer who was waiting for the

next interview. A full rank junior to Lindsay, yet he commanded the *Merlin*, a new and powerful fleet-destroyer which was lying quite near to *Benbecula*'s buoy. He watched Lindsay pass, his face curious. When he had left the room Lindsay could imagine the little scene. The young lieutenant-commander would ask politely who he was. The Chief of Staff's secretary would tell him. In the mind of the *Merlin*'s captain a whole new picture would form. Nobody to bother with. Just the captain of that old A.M.C. Looked all right, and seemed bright enough, but with a command like her he must have something wrong with him.

He stood stockstill in the deserted passageway, spent and despairing. *Damn them. Damn them all to hell.*

'Are you all right, sir?'

Lindsay swung round and saw the girl standing just inside the blackout curtain by the main entrance. As before she was muffled to the ears, and her feet and legs were encased in a pair of muddy rubber boots.

He stared at her for several seconds. 'Yes, thank you.' He tried to smile, seeing the doubt and concern in her eyes. 'A bit bushed, that's all.'

She took off her jaunty cap and shook out her hair vigorously. 'I saw you come in this morning.' She was still studying him, her eyes troubled. 'We all heard about what happened.'

A door opened and closed with a bang and another Wren, also heavily covered in duffel coat and scarf, passed Lindsay without a glance. As she reached the door the Wren called Eve Collins tossed her an ignition key and said, 'Thanks for relieving me early, Sue. Watch out for ice on the roads.'

The other girl paused and looked at Lindsay. 'Do it for me sometime.' Then she was gone, the blackout curtain swirling momentarily in a jet of cold air.

She said quietly, 'I'm glad you made it back all right, sir.'

Lindsay recalled the flashing headlights on the shore, the signalman who had seen them.

He said, 'One of the bunting tossers read your message when we left Scapa. It was nice of you to see us off.'

She grinned. 'Thank him for me, will you? My morse isn't too hot.'

Then she saw his expression and added huskily, 'Was *he* killed?'

'Yes.' He tried to shut it all from his aching mind. Ritchie's face. The wet oilskins by the rail. *We commit his body to the deep.*

He said abruptly, 'I wonder if you'd care to have a drink with me?' He saw the sudden surprise and added, 'Maybe we could get a meal or something?'

She replaced her cap very slowly. 'I'm sorry. I really am.'

'You've *got* a date?' It was all suddenly clear. The other Wren relieving her early. *Do it for me sometime.*

She did not smile. 'Something like that.' She looked away. 'I can break it though——'

'No. It's all right.' He thrust his hands into his greatcoat pockets, trying to sound casual. That it did not matter. He did not even know why it had all become so urgent and important. 'Forget it.'

The curtain swirled inwards again and a R.A.F. flight-lieutenant blundered into the lamplight, banging his gloved hands together.

'I guessed you'd take half the night to get changed! I've got a car outside. I'll run you to your billet.' He saw Lindsay and said awkwardly, 'Oh, sorry!'

She said, 'Jack, this is Commander Lindsay.' Then she turned to him again, her voice very quiet. 'The fighter boys are giving a dance at the field. Why don't you come, too? It might be a change from——' She looked at the flight-lieutenant. 'What do you say, Jack? It would be all right, wouldn't it?'

'Of course.' He did not sound very enthusiastic.

Lindsay smiled. 'I must get back to my ship. They'll be waiting to hear the news.' He looked at the R.A.F. officer and back to the girl. 'But thanks again. Enjoy yourselves.'

Then he was outside in the darkness, the icy wind driving down his throat, making his eyes water like tears.

In the passageway the flight-lieutenant spread his hands. '*So?*'

She tightened her scarf and frowned. 'So nothing. He's a good bloke, that's all.'

He grinned. 'A full commander, too. By God, Eve, I admire your sense of priorities!'

Out on the roadway Lindsay heard her laugh and the sound of the car driving away. He had made an idiot of himself, and it mattered. It mattered so much he could feel it like pain.

Aloud he said, 'You bloody fool. You stupid bloody fool!'

Then he quickened his pace and turned once more towards the sea.

———————

Lindsay was working at his desk when Goss, followed by Fraser, entered his day cabin.

'Sit, gentlemen.' He pressed the bell beside his desk and added, 'Nearly noon. We'll have a drink.'

He watched Goss's heavy features as he selected a chair, noting the deep lines around his mouth and eyes. It had been a busy time for the whole ship, but the effect on Goss was even more noticeable. Captain Lovelace had been right about the timing, he thought bitterly. *A week is about all you can expect.*

He looked at the two men and said slowly, 'I have just received our orders. We are at forty-eight hours notice for steam.'

Fraser muttered, 'A week and a day. That's all they've given us.' Then he grinned. 'Generous bastards!'

Lindsay turned to Goss. 'What about you, Number One? Are you all buttoned up?'

Poor Goss, he had taken the time in harbour badly. Lindsay had watched him arguing with engineers and workers from the repair ship, seen him following the mechanics and welders between the *Benbecula*'s decks like an old hen trying to protect its chickens from a pack of rampaging foxes. But for Fraser's excellent work on repairs while the ship had been returning to the Flow it was hard to see how they could have managed. The shell holes in the hull had been covered by new plates, and with the aid of fresh paint the outer damage would pass unnoticed to all but an experienced eye. Inboard, the repairs had been equally brief, a case of patch up and hope for the best, as one dockyard official had described it.

Jupp padded into the cabin and opened the drinks cabinet as Goss replied, 'I've done my best, but it's nowhere near ready. Those butchers have made more mess than they've repaired. We should have gone down to Greenock or Rosyth.' He glanced at the nearest scuttle and added harshly, 'The weather's worse, too.'

Fraser grimaced. 'Proper ray of sunlight, you are!'

Lindsay said, 'I believe we may be at sea for Christmas.'

He watched his words affecting each of them in different ways. He had been at sea for nearly every Christmas he could remember, but this was different. Most of the ship's company had not, and after the misery of the last patrol, Christmas in the Arctic wastes might seem like a final disaster. He followed Goss's stare to the scuttle. The sky was very pale and without colour. Inside the cabin it was humid with steam heat, but beyond the toughened glass the air would be like a razor.

Fraser asked mildly, 'Is it definite, sir?'

Lindsay glanced at Jupp's stooped shoulders and smiled. 'The chief steward informs me that it is so.'

Jupp bowed over the desk with his tray of glasses and

eyed him calmly. 'I saw the turkeys meself, sir. Bein' stacked up ready for Mr Barker's people to collect 'em.' He shook his head. 'A sure sign.'

Fraser grinned. 'Very.'

Goss did not seem to be listening. 'Same patrol?'

'No.' Lindsay held up his glass to the light. 'Further south-west than Uncle Item Victor. But that is just between us.'

Goss shuddered. 'Nearer Greenland. There'll be ice about.'

The three of them lapsed into silence, so that the muffled shipboard noises intruded like whispers.

Lindsay watched as Jupp refilled his glass and wondered if the chief steward had noticed he was drinking more lately. He should have gone ashore, if only to stretch his legs or to find a change of scene. But apart from two official visits to the headquarters at Kirkwall he had remained on board immersing himself in the business of preparing his ship for sea again. He knew he had stayed too much alone, that it had solved nothing.

He realised too that something had to be done to break the gloom which hung over his command like a threat, especially with the added prospect of Christmas at sea. He had granted shore leave as often as possible, but the libertymen had soon discovered the scope of enjoyment in Scapa was almost nil. There had been several fights, drunkenness and two cases of assault on naval patrolmen. Few of the defaulters brought before him for punishment had offered a reason for their behaviour, and he knew that all these things were just symptoms of frustration and boredom. The stark thrill of being spared *Loch Glendhu*'s fate, of hitting at the enemy, had soon vanished when back in harbour. Anywhere else and it might not have mattered. But here, in this dismal place it was taking its toll.

He said suddenly, 'I thought we'd have a party before we sail. It will help make up for Christmas.'

Fraser eyed him curiously. 'It'll pass the time.'

But Lindsay was watching Goss. 'It's rather up to you, Number One. If you think you've too much on your plate we'll scrub round it, of course.'

Goss stirred in his chair. 'I *am* very busy, sir.' He was pondering on Lindsay's words, his eyes far away as he continued, 'Who would be coming anyway?'

Lindsay tried to keep his tone matter of fact, knowing Fraser was watching him. He hoped Goss would not see through his little game as easily as Fraser was obviously doing.

He said, 'Oh, all the usual. Base staff, some of the people who have been helping us. That sort of thing.'

Fraser said over the rim of his glass, 'I think it might be too difficult. Number One's people have still got a good bit of clearing up to do. In any case, who'd want to come to a ship like this? There's a damn great carrier here now and——'.

Goss swung towards him angrily. 'That's all you bloody well know! How many ships like this one have *you* seen then, eh?' Some of his drink slopped on to his thighs but he did not notice. 'A carrier, you say? Well, that's just another warship, and most people are sick to death of them up here!'

Lindsay asked quietly, 'You're in favour?' He saw Fraser drop one eyelid in a brief wink.

Goss recovered some of his old dignity. 'Well, if you think——' He darted a glance at Fraser. 'Yes, I am, sir.'

'That's settled then. I'll leave it to you. Two days is not long to arrange it, but I expect you'll manage.'

Goss pushed his empty glass towards Jupp. 'Manage?' He frowned. 'I've seen the main saloon filled to overflowing in my day. A prince, his whole retinue, and some of the richest passengers we've carried, all eating and drinking fit to bust.' He nodded firmly. 'We'll show 'em.' He stood up violently. 'So if you'll excuse me, I think I'll find Barker. Go over a few things with him.' He did not mention the patrol at all. 'Carrier indeed! Who the hell wants to see that!' He left the cabin with unusual speed.

Fraser signalled for another drink and then said quietly, 'I've not seen him like that for years. My God, sir, you don't know what you've sparked off.'

Lindsay smiled. 'I hope you're right, Chief. This ship needs something, so we'll make a start with the party, right?'

Fraser grinned. 'Right.'

———————————

Lindsay did not have much time to think about the proposed party. Almost to the hour of its starting he was kept busy dealing with the ship's affairs as with growing speed sailing preparations were completed. Fresh supplies and ammunition. A new whaler to replace the one destroyed by shellfire, as well as the promised turkeys, which were whisked away by Barker's men to the cold storage room before any could go astray. And of course there were the new ratings who arrived in dribs and drabs in the ferries to take the places of more seasoned men needed elsewhere.

The *Benbecula*'s company watched the new arrivals with all the usual interest. The men who had made just one patrol, who had been drafted straight from shore training establishments, now stood like old salts and eyed the newcomers with a mixture of contempt and assured superiority. Lindsay had watched some of them from the bridge. Their brand-new greatcoats and gasmask haversacks, their regulation haircuts and general air of lost confusion marking them out from all the rest.

He had heard Archer, the chief boatswain's mate, bellowing at them, 'Come on then, jump about! Drop yer bags 'n'ammicks and get fell in while I gives you yer parts of ship!'

Archer seemed to have grown in size since the

commissioned boatswain, Tobey, had left for another ship, but quite obviously relished his new powers.

When one pale-faced recruit had said timidly, 'I thought we were coming to a warship, P.O., not a ——' he had got no further.

Archer had roared at him, 'This 'ere is an' armed merchant cruiser, see? Any bloody fool can 'andle a battleship, but this takes *seamen,* got it?' As he had been about to turn away he had added loudly, 'And I'm not a P.O., I'm the *chief bosun's mate,* so don't you bloody well forget it!'

The little seaman had tried to escape after the rest of the draft but Archer's voice had pursued him like an enraged walrus. 'An' get yer bloody 'air cut!'

It was dark in the Flow when Goss came to Lindsay's quarters. 'Ready for you in the wardroom, sir.'

Lindsay noticed Goss was wearing a new uniform and his cheeks were glowing from a fresh shave and bath. There was something else, too. A kind of defiance.

When they reached the wardroom Lindsay was astounded. It was difficult to believe he was in the same ship. Everything shone with polish and small coloured lights, and two long tables were groaning under such a weight of sandwiches, canapés and so many tempting morsels that he could pity the officers and their mess bills when the reckoning was made. Most of the stewards who had been with the company before the war were wearing their old mess jackets and maroon trousers, and as Lindsay followed Goss's massive figure towards the assembled officers he saw three other stewards waiting self-consciously with violins and a piano which had certainly not been present before.

Goss turned and faced him grimly. 'Well, sir?'

Lindsay kept his face impassive. 'It's not Navy, Number One.' Then he reached out and touched Goss's forearm. 'But it's bloody marvellous! I knew you'd do your best, but this is more than that!'

Goss stared at him uncertainly. 'You like it then?'

Barker appeared at his side, beaming. 'Just like the old days!'

Goss ignored him. 'You *really* like it, sir?'

'I do.' Lindsay saw Jupp making towards him with a tray. 'It's what I needed. What we all need in this bloody war!' And he knew he meant it.

Goss snapped his fingers at a steward and said, 'I heard a boat alongside. The first guests are arriving.' Then he strode away, his eyes darting across the laden tables to ensure nothing had been eaten.

Fraser watched him go and then said, 'You've made his day.' He looked at Lindsay searchingly. 'I'm drinking to you.' He lifted a glass. 'That was a damn nice thing you just did.'

In no time at all the wardroom seemed to get crowded with visitors. As the din of conversation and laughter mounted and the trio of musicians did their best to rise above it, Lindsay was conscious of the impression Goss's party was having. What had started almost as a joke was gathering way, so that he too could sense a kind of pride for the way this old ship, his ship, was hanging on to her past and so giving pleasure to the present.

Faces swam around him, handshakes and slaps on the shoulder marked each new arrival. Officers from the base and other ships. Some nursing sisters and the wives of senior officers and officials added the required feminine interest, and the plentiful supply of drink did the rest. There were several Wrens, too, but not the one he had been waiting to see. He knew it was pointless to try again, just as he realised he wanted very much to meet her once more before the ship sailed.

His own officers appeared to be enjoying themselves. de Chair, impeccable as ever in his best blue uniform, was entertaining two of the women. Stannard and Sub-Lieutenant Cordeaux seemed to be having a drinking contest, while Dancy was speaking gravely to a blonde nurse on the trials of being surrounded by so much literary material.

She was saying huskily, 'It must be marvellous to be a real writer.'

He looked at her and nodded, his eyes already glazed. 'It can also be a *great* responsibility.'

Even Emerson, the elderly warrant engineer, was coming out of his shell. He was talking with the wife of a dockyard manager, his voice loud with enthusiasm.

'Yeh. So I says to me old woman, what about a run to Margate? An' *she* says—' he paused to dab the tears from his eyes, '—*she* says, wot d'you think I am? A bloody rabbit?'

Behind him Lindsay heard Dancy's nurse ask, 'Is he really an officer?'

Dancy said thickly, 'One of my best, actually.'

And through and above it Goss moved like a giant, his voice carrying over all else as he received his compliments and replied to many of the questions.

'Yes, I recall the time when we were at Aden, that was quite a trip.' Or, 'She was the best paying ship in the line. Always popular on the Far East run, was the old *Becky*.'

Lindsay took another drink, trying to remember how many he had swallowed so far. Goss was really enjoying himself. It was just as if the opportunity to show what his old ship could do had released some of the pressure.

Jupp said quietly, 'There has just been a telephone call, sir. Captain Lovelace will be coming aboard shortly.'

But Lindsay was looking past him towards the door. Boase, the doctor, was greeting several latecomers and leading them to the tables. One of them was the Wren called Eve.

At first he could not be certain. Without her scarves and baggy coat she looked quite different. For one thing, she was much smaller than he had imagined, and her hair was cut very short, giving her a sort of elfin simplicity.

He pushed through the press of figures and saw Boase stiffen and say, 'Oh, this is the captain.'

She held out her hand. It was small and very warm. 'I know.'

Lindsay said, 'I'm glad you could come.'

She had hazel eyes, very wide. And she was studying him with that same mock gravity he had remembered so vividly from their first meeting in that wet, quivering staff car.

She said, 'It's like nothing I've ever seen. She's a *beautiful* ship.'

He realised with a start he was still holding her hand and said awkwardly, 'Here's a steward. Take a drink from the tray and tell me what you've been doing.'

She smiled up at him. 'Not much.' She lifted the glass. 'Cheers.'

Boase had sunk back into the crowd but Lindsay had not even noticed. He said, 'I'm sorry I was a bit stupid the other night. You must have thought——'

She interrupted quietly, 'I thought you looked worn out. I was sorry, too. About that dance.'

Lindsay glanced round. 'Have you brought him with you?' He forced a smile. 'He seemed a nice chap.'

'You hated him, and it showed!' She laughed at his confusion. 'But he's not with me.' The laugh wavered. 'He was a friend of Bill's. The one who was killed.'

Then she waved her glass to another Wren who was in deep conversation with Lieutenant Hunter. 'Watch it, Judy! You know what they say!' The mood had changed again.

Lindsay guided her to the bulkhead. 'We're leaving tomorrow, but I imagine you know. I was wondering. About that meal I promised you?'

She looked at him with new concern. 'Oh, I forgot to tell you. I've been drafted.'

'*Drafted?*' The word hung between them like a shutter.

'Well, I've been trying for ages to go on a signals course.

I should have gone when I joined, but I had a driving licence, you see.'

Lindsay did not see. All he knew was he was losing her almost before he had found her. 'Licence?'

She wrinkled her nose. 'Yes. So they made me a driver. You know how it is.' She staggered against his arm. 'Oops. I'm getting tipsy already!' Then she saw his face and added, 'Well, my draft-chit has at last arrived. I'm being sent on some new course.' She faltered. 'In Canada.'

Lindsay looked away. 'I'm very glad for you.'

'No you're not.' She rested a hand on his sleeve. 'Neither am I. Now.'

Canada. Not even where he could visit her. He cursed himself for allowing his disappointment to show. It wasn't her fault. It wasn't anyone's fault.

He said, 'You didn't come aboard to be miserable. Come and meet the others.'

She shook her head. 'I can only stay a little while. They're shipping me out tonight. I expect I'll be joining a convoy at Liverpool.' She was not smiling. 'Rotten, isn't it?'

'Yes.' He wanted to take her away. Free himself and her from the noise and enjoyment which hemmed them in like a wall. 'I shall miss you.'

She studied his face for several seconds. 'You mean it, don't you?'

Maxwell's polished head moved from the crowd. 'Sorry to interrupt, sir, but Captain Lovelace is here.' He kept his eyes on the girl. 'He has an important visitor with him.'

'Tell him I'll be right over.' As Maxwell hurried away he said urgently, 'You won't leave the ship without saying goodbye?'

She shook her head very slowly. 'No. Of course not.' She tried to bring back her cheeky grin. 'I'll go and yarn with your delicious doctor.' But somehow the grin would not come.

Lindsay moved through the crowd and found Lovelace speaking with Maxwell, his serious features breaking into a smile as he said, 'Ah, Lindsay, I'd like you to meet Commodore Kemp.'

The other guest was a sturdy, thickset man, who nodded abruptly and said, 'Quite a party. Never think you'd been in action, what?'

Lovelace eyed him coolly. 'No. You've done a marvellous job, Lindsay.'

Lindsay was still watching the commodore. There was something aggressive about him. Intolerant. Like his words. 'Are you joining the base, sir?'

The commodore took a glass from a steward and regarded it critically. 'I'm here to co-ordinate new strategy.' He glanced at Lindsay again. 'Still, this is hardly the time to discuss Service matters, what?' He did not smile.

Lindsay felt suddenly angry. Who the hell did he think he was anyway? He thought too of the girl, of the fading, precious minutes.

The commodore said abruptly, 'Where is that son of mine then?'

Kemp. Of course. He should have guessed.

'I'm afraid I don't know, sir.'

'*I* would want to know where every one of my officers was, at any time of the day or night.'

'Come along, sir, why not meet some of the other guests?' Lovelace sounded tense. 'I'm sure the captain doesn't bother about one more midshipman, eh?'

Kemp stared at him bleakly. 'I *want* to see him.'

Lindsay sighed. 'I'll send for him.' It was his own fault. After all, Kemp had come a long way to see his only son. It was not much to ask.

He heard the commodore say, 'Young fool. When I heard about his latest failure I thought I'd explode!' He stared round at the shining panels and glittering lights.

'Under these circumstances, however——'

Lindsay turned sharply, 'Are you here on official business, sir, or as a guest?'

Kemp looked at him with surprise. 'As a guest of course!'

Lindsay said quietly, 'Then, sir, may I suggest you start acting like one!' Then he turned on his heel and walked away.

The commodore opened and closed his mouth several times. 'The impertinent young——' He turned to Lovelace again. 'By God, there will be a few changes when I'm in control, I can tell you!'

Lindsay almost collided with Jupp as he pushed between the noisy figures by the door.

Jupp said, 'Beg pardon, sir, but the young lady 'as gone. There was a call from the shore. Somethin' about 'er draft bein' brought forward an hour.' He held out a paper napkin. 'She said to give this to you, sir.'

Lindsay opened it. She had written in pencil. *Had to go. Take care of yourself. See you in Eden. Eve.*

Then he hurried out and on to the promenade deck, the breath almost knocked from him by the bitter air. He found the gangway staff huddled together in their thick watchcoats, banging their hands and stamping their feet to keep warm.

The quartermaster saw Lindsay and said, 'Can I 'elp, sir?'

'The last boat, Q.M. Can you still see it?' Beyond the guardrail the night was pitch black.

The quartermaster shook his head. 'No, sir. Shoved off ten minutes back.' His breath smelt strongly of rum.

Lindsay felt the napkin in his hand and folded it carefully before putting it in his pocket.

'Thank you. Goodnight.'

The quartermaster watched him go and said to his companion, 'Funny lot.'

The bosun's mate looked at him. 'Who?'

The quartermaster reached for his hidden rum bottle. 'Officers, of course! Who the bloody else!'

Lindsay walked back into the noisy wardroom and noticed that Commodore Kemp was speaking to his son in a corner. Several of the guests were showing signs of wear, and when they reached the cold air outside they would know all about it.

He reached Goss's side and said, 'I'm going to my cabin, Number One. You take over, will you.'

Goss nodded, watching him strangely. 'Good party, sir.'

'Yes.' Lindsay looked at the door, as if expecting to see her there again. 'Very good party.'

Then he saw Jupp and said, 'I'll have some whisky in my cabin.'

'Now, sir?'

'*Now.*'

He walked out of the wardroom and climbed the companion ladder which now seemed very quiet and deserted.

8 A small error

The telephone above Lindsay's bunk rattled tinnily, and without switching on his overhead lamp he reached up and clapped it to his ear.

'Captain?'

Stannard sounded off guard. He had probably imagined Lindsay to be fast asleep.

'Time to alter course, sir.'

Lindsay held up his watch and saw the luminous face glowing in the darkness. Four in the morning. Another day.

'Very well, Pilot. What's it like up top?'

Not that it would have altered in the three hours since he had left the bridge. Nor had it changed much in the days and the weeks since they had slipped their buoy in Scapa. Ten days to reach the patrol area and another twenty pounding along the invisible lines of its extremities while the sea did everything possible to make their lives a misery. Even now, as he listened to Stannard's breathing and to the dull boom of waves against the hull, he could picture the water sluicing across the forward well deck, freezing into hard bulk, while the blown spray changed the superstructure and rigging into moulds of crude glass. Men frozen to the bone, slipping and cursing into the darkness with hammers and steam hoses, knowing as they toiled that they would be required again within the hour.

Stannard replied, 'Wind still nor'west, sir. Pretty fresh. It might feel easier when we turn into it.'

'Good. Keep me posted, Pilot.' He dropped the handset on its hook and lay back again on the pillow.

What a way to fight a war. Mile upon wretched mile. Empty, violent and cold. He heard feet overhead, the muffled clatter of steering gear as Stannard brought the old ship round on the southernmost leg of her patrol. Right at this moment of time Stannard's little pencilled cross on the chart would show the *Benbecula* almost five hundred miles south-west of Iceland, while some seven hundred and fifty miles beyond her labouring bows was the dreaded Cape Farewell of Greenland. It was not a patrol area, he thought. It was a wilderness, a freezing desert.

One more day and they would be in December, with still another month to go before they could run for home, for Scapa and its weed-encrusted buoys.

He turned on the bunk and heard the small pill jar rattle beneath the pillow. The sound was like a cruel taunt, and he tried not to think of Boase's reserved voice as he had handed them to him. Enough to make you sleep for four hours at least. Deep, empty sleep which he needed so desperately. Pitifully. Yet he knew he was afraid to take even one of them. In case he was needed. In case. . . . He rolled over to his opposite side and thought instead about opening a new bottle of whisky. It was no use. He could not go on like this. He was slowly destroying himself, and knew he was a growing menace to all those who depended on him at any hour of day or night.

Whenever he fell into the bunk for even a few moments the nightmare returned with the regularity of time itself. Again and again and again he would awake, sweating and frightened. Shaking and knowing he was beaten.

Perhaps if they were on convoy duty it might have been different. The daily check of ships under escort, the careful manoeuvres with massive merchantmen charging blindly through fog or pitch darkness for fear of losing the next ahead. The search for stragglers, and the triumph at watching the lines of weatherbeaten charges plodding past into harbour and safety.

But here there was nothing, and he knew it was affecting almost every man aboard. Tension flared into anger. Someone just a minute late on watch would be cursed by the waiting man with all the hatred and venom of an enemy. Lindsay tried to break the deadly monotony and discomfort by speaking daily to the ship's company over the new tannoy system. He occasionally left the bridge to do his rounds, to visit as many parts of the ship as he could between other duties, but he could feel the hopelessness of it just the same. Even the pathetically early Christmas decorations in some of the messes seemed to make a mockery of their efforts to stay sane.

The telephone jarred into his thoughts like a gunshot. It was Stannard again.

'Sorry to bother you, sir.' His Australian accent was more pronounced than usual. 'There's a westbound convoy altering course to the south-east of us. W/T office is monitoring all traffic as you instructed.'

'How far away?'

Stannard sounded vague. 'Approximately five hundred miles, sir.'

'Anything else?'

'Admiralty reports a deployment of seven plus U-boats converging ahead of convoy's original course, sir.'

'Very well. Keep a good listening watch.' He heard the line go dead.

As he lay back he thought of the countless times he had heard such warnings himself when he had commanded the *Vengeur*. Except that now there were more U-boats, bigger and better organised than before. He could imagine the heart-searching which would be going on at this moment as the commodore and escort commander of that unknown convoy examined and discussed the latest information. Alter course. Run further north to avoid the eager U-boats. Lose time certainly, but with luck the ships would be saved from destruction. U-boats rarely wasted their efforts and fuel by sweeping too far from the main convoy routes. And why should they? Their growing toll of sinkings was evidence of their harvest.

But in the Atlantic you could never be really certain. Time and distance, speed and visibility were so different here from the calm efficiency of the plotting rooms in the far off Admiralty bunkers.

But it was not *Benbecula*'s concern. The convoy, like all the others at sea at any given time, must depend on its own resources.

He closed his eyes and tried to dismiss it from his mind. But try as he might he could not put aside a sudden feeling of uneasiness. Doubt or instinct? It was impossible to describe.

He switched on the light and swung his legs off the bunk, feeling automatically for his sea boots. It was no surprise to hear the discreet knock at the outer door and to see Jupp's mournful face peering in at him. Perhaps he could not sleep either.

'Will you be wanting an early breakfast, sir?' His eyes flickered swiftly across the disordered bunk. 'I 'ave some coffee on the go.'

Lindsay shook his head, steadying his legs against the tilting deck. 'I think I'll make do with coffee for now.'

Jupp vanished just as quietly and returned in minutes with a pot of fresh coffee.

He said, 'Blowing a bit up top, sir.' He glanced with obvious disapproval at Lindsay's soiled and crumpled sweater. 'I could get you some more gear from my store.'

Lindsay smiled. 'Later.'

He swung round as the handset rang again. 'Captain?'

Stannard said, 'W/T office has just received a signal for us, sir. Top Secret. I've got Aikman on to it right away.'

Lieutenant Aikman, who was listed as boarding officer, had the additional chore of decoding the more secret and difficult signals, and would not thank Stannard for hauling him from his warm bunk.

Lindsay swallowed some coffee and then asked, 'Any news of the convoy?'

'Six more U-boats reported to the south of it, sir. I've marked 'em on my chart, so it also gives us a fair idea of the convoy's position.'

Lindsay nodded. 'Good. That was sensible.' There was more to Stannard than he had imagined.

He replaced the handset as Jupp said, 'Marvellous 'ow the Admiralty know all them things, sir.'

Lindsay shrugged. 'They've the Germans to thank for that. Admiralty intercepts signals from seagoing U-boats to German naval headquarters and passes the information on to the convoys. Got it?'

Jupp looked doubtful. 'Not quite, sir.'

Lindsay groped for the nearest dry towel and wound it round his neck. 'If a U-boat sights a convoy her skipper flashes the news to Germany. The German operations staff then signal all U-boats in the vicinity to home on to it like a pack of wolves.'

As he buttoned his jacket he was thinking of those submarines. Seven plus ahead of the convoy's previous course. Now six more to the south. It was a formidable force, but fortunately there was still time to take avoiding action. Thanks to the radio operators at the Admiralty.

Jupp handed him his cap and glasses. 'It's all too much for me, sir. Makes me feel old.'

Lindsay brushed past him. 'You'll never get old. You're like the ship. Rheumaticky but reliable!'

As he hurried up the companion ladder he realised with a start that it was the first time he had attempted to make a joke about anything since . . . he shut the other picture from his mind.

By the chart room he paused and glanced inside. Stannard was stretching across the big table, his fingers working deftly with dividers and parallel rulers. He made some small notations on the chart and then straightened his back. Seeing Lindsay in the doorway he said, 'Oh, good morning, sir.' He grinned. 'Although it's as black as a boot outside.'

Lindsay leaned on the table and studied the neat lines and bearings.

Stannard said, 'As far as I can make out the convoy has made a really drastic alteration of course.' He tapped the chart with his dividers. 'They are steaming almost nor-'west and really cracking it on.'

'What do we know about it, Pilot?'

Lindsay knew what the convoy's commodore was doing. He had already passed out of effective range of air cover from England and was heading further north in the hopes of getting help from the longe-range bomber patrols from Iceland. There were so many dead patches where aircraft could not reach to carry out sorties and anti-submarine attacks. Like the vast area now covered by *Benbecula*'s endless vigil.

Stannard said, 'I looked at the intelligence log, sir. Seems it's a fast westbound convoy. Only ten ships, according to the last information.'

The door banged open and Aikman, his pyjamas covered by a duffel coat, stepped over the coaming.

'Bloody hell, Pilot! Can't you let a bloke get some shut-eye!' He saw Lindsay and flushed. 'Sorry, sir!'

Lindsay smiled. 'I know how you feel.' He was still thinking about the convoy. 'What does the signal say?'

Aikman ran his fingers through his tousled hair. 'Three German heavy units have left Tromso, sir. Last reported heading south along the Norwegian coast. Further information not yet available.' He looked up as Lindsay turned to face him. 'There's a list of deployments too, sir.'

Lindsay took the long, neatly written signal and read it very slowly. It might be nothing. The enemy could be moving three important warships south to Kiel or to the

Baltic for use against the Russians. They had been *seen* steaming south, but that could have easily been a ruse to confuse the Norwegian agents who must have flashed the news to the Admiralty in London. Perhaps they were going to make another attempt to break into the Atlantic in strength. He ran his eye over the deployment information. A cruiser squadron was already on its way from Iceland, and more heavy units had left Scapa Flow. He found he was reading faster as the mental picture began to form in his mind. Almost every available ship was being sent to forestall anything which the three German units might attempt. He thought of the deserted buoys at Scapa. The place would really be stripped bare now.

He looked at Stannard. 'I want you to make notes on this signal. You'll need help with it, so I'll stay on the bridge awhile until we hear something more.'

Stannard nodded and picked up a telephone. He said, 'Bosun's mate? Get the navigator's yeoman double quick. And tell Midshipman Kemp I want him here, too.' As he dropped the handset he was already searching through his chart folios until with a grunt he dragged one out and laid it on the smaller chart table by the bulkhead. 'Just so as I can plot what's happening off Norway, sir.' He grinned and added, 'Not that we'll be involved, but it helps to pass the time.'

Lindsay eyed him gravely. 'Good thinking. But don't bank on the last part too much.'

As he walked towards the wheelhouse Lindsay was thinking of the carefully detailed information in the signal. What Stannard did not yet realise was that apart from *Benbecula* and two patrol vessels in the Denmark Strait there was hardly a single ship within five hundred miles of the convoy and its escorts.

He found Dancy standing in the centre of the bridge staring straight ahead through a clearview screen. Beyond the toughened glass there was little visible but the dark outline of the forecastle framed against the oncoming ranks of white-topped waves. Past the pale crests there was complete darkness, with not even a star to show itself through the thick cloud.

Dancy stiffened as Lindsay lifted himself on to the chair.

Lindsay remarked, 'How is the ice on deck, Sub?'

Dancy replied, 'The middle watch had it cleared before we came up, sir. But there is some forming below Number Two gun mounting, I think. I'll get the hands on it in half an hour.' He hesitated. 'If that is all right, sir?'

Lindsay looked at him. How much more confident Dancy had become. Probably through working with Stannard.

'Fine,' he said.

Stannard entered the wheelhouse a few minutes later but he was no longer so untroubled. 'I've marked all of it on the charts, sir.' His palm rasped over his chin. 'If those three jokers make a go for the Atlantic, which way will they come, d'you reckon?'

Lindsay shrugged. 'They'll know they've been seen on the move and will not waste time trying for the Denmark Strait this time. Quite apart from the problems of drifting ice, they'll imagine we've a mass of patrols there already waiting for them.'

Stannard said quietly, 'If they only knew!'

Lindsay nodded. 'My guess is they'll head for the Rose Garden.'

'Sir?' Dancy sounded puzzled.

Stannard understood. 'That's the area between Iceland and the Faroes, you ignorant oaf!'

Dancy replied carefully, 'All the same, it'll be hard to slip past our ships, surely?'

'Over four hundred miles, Sub?' Lindsay looked away. 'It's a pretty wide gap.'

He settled back in the chair and waited until the others had moved away. He did not want to talk. He wanted to think, to try and explain why he felt so uneasy. Involved.

On the face of it, Dancy's youthful optimism should be justified. The Navy had been planning for such an eventuality since the *Bismarck*'s breakout. But this was a very bad time of the year. Visibility was hopeless and air cover restricted accordingly. It was just possible the Germans might make it. If so, where would they go, south to prey on the convoys from the Cape, or further west in search of more rapid results?

Aikman entered the wheelhouse, his eyes glowing faintly in the shaded compass light. 'Another signal, sir. Two more U-boats reported to south of convoy.'

Stannard snapped, 'Give it to me. I'll put it on the chart.'

Lindsay's voice stopped him by the door. 'While you're there, Pilot, get me a course and speed to intercept the convoy.' He hesitated, feeling Stannard's unspoken warning. 'I mean to intercept the convoy *if* it comes as far north as our patrol limit.'

Stannard said, 'Right away, sir.'

Aikman asked, 'They'll never come right up here, surely, sir?'

Lindsay looked at him. 'Wouldn't you if you had fifteen odd U-boats coming after you?'

Aikman nodded glumly. 'I suppose so.'

Somewhere below the bridge the tannoy speaker squeaked into life. 'Cooks to the galley! Forenoon watch-keepers to breakfast and clean!'

Lindsay looked at his watch. Nearly three hours since Stannard had called him on the telephone about the change of course. It seemed like minutes.

Stannard came back and said, 'Course to intercept would be one hundred degrees, sir. Revs for fifteen knots.' He paused, his voice empty of everything but professional interest. 'If the convoy maintains its present course and speed we should make contact at 2000 tonight.' He stood back, his face hidden in shadow as he waited for Lindsay's reaction. Then he added slowly, 'Of

course, sir, we'd be out of our allotted area by noon if you
decided to act on it.'

'Yes.' He thought of the two lines which Stannard must
have drawn on his chart. Two converging lines. One the
Benbecula, the other a handful of desperate, valuable
ships. The convoy's original track was straddled by U-
boats. To the south the gate was also closed. But if the
convoy came further north and the German heavy units
burst through the patrol lines, they would need all the
help they could get.

He said, 'Very well. Bring her round to one-zero-zero.
Call up the chief before you ask for maximum revs, but
warn the engine room what to expect.'

He could feel the sudden expectancy amongst the
shadowy figures around him. Moments before they had
been lolling and swaying with the regular motion, half
asleep and dull with boredom. His words had changed all
that in an instant.

'Port fifteen.' Stannard rested one hand on the gyro,
his eyes watching the quartermaster as he began to turn
the wheel.

Below decks, as the forenoon watchkeepers queued for
their greasy sausages and powdered egg, their sweet tea
and marmalade, they would feel the difference and cling
to their mess tables until the turn was completed. Only
the seasoned men would guess what was happening. The
others would merely curse the officers on the bridge for
deliberately trying to ruin their breakfast.

'Midships.' Stannard had his eye down to the gyro.
'Steady.'

'Steady, sir. Course zero-nine-five.' The quartermaster
sounded breathless as the ship rolled heavily across a
steep trough.

'Steer one-zero-zero.' Stannard looked up as small
tinkling sounds echoed above like tiny bells. More ice
forming on the control position and rigging made by the
spray flung high over the bows.

A telephone buzzed and Stannard said, 'Yes, Chief.' He looked at Lindsay. 'For you, sir.'

Fraser sounded irritable. 'What's all this I hear about full revs, sir?'

Lindsay turned his back to the others and spoke very quietly into the mouthpiece. 'There may be a convoy coming into our pitch, Chief. There are three bandits at large from Norway and a whole pack of U-boats to the south. I thought our presence might cheer 'em up a bit. Pilot will give you the details. I just wanted you to know the rest of it first.'

There was a long pause. 'Aye, sir. Ring down when you're ready. I'll give you everything I've got.'

Lindsay handed the telephone to Stannard and said, 'I'm going below. I have a feeling this is going to be a long day.'

Two hours later Jupp stood beside Lindsay's table and eyed him with grave approval. Lindsay had shaved, taken a quick shower, and had allowed Jupp to supply him with a freshly laundered sweater. But it was the fact that he was eating his first complete breakfast since taking command which was obviously giving the steward so much pleasure. He even felt better, but could discover no cause for it.

Beyond the bulkhead he could hear hammers banging away the ice and the squeak of metal as the gun crews tested their weapons and made sure the mechanism had not frozen solid overnight. It was still dark on deck, and would be for most of the day. He could feel the ship's stern lifting slowly to the following sea, while the bows crashed and vibrated like dull thunder, throwing up the spray in long tattered banners as high as the foremast derricks.

There was a tap at the door and Petty Officer Ritchie stepped over the coaming, his cap beneath his arm. He too looked brighter and more relaxed than Lindsay could remember. Perhaps, like himself, he craved to be doing something, if only to keep his inner hurt at bay a while longer.

'Good morning, Yeoman. Anything new?'

Ritchie took a pad from his pocket. 'Not much, sir. No more U-boat reports. And there's nothin' about the three Jerry ships neither.' He leafed through the pad. 'Bad weather over the Denmark Strait, so all air patrols is grounded.'

'That follows.' Lindsay gestured to Jupp for some more coffee.

Ritchie added, 'Some more information about the convoy, sir. Ten ships and three escorts.'

'Only three?'

Ritchie grimaced. 'Well, sir, it's a fast convoy apparently. Mostly tankers in ballast and two personnel ships. One of 'em's got a party of Wrens aboard it seems. A complete signals course.'

Lindsay stared at him, suddenly ice cold. It was more than a coincidence, surely. The feeling. The nagging instinct that something was wrong. Like the dream. Only this time it was real.

'Give it to me.' He took the pad, his eyes darting across Ritchie's round handwriting as if to see something more than the bare details.

Ritchie watched him curiously. 'I did 'ear they was sendin' some Wrens to Canada, sir. Wouldn' 'ave minded an instructing job out there.'

Lindsay stood up. 'Get back to the bridge, Yeo, and tell the W/T office I want every channel open. Anything,' he paused, holding Ritchie's eyes with his own, '*anything* they hear I want to know about. Then pass the word for Lieutenant Stannard to report to me.'

Ritchie looked as if he were about to ask a question, but as he glanced past Lindsay he saw Jupp give an urgent shake of the head and decided against it.

Jupp watched the door close and asked, 'More coffee, sir?' When Lindsay remained staring at the bulkhead he added gently, 'She'll be safe, sir. They'll not take chances with a ship full of women.'

Lindsay turned slowly and looked at him. Poor Jupp, what did he know of the Atlantic?

He said quietly, 'I expect you're right. And thank you.'

Jupp had been expecting Lindsay to fly at him for his foolish comments and had been prepared for it. But he had been determined Lindsay should not be dragged down by the sudden despair which was stamped on his face. The fact that Lindsay had spoken so quietly was in some ways much worse. Jupp was deeply moved by the discovery, as he was troubled by the realisation he could do nothing to help.

———————

In his private office below the bridge Lieutenant Philip Aikman carefully locked the secret code books inside his safe and took a quick glance at himself in the bulkhead mirror. He was past thirty, and occasionally worried about a certain flabbiness around his chin and waist. He liked to take care of himself whenever possible, but with the *Benbecula* rolling drunkenly through trough after trough it was not easy to exercise in comfort and work up a sweat without being watched by prying eyes.

Unlike most of the other officers aboard, Aikman really enjoyed his appointment to the ship. *Benbecula* was not involved with complicated manoeuvres of fleet actions. She was remote from all but the rarest chances of air or U-boat attack, which suited him just fine.

He slipped into his duffel coat and arranged his cap carefully on his fair hair at what was a jaunty angle, but not enough to draw sarcasm or a harsh reprimand from Goss.

In civilian life Aikman had been manager of a small but busy travel agency in the London suburbs. Holidays for middle class families in Brighton and Torquay. Weekends for the less fortunate in Southend and Selsey

Bill. It never varied very much except when someone came to see him for advice on something more daring. France or Italy. A cruise to the Greek Islands or the ski slopes of Switzerland. Aikman knew every place, almost as if he had visited each one himself.

His education was scanty, but he made up for it by his sharp attention to detail and manner. He watched and listened to those who came to his shop to book their holidays, and never pushed himself further than was necessary to gain more information from them when they returned to tell him of his satisfactory, or otherwise, arrangements.

Deep inside he yearned to be part of the world he sold and traded in his shop. That unreal world of laughing girls on posters holding beach balls and calling you to sunshine and endless enjoyment. Of the white-hulled liners anchored in glittering bays and harbours, surrounded by boats of eager wogs and, of course, more smiling girls.

When war came he volunteered for the Navy without really knowing why. He never lost a chance in seeking someone who could help him reach his new goal, a commission, and when luck came his way he seized it with both hands. In the early months, the phoney war as it was called by all those not made to fight in it, there was much confusion, as a peacetime Navy became swollen in size and purpose. By chance he saw and confronted one of his old customers, a retired captain of some age who was now back in the Service, and like it had become larger than life. Aikman had always flattered him, and when the old captain asked casually if he was interested in a job on Contraband Control, Aikman jumped at it.

One advantage Aikman had over the younger officer candidates was that he had experience of life outside the Navy or some public school. Without a blush he completed his forms, adding a list of languages which he spoke fluently and more of which he had a fair

knowledge. In fact he spoke only one, his own, and even
that was limited. But as he had told his customers often
enough. 'Everyone speaks English!' His supreme confidence and smooth acceptance of his new work somehow
carried him through. In the early part of the war, when
maritime neutrals still outnumbered the combatants, he
was required to board and search their ships to make sure
no war materials were being smuggled to the enemy. To
his surprise, he found everyone *did* speak English, well
almost, and when a rare ignorance spoiled his approach
Aikman would soon discover another officer or a steward
who could give him his necessary information. In fact, he
did so well he gained a second stripe almost before the
first one had become tarnished.

But when he was transferred to a troopship and later to
Benbecula he felt a pang of relief. Luck could not last
forever, and here he was really safe. The officers were
nicely mixed, and only a few like Maxwell, the gunnery
officer, and Goss, the first lieutenant, ever bothered him.
He had not a specified job, other than as boarding officer,
until of course the captain had made him his senior
decoding officer, an untouchable and unreachable position. It suited him very well indeed.

He stepped over the cabin coaming and winced as the
wind smashed him back on the wet steel. Over the
weather rail the sea was sinking and then surging high
against the hull, and he had to run like mad to reach the
bridge ladder without getting soaked.

He entered the chart room and shook his cap carefully
on the deck. Stannard was not there, and only Midshipman Kemp and Squire, the navigator's yeoman, were
working on the two charts.

Kemp was well bred, you could see it in the fine clear
skin and sensitive mouth. He had an important father
too, Aikman had learned from someone, and he guessed
there might be a next step for him there if he played it
carefully.

He said casually, 'I've just decoded that last top secret one.' He laid the pad on the chart. 'It states, two repeat two of the German heavy units have entered the Skager-rak, so you'd better note it in the pilot's log.'

Kemp looked up, his eyes rimmed with fatigue. 'Just two of them?'

Aikman gave a grave smile. 'It stands to reason that if two of them have gone to earth the other will be close behind.' He shrugged. 'If not, I imagine the Home Fleet can take care of that bugger!'

Kemp thrust the pad to Squire. 'You do it, will you?'

'I said as much to Pilot.' Aikman yawned hugely. 'When he got me out of my pit at the crack of dawn. Still, there you are.'

He walked to a salt-stained scuttle and peered down at the leaping, jarring wave crests. It was just past noon, yet the sky was dull grey, like a London fog in winter. He watched the rivulets of spray running down the glass and freezing into small distorted worms.

'Nasty. But I've seen worse.'

Behind his back Squire looked up and grinned. Pomp-ous twit. Sounded like a proper old sea-dog. He lowered his head again and reached for his pencil. Squire had been a merchant seaman, but now that he was officially in the Royal Navy for the duration of the war was as determined as Aikman to better himself. There the simi-larity ended. He was a dark haired seaman of twenty-eight years, with the quiet good looks of a scholar rather than a sailor. He had worked hard and had gained the coveted appointment as Stannard's personal yeoman, a step, as the Australian had explained more than once, which would land him a bit of gold lace if he kept his nose clean. So there it was.

He paused, the pencil in mid air. He was too tired. Too worn out by the cold and damp of his endless visits to the bridge. He tried again.

As Aikman walked across the passage to visit the W/T

office Squire said quietly, 'These two Jerry ships, sir. How can they be in the Skagerrak?'

Kemp, who had been brooding about his father and their last angry confrontation, turned and looked at him warily. 'Why not?'

Squire studied him thoughtfully. He liked Kemp, but as an officer he was bloody useless.

Patiently he said, 'If three of them left Tromso last night, how can two have reached as far south as Denmark in that time?' He put down the pencil. 'It's not possible, sir, unless they grew wings!'

Aikman's voice was loud in the passageway and Squire said, 'You'd better tell him, sir. It could be important.'

'Tell him what?' Aikman was back, smiling at them with assured ease.

Kemp looked at the signal pad. 'The yeoman says that these ships could not have reached the Skagerrak so quickly, sir.'

'What?' Aikman was still smiling. 'That's bloody rubbish, lad.' He crossed to the table. 'If their lordships tell us they've got there, then who are we to question them, eh?' He laughed. 'Would you like me to make a special signal to the First Sea Lord? Tell him that Mr Midshipman Kemp and Acting Able Seaman Squire are of the opinion his information is all to hell?'

Kemp dropped his eyes. 'I was only saying what——'

Squire interrupted, 'I think you should check the original signal, sir.'

'Do you?' Aikman felt a sudden twinge of alarm. They were all reacting wrongly. He was losing control. 'As it happens, Squire, I do not require any advice on my department!'

'Sir.' Squire looked away, hurt and suddenly angry. What the hell was the matter with Aikman? He glanced at Kemp's strained face. And he was little better. He should have spoken out, done the job Stannard had entrusted him with.

He said stubbornly, 'When the navigating officer returns, sir, I shall have to tell him.'

'You *do* that small thing, Squire!' Aikman shot him a withering stare. 'I may have some things to tell him, too!' He stamped out of the chart room and slammed the door.

Kemp shrugged. 'Phew, you've really upset him now.'

Squire did not look at him. The first thing he had done wrong. Spoken out against an officer. He must be mad. Even Stannard would be unable to wipe that from his record.

At that very moment Stannard was standing beside Lindsay's tall chair, his eyes fixed beyond the bows and the steady panorama of cruising wave crests.

He said, 'Well, sir, I have to tell you that we should make a turn. Even allowing for dead reckoning and little else, I'm sure we're miles over our patrol line.'

Lindsay nodded slowly. Stannard was right, of course. All the forenoon as he had sat or paced the creaking, staggering bridge he had listened to the intermittent stream of incoming signals. The convoy had made another turn to westward, its commodore apparently satisfied the U-boats had given up the chase. There had been several reports of ice to the south and south-east of Cape Farewell from the American ice patrols, but every captain had to be prepared to take avoiding action in these waters.

He replied, 'Well, if anything had happened we'd have been better placed to go and assist.' It sounded as lame as he knew it was.

Aikman strode on to the bridge and reported, 'Two enemy units have been sighted in their own waters, sir. The third is still unaccounted for.'

Stannard grinned. 'That settles it then. I'll go and lay off a new course.'

Lindsay glanced at Dancy. 'Ring for half speed.'

He settled down again in the chair and thought of the

convoy and the party of Wrens who were probably quite unaware of their momentary danger.

He realised that Aikman was still beside him, and when he turned saw his face was deathly pale, as if he was going to be sick. 'What's wrong?'

Aikman spoke between his teeth. 'There's been a mistake, sir. Not important now as the enemy ships are back in safe waters, but——'

Lindsay asked, 'What sort of mistake?'

'I was called here this morning and told to decode that first signal.' He was speaking mechanically, as if he had lost control over his voice. 'I was tired, I'd been overworking, you see, sir, and I must have confused the times of origin.'

Lindsay gripped the arms of the chair. 'You did what?'

'Well, sir, it was just a small slip.' A bead of sweat ran from under Aikman's cap. 'But the three German ships left Tromso twenty-eight hours *earlier* than I calculated.'

Lindsay saw Dancy watching him over the gyro, his face like a mask.

'But two of them are back in their own waters.' Lindsay forced himself to speak gently, knowing Aikman was near breaking. 'Is *that* part right?'

Aikman nodded. 'Yes, sir.'

The sliding door at the rear of the wheelhouse crashed open and Stannard said harshly, 'Own waters be damned! They're in the Skagerrak, and that was how Squire knew *he,*' Stannard pointed angrily at Aikman's rigid shoulders, 'had made a cock of the decoding!'

'Easy, Pilot!' Lindsay slid from the chair, his mind working wildly. 'This won't help anything.'

Stannard crossed the bridge and said to Aikman, 'You stupid bastard! Why the hell did you take so long to find out?'

Aikman faced him, his lips ashen. 'Well, they're back now, so what are you trying to make trouble for?'

Lindsay's voice silenced all of them. 'In twenty-eight

hours quite a lot might have happened.' He looked at Stannard. 'See what you can find out about the convoy.' Then he looked at Aikman. 'I just hope to God I'm wrong. If not, you'd better start praying!'

Aikman walked from the wheelhouse, his eyes unseeing as Stannard came back from the W/T office.

He said quietly, 'Convoy is now steering two-seven-five, sir. Fifteen knots. Should pass within fifty miles of our southernmost leg at 2000.'

Lindsay waited, knowing there was more.

'A Swedish freighter reported sighting an unidentified ship in the Denmark Strait the night before last, sir. That is all the information available.'

Lindsay walked past him and gripped the rail beneath a clearview screen. Almost to himself he said, 'So while every available ship is out searching for the three from Tromso, one other slips quietly through the Denmark Strait. He's been there, sitting patiently and waiting while the U-boats did the hard part for him.' He swung round on Stannard and slammed one fist into his palm. 'Like beasts to the slaughter!'

Stannard stared at him. 'Oh, my Christ!'

Lindsay turned away. 'Bring her round on to your new course. Maximum revs again, and I'll want the hands to exercise action stations in thirty minutes before the light goes!'

He gestured to a bosun's mate. 'Get the first lieutenant and gunnery officer.' As the man ran to his telephone he looked at Dancy. 'And you, Sub, pray for a snowstorm, anything, if you've nothing else to do.'

Below in his small office Aikman sat on the edge of his chair, the knuckle of one finger gripped tightly between his teeth to keep himself from sobbing aloud. The mistake which he had anticipated and then ignored had at last found him out. He still did not understand exactly what had happened up there on the bridge, but knew it was far more terrible than even he imagined.

Overhead a tannoy speaker blared, 'Hands will exercise action in thirty minutes. Damage control parties will muster on A deck.'

Aikman stared at the speaker, his eyes smarting from the strain. What the hell was happening? There was no real danger now, surely? Two ships had been found, and probably the other one too by now.

Tears ran unheeded down his cheeks. That fool Stannard and his stupid, crawling yeoman were responsible. The signal could have been filed and forgotten like so many others. And now, whatever happened, his small world was broken and lost to him forever.

9 The trap

Lindsay made himself sit very still in his chair as the deck lifted, hesitated and then swayed through another steep roll. Apart from the shaded compass lights the bridge was in total darkness, and because the sea had moderated during the afternoon and evening the ship-board noises seemed all the louder. Steel creaked and groaned as if in pain, and above the bridge the long necklaces of iced spray on stays and rails rattled and tinkled in tuneless chorus.

The *Benbecula* had turned in a great arc, so that she was now heading once again towards the southern extremity of Greenland. All afternoon they had listened to the crackle of morse from the W/T office and watched the mounting clips of signals. The third German ship, a cruiser, had at last been sighted entering the Skagerrak like her consorts, so whatever doubt had remained in Lindsay's mind had almost gone. This was no slapdash operation for morale or propaganda purposes. The German navy was showing what it could do when it came to co-operation between all arms of the service.

But for the twenty-eight hours delay things might have been very different. He could have taken *Benbecula* at full speed to the northern span of her patrol area, where there was the best chance of contacting any ship which might come through the Denmark Strait. If only the neutral freighter had reported seeing the fourth ship earlier, but the unknown vessel had made good use of time and the carefully planned ruse to draw off the Home Fleet's reserves, and by now could be almost anywhere.

The Admiralty was suspicious, too. *Benbecula* had

received more signals giving details of the convoy's
course and approximate position. The best Lindsay
could do was to keep on a slowly converging track,
putting his ship between the convoy and whatever was
likely to come down from the north-east.

The ten ships and their escort were now in a position
on *Benbecula*'s port bow. It was impossible to fix the exact
distance. It could be thirty or one hundred miles away.

He watched the spray lift over the stem and drift lazily
towards the revolving screens, saw the quick pinpoint of
light from one of the guns as a quarters officer made
some frantic inspection in the freezing air. The sea was
very much calmer, moving towards them in a great
humped swell with only an occasional whitecap to betray
its anger. There were several reports of ice, and Lindsay
knew the smoother surface was evidence enough that
there was some quite near. He half listened to the
engines' muted beat and imagined Fraser on his footplate, watching the dials set to the present reduced speed
and waiting to throw open the throttles at a second's
warning.

He thought too of the girl out there in the blackness. It
seemed incredible that it could be so. She was probably
fully dressed and in her lifejacket, talking quietly and
listening to the unfamiliar orders and sounds around
her. One good thing was that the convoy consisted of fast
ships. It was not much but. . .

He turned on his chair and rapped, 'Time?'

A signalman said, 'Twenty-one 'undred, sir.'

Feet thumped overhead where Maxwell and his fire
control team had been sitting and shivering for several
hours.

He darted a quick glance around the bridge. Dancy
and Petty Officer Ritchie. Stannard just by the rear door,
and the signalmen and messengers arranged at telephones and voicepipes like so many statues. The
coxswain was leaning slightly over the wheel, his heavy

face set in a frown of concentration as he watched the
ticking gyro repeater. The tension was almost a physical
thing.

Watertight doors were closed, and apart from the
bridge shutters every hatch and scuttle was tightly sealed.

Lindsay felt his stomach contract painfully and realised
he had not eaten since breakfast.

The buzz of a telephone was so loud that a seaman gave
a yelp of alarm.

Stannard snatched it and then said quickly, 'Signal
from convoy escort to Admiralty, sir.' He paused, listening to the voice from behind the W/T office's protective
steel plate. *'Am under attack by German raider. One escort in
sinking condition. Am engaging.'* He swallowed hard.
'Require immediate repeat immediate assistance.'

Lindsay did not turn. 'Full ahead both engines.'

Stannard shouted above the jangle of telegraphs.
'Admiralty to Benbecula, *sir. Act as situation demands. No
assistance is available for minimum of twelve hours.'*

Dancy whispered, 'God!'

Another telephone buzzed and Lindsay heard Dancy
say, 'Masthead. Yes. Right.' Then he said, 'Gunflashes at
Red two-oh.'

The bridge was beginning to vibrate savagely as the
revolutions mounted.

Then Stannard again. 'Admiralty have ordered convoy
to divide, sir.'

Dancy called, 'Masthead reports that he can see more
flashes, sir.'

'Very well.'

Lindsay forced his spine back into the chair, willing his
mind to stay clear. The flashes were a guide, but with the
low cloud and possibility of ice about it was impossible to
gauge the range.

The control speaker intoned, 'We can see the flashes
too, sir. No range as yet.'

With the freezing spray splattering over the bridge it

was hardly surprising. Maxwell's spotters probably had their work cut out to keep even the largest lens free of ice.

'Any more news from the escort?'

'No, sir.' Stannard had the handset against his ear.

Lindsay pounded the screen slowly with his gloved fingers. Come on, old girl. *Come on.* He recalled the words from the Admiralty. *Act as situation demands.* Would they have said it if they had known *Benbecula* was so close?

Dancy asked quietly, 'D'you think it's the same one that sank *Loch Glendhu,* sir?' He sounded hoarse.

'Yes. That last effort was just a rehearsal. Maybe this is, too.'

Someone gasped as a bright orange light glowed suddenly in the blackness ahead. It seemed to hang like a tall, brilliant feather of flame, until with equal swiftness it vanished completely.

Stannard said, 'That's one poor bastard done for.'

Maxwell's voice made him look round at the speaker. 'Approximate range is three-double-oh, sir. Bearing Red one-five.'

Lindsay clenched his fingers to steady himself. Fifteen miles. It might as well be double that amount.

Stannard was by his side again. 'We're a lot closer than I calculated, sir.' He seemed to sense Lindsay's despair and added, 'We might still be able to help.'

Another bright flash against the unmoving backcloth. This time it seemed to last for several minutes so that they could see the underbellies of the clouds shining and flickering as if touched by the fires below.

Out there ships were burning and men were dying. Lindsay stared at the shimmering light with sudden anguish. It had been so well planned, with the methodical accuracy of an assassination.

The fire vanished, as if quenched by a single hand.

Lindsay looked away. If she was in that ship, please God let it have been quick. No terror below decks with the ship falling apart around her. No agony of scalding steam, of shell splinters. Only the freezing sea, just for this once being merciful.

Stannard took the handset from a messenger before it had stopped buzzing. 'To us from Admiralty, sir. Convoy has divided. The two personnel ships with the commodore aboard have turned north. The tankers and remaining escort have headed south.' He sounded surprised. 'Enemy has ceased fire.'

Lindsay stood up and walked slowly across the violently shaking gratings. Of course the German had ceased fire. He had destroyed two or more in the convoy. The U-boats would be waiting for the tankers now. The raider could take his time. Follow the two helpless ships as far as the ice, and then. . . .

He swung round, his tone harsh. 'Come to the chart room, Pilot. We'll alter course immediately.'

'Are you going after them, sir?'

Lindsay looked at him. 'All the way.'

Ritchie watched them leave the wheelhouse and then crossed to the gyro, straddling his legs as the ship crashed violently in the heavy swell.

'What d'you think, Swain? Will we make it?'

Jolliffe's face remained frozen in the compass light like a chunk of weatherworn carving. 'I'll tell you one thing, Yeo. If we gets stuck up there in the bleeding ice it'll be like shooting fish in a barrel.'

Dancy heard his words and walked quickly to the forepart of the bridge. He watched the spray rattling against the glass and thought of men like Jolliffe and Ritchie. Professionals, yet they were worried. He gripped the rail and shivered uncontrollably. Knowing he was at last afraid.

Down in the ship's damage control section Goss sat in a steel swivel chair, his hands on his thighs, his head jutting forward as he stared grimly at the illuminated ship's plan on the opposite bulkhead. This compartment had altered very little since her cruising days, and apart from additional titles and new functions, the plan, the various sections throughout the hull had not changed. Coloured lights flickered along the plan showing watertight compartments and bulkheads, stores and holds, the complex maze of passageways and shafts which went into the body of a ship.

The damage control parties had been at their stations for hours, and behind him Goss could hear some of the stokers and seamen chattering together, their voices almost lost in the pounding rumble of engines and the whirr of fans.

In another seat at the far end of the plan sat Chief Petty Officer Archer, his head lolling to the unsteady rolls, his cap tilted to the back of his head as he waited with the others for something to happen.

Goss did not like Archer, and already there had been several flare-ups between them. With Tobey, the ship's boatswain, who had been drafted to *more important duties,* as the dockyard had explained, Goss had got on very well. Not on a sociable level, of course, but professionally, which was all Goss required in any man. Tobey was a company officer, one who had served in the line for many years, most of them in the *Benbecula.* He *knew* the ship, every rivet of her, like his own skin, and had nursed her over the thousands of miles they had steamed together. Being sparing with paint and cleaning gear, avoiding waste in materials by keeping an eagle eye on the seamen to make sure a proper wire splice was used instead of merely signing a chit for a whole new length of it. But at all times he had kept the ship perfect, a credit to the company.

He darted a glance at Archer. He on the other hand was a regular Navy man. He knew nothing of making do with meagre resources, with a clerk in the company office checking every item and expense. He had lived off the

taxpayer for too long, and cared nothing for economy.
When Goss had got on to him about the constant increase
of rust streaks on the superstructure, Archer had merely
ordered his men to slop on more paint. Hide it, cover it
up, until somebody else made it his business to deal with
properly. Someone else, in Archer's view, was the dockyard, any dockyard. He was not concerned.

He sat bolt upright in his chair as the deck and fittings
gave a sudden convulsion, and above the engines' confident beat he heard a drawn-out, menacing roar.

A seaman called, 'What was that, Chief?'

Archer looked at Goss, his eyes anxious. 'I'm not sure.'

Goss listened to the sound as it faded and then stopped
altogether. 'We must be pushing through some drift
ice.'

He licked his lips. The captain must be stark, staring mad
to drive the ship like this with ice about.

Archer said quietly, 'Well, I expect they know what
they're doin'.' He did not sound very convinced.

A door opened and a seaman staggered into the compartment carrying a huge fanny of cocoa. Feet scraped
and mugs clattered as the men hurried to meet him, their
concern temporarily forgotten.

Goss glared at the clock. It was six in the morning. Nine
hours since the bridge had reported sighting gunflashes
and had rung down for full speed. The old *Becky* must
have covered nearly a hundred and forty miles in that
time, and it was a wonder the boilers hadn't burst under
the strain. A further scraping roar echoed around the
hull, and he gripped the arms of his seat as he pictured
the surging slabs of ice dashing down the ship's flanks,
fading into the wash astern.

He could feel his palms sweating, and knew from the
stricken silence behind him that the others were watching
him.

He said gruffly, 'She can take more than this, so get on
with your bloody cocoa!'

Goss tried to shut them all from his mind, close them
out, as he often did when he was worried. He thought
back to that last cruise, before the war had changed
everything. Even by looking at the damage control plan
he could bring back some of it. The passengers had often
come down here on one of the little conducted tours
which had always been so popular. The ladies in the silk
dresses, with tanned shoulders, the men in white dinner
jackets wafting the scent of rich cigars as they listened to
some earnest junior officer explaining the ship's safety
arrangements. It had all been a bit of a joke to them, of
course. Like the boat drill, with the stewards taking as
many liberties as they dared when they *assisted* some of
the younger women with their lifejackets. But Goss had
never looked on it as anything but deadly serious. He had
been in one ship when fire had broken out and the
lifeboats had been lowered with minutes to spare. An
ugly episode. He looked along the plan, his eyes dark. In
those days, of course, one of the main points to be
watched was the watertight door system. It did not actually *say* anything about it on the plan, but Goss had known
that if *Benbecula* had begun to sink it would have been his
job to ensure the emigrants and other poorer passengers
were not released by his system of doors until all the first
class had been cleared into the boats. He had always
disliked the tours down here, just in case some clever
bastard had noticed the obvious.

He felt the chairback pushing against his spine and saw
a pencil begin to roll rapidly from the table. The helm
had gone over, and fast. He thrust himself forward and
gripped the table, as with a grinding vibration more ice
came roaring against the ship's side. But this time it did
not pass so quickly. Even as he staggered to his feet the
whole compartment gave a tremendous lurch, so that
men fell yelling and cursing amidst the widening stain of
spilled cocoa. An overhead light flickered and went out,
and flecks of paint chippings floated down like a toy

snowstorm. The deck shook once more and then the noise subsided as before.

But Goss was already reaching for his array of buttons, his eyes fixed on the neatly worded compartment on the port side where a red emergency bulb had begun to flash.

'Pumps! Come on, jump to it!' He snatched up a telephone and shouted, 'Give me the bridge.' He saw Archer and a mechanic fumbling with the pump controls and added violently, 'Yes, the *bridge*, you bloody idiot!'

Benbecula had hit hard and was flooding. It was all he knew. All he cared about.

'Bridge? Give me the captain!'

Lindsay watched the foreshortened figures of some seamen slipping and sliding across the forward well deck. Because of the thin coating of ice their black oilskins made them stand out like so many scurrying beetles as they began work with their hammers to clear the wash ports and scuppers before the task became impossible.

Dancy was saying, 'Masthead? Yes, you can be relieved now.'

Lindsay thought briefly of the masthead lookout. Even with his electric heater he had to be relieved every hour if he was to keep his circulation going. He peered at his luminous watch. Six o'clock. It did not seem possible they had been charging through the darkness for so many hours. He walked to the port side to watch as more fragments of broken ice materialised out of the black water and swirled playfully along the side. Nothing dangerous, in fact it was unavoidable. It looked more menacing than it was, and in the darkness gave an impression of great speed and size.

Stannard said, 'We should sight something soon.' But nobody answered.

Hardly anyone had said much as hour by hour the ship

had pounded into the night. The noise and violent shaking had thrown most of them inwards on their own defences, and even the men with cocoa and huge chunky sandwiches who had come and gone throughout the agony of waiting had passed without more than a quick, anxious word.

Stannard said, 'I'd like to go and check the chart again, sir.'

'Yes.' Lindsay thrust his hands into his pockets, feeling the gratings under his sea boots jerking as if being pounded by unseen hammers. 'Do that.'

Maybe the German had indeed turned away and run for base. He might think the Home Fleet was better deployed than it was, and feared a quick and overwhelming reprisal. And where were the two ships?

A telephone buzzed and a messenger said urgently, 'It's the doctor, sir.'

Lindsay tore his mind from the mental picture of the chart, the course which he and Stannard had evolved to contact the two ships.

'What does *he* want?'

The seaman, hidden in the darkness, answered, 'He asked to speak with you, sir.'

Lindsay swore silently and groped his way across the deck. It was slippery from the constant comings and goings of slushy boots, and added to the streaming condensation from deckhead and sides it filled the bridge with an unhealthy, clinging humidity.

He snatched the handset. 'Captain. Can't it wait?'

Boase sounded edgy. 'Sorry, sir. It's Lieutenant Aikman. He's locked himself in his cabin. One of my S.B.A.'s tried to make him open the door. I think he's upset.'

'*Upset?*' The word hung in the air like one additional mockery. 'What do you want me to do, for God's sake?' Lindsay made an effort to steady his voice. 'Do you really think he's in trouble?'

Boase replied, 'Yes, sir.'

As Lindsay stood with the telephone to his ear, his eyes staring at Ritchie's shadowy outline by the nearest window, the hands of the bulkhead clock showed eight minutes past six.

At that precise moment in time several small incidents were happening simultaneously. Small, but together they amounted to quite a lot.

Able Seaman Laker, known to his messmates as Dracula because of his large protruding teeth, was just being relieved from the crow's-nest by a seaman called Phelps. As they clung together on the swaying iron gratings outside the pod Laker was shouting in the other man's ear about the stupid, bloody maniacs who had fitted such a piddling little heater for the lookout's survival. Neither of them was paying much attention to the sea beyond the bows.

On the forward well deck another seaman fell from a bollard and slithered like a great black crab across the ice and came up with a thud against a hatch coaming, dropping his hammer and yelling the most obscene word he could think of at such short notice.

The lookouts on Numbers One and Two guns turned to watch him, drawing comfort from the man's clumsy efforts to regain his feet, while the rest of the deck party paused to enjoy the spectacle as well.

On the bridge Dancy was remembering Aikman's stricken voice, his pathetic self-defence under Stannard's anger and the captain's questioning. He had not heard what Boase was saying, but he could guess. He did not know Aikman very well, but realised probably better than the others that he was, like himself, acting a part which had suddenly got beyond him. He turned to peer at Lindsay's vague outline at the rear of the bridge, wondering what it was Aikman had done to excite Boase and make him risk disturbing the captain.

All small incidents, but as Dancy turned once more to his clearview screen he saw in that instant what a momentary lack of vigilance had created. Looming out of the darkness was a solid wedge of ice. In his imagination he had often pictured icebergs as towering and majestic, like white cathedrals, and for several more seconds he was totally incapable of speech or movement.

Then he yelled, 'Hard astarboard!' He heard the wheel going over, the sudden gasps of alarm, and then added wildly, 'Ice! Dead ahead!'

Lindsay dropped the telephone and hurled himself towards the screen, his voice sharp but level as he shouted, 'Belay that! Wheel amidships! Both engines *full astern!*'

Ignoring the clang of telegraphs, the violent response of reversed screws and the clamour of voices from all sides he gripped the rail and stared fixedly at the oncoming wedge of ice. It was difficult to estimate the size of it. It was not very high, probably about ten feet, and some eighty feet from end to end. Against the dark backcloth of sea and clouds it appeared enveloped in vapour, like ice emerging from a giant refrigerator. He felt the engines shaking and pounding in growing strength to stop the ship's onward dash, and found himself counting seconds as the distance continued to shorten. Dancy should not have put the helm over. If the ship had hit an ice ledge with her bilge it would slit her open like one huge can. But if he had not even seen it the ship would have smashed into it at full speed, with terrible results.

Stannard came running across the bridge, then stood stockstill beside him, his voice strangled as he said, 'We're going to strike, by Jesus!'

It seemed to take an eternity for the ice to reach them. The engines were slowing them down, dragging like great anchors so that the bow wave was falling away even as the ice became suddenly stark and very close, the jagged crest of it looming past the port bow as if drawn by a hawser.

The crash, when it came, was muted, but the sensation

transmitted itself from the keel to the flesh and bones of every man aboard.

The ice turned slowly as the ship surged against it, making a kind of clumsy pirouette with pieces breaking adrift and sliding haphazardly into the dwindling bow wave.

'Stop engines!'

Lindsay ran to the port door and tugged it open. As he hurried to the unprotected wing he felt the wind across his face like a whip, and under his gloved hands the rail was like polished glass. He watched the ice moving away while the ship idled forward sluggishly, the deck under his feet very still, as if the ship herself was holding her breath, feeling her hurt.

There was more ice nearby but just small fragments as before. It was a piece of bad luck which had brought that one heavy slab across their path without anybody sighting it.

Stannard called, 'First lieutenant's on the phone, sir.'

Lindsay strode into the bridge again, feeling the heated air enclosing him like a damp towel.

Goss was very brief. 'Flooding in Number Two hold, sir. I've got the pumps working on it, and I'm waiting for a report from the boiler room. Their main bulkhead is right against that hold.' He paused and then said thickly, 'I knew something like this would happen.'

'Any casualties?'

'I don't know yet.' The question seemed to catch Goss off guard.

'Well, get on with it and let me know.' He replaced the handset very slowly.

He knew what Goss was thinking. What most of the others were probably thinking, too. That their captain was still unfit for command. Even this one. Especially this one. He felt the pain and despair crowding his brain like blood and he had to turn away from the others, even though they could not see his face.

Jolliffe said, 'We're drifting, sir. Ship's head is now three-three-zero.'

Stannard said quickly, 'Very well, Cox'n.'

A messenger called, 'Engine room reports no damage, sir.' He gulped. 'To the bulkhead, I mean, sir.'

Stannard remarked softly, 'Once saw a great berg down off South Georgia. Big as Sydney bridge it was, and all covered with little penguins.'

Lindsay said flatly, 'Penguins?' He did not even know he had spoken.

'Yes. There were these small killer whales about, you see, and the penguins would push one of their cobbers off the berg every so often as a safety measure. If the little chap survived they all dived in. If he was eaten they'd just wait there like a lot of unemployed waiters and stand around a while longer before they pushed another one over the edge.'

Nobody laughed.

Lindsay thought suddenly of Aikman, and was about to tell Stannard to call up the doctor when Ritchie snapped, 'Listen! I 'eard a ship's siren!'

Once more Lindsay was out in the freezing air, as with Ritchie and Stannard he blundered through the opposite door and on to the starboard wing.

'And there's another!' Ritchie was peering over the wing like a terrier at a rabbit hole.

Stannard said quickly, 'Same ship.' He too was bending his head and listening intently. 'When I saw those penguins I was doing a spell as third officer in a whale factory ship. Some masters used their sirens to estimate the closeness of heavy ice. Bounce back the echoes, so to speak.'

Lindsay heard it again. Mournful and incredibly loud in the crisp air. The echo threw back its reply some ten seconds later.

Dancy joined them by the screen. 'I——I'm sorry about that helm order, sir. I lost my head.'

Lindsay did not take his eyes from the bearing of the siren. 'You were quite alone at that moment, Sub.' He heard Dancy's breathing, knew how he was suffering. 'And if we had not stopped the engines we would have drowned out that siren.'

'Damage control says the pumps are holding the intake, sir. No apparent danger to boiler room bulkhead.' The seaman waited, gasping in the cold air. 'And only one casualty. Man on A deck broke his wrist.'

Lindsay nodded. 'Good.' He tried to rub the ice from the gyro repeater below the screen but it was thick like a Christmas cake. 'We'll try and close on that siren, Pilot. Warn control in case of tricks. And we'll have some extra lookouts on the boat deck.'

Stannard was listening to his voice when his face suddenly lit up in a violent red flash. The savage crash of gunfire echoed across the water, lighting up the scattered patches of ice, painting them with scarlet and yellow as again, and again the guns tore into the darkness, blasting it aside in short, violent cameos.

Lindsay dashed through the open door, his glasses banging against his chest as he shouted, 'Half ahead together!' Around him men were slamming the new steel shutters, and he added, 'Leave the centre one!' As he cranked it open he felt the air clawing his face and lips, heard the sudden surge of power from the engines as once more the ship began to push forward.

'Steer for the flashes, Cox'n!'

He tensed as a ball of fire exploded and then fanned out to reveal the outline and angle of a ship. She was less than two miles away, her upper deck and superstructure burning fiercely in a dozen places. There was ice all around her, small fragments and heavier, more jagged prongs which seemed to be enclosing her like a trap. Another ripple of flashes came from her opposite beam, and Lindsay saw the telltale waterspouts shooting skywards and one more bright explosion below her bridge.

The siren was bellowing continuously now, with probably a dead man's hand dragging on the lanyard, but as the *Benbecula* gathered way Lindsay thought it sounded like a beast dying in agony.

Crisp and detached above the din he heard a metallic voice intone, 'Control to all guns. Semi-armour-piercing, load, load, load.'

More thuds and clicks below the bridge, and somewhere a voice yelling orders, shrill and momentarily out of control.

'Target bears Green two-oh. Range oh-five-oh.'

Lindsay raised his glasses as Maxwell's voice continued to pass his information over the speaker. Five thousand yards. Maxwell's spotters had done well to estimate the range on the flashes alone.

'Port ten.' He watched the ticking gyro. 'Midships. Steady.'

Jolliffe replied heavily, 'Steady, sir. Three-one-zero.'

Almost to himself Lindsay murmured, 'That'll give the marines a chance to get on target, too.'

More flashes blasted the darkness aside and joined with those already blazing on the helpless ship. He could see her twin funnels, the great pieces of wreckage falling into the fires and throwing fountains of sparks towards the clouds. Not long now.

To Dancy he snapped, 'Pass the word to prepare that signal for transmission.'

Stannard said thickly, 'Aikman's got the code books, sir.'

Lindsay kept his glasses trained on the other ship. Was it a trick from the reflected fires, or was she starting to settle down?

He said harshly, 'Tell the W/T office to send it plain language. What the hell does it matter now?'

Stannard nodded and handed his pad to a messenger. 'Give this position to the P.O. Tel. He knows what to do.'

Maxwell's voice again. 'Starboard battery stand by.'

Lindsay lowered his glasses. 'Open fire.'

Maxwell waited until the hidden raider fired again and then pressed his button. The bells at each mounting had not rung for more than a split second before all three starboard guns roared out together, their long tongues flashing above the wash alongside.

Lindsay held his breath and counted. He shut out the bellowed commands, the click of breech blocks and the chorus of voices on the intercom. Someone at the Admiralty would be listening to all this, he thought vaguely. They would be plotting Stannard's position and rousing out some senior officers from their camp beds in the cellars. *From Benbecula to Admiralty. Have sighted enemy raider. Am engaging.*

Not much of an epitaph. But it might be remembered.

'Up five hundred. Shoot!'

Again the guns belched fire and smoke, the bridge jerking violently as the shock made the steel quake as if from hitting another berg.

'The other ship's going down, sir!' Dancy was shouting, his voice very loud after the crash of gunfire.

'Yes.'

Lindsay watched rigidly as the stricken ship began to tilt over towards him. She must have been hit badly, deep inside the hull, and the fires which he had imagined to have begun on her superstructure had in fact surged right up through several decks. He could see the gaping holes, angry red, the criss-cross of broken frames and fallen masts, and found himself praying there was nobody left to die in such horror.

More distant flashes, and this time he heard the shells pass overhead almost gently, the high trajectory making them whisper like birds on the wing.

Maxwell's bells tinkled again, and seconds later Lindsay heard him shout, 'One hit!'

A fire glowed beyond the sinking ship, just long enough for Maxwell's guns to get off another round each.

Then it died, and Lindsay guessed the enemy had turned end on, either to close with this impudent attacker or to run, as before.

He would have picked up the short signal and would probably be wondering what sort of ship he was tackling. Benbecula's name was not on the general list, as far as he knew, and it might take the German time to realise what was happening.

'Enemy has ceased fire, sir.' Maxwell seemed out of breath.

'Very well.' Lindsay watched the dark line of the other ship's hull getting closer and closer to the sea. 'Tell Number One to prepare rafts for lowering.'

Dancy asked, 'Will we stop, sir?'

Lindsay rubbed his eyes and then raised the glasses again. 'Not yet.'

A sullen explosion threw more wreckage over the other ship's side, and he imagined he could see a flashlight moving aft by her poop. One lonely survivor, he thought dully.

'Slow ahead together.' He heard men pounding along the boat deck. 'Starboard fifteen.' He watched the steam rising like a curtain, and knew the sea was exploring the damage, quenching the fires too late.

As if from a great distance he heard Stannard say, 'We *can't* stop yet, Sub. We'd be sitting ducks if that bastard is still about.'

'Yes, I understand.' But from his tone it was obvious Dancy did not. Like the others, he was probably thinking of the people who were trying to escape the flames only to face being frozen to death in minutes.

Lindsay climbed on to his chair and stared through the slit in the steel shutter. The slit was glowing red from the other ship's fires, like a peephole in a furnace door. Like a fragment of hell.

He looked at the gyro repeater again. 'Midships.'

They had almost crossed the ship's stern when with a

great roar of inrushing water she turned over and dived, the fire vanishing and plunging the sea once more into darkness.

Lindsay looked at his watch. Seven fifteen.

'Prepare both motor boats for lowering, Pilot. Each will tow a raft. Number One will know what to do.'

'I can see some red lights on the starboard beam, sir.' Ritchie lowered his telescope. 'Might be in time for 'em.'

'Yes.'

Lindsay heard the rumble of power-operated davits, the protesting squeaks from the falls as the two motor boats jerked down the ship's side. If their motors would start under these conditions it would be a miracle.

'Ready, sir.'

'Stop engines.'

Another set of sounds as the boats were slipped and took the released rafts in tow. Both motors were working, and Lindsay thanked God for an engineer like Fraser who kept an eye on such details.

'Sky's a bit brighter, sir.' Stannard looked at Lindsay's unmoving outline against the shutter.

The enemy had gone. Lindsay did not know how he could be sure, but he was. Slipped away again. Just like that last time. Leaving death in his wake. Blood on the water.

He stood up suddenly. 'Yeoman, use the big search-light. Tell the gunnery officer to expect an attack, but we'll risk it.'

He walked to the door and then out on to the open wing. The searchlight's glacier blue beam licked out from the upper bridge like something solid, and as it fanned down across the heaving water where the two boats and their tows stood out like bright toys, he saw the endless litter of flotsam and charred wreckage. Chairs and broken crates, empty liferafts and pieces of canvas. Here and there a body floated, either spreadeagled face down in the water or bobbing in a lifejacket, its eyes like small stones as the beam swept low overhead.

There was a stench of oil and burned paint, and as the boats moved apart to begin a closer search Lindsay stood and waited, his body almost frozen with cold, but unable to move.

Stannard strode on to the gratings and said, 'The first lieutenant has reported that Aikman has tried to kill himself. Cut his wrists with some scissors. But he's still alive, sir.' He stared past Lindsay as a boat stopped to pull someone aboard.

Lindsay nodded. 'He couldn't even do that properly, could he?'

He too was watching the motor boat as it gathered way again towards another dark clump in the water. The other personnel ship was probably further to the north-west, waiting for some light before attempting to brave the ice and the possibility of a new attack. She would have seen the gunfire, and may have thought it was a second enemy ship making the assault.

A torch stabbed across the water and Ritchie said, 'One boat 'as got eleven survivors, sir.' He turned as the second boat's light winked over the lazy swell. 'She's got eighteen, though Gawd knows 'ow she's managed to cram 'em in.'

Lindsay wanted to ask him to call up the boats, to ask what was uppermost in his mind. But he was afraid. Afraid that by showing his fear he might make it happen. She could be in the other ship. Frightened but safe. Safe.

The search continued for a full hour. Round and round, in and out of the great oil stain and its attendant corpses and fragments.

'Recall the boats.' Lindsay wiped the ice rime from his eyebrows, felt the pain of cramp in his legs and hands. 'Tell the sickbay to be ready.'

Entry ports in the hull clanged open and ready hands were waiting to sway the first survivors inboard.

Goss came to the bridge and said, 'Boats secured, sir.

I've had to abandon the two rafts. They're thick with ice.
I'd never get them hoisted.' He watched Lindsay and
then added, 'There are five women amongst 'em. I don't
know if they'll survive after this.'

Lindsay gripped the screen. So the Atlantic had
cheated him after all. He said, 'Take over the con and get
under way. I'm going below.'

By the time he reached the sickbay he was almost
running, and as he stumbled past huddled figures
cloaked in blankets, the busy sickberth attendants, he saw
a young girl sitting on a chair, hair black with oil, her
uniform scorched as if by a hot iron, her face a mass of
burns.

Boase looked across her head and said tersely, 'We'll do
our best, sir.'

Lindsay ignored him, his face frozen like a mask as he
stared around at the scene of pain and survival. One body
lay by the door covered in a blanket. One bare foot was
thrust into the harsh light, and with something like
madness Lindsay pulled the covering from the girl's face.
She was very young, her features pinched tight with cold,
captured at the moment of death. The sea water had
frozen around her mouth and eyes so that she seemed to
be crying even now. He covered her face, and after a
small hesitation pulled the blanket over the protruding
foot. As his fingers touched it he felt the contact like ice
itself.

Without another word he turned and began the long
climb to the bridge. The engines were pounding again,
leaving the fragments floating and bobbing astern in
their wake. She was with them. Back there in the Atlantic.
Alone.

Take care, she had said. Will see you in Eden.

He reached the bridge and said, 'Fall out action stations
and secure.' He looked at Stannard. 'We will steer north-
east for an hour and see what happens.'

Stannard asked quietly, 'What about Aikman, sir?'

Lindsay did not hear him. 'Take over, Number One. I'm going below for half an hour.' He left without another word.

Goss grunted and walked to the empty chair. Stannard sighed and turned towards his chart room.

Only Ritchie knew what was wrong with the captain. Jupp had explained. Not that it helped to know about it, Ritchie thought.

10 Christmas leave

Lindsay removed his cap and tucked it beneath his arm as he stepped into Boase's sickbay. A week had passed since the survivors had been pulled aboard, and in that time the doctor and his staff had done wonders. Three of the survivors had died of their injuries and two more were still dangerously ill, but under the circumstances it was a miracle any had endured the fires and the freezing cold.

Boase was washing his hands, and hurried across when he saw Lindsay. He looked very tired but managed to smile and say, 'Nice of you to look in, sir.' He eyed Lindsay's strained features and added, 'Wouldn't do you any harm to rest for a bit.'

Lindsay looked around the long sickbay. The neat white cots, an air of sterile efficiency which he had always hated. The five girls had survived, and that was the biggest surprise of all. Maybe they were tougher than men after all, he thought wearily. Four of them were sitting in chairs, watching him now, dressed in a colourful collection of clothing which the ship's company had gathered. The fifth Wren was in a cot, her burned face hidden in bandages, her hands outstretched to the sides of the blankets as if to steady herself. She had nice hands, small and well shaped. Boase had told him she cried a lot when the others were asleep, fearful of what her face would be like when the bandages came off.

All told there were only thirty survivors. From what he had gleaned Lindsay had discovered the ship had carried a company of one hundred and fifty as well as some forty Wrens en route for Canada.

He cleared his throat. 'As you know, we have been ordered to proceed direct to Liverpool, where you will be landed and my ship can receive repairs.'

Lindsay looked slowly around the watching faces. The Wrens, their eyes just a bit too bright. Holding back the shock which would grow and sharpen as thankfulness for survival gave way to bitter memories for those who had died. The men, young and old alike, some of whom had probably been bombed or torpedoed already in the war, watching him, recalling their own moments, like the ones when a motor boat had come out of the searchlight's great beam to snatch them to safety.

He continued, 'I have just received another signal from the Admiralty. The Japanese have invaded Malaya, and yesterday morning carried out an air attack on Pearl Harbour in the Pacific.' He tried to smile as they stared at each other. 'So the Americans are in the war with us. We're not alone any more.'

He nodded to Boase. 'I'll leave you in peace now.'

Lindsay did not even know why he had come down to tell them the news. Boase could have done it. It was just as if he was still torturing himself by wanting to be near someone who had been with Eve when she had died. What did Malaya and Pearl Harbour mean to them at this moment anyway? The sea was all they understood now. During the night, before sleep relieved them, they would be thinking of it just beyond the sides of the hull. Waiting.

He recalled the atmosphere in the sickbay when *Benbecula* had sighted the second personnel ship two days after the attack. She had been edging through some drift ice, and her relief at seeing *Benbecula*'s recognition signals had been obvious to everyone aboard. Except here, in the sickbay. Was it that they felt cheated? Did they think it so cruelly unfair that their friends had been slaughtered while the other ship had escaped with little more than a bad scare? It was hard to tell.

The other ship had been ordered to Iceland and would

be in Reykjavik by now with another escort. *Benbecula* had not been short of company either. As she turned and steamed south once more she had been watched by two long-range aircraft, as well as a destroyer on the far horizon. But it was all too late. And the evidence of it lay and sat around him listening to him as he said, 'And remember, you'll all be having Christmas at home.' He turned to leave, the words coming back to mock him like a taunt. Christmas at home.

Something plucked at his jacket and when he looked down he saw it was the Wren's hand, the girl with the burned face.

As he bent over the cot he heard her say, 'Thank you for coming for us.' He took her hand in his. It felt hot. She said, 'I saw you when I was brought here. Just a few seconds——'

Boase shook his head. 'That's enough talking.'

But her voice had broken Lindsay's careful guard like a dam bursting. Still holding her hand he asked gently, 'Did you know Wren Collins? Eve Collins?'

'I think so. I think I saw her by the lifeboats when——' She could not go on.

Lindsay released her hand and said, 'Try and sleep.' Then he swung round and hurried from the sickbay with its clean, pure smells and shocked minds.

He found Goss and Fraser waiting for him outside his day cabin. 'Sorry you were kept so long.' He could not look at them. 'I just wanted to go over the docking arrangements at Liverpool.' He remembered the other thing and added quietly, 'By the way, Number One, you told me when I took command that one of *Benbecula*'s sister ships was an A.M.C. in the Far East.'

Goss watched him closely. 'The old *Barra,* sir. That's right.'

'Well, I'm afraid she's been sunk by Jap bombers off Kuantan.'

He saw Goss's face crumple and then return swiftly to

the usual grim mask. 'That's bad news, sir.' It was all he said.

Lindsay could feel the agony inside his skull crushing his mind so that he wanted to leave the others and hide in his sleeping cabin.

In a toneless voice he said, 'Right then, we'll start by discussing the fuel and ammunition. We must arrange to lighten ship as soon as we pick up the tugs.'

Fraser took out his notebook but kept his eyes on Lindsay's face. You poor bastard, he thought. You keep fighting it and it's tearing you apart. How much more can you take?

Goss was thinking about the *Barra*. He had been third officer in her so many years back. Her picture hung in his cabin beside all the others. Now she was gone. He looked desperately around the cabin. *Benbecula* could go like that. In the twinkling of an eye. Nothing.

Lindsay was saying, 'And there's the matter of leave. We should get both watches away for Christmas with any luck.'

Goss said, 'I'd like to stay aboard, sir.'

Fraser looked at him. Oh God. Not you, too.

Lindsay made a note on his pad. 'Right then. Now about Number Two hold——'

In his pantry Jupp listened to the muted conversation and walked to a scuttle. Below on the promenade deck he saw a figure in a duffel coat walking slowly aft. He knew from the bandaged wrists it was Lieutenant Aikman. He saw two seamen turn to watch Aikman as he shambled unseeingly past them, and wondered how he would be able to survive after this.

He returned to his coffee pot and hoped Fraser at least would remain and talk with the captain. He had seen what the girl's death was doing to Lindsay and knew he must not be left alone. He had heard him whenever he had turned into his bunk, which was not often. Fighting his nightmares and calling her name like a lost soul in hell.

Whenever he was alone Lindsay seemed to be searching through his confidential books and intelligence logs, totally absorbed, his eyes filled with determination, the like of which Jupp had never seen.

Maybe when the ship was in dock the captain would find some comfort at home. He frowned as he recalled hearing that Lindsay had no proper home to go to.

The bell rang, and with a flourish he picked up his coffee pot and thrust open the pantry door. Something might turn up. And until it did, Jupp would make sure Lindsay would have his help, just as long as he needed it.

The wardroom stove glowed cheerfully across the legs of the *Benbecula*'s officers as they waited for the stewards to open the bar. The ship felt rigidly still, for she was moored to a wharf awaiting the next move to dry dock, and some of the officers glanced repeatedly through the rain-dashed scuttles as if unable to accept the fact. Murky grey buildings, motionless in the rain, instead of a tossing wilderness of angry wave crests. Tall cranes and gantrys and the masts of other ships, instead of loneliness and complete isolation.

Dancy listened to the clink of glasses and squeak of bolts as the stewards opened their pantry hatch, and tried to think of some special, extravagant drink to mark his return to the safety of harbour. While the ship had crept through the morning drizzle and mist and tugs had snorted and puffed importantly abeam, he had watched the great sprawling mass of Liverpool opening up before him with something like wonder. There had been little for him to do at the time so he had been able to let his ready imagination encompass everything he saw and felt. Relief, sadness, excitement, it had all been there, as it was now. Around him on the bridge he had watched his companions, faces and voices who had become real and very close to him. Stannard at the gyro taking careful, unhurried fixes while the ship glided up channel. Ritchie and his signalmen peering through their glasses at the diamond-bright lamps which winked from the shore. Down on the forecastle he had seen Goss waving his arms as he strode amongst the busy seamen at the wires and fenders, while from the upper bridge the pipes shrilled and twittered in salute to passing or anchored warships. Cruisers and sturdy escort vessels. Destroyers and stumpy corvettes, all showing marks of the Atlantic weather, the seasoned look of experienced and hard-used warriors.

Lindsay had been sitting in his chair for most of the time. He had seemed very remote, even aloof whenever someone had attempted to make personal contact with him. But Dancy had watched him, nevertheless, and had tried to draw from him some of the strength he seemed to give. He had seen the twin towers of the Royal Liver building loom above the mist and had felt the infectious excitement and purpose of this great port. Headquarters of Western Approaches Command, it was also one of the main doors through which came the very life blood of a country at war.

Stannard crossed to his side and held his hands above the glowing stove. 'Well, Sub, we've made it. All snug and safe. Until the next bloody move!'

He sounded relaxed, and Dancy envied him for it. Stannard was really important, a man who could work out a position when there was neither star nor sun to help him. When the deck was trying to stand on end while he plotted and brooded over his charts and instruments.

A steward said, 'Orders please, gentlemen.'

Dancy and Stannard stood back to wait for the first rush to subside.

'What do you think about the Japs, Pilot?'

Stannard looked at him thoughtfully. 'God knows. We were always told that if Malaya or Singapore were attacked the enemy would come from the south.' He shrugged. 'Still, I guess they've got it in hand by now. When I think of the places I've been out East, it makes me puke to picture those little yellow bastards clumping all over them.'

Then he brightened and added, 'Now, about that drink. Have it on me.'

Dancy frowned. 'A brandy and gin.'

Stannard stared at him. *'Mixed?'*

'Mixed.'

'You greedy bastard!' Stannard waved to a harassed steward. 'I hope it chokes you!'

The door banged open and Goss marched towards the fire.

Stannard asked, 'How about joining us, Number One?'

Goss did not seem to hear. Turning his back to the fire he barked, 'Just pipe down a minute, will you!'

They all paused to look at him, suddenly aware of the harshness in his tone.

Goss said, 'We've just had news from the Far East. The Japs are still advancing south into Malaya.' He swallowed hard. 'And they've sunk the *Prince of Wales* and *Repulse.*' He did not seem able to believe his own voice. 'Both of 'em. In less than an hour!'

'Jesus.' Stannard stared at Dancy. 'Those two great ships. How the hell *could* they wipe them out so easily?'

Goss was staring into space. 'They had no air cover and were overwhelmed by enemy bombers.'

'It's getting worse.' Stannard downed his drink in one swallow. 'I thought it would have been a fleet action at least.' He sounded angry. 'What's the matter with our blokes out there? No air cover, they must be raving bloody mad!'

Goss continued, 'There'll be leave for three weeks. If you'll all see Lieutenant Barker about your ration cards and travel warrants after lunch we can get it sorted out without wasting any more time.'

Dancy looked at his glass. Goss's news had left him confused and feeling vaguely cheated. They had done so much, or so it had seemed. The quick, savage gunfire in the darkness, the handful of gasping, oil-sodden survivors, it had all been part of something special. The brief announcement about the two great capital ships sunk in some far off, unknown sea had changed it in an instant. That was the real war, the swift changing balance of sea power which could and might bring down a country, a way of life for millions of people. It made his own part in things appear small and unimportant.

Stannard said quietly, 'Drink that muck, Sub. I think I feel like getting stoned.'

Dancy touched the drink with his tongue. It tasted like paraffin.

Stannard was saying, 'My brother's out there in an Aussie battalion.' He looked away. 'To think his life depends on those stupid Pommie brasshats!' He faced Dancy and smiled. 'Sorry about that. You're quite a nice Pommie, as it happens.'

Dancy watched him worriedly. 'Thanks.'

Then he said quickly, 'What about coming home with me, Pilot? My people would love to fuss over you. Christmas is pretty quiet but——' He hesitated, realising what he had done. All his carefully built up disguise as the intrepid writer would be blown to ashes when Stannard met his parents.

Stannard eyed him gravely. 'No can do, Sub.' He was thinking of the girl he had met on his last leave in London. She had a small flat in Paddington. He would spend his leave with her. Have one wild party and make it last until the leave was over. He added, 'But thanks all the same. Maybe next time, huh?'

Dancy nodded, relieved and saddened at the same time. He could imagine what Stannard had in mind. And he thought of his own house. The Christmas decorations, his mother complaining about rations, his father telling

him how the war should be waged, where the government were going wrong.

He said, 'Maybe we could meet up somewhere? Just for
a drink or something.'

'Yeh, why not.' Stannard grinned lazily. 'I'll give you a
shout on the blower when I get fixed up.' She would
probably have forgotten him by now anyway. But she was
a real beaut. Long auburn hair, and a body which seemed
to enfold a man like silk.

A steward called, 'Ambulances 'ave arrived to take your
people away, sir.' He waited until Boase had extracted
himself from the group by the bar. 'The P.M.O. is comin'
aboard.'

Dancy said, 'Let's go and see them leave, Pilot.'

Stannard nodded. 'I was feeling very sorry for myself
just now.' He nodded again. 'We'll go and cheer them up
a bit, eh?'

They grabbed their caps and hurried to the promenade deck. There were plenty of the ship's company
with the same idea, Dancy noticed. A ragged cheer
greeted the first of the survivors, as on stretchers or
walking with white-coated attendants from the base hospital they started to move towards the gangway.

Stannard muttered quietly, 'Oh Jesus, there's Aikman.'

Dancy turned and saw the lieutenant walking slowly
along the deck, a suitcase in his hand, a sickberth petty
officer following him at a discreet distance.

Stannard bit his lip. Aikman was going ashore for
observation. That was typical of Lindsay, he thought.
Most other skippers would have slapped him under
arrest to await court-martial for negligence and God
knows what else. But Lindsay seemed to realise Aikman
could not be punished more than he was already. He
would probably be kept in hospital and then quietly
dropped. Kicked out. Forgotten.

He said impulsively, 'Poor bastard.'

Dancy looked at him, recalling Stannard's bitter anger

on the bridge. His contempt for Aikman's pathetic efforts
to cover his mistake.

Stannard strode forward and asked, 'You off then?'

Aikman stopped as if he had been struck. When he
turned his face was very pale, his eyes shadowed by dark
rings, like a man under drugs.

He said thickly, 'Yes. I——I'm not sure quite what——'
He could not go on.

Dancy watched Stannard, wondering what he would
say next. Aikman looked terrible, far worse than
immediately after he had tried to kill himself. He had
remained in his cabin, one of Boase's S.B.A.'s with him
the whole time. Now he was slipping away, with not even
a word from the other officers.

Stannard thrust out his hand and said quietly, 'Good
luck, mate. I'm sorry about what happened.' He turned
away as if to watch the ambulances on the jetty. 'Could
have been any one of us.'

Aikman seized his hand and said brokenly, 'But it
wasn't. It was me.'

There were tears running down his cheeks, and the
petty officer said cheerfully, 'Come along, sir, we don't
want to keep 'em all waiting, now do we?'

Dancy looked at Stannard. It was like hearing a teacher
speaking to a backward child. He said quickly, 'So long,
sir.' Then he saluted and watched Aikman being led
down the gangway and into one of the ambulances.

Stannard said, 'When you're in a war you think sometimes you might get bloody killed or have a bit shot out of
yourself.' He shook his head as they turned back towards
the wardroom. 'You never think about this side of it.'

Lindsay's cabin was filled with swirling tobacco smoke
and the smell of whisky. The dockyard officials in their
blue serge suits, some officers from the base engineering

department, a lieutenant of the intelligence section, there seemed to be an endless array of alien faces.

He held a match to his pipe and watched the flame quivering above the bowl. It was shaking badly, and he had to force himself to hold it still. He saw Fraser talking with another engineer and knew from the slur in his voice he was halfway to being drunk. Lindsay had already had more drinks than he could remember yet felt ice-cold sober. He did not even feel tired any more, just numb. Empty of anything which he could recognise.

Lindsay had been down to see the survivors over the side and had spoken to most of them. A handshake here, a quick thumbs-up there. They had all responded by playing their allotted roles. It was the unspoken word and unmade gesture which had moved him. The glances from some of the Wrens as they had looked down at the solid, unmoving jetty. The wounded sailor on a stretcher who had looked up at the grey sky and had stared at it with something like awe. And the girl with the bandaged face who had been carried by two S.B.A.'s on a kind of chair over the gangway with all the others.

It was almost as if she had sensed Lindsay was there, and had reached out to hold his hand. Nothing more. Just a quick contact, not even a squeeze, but it had told him so much.

Now they were all gone and the old ship was waiting patiently for the next phase to begin. Repairs and all the indignities of dry dock. Then back again. To the Atlantic.

If Goss had not been so determined to stay with the ship he knew he would have done so. He did not want to go anywhere else. Not to spend his leave in some hotel with all its Christmas noise and urgent gaiety. He would have to go somewhere. He thought of Aikman's face as he had explained what was arranged for him. But you never knew with men like Aikman. He might go under completely. He could just as easily grow a new outer covering and start all over again. Given time, he might even believe he had been blameless, that everyone else had caused the mistake. Lindsay hoped it would be the latter. Aikman was too weak and insecure to carry the brand entirely for what had happened.

He realised with a start that the earnest young lieutenant from Intelligence was speaking to him.

'I shall make a *careful* study of all your considerations, sir.' He nodded gravely. 'I feel sure that something very useful may come of them.'

Lindsay regarded him evenly. The lieutenant was a temporary officer with a beautifully cut uniform and perfect manners. Perhaps a journalist in peacetime who had found his niche on the staff. He certainly appeared to be enjoying his role. He even spoke with a conspiratorial confidence, like some master-spy in a pre-war film.

Lindsay found himself wondering why he had bothered to compile such a lengthy report. Probably to retain his own sanity. He knew he needed some new purpose if he was to keep from cracking apart. And if hatred was a purpose then he might be halfway there.

He said, 'I believe that if we can discover more about the German raider, the man who commands her, then we might learn something.' He stopped. It was obvious from the lieutenant's polite smile he was already thinking of something else. He added, 'With the Japs in the war we won't be able to rely too much on American protection on the other side of the Atlantic. They'll need all their spare ships in the Pacific until they can get on their feet again.'

The lieutenant looked at his watch. 'I am sure we can rely on that very point being watched by the powers-that-be, sir.'

'I'm sure.' Lindsay signalled to Jupp with his empty glass. 'Like they watched the Denmark Strait and the fjord where this bastard raider was anchored. Oh yes, I'm sure we can rely on *them.*'

Fraser said unsteadily, 'What about some food? My guts feel like a rusty oil drum.'

The sudden silence which had followed Lindsay's angry outburst broke up in laughter, and Lindsay saw Fraser watching him grimly.

The lieutenant stood up and said, 'Well, I'll be on my way, sir.' He forced a smile. 'I'm sure you're sincere, sir, but——'

Fraser took his elbow and pulled him away from the table. 'Look, sonny, if you want to play games, that's all right with me.' He tried to focus the lieutenant with his eyes. 'But don't come aboard *this* ship and try it, see?' He gestured with his glass, whisky splashing across the carpet. 'That man you were being so bloody patronising to has done more, seen more and cares more than you'll ever know! While you sit on your bum, sticking pins in some out of date map, it'll be men like him who get on with the job!'

The lieutenant looked down at him, aware that some of the civilian dockyard men were grinning at his confusion. 'Well, *really!* I don't see there's any occasion to speak like that.'

Fraser lurched away. 'Piss off!' He collapsed into a chair and added as an afterthought, 'And stick *that* on your bloody map!'

The others were leaving now. Most of them were used to dealing with men like Fraser. Western Approaches was unkind to those who served there. Death and constant danger had long since pared away the outward niceties and veneer of normal behaviour.

When they had all gone Lindsay said, 'Chief, I think you are one of the most uncouth people I have ever met.'

Fraser grinned. 'Could be.' He was unrepentant.

Lindsay held out his glass against the grey light from a scuttle. 'You'll be going home as soon as we've docked, I suppose.'

Fraser nodded. 'Aye. I'll have a good row and get this damn ship out of my system.' He grimaced. 'Still, I'll be there for Hogmanay. The wife'll have forgiven me by then.'

'Do you always have an argument when you go on leave?'

Jupp said, 'I think the chief engineer 'as dropped off, sir.' He removed the glass from Fraser's limp hand and added, 'I'll bring 'im some black coffee.'

Lindsay stood up. 'No. Let him sleep. He's done enough for ten men. His second can take over when we shift berth.'

'And when will that be, sir?'

'Tomorrow. Forenoon.'

Lindsay listened to the mournful bleat from some outgoing tug. It reminded him of the sinking ship. The siren going on and on as the shells blasted her apart.

He could hear muffled laughter from the wardroom and imagined them making plans for their unexpected leave. Wives and parents, girl friends and mistresses. Dancy's iceberg, as it had come to be known, had done them all a bit of good. Well, most of them. There were some, like Ritchie, who had nowhere to go. Wanted nothing which might remind them of what they had lost. And there was Goss. He had nothing but the ship, or so it appeared.

He said, 'I'm going ashore.' He had spoken almost before the idea had come to him. He had to get away, just for a few hours. Go where he knew no one and could find a moment of peace. If there was such a thing.

Jupp regarded him sadly. 'Aye, aye, sir. I'll run a bath for you.'

He hurried away to lay out Lindsay's best uniform and to make him some sandwiches, knowing the captain would not wait for a proper meal.

Lindsay walked to a scuttle on the outboard side and watched a rusty freighter being edged by tugs into the mainstream. But he was thinking of the signal and of the two ships lost on the other side of the world. Especially the *Prince of Wales*. He could see her clearly in his mind as she had been at Scapa Flow.

The memory of that windswept anchorage brought it all back again in an instant. The staff car. The girl with her duffel coat and jaunty cap.

He was still thinking about her as he left the ship and walked slowly along the littered jetty, his greatcoat collar turned up against the drizzle.

By a crouching gantry he paused and looked back. *Benbecula* seemed very tall and gaunt, rising like a wet grey wall above the winches and coiled mooring wires, the nameless piles of crates and the clutter of a seaport at war. From this angle her list to starboard was all the more apparent, so that she appeared to be leaning against the wet stonework, resting from the ordeal which men had thrust so brutally upon her.

How was it that Lieutenant de Chair had described her? *Long-funnelled and rather elderly.* It suited the old ship very well, he thought wearily.

Right aft an oilskinned seaman readjusted the halliards on the staff so that the new ensign flapped out with sudden vigour against the grey ships and sky beyond. But it took more than a flag to change a ship into a fighting machine. Just as it needed something extra to transform men into one company. Like Aikman, he thought. You could not expect a man to catch the same train to work day after regular day and then change into a dedicated, professional fighter. He strode on towards the gates. And when it was all over, would Aikman and Dancy, Hunter and Boase, and those like them, ever be able to break free from all this and return to that other, almost forgotten existence?

Then he stopped and took another look at his ship. It was up to him and the *Benbecula* to try and make sure they got the chance, he thought.

He showed his identity card to the dockyard policemen and then stepped outside the gates, suddenly confused and uncertain. Perhaps he was wrong. Maybe he was the one to be pitied and who needed help.

Some sailors disentangled themselves from their girl friends and saluted him as he passed, and he tried to read their faces in that small moment of contact.

Respect, envy, disinterest. He saw all and none of it. They were home from the Atlantic and were making the best of it. In a way, that answered his question, and he quickened his pace to look for a taxi.

11 Memories

During the forenoon of the second day in January 1942, His Majesty's Armed Merchant Cruiser *Benbecula* was warped from dry dock and made fast to her original jetty. In Western Approaches Command her appearance excited little comment, and if there was any reaction at all it was one of impatience. Impatience to be rid of her so that the dock, jetty and harbour services could be used again for the procession of damaged ships which came with every incoming convoy.

All leave for the ship's company was due to expire at noon, and as officers and ratings returned to Liverpool, with varying degrees of reluctance and according to the success or otherwise of their unexpected freedom, they could only stare at their floating home with a mixture of surprise and apprehension. For in their absence the old ship had shed her drab grey, and now rested at her moorings with an air of almost self-conscious embarrassment. From stem to stern, from the top of her single funnel to the waterline she was newly covered with dazzle paint. Green and ice-blue, strange angular patches of black and brown made it difficult to recognise her as the same ship. Only her list remained to prove her true identity, and as one amazed stoker remarked, 'She looks like some old Devonport tart in her daughter's summer dress!' There were other comments even less complimentary.

Lindsay had returned from leave several days earlier, and as he sat in his cabin studying the piles of stores folios, signals and the latest Admiralty Fleet Orders he heard some of the raised voices and remarks, and could appreciate their concern.

As usual, nobody knew what role was being cast *Ben-becula*'s way. It was someone else's department. The dock-yard people had made good the damage below the water-line and had added some of the extra refinements he had been asking for since taking command. There was an additional pair of Oerlikons on the boat deck, which he had *not* requested, so it rather looked as if the ship would be working within reach of enemy aircraft, at least for some of the time. Fresh armour had appeared abaft the bridge and wheelhouse, previously regarded as a very tender spot should an attacker be fortunate enough to approach from astern. Several new liferafts, an additional generator in the engine room and a generous repainting job in the lower messdecks showed the dockyard manager had not been idle, even allowing for Christmas.

For Lindsay the leave had been a strange and frustrat-ing experience. Far from seeking seclusion in some hotel as he had first considered, he had instead gone south to London. After several attempts he had managed to obtain an interview at the Admiralty with a fairly senior intelli-gence officer. As he had expected, the department had heard nothing from the suave young lieutenant in Liver-pool, nor did they know anything of Lindsay's report and suggestions about the German raider. Looking back, the intelligence officer had been extremely courteous but vaguely unhelpful. He had known very little about the raider, other than she was the *Nassau* which had sunk *Loch Glendhu* as well as the recent losses. She had not returned to Norway, and even now, as Lindsay sat staring at the littered desk, nobody had heard or seen anything of her at all.

But when Lindsay had persisted with his theme, that the Germans were planning another series of widespread attacks on Allied commerce to thin the resources of escort vessels and air patrols as well as to aid their new Japanese

ally, the officer had been more definite. He was being
hard-pressed to the limits of his department. There was no
evidence to suggest that Lindsay was right. And anyway,
the war was quite difficult enough without adding to it with
ifs and *maybes*.

Lindsay groped for his pipe, remembering London.
The ruined buildings, the gaps in small terraced houses
where the bombs had carved a path like some giant axe.
Sandbags around stately Whitehall offices, policemen in
steel helmets, the blackout, and the wail of air-raid sirens,
night after night, with hardly a break.

The people had looked tired and strained, as with each
new day they picked their way over rubble and firemen's
hoses to queue with resigned patience for buses which still
somehow seemed to run on time.

And everywhere there were uniforms. Not just the
three services, but all those of the occupied countries as
well. Poles and Norwegians, Dutch and Czechs, whose
alien uniforms seemed to show the extent of the enemy's
successes.

When not waiting in an Admiralty lobby or going
through the latest intelligence reports in the operations
room, Lindsay had found himself walking. He still did not
know how far he had walked nor the full extent. The East
End and dockland. Green Park and the scruffy gaiety of
Piccadilly. Quiet, faceless streets south of the river, and the
proud skyline of the city darkly etched against the night
sky with its criss-cross of searchlights and sullen glow of
burning buildings. He had been bustled into an air-raid
shelter by an indignant warden who had shouted, 'Who do
you think you are, mate? God or something? You'll get
your bloody head blown off if you walk about while there's
a raid on!'

He had sat on a bench seat, his back against the cold
concrete, while the shelter had quaked and trembled to
the exploding bombs. Beyond the steel door, where the
same warden had stared at him fixedly as if to discover the

reason for his behaviour, he had heard the clang of fire bells, the shrill of a police whistle. But inside the crowded shelter he had found the same patience, the sense of oneness which had made such a mark on his memory.

From the day he had entered the Navy as a cadet Lindsay had been trained in all matters of the sea and, above all, sea warfare. Ship-handling and seamanship, gunnery and navigation, the complex management of groups of vessels working together in every conceivable condition which past experience and history could offer.

Nobody had said anything about the other side of it. At Dunkirk and Crete, Norway and North Africa, the lessons had been hard and sharp. Terrified refugees on the roads, scattering as the Stukas had sliced through them with bombs and bullets. Soldiers queueing chest-deep in the sea to be taken off devastated beaches by the Navy, which like London buses always managed to reach them in time. But at what a price.

The loss of his own ship, the agonising memory of the sinking transport which refused to leave him in peace, had all left their scar on Lindsay. But this last visit to London had shown him more than anything else that he knew nothing of the other war at all. It was not a battle to be contained in a gun or bombsight, with an enemy beyond reach or personality. It was right here. It was everywhere. No one was spared, and he knew that if these people with whom he had shared an air-raid shelter and all the others like them were to lose faith and hope the end was even closer than some imagined. It was amazing they had not given up already, he thought. Yet in the battered pubs with their shortages and watery beer he had heard plenty of laughter and optimism. Although on the face of it he could find no reason for either. The war was going badly, and the first breath of relief when it was learned that, willingly or otherwise, the Americans were now firm allies, was now giving way to an awareness that the real struggle had not even begun.

Even the newspapers found it hard to explain the daily events in Malaya. In a month the Japanese had driven almost the full length of the peninsula, smashing resistance and leaving a wake of horror and butchery which was impossible to measure.

During his leave Lindsay had toyed with the idea of finding out where Eve Collins had lived. He would visit her parents. Would make and hold on to some small comfort by the contact. He had dismissed the idea almost immediately, despising himself for his own self-pity. What would he have said? That he saw the ship burn with their daughter condemned to a hideous death? That he was there, a witness who should have been able to help but could not?

No, it was better to leave them to their own resources. After the harsh cruelty of an official telegram they would have to draw upon each other for strength. With time, even this unreality might ease and they would be able to think of her memory without pain, as countless others were having to do.

There was a tap at the door and Goss walked heavily into the cabin.

He said, 'Eight bells, sir. Still seven absentees, but there's been a train delay. They might be on that.' He opened his notebook. 'One call from the R.N. hospital. Able Seaman McNiven is detained in the V.D. wing for treatment.' He closed it with a snap. 'I've detailed another A.B. to replace him as quartermaster, sir.' He did not sound as if he cared much about McNiven's unhappy predicament.

'Thank you.' Lindsay eyed him steadily. Goss looked very strained, and he could imagine his feelings about the ship's new appearance. 'I expect we shall be getting our orders shortly.'

Goss nodded. 'Yes.'

It was as hard as ever to make contact with Goss.

Lindsay said, 'We will be taking on fuel and ammunition

this afternoon. We'll work into the dog watches if necessary. If there's an air-raid on the port we don't want to be sitting ducks.'

In the distance he heard a man laugh, and pictured the returning hands far below his chair as they struggled out of their best uniforms, folding them carefully into kitbags and lockers until the next time. They would all be telling each other of their leaves. Their conquests and their failures. Their families and their expectations for the next leave. It was always the same.

Goss said suddenly, 'I've been ashore a few times. Made it my business to find out where we're going next.'

Lindsay asked, 'Discover anything?'

He sighed. It seemed to come from his very soul. 'Snotty lot of bastards, sir.' His eyes gleamed. 'But I did hear we might be going south.'

Lindsay nodded. 'Could be.' He had already noted the extra fans and ventilation shafts, and the bright dazzle paint pointed to something more than another Icelandic patrol. He realised too that he did not care where it was, except for one thing. The faint, impossible chance of meeting that raider again.

Goss said, 'If we do.' He moved slightly so that Lindsay could no longer see his face. 'I don't think we'll ever get back.'

Lindsay turned in his chair. Goss was deadly serious. As he always was. He was also more troubled than he had ever seen him.

Goss continued in the same empty tone, 'While you were away, sir, they got the old *Eriskay*. Torpedoed her. Didn't say where.'

Without asking, Lindsay knew the ship must be another of Goss's old company.

Goss said, 'Only three left now.' He moved restlessly to a scuttle, his face very lined in the grey light. 'They'd no right to put them where they can't survive. It's always the same.' He turned, his eyes in shadow. 'The big warships

swing round their buoys in harbour. The best destroyers
stay with 'em just in case they might be in danger. While the
poor bloody escorts which should have been on the scrap-
heap years ago,' he took a deep breath, 'and ships like the
Becky are made to take the brunt of it!' He clenched his big
hands as if in pain. 'It's not bloody right, sir! It's not bloody
fair!'

Lindsay watched him gravely. Goss's sudden outburst
was both vehement and moving. He knew he was hitting
not only at the nameless warships but at the Service which
controlled them. Perhaps indirectly at him, too.

'I've seen people in London, Number One, who are in
much the same position. They've no choice.' He hardened
his voice. 'Any more than we have.'

Goss recovered himself. 'I know that.'

The deck gave a delicate tremor, and Lindsay wondered
if Fraser was already in his engine room, testing some
machinery or the new generator.

He said, 'Well, carry on, Number One. We'll make an
early start after lunch.' He saw Ritchie peering in the door
and added, 'Come in, Yeo.' He watched Goss stride past
Ritchie and wondered why he could not face the inevitable.

Ritchie said, 'New batch of signals, sir.'

'Thanks.' He flicked over the top one. 'Good leave?' He
looked up, seeing the distress on the man's round face,
cursing himself for his stupidity. 'I'm sorry. That was
bloody unforgivable.'

Ritchie smiled. 'S'all right, sir.' He added, 'I'm not sorry
to be back.' He glanced around the cabin. 'I stayed at the
Union Jack Club. Better'n nothing, I suppose.'

Lindsay thought of his own leave. The endless walking,
the visits to the Admiralty. The nights when he had at last
made good use of Boase's pills. Now, with the ship needing
him once more, he wondered what the first night would
bring. Perhaps he would be safe.

Ritchie said, 'Signal 'ere from H.Q., sir. Ops officer

comin' aboard at 1400.' He added quietly, "'E's bringin' the commodore with 'im.'

Lindsay looked up. 'Kemp? I thought he was staying at Scapa?'

Ritchie shrugged. 'You know 'ow it is in the Andrew, sir. They give you tropical rig and sends you to the Arctic. Train you for torpedoes and make you a cook!' He grinned. 'They call it plannin'!'

Lindsay smiled up at him. It was good to see him again. Something familiar. To hold on to.

'We shall just have to see what it is in our case.'

'There's another signal about A.B. McNiven, too.' Ritchie leaned over to open the pad. 'A shore patrol caught 'im breakin' into a chemist's shop. Poor chap probably thought 'e could cure a dose with stickin' plaster.' He became formal again. 'An' Mr. Aikman's replacement is due this afternoon.'

Jupp entered the cabin and hesitated. 'Pardon, sir.'

Lindsay stood up. 'I think we'll have a drink.' He looked at Ritchie. 'What about it, Yeoman? Just to start things off again.'

Ritchie grinned. 'Well, if you say so, sir. Never bin known to refuse.'

Jupp darted a quick glance at Lindsay and saw the smoother lines around his mouth and eyes. The tablets had done some good then. He looked at the petty officer as he stood beside the desk, pleased yet awkward with the captain's invitation. He thought too of Ritchie's family photographs in the P.O.'s mess and wondered how he had endured the past three weeks.

He straightened his stooped shoulders. 'Comin' right up, sir. An' as we're safe in 'arbour, the *best* glasses!'

Immediately after lunch, while the cranes dipped and swayed back and forth overhead, the ship's company turned to for work. There was a keen wind across the port and they needed little encouragement to make the business of loading stores and ammunition as brisk as possible.

On the outboard side an oiler nestled against the fenders while the pulsating fuel hoses pumped *Benbecula*'s life-blood into her bunkers, her skipper already watching other ships nearby with signal flags hoisted to show they too were demanding his services.

Throughout the ship, above and below decks, officers and ratings busied themselves with their allotted duties, their faces absorbed as they relived some incident or memory of their leave.

Fraser stood by the guardrail above the oiler, his gloved hands on his hips as he watched the chief stoker checking the steady intake. He had done it so often, in so many ports, he could gauge the fuel supply almost by the jerk of the hoses. He was thinking of his family in Dundee. It had all turned out to be quite different from what he had expected. For years he had been almost a stranger in his own home. A man who came and went, season by season. Back and forth to the other side of the world, a life which he could share with no one outside whatever ship he happened to be serving.

But this time he had been shocked to find his wife was suddenly growing old. And his two children had seemed like strangers, even embarrassed by his forced familiarity. There had been no tours around the pubs as in the past. No quiet anger on his wife's face as he staggered home in the early hours. For three whole weeks he had tried to make up for it. Had tried to rediscover what he had never known he had possessed. She had understood. No arguments. No quarrels about other ships' officers who lived in the district, whose wives had always told her how well their men were doing. Better ships than Fraser's. Promotion, more opportunities, fancy jobs on shore or in some harbour authority.

It had been a close, warm Christmas, and unlike any other leave when New Year had been involved, neither

Fraser nor his wife had budged from their fire. As they had listened to the welcome to the New Year on their radio they had held hands, both realising perhaps that it was not merely the end of a year but also of this leave.

He had heard himself say, 'If anything happens to me, will you let young Jamie follow the sea if he's so inclined?'

Their son was eleven but had seemed so much older this time.

She had replied, 'Don't talk like that, Donald. It's not like you to fret so. What have they done to make you like this?'

'I didn't mean to worry you, lass.'

She had poured him a full glass of whisky. 'Drink this, Donald. Jamie's like his father. I'll not stop him.'

And when he had made to leave he had stared around their small house as if trying to remember everything at once. Then he had kissed her and had gone down the path without looking back.

The chief stoker squinted up at him, his eyes red in the wind. 'That feels better, eh, sir? The old girl'll take us anywhere!'

Fraser regarded him dourly. 'She'd bloody well do just that, Usher! I'll not forgive her if she conks out now!'

Above on the boat deck Lieutenant Maxwell was staring up at the twin mounting which had appeared abaft the bridge superstructure.

His assistant, Lieutenant Hunter, was saying, 'I've checked the communications, sir, and the siting of the mounting is quite good, too.' He was careful to say little, knowing how scathing Maxwell could be.

Maxwell bobbed his bullet head. 'Good. Fine. As it should be.' He had hardly heard a word Hunter had said.

He still could not accept it. It was like a bad dream which refused to be broken even when the sufferer was endeavouring to burst awake and free himself from it.

If he had telephoned first he would never have known. He felt the sweat gathering under his cap, hot in spite of the bitter wind. He rarely bothered to telephone or send a letter about leave. Decia, his wife, always seemed to be home anyway. She had money of her own, plenty of it, thanks to her rich father, and was quite content to entertain her friends rather than go visiting.

It might have been going on for months. Years. He felt the anxiety and disbelief churning his insides as if he were going to vomit.

On the last link of his journey down to Hampshire the train had been held up for several hours because of a derailment further along the line. Without lights or heating, the occupants of his compartment had sat in resentful, shivering silence. Then when at last he had reached his station there had been no taxi or hire-car available. The aged porter had said sourly, 'Don't you know there's a war on?' Stupid old bastard.

Maxwell had been almost out of breath by the time he had walked the five miles to his house. His case had been heavy, filled mostly with duty-free cigarettes and a length of silk which he had obtained in Liverpool from an old contact. For Decia.

Inside the front door the house had been as quiet as a grave, and for a few moments more he imagined she might have been away. The housekeeper lived out, for now that factories and the services offered either better money or a more exciting life, servants were almost impossible to find. Decia often complained about this fact, as she did about other things, too.

Then he had heard her laugh. A long, excited, sensuous sound.

He did not remember running upstairs or how long he had waited outside the bedroom door. In his mind he could only picture the scene captured in the bedside lights like some hideous tableau.

Decia sitting up and staring at him, her naked body like gold in the lamplight, her hair across her shoulders in a way he had never seen before. And the man, open-mouthed and transfixed, one hand still thrust against her thigh. He had tumbled from the bed, blurting out senseless, meaningless words, groping for his trousers, falling, and then sobbing with terror as Maxwell crossed to his side.

The worst part of it was that Maxwell had been unable to hit him. Maybe in his heart he had known that if he had once started he would have killed him there and then. The man was paunchy and ridiculous. Not even young, and had been in tears as he had babbled for forgiveness.

Maxwell had slammed the door behind him, hearing the man stumbling downstairs, the sounds of his feet across the gravel drive, and then silence.

In the bedroom there had been no sound either. Just her breathing and his own heart pounding into his ribs like a hammer.

'Why?' The one word had been torn from him even before he had recovered his reason. 'In Christ's name, *why?*'

Instead of trying to cover her body she had leaned back, her eyes suddenly calm again.

'Why not? Did you imagine I'd be able to go on living like this without a *man?*'

Maxwell had turned towards the door. 'Man? You call that a man?'

She had said, 'He made a change.'

Even as he stood stockstill below the twin Oerlikons Maxwell could not believe. She had not been afraid or repentant. Had not even bothered to conceal what she had done, perhaps many times with others.

'You bitch!' He had almost choked. 'You bloody, spoiled whore!'

Still she had not flinched, and when she had spoken her voice had been scathing, taunting.

'What did you expect? That I could just sit here while you go playing the little hero again? But for this war you'd still be living on my money, pretending to be the retired gentleman, when we both know you were thrown out of the Navy! I'm only surprised they took you in the first place!' She had mocked at his anguish. 'God Almighty, *look* at you! No wonder we're losing the war!'

'I was not thrown out.' He had heard his excuses pouring from his lips, just as he had told them to himself over and over again. 'It was an accident. Someone else——'

'Someone else? Oh, it would be. It always is when you make a mistake.'

She had let her shoulders fall back over the pillows, her perfect breasts firm in the bedside lights.

'You're a failure. Just as you're a failure in bed!'

He had almost fallen on top of her, his eyes blinded with tears and desperation, his hands groping for her as he had pleaded, 'You're wrong. You know you are. I've had bad luck. I've tried to make you happy.'

And all the time she had just laid there, her eyes almost disinterested as she watched his hands running over her shoulders and breasts.

'You make me sick.'

Everything else had been lost in a blur. Like a film out of focus. He could still hear himself screaming down at her, saw her amused contempt change to sudden fright as he had swung back his arm and then struck her across the mouth. She had rolled on to her side, gasping with pain, only to rock back again as he had hit her once more. How many times he had struck her he could not recall. But he could see her doubled over the side of the bed, her cheeks puffed and swollen, her beautiful lips running with blood.

That last sight had frozen him, chilled his fury as if he had been drugged. Hesitantly, almost timidly he had put one hand on her quivering shoulder.

Before he could speak she had turned and looked up at him, her hair disordered across her bruised face, partly hiding one eye which was already closing from his blows.

'Better now, little man?' The tears had been running down her face to mingle unheeded with the blood on her lips. Perhaps she had expected him to kill her and no longer cared.

Maxwell remembered only vaguely leaving the house. Even as he made to close the front door he had heard her call after him. Just one word which hung in his brain even now. *'Bastard!'*

The leave had been spent in a small hotel. He had tried phoning her. Had even written several letters and then torn them up. After having her telephone hung up on him he had tried to get drunk. He had almost gone mad in his hotel room, drinking and going over it all again and again. The nightmare had been made worse by the other hotel guests singing Christmas carols, their curious or amused stares as he had sat at his table for an occasional meal. Once he had taken out her picture from his wallet and torn it in half, cursing her and her beautiful body until someone had banged on the wall and yelled, 'Pipe down, chum! Who've you got in there? A bloody tiger?'

The sudden interruption had sobered him, and with pathetic despair he had dropped to his knees, gathering up the fragments of her picture, and had tried to fix them together as he had mumbled her name.

Hunter watched him carefully. He disliked Maxwell but his present mood was almost unnerving. Perhaps he had gone round the bend. It could happen, they said. Or maybe he had heard some bad news.

He asked, 'Everything all right at home?'

Maxwell turned on his heels like a bullfighter, his face screwed up with sudden anger.

'You mind your own damn business, right? Do your job and keep the guns in order, that's all I want from you!' He swung away and marched violently towards the bridge, his shoes clicking across the worn planking as if he were on parade.

Hunter shook his head and smiled to himself. That was

more like it. Better the bastard you knew than some nut case.

Lieutenant de Chair was passing and drawled, 'Back to normal, I see?'

Hunter grinned. 'One big happy family.'

The marine lieutenant rested his hands on the guardrail and watched a staff car driving towards the main gangway.

'Let's hope it stays that way, old son.'

A marine driver opened the car door and a stocky figure climbed out to stare up at the ship's side, the dull light glinting on his oak-leaved cap and the single broad stripe on his sleeve.

de Chair added quietly, 'I should tell young Kemp to watch out.' He walked casually aft saying over his shoulder, 'Some sort of god has just arrived!'

———————

Commodore Martin Kemp selected an armchair and sat down very exactly. Without his cap he became just as Lindsay had remembered him from the wardroom party at Scapa. Stocky, even heavily built, he looked like a man who took some pains over his appearance. His features were very tanned, so that his keen blue eyes and the few remaining wisps of grey hair stood out as if independent from the rest of the mould.

He said briskly, 'I expect you're wondering why I've come bursting in like this. I *could* have arrived quite unannounced, of course.'

Lindsay watched him impassively. The *of course* was somehow typical of the man, he thought.

He said, 'I would be ready to receive you at any time, sir.'

Kemp grunted. 'Yes. I expect so. Wasn't trying to catch you out.'

'Would you care for some refreshment, sir?'

He shook his head. 'No time.' He studied Lindsay calmly. 'But if you feel *you* would like a drink, don't let me stop you.'

Lindsay sat down and tried to relax. He must not let Kemp get under his skin so easily.

'What is it you want to see me about, sir?'

Kemp interlaced his fingers carefully across his stomach. Lindsay noticed how erectly he sat in the chair. There was not a crease in his uniform, and he guessed that he made a point of appearing alert whenever he was with his subordinates.

'As you know, Lindsay, I have been doing a good deal of work on co-ordination.' A small sigh. 'A hard, thankless task.'

'I did hear something about it, sir. But I've been away for several weeks, and of course there has been leave for the whole ship since we came to Liverpool.'

Kemp's eyebrows lifted. 'Away? Oh yes. The patrol.'

Lindsay took out his pipe and gripped it until Kemp's casual dismissal of the patrol faded into perspective. Perhaps being recalled to the Service after retirement, the fast-moving rate of the war, the sudden jump into his new work were hard to bear for him, too. There were plenty like Kemp. So grateful to be needed again, yet unwilling to bend in the face of the changes which war had hurled against the country and the world.

Kemp continued, 'That was a bad show about the convoy. Its commodore did not throw much light on the matter.' He shrugged. 'Past history now.'

Lindsay thought of the girl with the bandaged face. The blazing ship, and that last pathetic signal from the convoy escort. *Am engaging.*

He said quietly, 'It was murder. In my opinion, our people will have to start thinking like the enemy and not of acting out the war as if it is a game.' He could feel his hands trembling. 'To see men die and be helpless to aid them was bad enough. To know it was because of carelessness makes it all the worse.'

Kemp smiled. 'You are still on your hobby horse? I've been hearing about your assault on the Admiralty. I'd have thought you'd find a better way of spending your leave.' He shrugged. 'No matter. I came to tell you your new assignment. Not partake in amateur strategy.'

Lindsay replied, 'You don't believe that ships and men's lives are important then, sir?'

Kemp smiled again. He looked more at ease than when Lindsay and the side party had met him at the gangway.

'Look, Lindsay, you've had a bad time. I make a point of knowing everything there is to know about my officers. Especially *commanding* officers.'

Lindsay looked away. *My* officers. So Kemp was taking the reins.

He said, 'I am involved, sir. I cannot just ignore it.'

'Of course not. Admirable sentiment. However, you must allow me to understand the overall position and what must be done to contain whatever the Hun intends to do.'

Lindsay watched him with sudden realisation. There was something old-world about Kemp. He may have been able to obtain this new appointment through his past knowledge or record, but his manner, his form of speech were as revealing as a Cockney barrow-boy trying to masquerade as a bishop. The *Hun*, for instance. It had a First World War, Boys' Own Paper ring to it. God, if Kemp thought he could introduce cricket into the Atlantic he was in for a shock. He felt the anger rising like a fever. But Kemp would not be the one to suffer.

'Drastic situations call for drastic measures, Lindsay. I will be speaking with everyone concerned tomorrow, but I felt you should be put in the picture first.' He hesitated. 'Well, I mean, this ship is hardly a front-line warrior, eh?'

Lindsay said quietly, 'They are using old pleasure boats,

paddle-steamers for minesweeping, sir. China river gun-boats for covering the army's flanks in the Med. *Benbecula* is not alone when it comes to unpreparedness.'

'Well, we can't all have the plum commands.' Kemp's smile was still there but it was without warmth. 'We need every ship we can get. Every man-jack who can serve his country to step in and fill the breech.'

Lindsay wanted to laugh. Or cry. 'And the breech *is* a big one, sir.'

Kemp let his hands move up and outwards to the arms of his chair. 'I think I am a tolerant man, Lindsay. Do not overtax me. There is vital work to be done and without wasting any more time.' He stood up and walked to a scuttle. 'The situation in Malaya is grave, more so than I would have thought possible. Of course I realise the Japanese have only been facing our native troops for much of the campaign, but I still feel that in my early days we would have given any attacker out there very short shrift indeed.'

Lindsay watched his profile. Native troops. Why not just let him talk. Get it over with and send him away happy.

Instead he said abruptly, 'The troops are from many parts of the Commonwealth. Indians and Australians, as well as our people. I understand the Indian infantry have not been trained in tank warfare. Have never even seen one. They were told no attacker could use them in the jungle. I suppose the Japs didn't know that though.'

Kemp swung round. 'That's probably a damned rumour!' He calmed himself with a quick effort. 'One thing is certain, however. Singapore will be held. It is a sad business to lose so much of Malaya, but with Singapore made even stronger than before we can soon retake the initiative on the mainland.'

Lindsay massaged his eyes. What was Kemp saying? That *Benbecula* was to go to the Far East? If so he was deluding himself more than ever.

Kemp became very grave, so that his eyes seemed to sink into the wrinkles like bright buttons.

'Reinforcements will be sent forthwith. A fast convoy is being mustered and will sail in four days. It is a vital convoy. Armoured vehicles and anti-aircraft weapons. Troops and supplies, and everything else they'll need for a siege.'

Lindsay tensed. 'Around the Cape, sir?'

'Of course. Did you imagine I would direct it through the Med. to Suez? We'd have every bomber and submarine attacking it all the way.'

Lindsay replied, 'I know, sir.'

'Non-stop to Ceylon.' Kemp seemed satisfied Lindsay was now in full agreement. 'From there the troops and supplies will go on in smaller ships with fresh escorts. The FOIC in Ceylon is ready to act and will get them moving within two days of our arrival.' He rubbed his hands. 'That will keep the moaning minnies quiet when they see what can be done with a bit of initiative and drive.'

Lindsay said, 'It's thirteen thousand miles to Ceylon, sir. Even allowing for minimum changes of course to avoid U-boat attacks, breakdowns and delays it will take nearly seven weeks to get there.'

'*Really?*' Kemp's eyebrows seemed to rise a full inch. 'I am glad you have such a quick grasp of routes and distances. But I hope you are not suggesting that Singapore will have sunk without trace before that time?' He laughed quietly. 'And there will be no delays. This is an important job. We will have a heavy escort, and will go through regardless of what the Hun can throw our way.'

Lindsay stood up. 'Look, sir, my idea about this German raider was not just born on the spur of a moment. I believe it is the start of something fresh. Something which could put our convoys into real danger. We're fighting on two oceans now. Even the Americans can't be expected to help us until they've replaced some of their losses at Pearl Harbour.'

Kemp picked up his cap and eyed it critically. 'I am not concerned with the American Navy, Lindsay. How they fight their war is their affair. Personally I have greater respect for the Japanese. I worked with them in the last war. Courageous, plucky little chaps. Plenty of guts.' He sighed. 'But fate can be unkind, as we have seen.'

Lindsay could feel his mind reeling. It was like part of a badly acted play. Dinner jackets in the jungle. The captain on his bridge saluting as the ship went down.

He said, 'I'm afraid I can't agree, sir.'

'That is hardly my worry, Lindsay.' He smiled grimly. 'I know you're fretting about having this old ship to command. With any sort of luck I may be able to help towards something better.' His smile vanished. 'But I intend to see that my arrangements *work*. I do not expect to hear any more of this defeatist talk from you or anyone else.'

Lindsay followed him from the cabin. 'Would you like to see your son, sir?'

Kemp did not turn. 'When he has achieved something worthwhile, yes. Then I'll see him with pleasure.'

Lindsay saluted as Kemp hurried down the gangway and then turned abruptly towards the bridge. The commodore had a new appointment and expected everyone to work, or die if necessary to make it a success.

He stopped and looked up suddenly at the masthead pennant flicking out to the wind. He had just remembered Goss's words. *I don't think we'll ever get back.*

Then he thought of the commodore and quickened his pace again. I'll get them all back, if it's only to spite that pompous fool, he thought.

And if Commodore Martin Kemp was coming along for the ride he might at last realise what he was up against. Or kill all of us.

Jupp was waiting for him and said, 'South Atlantic then, sir?'

Lindsay sat down wearily. 'Who says?'

Jupp showed his teeth. 'Some fur-lined watchcoats 'ave just arrived, sir. The pusser 'as 'ad 'em on order for weeks.' He spread his hands. 'If they sends us that, then we just 'ave to be goin' to the sunshine, it stands to reason.'

Lindsay nodded. 'Except for the word *reason*, Jupp, I'm inclined to agree.'

12 Convoy

'Forenoon watch closed up at defence stations, sir.' Stannard saluted formally and waited for Lindsay to comment.

Lindsay glanced at the gyro repeater and then climbed on to his chair and stared at the grey horizon for several seconds.

'Very good, Pilot.'

He waited for Stannard to move away again and then lifted his glasses to study the regularly spaced lines of ships. The convoy had been at sea for four whole days and as yet without a sign of trouble. The first two days had been very rough with gale force winds and visibility down to four miles. Maybe the U-boats had run deep to stay out of the savage buffeting which such seas could give their slender hulls, or perhaps they had just been lucky. The convoy was small but weighty nonetheless. The ships were steaming in three columns, the centre one being led by a modern heavy cruiser mounting twelve six-inch guns, a formidable looking vessel which represented the main escort. She was followed by two oil tankers and then the most hated member in the group, a large ammunition ship which steamed directly ahead of the *Benbecula*. The two outer columns were led by troopships, followed at prescribed intervals by freighters, the decks of which were covered by crated aircraft and armoured vehicles of every kind. They were well down in the water, and Lindsay guessed their holds were also crammed to capacity.

The destroyer escort was impressive. Six of them, none more than a year old, an unusual state of affairs with so many shortages elsewhere, and evidence of the importance placed in the convoy's safety and protection.

It was strange how the weather had eased. That too was rare for January. The horizon was sharply defined and very dark, and as Lindsay steadied himself in his chair he thought it made *Benbecula*'s list all the more obvious. The horizon line appeared to be on the tilt with the ships balanced on it and in danger of sliding uncontrollably abeam.

He readjusted the glasses to watch one of the escorts zig-zagging some five miles ahead of the convoy. He could see the great white surge of her bow-wave creaming away from her raked stem, the lithe hull almost hidden as she sped protectively across the convoy's ponderous line of advance. Just the sight of her plucked at his mind and made him remember his own destroyer and the others which he had served before her. Fast, aggressive and graceful. They above all had managed to retain the dying art of ship design. The cruiser on the other hand was like some grey floating fortress. Bridge upon bridge, her triple gun mountings and secondary armament giving her an air of massive indestructibility.

Some signal flags broke from the yard of the troopship leading the starboard column. The commodore was urging some unfortunate captain to keep station or make better speed. He could picture Kemp up there, revelling in his new power. It was to be hoped he was equally aware of his great responsibility.

All around them the horizon was bare, with the enemy-occupied coastline of France some thousand miles away on the port beam. Apart from the distant shapes of the prowling destroyers the sea was theirs alone. Not even a gull, let alone a spotting aircraft to break the dull overcast sky as a warning of impending danger.

Seventeen ships in all. He saw some anti-aircraft guns

aboard the cruiser swivel skyward, their crews going through the daily drills. Unconsciously he touched the gold lace on his sleeve. She was the *Madagascar,* nine thousand tons, and capable of tackling almost anything but a battleship. Had things been different he might have been on her bridge right now, or one like it. Doing what he had been trained for. What he had lived for.

He looked round the bridge, seeing the worn panelling, the usual scene of watchkeeping monotony. Quartermaster on the wheel, telegraphsmen swaying with the easy roll, their eyes lost in inner thought. A signalman was sitting on a locker splicing a worn halyard, and Ritchie was leafing through the morning watch reports with little on his face to show what he was thinking. A bosun's mate, a messenger gathering up the chipped enamel mugs, everything as usual.

Dancy was out on the open wing, his glasses trained on one of the ships. Stannard leaned against the screen, his face set in a tight frown.

Lindsay eased forward to watch some seamen who were working on the well deck, taking the rare opportunity to dab on some fresh paint under C.P.O. Archer's baleful eye. It was very cold, but after the ice and the constant hazards of working on a slippery deck with seas breaking over their numbed bodies they would find it almost normal.

He lifted his glasses and trained them on the commodore's ship. She was the *Cambrian,* a handsome twin-funnelled liner which had once plied between England and South America. Commanding the *Benbecula* had made a marked difference where merchant ships were concerned. Before, Lindsay had seen them as charges to be protected. Names on a convoy list to be chased or reprimanded as the occasion demanded. The slow ones, and those which made too much smoke. The ones who strayed out of their column or crept too close on the next ahead. With so many ex-merchant service people around

him every day and night he was seeing them differently.
They spoke of their past records, their cargoes and
passengers. The carefree cruises or months in harbour
without charter, and the dockside thronged with unemployed, hungry seamen. Rogue ships and bad skippers.
Fast passages or valuable time and freight lost while
searching for some other ship in distress. Shifting cargo
in a Force Nine gale, miserly captains who kept their
crews almost on starvation diet for their own ends. It was
so remote from the regulated world of the Royal Navy. It
was like re-learning everything just by listening to others.

Stannard had worked in a whaling fleet and on the
frozen meat trade before joining the company. The
second engineer, Lieutenant Dyke, had originally gone
to sea in a Greek ship running guns to the Republicans in
the Spanish Civil War. To them the ships they met in
convoy were like old faces, old friends, with characters to
match.

Stannard was studying the next ship ahead. 'Down two
turns.' He looked at Lindsay and gave a wry smile. 'Don't
want to be too near that joker if she gets clobbered.'

Lindsay nodded. He had seen an ammunition ship go
up. She had been two miles away, yet the noise, the savage
pressure on his ears had been almost unbearable. One
great ball of fire, rising and expanding like another sun.
When the smoke and steam had faded there had not even
been a stick or spar to mark where the ship had been.
What sort of men were they, he wondered, who
would go to sea again and again knowing they were the
targets?

He saw a small hatch open on the forward hold and
Lieutenant Barker clambering on deck to stand shivering
in the wind. He had been checking his stores again, no
doubt. He did not seem to trust anybody where they were
concerned. Barker had returned from leave in a very
shaken state of mind. Lindsay had heard that he had
some private property in England. Boarding houses or

something of the sort. But when he had gone to make his usual inspection of his other source of income he had been horrified to find them commandeered by the military. Every room filled with soldiers. Paint scratched, floorboards used for firewood. The havoc had been endless. Jupp had casually mentioned it to Lindsay. It seemed to amuse him.

A destroyer on wing escort turned in a wide arc to begin another zig-zag and he watched her with silent fascination. Then he remembered that she was the *Merlin* and recalled her young commander waiting in the office at Scapa. That day when he had seen Lovelace. When he had met the girl in the passageway. He thrust his hands into his pockets and stared fixedly at the sloping horizon. It seemed so long ago. And it felt like yesterday.

'Signal from commodore, sir.' Ritchie was wide awake. 'Alter course in succession to two-two-zero.'

'Acknowledge.' He heard Stannard moving swiftly to the gyro.

Ritchie steadied his telescope. 'Execute.'

Like ponderous beasts the ships moved slowly on to their new course. A destroyer swept down between the lines, a signal lamp flashing angrily at a rust-streaked freighter which had edged badly out of station. As she dashed abeam of *Benbecula* her loud-hailer echoed across the churned water, 'You have a bad list, old chap!'

Stannard snatched a megaphone and ran to the open wing. 'You have a loud voice, *old chap!*' He sounded angry.

Lindsay watched him thoughtfully. Like Fraser, Stannard was often quick to malign the *Benbecula*. But if anyone else tried it he became protective, even belligerent.

He came back breathing hard. 'Stupid sod!'

Lindsay asked, 'Have you heard how your brother is getting on?'

'Not much.' Stannard stared gloomily towards the

nearest ship. 'He is always a cheerful cuss. I think he *enjoys* being in the army.'

Lindsay could tell Stannard wanted to talk. He seemed on edge, different from before his leave.

'Your people are in Perth, I believe?'

'Yeh. My dad runs a sale and repair business of agricultural gear. He'll be missing young Jason, I guess. He's twenty-five almost. It was bad enough for my folks when I scarpered off to sea.' He turned his head sharply. 'Watch your helm, quartermaster! You're snaking about like a whore at a christening!'

'Aye, aye, sir.' The man sounded unmoved. Nobody seemed to mind Stannard's occasional bursts of colourful language.

He continued, 'Most of Jason's mob come from Perth or nearby.' He gave a brief smile. '*Nearby* means a coupla hundred miles either way in Aussie.'

Lindsay thought of the news reports, the confused despatches he had read in the London papers. It sounded as if the Japs were right across the Malay Peninsula, cutting it into halves with a line of steel.

Ritchie called, 'Signal from *Merlin*, sir! Aircraft bearing zero-eight-zero!'

Before anyone could move the control tannoy reported, 'Aircraft at Red one-four-oh. Angle of sight one-oh.'

Stannard said harshly, 'That *Merlin* must have good RDF. She's two miles on our starboard quarter.' He shook his fist at the deckhead. 'Why the hell don't they give us something better? We might just as well have a pair of bloody opera glasses!'

Lindsay strode to the port wing and levelled his glasses over the screen. It was not hard to see it now. A black splinter etched against the sky, seeming to skim just clear of the horizon line itself.

He heard Dancy at his side fumbling with his glasses. 'Don't bother, Sub. It'll be a Focke Wulf reconnaissance plane. Long-range job. It'll not come within gunshot unless by accident.'

Very faint above the sea noises and muffled engines Lindsay heard the far off notes of a bugle. The cruiser was doing things in style. Within seconds the A.A. guns would be cleared away and tracking the distant aircraft. It was always good experience for the crews. He rubbed his eyes and lifted the glasses once more to watch the enemy aircraft. How small it looked and near to the sea. Both were illusions, as he knew from bitter experience. The Focke Wulfs were like great eagles, huge whenever they came near enough to be seen properly. They could cover many hundreds of miles of ocean, where there were no fighter planes to pluck them down and no guns to reach them as they circled so lazily around a convoy, their radio operators sending back the vital information. Position, course and speed. It never varied. Even now, somewhere out there in the grey Atlantic a U-boat commander would be awakening from a quick nap by one of his officers shaking his shoulder. *Convoy, Kapitan.* And the signals from his H.Q. would waste no time either. Attack, attack, attack.

'Signal from commodore, sir.' Ritchie stood in the doorway. 'Maintain course and speed. Do not engage.'

Do not engage. Lindsay felt despair like pain. What did the bloody fool imagine they could do?

Dancy said, 'Is it bad, sir?'

'Bad but not critical, Sub.' He looked at him calmly. 'We will be altering course at dusk. That may throw them off the scent. If we can keep up this speed we should soon be out of range even of that high-flying bastard!' He had spoken with unconscious venom and realised Dancy was watching him with obvious surprise. Surprise that the cool-headed commander should possess any feelings. That he could hate. He added slowly, 'He'll keep up there as long as he can. Flying round and round and watching us. He may be relieved by one of his chums. It happens.'

Dancy turned towards the distant cruiser. 'She's got an aircraft, sir. I saw it on the catapult.'

Lindsay laughed. 'A poor old Walrus. Better than nothing, but that bastard would have it down in flames before you could blink.'

'Makes you feel a bit naked, sir.'

Lindsay walked towards the wheelhouse. 'Keep an eye on him, Sub. I'm going to check the chart.'

Dancy stood at the end of the wing watching the aircraft. How slow it seemed. But it was very real. The enemy. Something you could see. Not like the haphazard flash of guns in the night. The terrible leaping reflections on the ice as a ship had burned and died before his eyes. There were real Germans over there. Sitting on little stools. Drinking coffee perhaps as they peered towards the convoy. How would the ships look, he wondered? Little dark shapes, betrayed by their long white wakes and a haze of funnel smoke. Impersonal. Remote. Did they hate the men in the convoy? Did they feel anything at all as they listened to the plane's operator hammering away at his morse key?

He thought suddenly of his leave. His mother had prompted, 'Go on, Mike, tell us what it was like.' She had laid the table, spread out the best cups and plates. The sandwiches and home-made cakes. His sister and her boy-friend had been there too. His father and one of his friends from the bowling club at the Nag's Head at the end of the road. Tell us what it was like. . . .

He had tried to describe the ship, the first sight of floating ice, the party at Scapa. He had started to tell them about the captain. About Lindsay who had just left his side.

His mother had remarked, 'I expect he's a proper toff, eh, Mike? Not one of our sort.'

His father had eyed her reprovingly. 'Now, Mother, Mike's as good as anyone now that he's an officer.'

It had ended there, or almost. His mother had started

on about the reduced rations, how hard it had been to get enough even for this welcome-home tea party. They should have more consideration for those who had to stay at home and *take it.*

His father had got out his *Daily Mail War Atlas.* 'In my opinion, we should never have trusted the Froggies. It was just the same in the last lot. No guts, the lot of 'em.'

Dancy had recalled Lindsay's face at the burial parties. His quiet voice. And all at once he had not wanted to tell them anything. To share what they could never understand because they did not really want to.

Stannard came out on the wing and screwed up his eyes to search for the aircraft. It was almost abeam, parallel with the port column of ships.

'He's flaming confident.' He looked sideways at Dancy's grim face. 'I hope he runs out of gas without noticing!'

They lapsed into silence, watching the Focke Wulf until it was hidden by a freighter and the overlapping superstructure of the leading troopship.

Dancy said uneasily, 'With an escort like ours we *should* be all right.'

'Too right. The destroyers can cope with the subs. And the big cruiser can beat the hell out of the captain's raider.'

'Is that how you see it?'

'The raider?' Stannard shrugged, remembering with sudden clarity Lindsay's agonised voice on the telephone as he relived the nightmare or whatever was trying to destroy him. 'Every man has to have something in a war. Something to hate or hope for. A goal, personal ambition, who knows?' He glanced round quickly to make sure the nearest lookout was out of earshot. 'Sorry I couldn't give you a ring, Sub. Got a bit involved. You know how it is. Still, I expect you had some little sheila to keep the cold out, eh?'

Dancy tried to grin. 'I did all right.' He did not want to

think of his leave. Or how hurt he had been when
Stannard had failed to call him on the phone. Just for a
drink. Anything. He watched Stannard's clean-cut
profile. Lucky devil. There was something about him. A
sort of carefree recklessness which would appeal to
women very much, Dancy decided.

The closest he had got to female company had been a
friend of his sister. They had made a foursome, which
had of course included his sister's boy-friend. He was not
in the armed forces but employed on some reserved job
in an aircraft factory. Plenty of money, a loud laugh, and
his sister appeared to adore him.

The other girl had been called Gloria. They had gone
to a local dance, and Dancy had been so desperate for
enjoyment that once again in his young life he had mixed
his drinks. Recklessly he had invited the girl back to his
home. His sister and her friend had vanished halfway
through the dance so he had the sitting room marked
down in his mind as a suitable place for improving his
relationship with Gloria. She was young and quite pretty
and had giggled nervously when he had said casually,
'We'll have a tot together. Some of the real stuff I brought
back with me.'

The warmth of the fire, the scent of her hair and body,
the gin, all seemed to combine against him. When he had
kissed her it had still appeared to be going well enough.
When he had put his hand on her breast she had pushed
him frantically away, jumping up with such force that the
gin and glasses had scattered over the floor with a crash
loud enough to wake the dead.

It had in fact awakened Dancy's mother. He could see it
all clearly in his mind as if it was happening this very
instant. Feel the humiliation and embarrassment as his
mother had switched on all the lights and had stood in the
doorway in a dressing gown, her hair in curlers, as she
had snapped, 'I don't expect this sort of thing in *my*
house! I don't know what sort of people you've been

mixing with in the Navy, but I'll not stand for filth under this roof!' To make it worse, Gloria had been violently sick. Altogether it had not been a successful leave by any standards.

Stannard raised his glasses and studied the ammunition ship for several seconds. 'Check her bearing again, Sub. I think she's off station.'

He heard Dancy return to the wheelhouse and sighed. I must be losing my touch, he thought. He had never believed in coincidence, love at first sight, we were meant for each other, and all the other sentiments he had heard voiced in so many ports of call.

But it had happened to him. Just like that. There was no future for either of them. It was hopeless. Best forgotten. Equally he knew he was involved completely. No matter which way it ended.

He had had a couple of drinks at the railway hotel before getting a taxi to the flat. It was all exactly as he had remembered. As he had nursed it in his aching mind throughout the patrols and the freezing watches, the sights of death and pitiful survival.

But another girl had opened the door. When he had identified himself she had said calmly, 'Oh, *she* left some weeks back.'

Stannard had been dumbfounded. No message. Nothing. Not even a goodbye.

The girl had said, 'But if you like to come back in an hour I'll be free.' She had smiled, and in that instant Stannard had realised his dream had been something more than he had bargained for. 'We're kept pretty busy you know.' She had reached out to touch his shoulder strap. 'But for a nice lieutenant like you I'll break all the other appointments, okay?'

He had left without a word, his mind a complete blank.

As he had reached the stairway she had called after him, 'What d'you expect? Betty Grable or something, you stuck-up bleeder!'

And then, a few days later, as he had been walking aimlessly down a London street searching for a bar he had visited some years before, an air-raid had started. Within minutes, or so it had seemed, bombs had begun to rain down, the far end of the street had been filled with dust, smoke and crashing debris. With vague, scurrying figures he had run into a shelter, amazed that he had seemed to be the only one who did not know where to go or what to do.

The All Clear had sounded thirty minutes later. It had been a hit-and-run raid, a warden had said in an authoritative tone. 'Lost 'is bleedin' way more likely!' a disgruntled postman had suggested.

But when Stannard had emerged from the shelter it was almost dark, and as the other strangers had melted away in the gloom it had begun to pelt with rain.

It was then that he had noticed her. She had been standing under the doorway of a bombed shop clutching a paper bag against her body and staring at the rain in dismay. Without hesitation he had taken off his greatcoat and slung it across her shoulders before she could protest.

'Going far? Well, I'll walk you there, if you like. We'll be company for each other if there's another raid.'

And that was how it had all begun. She lived at a small house in Fulham, close to Putney Bridge. At the door she had looked at his dripping uniform and had said quietly, 'Would you like to come in for a minute? I owe you that at least.'

Her name was Jane Hillier, and she was married to a captain in the Royal Armoured Corps.

As Stannard had given her his jacket to hang by the fire he had seen her husband's picture on the sideboard. A nice looking chap standing with some other soldiers in front of a tank.

'I'd offer you a meal but I'm afraid I've only got some Spam until the shops open tomorrow.'

She was dark and slim, and very attractive. She had

opened the rain-splashed parcel and taken out a small, brightly coloured hat.

'I was being extravagant. I wanted everything to be just right.'

Stannard had glanced at the photograph but she had said quickly, 'No, he's all right. It's not that. But he'll not be coming home. Not yet anyway. He's in the Western Desert. I've not seen him for two years.'

Stannard had walked to his suitcase. 'I've got something better than Spam. I was bringing it for——'

Then she had smiled. For the first time. 'So we were both let down?'

Try as he might, Stannard could not remember the exact moment, the word or the sign which had brought them together.

As he leaned against the screen watching the distant aircraft while it reappeared around the port quarter all he could recall was her body, naked in his arms, her fierce passion as she had given herself, pulling him to her as if there were only minutes left before the world ended. Outside the room the sirens had sounded and some-where more houses had been bombed to fragments. Once, as Stannard had lain awake staring up into the darkness he had felt her crying against his shoulder, very softly, like a child. But she had been asleep, and he had wondered if, like himself, she was thinking of that other man, the face in the photograph, somewhere in the desert with his tank.

The next day he had collected his things from his hotel and had stayed at the little house near Putney Bridge until the end of his leave.

She had said, 'I'm not sorry for what we did. You know that, don't you?'

As he had stood by that same front door a lorry packed with soldiers had rattled past the house, and Stannard had heard the wolf-whistles and cheerful yells of admira-tion with something like hatred.

'It wasn't just because you, *we* were lonely. You must know that, too.' The seconds had ticked away. Where were the words when you needed them? 'I don't know how, Jane. But we'll sort this out. I must see you again. *Must.*'

On the crowded train he had tried to rationalise his feelings. Collect his arguments. It was over. An episode, inevitable in this bloody war. He had wanted her. She had been starved of love for two years. That was all there was to it.

When Lindsay had told him of the convoy and the long haul around the Cape to Ceylon he had tried again. Time and distance would end it. But in his heart he knew he would have to see her again, if only to be sure.

Feet moved on the gratings and Lindsay said, 'We've had a signal from Admiralty, Pilot. Four plus U-boats in our vicinity. You'd better put your plotting team to work.' He watched Stannard's strained face. 'You bothered about something?'

Stannard looked at him. 'I'm okay, sir.' He forced a grin. 'Just thinking that I *could* have stayed with my dad selling tractors instead of all this!'

Lindsay watched him leave. He's like the rest of them. Like me. Sick and tired of being on the defensive. Worn out by retreat and vague plans for hitting back at an invisible enemy.

'Signal from commodore, sir.' Ritchie grimaced. 'To *Benbecula*. Make less smoke.'

'Acknowledge, Yeoman.'

Lindsay glanced up at the tall funnel, garish in its new paint. No more smoke than usual. No more than anyone could expect from a ship which should by rights be ending her days quietly somewhere in the sun. Where war meant only a fight for better freight or cheaper running costs.

Maybe the commodore had seen in the curt Admiralty signal some small hint of what he was up against. Not pins

and paper flags on a map. Not a glib daily communique
for the press and the civilians who were *taking it* as best
they could. Out here it was very real. A killing ground
where there were no rules and no standards. A place
where the horizon never seemed to get any nearer, where
the only quick escape was straight down, to the bottom.

He saw two destroyers wheeling in a flurry of spray and
foam to take station on the port quarter, to begin yet
another sweep, listening for the unseen attacker, preparing to strike and kill if the opportunity offered itself.

He glanced at his watch. There was still plenty of time.
The hunters and the hunted knew their various skills,
just as they understood how easily their roles could be
changed.

'I'm going below, Pilot. Call me if you hear anything.'

Stannard watched him climb down the bridge ladder.
Then he turned and stared at the hard horizon. The little
house so close to Putney Bridge suddenly seemed very
far away. A memory, which somehow he must hold on to.
No matter what.

———————

It was at dusk when the first torpedoes streaked into
the convoy. During the afternoon there had been numer-
ous reports of U-boats in the vicinity, and later still a
destroyer, the *Merlin,* had made a contact.

Aboard the *Benbecula* at the rear of the convoy the
hands had been sent to action stations, but with nothing
to do but wait had stared into the gathering gloom,
listening to the thundering roar of depth-charges. They
had seen tall columns of water bursting skyward even as
the destroyer had swung round for another run-in across
the hidden submarine. She had soon been joined by the
other wing escort, and again the charges had thundered
down, the explosions booming against the *Benbecula*'s
lower hull as if she too was under attack.

In the engine room Fraser had seen several of his men

pausing at their work to look up at the oil-streaked sides, imagining perhaps that a torpedo was already speeding towards them.

On the bridge it was all remote and vaguely disconnected with attack or defence. The three lines of ships plodded on towards a darkening horizon while the other destroyers tore back and forth like nervous dogs around a valuable flock of sheep.

Merlin had reported she had lost contact. There had been some oil sighted but no one paid much attention to that. The U-boat might have been damaged. It could have been a ruse to allow her commander to take evasive action. Either way, *Merlin*'s swift attack had given the convoy more time.

Lindsay sat on his tall chair and watched the ships on either bow. They were already losing their identity as darkness closed in. They were moving faster now, making a good fourteen knots in response to the commodore's signals.

Dancy said, 'It looks as if we may have given them the slip this time, sir.' He sounded very tired.

Lindsay shrugged. 'If the escorts can keep them down, yes. But if they surface they can make a fair speed, too.' He looked at Dancy. What with having the forenoon watch and being called to his action station on the bridge soon afterwards he was showing the strain.

Stannard snatched up a handset as its shrill cry shattered the stillness in the enclosed bridge.

He swung towards Lindsay, his voice urgent. 'Masthead reports torpedoes approaching on the port quarter, sir!'

Lindsay jumped from his chair. 'Full astern!'

When he reached the bridge wing he saw the pale white lines cutting across the dull water, his brain recording their bearing and speed even as he noted the urgent flash of signal lamps, the muffled squawk of the R/T speaker as the alarm ran like wildfire along the lines of ships.

'Stop engines!'

He craned over the screen, straining his eyes to watch the nearest track as it sped straight for *Benbecula*'s port bow. Nothing happened. The nearest torpedo must have missed the ship by less than twenty feet.

'Resume course and revs, Pilot!'

He waited a few more seconds, half expecting to see another torpedo coming out of the gloom. Slamming the engines astern for just those few minutes must have thrown the enemy's sights off balance.

There was a single, muffled explosion which seemed to come from miles away, like thunder on a range of hills. As he ran through the bridge to the starboard wing he saw a searing column of fire, bright red against the clouds, a billowing wall of smoke completely hiding the victim from view.

Lindsay crouched over the gyro repeater on the bridge wing and took a quick bearing. The torpedo must have run diagonally right through the convoy, hitting a freighter just astern of the commodore's ship. There were no more explosions, and he guessed the U-boat commander had fired at extreme range, fanning his torpedoes in the hopes of getting a lucky hit.

Depth-charges boomed and echoed across the water, and over the R/T Lindsay heard an unemotional voice say, 'Have contact. Am attacking.'

The freighter astern of the torpedoed ship was already swinging wildly out of line, the side of her tall hull glowing scarlet in the flames of her burning consort, the fires reflecting in her scuttles and ports so that her cabins appeared to be lit from within.

A destroyer was charging down the lines of ships, and faintly above the grumble of depth-charges and engine room fans Lindsay heard her loud-hailer bellowing, 'Keep closed up, *Pole Star*! Do not heave to!'

Stannard said thickly, 'God, look at her!'

The stricken freighter was beginning to heel over, and

in the leaping flames and sparks it was possible to see the deck cargo starting to tear adrift and go crashing through the tilting steel bulwarks as if they were matchwood. Army lorries lurched drunkenly overboard, and from aft another column of fire burst out of a sealed hold, the flames licking along the upper deck and setting several lifeboats ablaze.

The destroyer swept down *Benbecula*'s side, her wash surging against the hull plates like a great wave breaking on a jetty. Just briefly before she vanished astern Lindsay saw her gun mountings swinging round and the crouching seamen on her quarterdeck beside the depth-charge racks.

Dancy called, '*Pole Star*'s stopping, sir.'

Someone else said hoarsely, 'He's going to try and pick up survivors!'

Lindsay gripped the screen and watched the sinking freighter swinging helplessly abeam in the heaving water. The other ship, *Pole Star*, obviously intended to ignore the escort's order, and already he could see a boat jerking down its falls, so clear in the reflected fires it could have been midday.

'Starboard ten.' For a few seconds nobody moved or spoke.

Then Jolliffe said, 'Starboard ten, sir. Ten o' starboard wheel on.'

Lindsay watched the bows swinging very slowly towards the burning ship. 'Midships.' The bows were still edging round until the motionless *Pole Star* suddenly appeared in direct line with the stem.

'Steady.' Lindsay hurried out on to the wing again. Over his shoulder he snapped, 'Yeoman, make to *Pole Star*. Resume course and speed. Do not stop.'

He heard Ritchie's shuttered lamp clicking busily but kept his eyes fixed on the ship ahead.

Stannard exclaimed, 'We'll ram her if we keep on this course, sir!'

'Exactly.' Lindsay did not move.

Several miles astern a starshell burst almost level with the clouds, and he heard the immediate crack of gunfire. That destroyer must have caught one on the surface.

Ritchie said, '*Pole Star* requests permission to pick up survivors, sir.'

'Denied!'

Stannard looked at Dancy's stricken face and shrugged. If Lindsay did not check *Benbecula*'s onward charge they would hit the other ship fine on her port quarter. At nearly fifteen knots, *Benbecula* would carve through her poop like an axe into a tree.

'*Pole Star* is under way again, sir.' Ritchie had to clear his throat before adding, 'She's turnin'!'

'Port fifteen.'

Lindsay stayed by the screen, his heart pounding in time with the engines. The *Pole Star*'s master had ignored a necessary signal to try to save a few lives. It had taken the sight of *Benbecula*'s massive bows to make him change his mind. As the freighter turned heavily on to her proper course the sinking ship drifted into view down her starboard side. Lindsay watched the blazing hull fixedly as if under a spell. When *Pole Star* moved clear it was like the opening door of a furnace. Most of the freighter was ablaze now and she was going down by the stern, her poop and after well deck blanketed in steam as the beam sea eddied and swirled over the heated metal.

A signalman called, 'Sir! There's men in the water! I can see 'em by a raft!'

Ritchie said harshly, 'Just you watch the commodore's ship, Bunts!'

But the signalman turned towards him, his voice breaking. 'But, Yeo, there's blokes down there! I saw one wavin' at us!' He sounded close to tears.

Ritchie strode across the vibrating gratings and gripped his arm. 'Wot d'you want us to do, lad? Bloody well stop and get *our* arse blown off!' He swung him almost savagely. 'Up at the 'ead of the convoy there's two troopers with Gawd knows 'ow many squaddies on board, see? If we're goin' to get through we've got to stick together!'

The signalman was little more than a boy. 'I know that, Yeo.' He dashed one hand across his eyes and picked up his Aldis lamp. 'It's just that——'

Ritchie interrupted gently, 'You don't 'ave to spell it out, lad.' He sighed as the signalman moved slowly to the opposite side of the bridge. Away from the drifting inferno which was now almost abeam. He could feel the furnace heat on his face through the wheelhouse door, caught the foul stench of charred paint and woodwork. A ship dying. One more for the scoreboard.

The bosun's mate by the voicepipes said bitterly, 'Look at the skipper. Just standin' there watchin' 'em fry! The cold-blooded bastard!'

Ritchie pivoted on his heels and thrust his face within inches of the seaman's. 'If I 'ear you talk that sort of squit again I'll 'ave you on a charge!' He turned slightly to watch Lindsay's head and shoulders silhouetted against the angry glare. ''E's worth twenty of your sort, an' you'll eat your bloody words if you lives long enough!'

Lindsay heard none of it. He watched the other ship's bows begin to rise slowly above the litter of drifting flotsam, heard the dull roar of inrushing water, the screech of machinery tearing free to crash through the burning hull to speed its end. Some sort of fighter plane had broken from its crate and was suspended across one of the blazing holds. In the red glow it looked like a charred crucifix, he thought dully.

With a final roar the ship slid steeply under the surface, leaving a maelstrom of exploding air bubbles and frothing foam. Then nothing.

A messenger said, 'Captain, sir. From W/T office. Six plus U-boats in convoy's vicinity.'

Stannard snapped, 'Very well. Tell my yeoman in the chart room.'

He walked out to the wing, sucking in the cold air like a man brought back from drowning.

He said, 'Poor bastards. D'you think the escorts will be able to find any of them, sir?'

Lindsay's shoulders seemed to sag. 'Listen.' Astern the depth-charge explosions were rising to a drumming crescendo.

Stannard opened his mouth and then closed it, his mind suddenly sickened. The depth-charges would do what the torpedo had failed to accomplish. He had seen many hundreds of dead and gutted fish left in the wake of a depth-charge attack. Men in the water would fare no better, except they would know what was coming.

Lindsay continued to stare astern, his mind still cringing from the suddenness of death. He should be used to it. Hardened, as his half-trained company imagined him to be. But you never did get used to it. Close the ranks. More speed. Don't look back. His mouth twisted in a tight smile. That was the most important bit. Don't ever look back.

Stannard saw the smile and said quietly, 'I'm sorry, sir. I didn't understand.'

Lindsay turned his back on the sea and looked at Stannard's dark outline against the dazzle paint.

'Stop thinking about those men, Pilot.' He saw Stannard stiffen and added coldly, 'Another few feet and it would have been us. Think about that and about how you would have reacted then.'

An hour passed with nothing to break the regular beat of engines, the sea noises beyond the bridge. In the new darkness it looked as if the lines of ships had drawn closer together for mutual support. Another illusion.

Ritchie found Lindsay in his chair. 'From escort, sir. No survivors.'

Half to himself Lindsay said, 'And no U-boat sunk.'

'No, sir.'

Lindsay turned in the chair. 'Pass the word to

Lieutenant Barker to get some hot soup around the ship for all hands. Sandwiches as well.'

As Ritchie beckoned to a messenger Lindsay heard Stannard mutter, '*He* should have thought of that already himself!'

Lindsay turned and stared at the screen, the black blob of the ammunition ship's stern which seemed to be pivoting on *Benbecula*'s jackstaff.

'Pilot, come here.'

'Sir?' Stannard crossed to the chair.

Lindsay kept his voice very low. 'You have the makings of a good officer, a *naval* officer I'm talking about now.' God, how difficult it had become to keep his voice level. 'You are a good navigating officer too, and God knows that's something in a ship like this.' He turned and studied Stannard's face, pale in the darkness. 'But try not to be too clever for your own good. Don't get too hard or you'll grow brittle. Brittle enough to break when you're most needed.'

'I only meant——'

'I don't give a damn what you meant! For all you know, Barker may be dealing with the men's food right now. He may just as easily have fallen down a hatch and broken his neck.'

Stannard said abruptly, 'I *have* apologised.'

'That's fine then.' Lindsay turned back to the screen. 'Just one thing more, and then carry on. If a piece of Krupp steel comes through that screen or a shell bursts above your head on Maxwell and his spotters, things could change for you and *fast*.' He waited a few more seconds, feeling Stannard's resentment and uncertainty. 'You will be in command at that moment. Alone on this bridge maybe. Perhaps for just a few seconds until the next shell. Or maybe you'll have to nurse this old tub a thousand miles without help from anyone.'

Stannard nodded slowly. 'I think I *do* understand, sir. I'm sorry.' He smiled sadly. 'When you've always had a

captain or someone to give orders and get you out of a
jam it's hard to see yourself in that position.'

Lindsay nodded and took out his pipe. 'We'll say no
more about it.'

But Stannard said, 'I was wrong about Aikman, too. I'll
never forget how he looked when he left the ship.'

'I was the one who made the mistake, Pilot.' He heard
Stannard's quick intake of breath. 'Surprised? That I can
be wrong?' He gave a short laugh. 'I used to think much
the same about my first captain. He died at Narvik. He
turned out to be just a man after all. Like the rest of us.'

Dancy called, 'The first lieutenant's on the phone, sir.
Wants to know if he can fall out action stations.'

'No.' As Dancy turned back to his telephone he added
quietly, 'Cold and uncomfortable it may be. Cursing my
name and birth they most certainly are. But if we catch a
torpedo I want our people, or as many of them as
possible, *on deck*, where they've got a chance.'

Jupp appeared at the door behind the helmsman
carrying a tray. "Ot cocoa, sir?'

Lindsay looked at Stannard, feeling the nervous tension dragging at his mind like one huge claw. 'You see,
Pilot? Someone remembered us!'

Stannard walked to the starboard side where Dancy
was peering through his night-glasses at the ship ahead.

'I wish you'd heard some of that, Sub.' He kept his voice
very quiet. 'Sometime in the future you could have tried
to write it all down.'

Dancy lowered his glasses. 'He cares, doesn't he?'

Stannard nodded slowly. 'By Christ, and how he cares.
I saw his face when we steamed through those wretched
devils in the drink back there. I've sailed with some
skippers in my time, but never anyone like this.'

Dancy said simply, 'I was scared to death.'

Stannard took a cup of cocoa from Jupp and held it in
his gloved hands. And so was he, he thought wearily.
Lindsay was making himself watch those men die with

something like physical force. Testing his own reserves and hating what he was doing.

He thought suddenly of a captain he had once served in a ship on the meat-run from Australia. They had gone to assist a Portuguese vessel which had lost her rudder in a storm off Cape Finisterre. And what a storm. Stannard had been a green third officer at the time, and the thought of standing by a crippled ship in such mountainous seas had made him swear it would be his last voyage, if he ever managed to reach port. The old captain had stayed on the bridge for three days without a wink of sleep, never resting until they had lifted off every man from the stricken ship. And that was after several attempts to take her in tow.

There had been a doctor travelling as a passenger on board at the time and Stannard had heard him say to the skipper, 'You *must* get some rest! Or *your* life will be in danger next!'

The skipper, a man of few words on most occasions, had regarded him indifferently. '*My* life, doctor?' He had walked up the pitching deck to the screen again. 'My life is obligations. Nothing else counts.'

Stannard had had his own troubles at the time and had not fully grasped the significance of those words.

He watched Lindsay as he craned over the gyro repeater, the unlit pipe still jutting from his mouth. But he understood now well enough. Perhaps better than any other man aboard.

13 Abandoned

Thirteen days out of Liverpool found the convoy steaming due south, with the Cape Verde Islands some three hundred miles on the port beam. All the colours had changed, yet few aboard the *Benbecula* had noticed the exact moment the transformation had come about. Instead of leaden grey the sea had altered its face to a deep blue, and above the spiralling mastheads the sky was of paler hue with just a few frayed banners of cloud to break its washed-out emptiness.

Lindsay sat in his chair feeling every movement as the ship heaved up and over in an uncomfortable corkscrewing motion. There was a stiff breeze to ruffle the blue water with a million busy cat's-paws, and with a quarter sea to add to the ship's plunging lifts and rolls he could feel the chair pressing into his body as if the bones were pushing through his skin.

Thirteen days. Long days and longer nights, with hardly a break for the men who came and went about their duties like dull-eyed robots.

Not only the weather had changed. The convoy was steaming in just two lines, and it was smaller. The day after the first ship had been torpedoed the *Pole Star* had received a similar fate. Except that the attack had been better planned and controlled, possibly by three U-boats simultaneously. She had taken two torpedoes in her side and had started to sink in minutes. Even before the bow-wave around her rust-streaked stem had died away a third torpedo had struck her dead amidships, blasting her into halves, the forepart sinking immediately, the stern section remaining afloat just long enough for a destroyer to scrape alongside and lift off the remaining survivors. That same day one of the escorts had been hit, the explosion shearing off her forecastle as cleanly as a giant welding torch, laying bare her inner hull for a few more minutes until she rolled over and disappeared with her straight white wake still marking where she had dived.

Encouraged by their success the U-boats had made a surface attack under cover of darkness, only to be caught and pinned down by starshells from one of the other destroyers. She had dropped far astern of the convoy to pick up some survivors sighted by the cruiser's Walrus flying-boat. In fact, they were from some other convoy, and they had *not* survived. Eight men in a scarred lifeboat who had not waved or cheered as the destroyer had come to find them. They must have been dead for several weeks. Just drifting with the currents and winds, already forgotten by the living world they had left behind.

The destroyer had chased after the convoy and even as she had been about to make the recognition signal had detected the surfaced U-boats directly across her bows.

In the eerie glare of drifting flares she had opened fire with every gun which would bear. One U-boat had managed to dive without being hit, but another had been seen to receive several shells so close alongside it was more than likely she would never reach home. But the third had been even less fortunate. In the eye-searing flares her commander may have misjudged the destroyer's bearing and distance. Or perhaps his stern tube had been unloaded and he was trying to engage with his bow torpedoes. Whatever the reason for his sudden turn, the result of it had been swift and definite.

At twenty-five knots the destroyer had rammed her just abaft the conning tower, riding up and over the low

whaleback of her casing with a scream of rending steel
which had been heard even aboard the *Benbecula*. Like a
gutted shark the U-boat had rolled over, breaking apart
as the destroyer continued to grind and smash across
her.

When daylight came the men on the rearmost ships of
the convoy had lined the guardrails to cheer the victorious destroyer, the sound wild and almost desperate as she
had turned away for the dangerous passage to Gibraltar.
With her bows buckled almost to her forward bulkhead
and her forecastle gaping open to the sea she would be
out of the war for some time to come. She had made a sad
but defiant sight as her low silhouette had finally faded
astern, and there were few men in the convoy who had
not prayed for her survival.

Nothing else had occurred for two whole days. Then
one of the tankers had been hit by a long-range torpedo,
her cargo spilling out around her broken hull like blood,
until with a great roar the oil had caught fire, encircling
the ship in a wall of flames which had almost trapped one
of the escorts which was attempting to pick up some of
her crew.

Lindsay put a match to his pipe and tried to concentrate his mind on the ships ahead. Without such constant
effort his eyes seemed to droop, so that he had to drag
himself to his feet, move about like some caged animal
until his circulation and brain returned to life.

Thirteen days. Two escorts gone and three merchant
ships. The two remaining lines were led by the commodore's troopship, *Cambrian,* and the cruiser *Madagascar.*
Just four ships in each line, with *Benbecula* now steaming
directly abeam of the ammunition freighter. The early
fear of having her in the convoy, and so close to the
Benbecula for most of the time, had given way to a kind of
nervous admiration. Day in, day out, through the U-boat
attacks and the desperate alterations of course and speed,
she was always there. Big and ugly like her name,

Demodocus, she had, according to Goss, been sailing under almost every flag in the book since she had been laid down some four years before the Great War. A coal-fired ship, she was usually on the receiving end of some caustic signal about making too much smoke, but either her master didn't give a damn or as Fraser had suggested, her chief engineer had his work cut out just to keep the boiler from bursting.

He saw some off-watch seamen sprawled on the forward hold cover. In the bright sunlight their faces and bared arms looked very pale, almost white. He was thankful that for the past twenty-four hours there had been neither an attack nor any more reports of U-boats from the Admiralty. The hands had been able to get some rest, enjoy a properly cooked meal, and above all to be spared the jarring clamour of alarm bells.

He could hear Stannard moving about the chart room. It was not his watch, so he was probably getting his personal log up to date.

Lieutenant Maxwell had the forenoon watch, and he was out on the port wing staring at the ammunition ship, his cap tilted over his eyes against the glare. His assistant, Lieutenant Anthony Paget, did not seem to know where to stand. Afraid perhaps of disturbing his captain he stayed on the starboard side of the bridge, but at the same time he seemed unwilling to stray out of Maxwell's vision, just in case he was needed.

Paget was Aikman's replacement. He appeared a pleasant enough chap, Lindsay thought. He had obtained his watchkeeping certificate in a corvette but had been in the Navy for only eighteen months. Before the war he had been a very junior partner in a firm of solicitors in Leeds. It was his father's business, otherwise he might have found it more difficult to get that far, Lindsay decided. He seemed rather shy and hesitant, and his previous captain had written in his personal report, 'Honest and reliable. But lacks qualities of leadership.'

But he was one of *Benbecula*'s lieutenants now, and more to the point, his watchkeeping qualifications would help to spread the load more evenly in a wardroom where most of the junior officers had no experience at all.

Petty Officer Hussey, the senior telegraphist, walked to Lindsay's side and saluted.

'Just the usual bulletins, sir. No U-boat reports.' He flicked over the neatly kept log. 'It seems that the Japs are still advancing though.' He held the log in the sunlight and squinted at it. 'Says that they've reached a place called Batu Pahat.' He grinned. 'Could be in Siberia as far as my geography is concerned, sir.'

The rear door slammed back. 'What was that?' Stannard stood in the reflected sunlight, his brass dividers grasped in one hand.

Lindsay said quietly, 'Batu Pahat.'

Stannard seemed to stagger against the voicepipes. 'But that's only sixty miles from Singapore, for God's sake! It can't be true. No army could move that fast!'

Paget said timidly, 'It's in the south-west corner of Malaya, sir.'

Stannard looked at him unseeingly. 'I know.'

Paget nodded eagerly. 'I read somewhere that there's a prosperous coastal trade for rubber and——.'

Lindsay said, 'Would you ask the chief bosun's mate to come to the bridge, please?'

As the lieutenant scurried for the rack of telephones Stannard said, 'Thanks, sir. You didn't have to do that. He didn't mean anything by it.'

'I know.' Lindsay watched him gravely. 'But sometimes one extra word is enough to drive a man mad.' He smiled. 'I expect your brother has been pulled out by now anyway. If Singapore Island is to be the real holding-point it would be the obvious thing to do.'

Stannard nodded. 'I guess so. But all these reports.' He shook his head. 'Surely to God the people in charge out there can see what's happening?'

Lindsay looked away. 'Some people never read the words, Pilot. They just check the commas!' He rubbed his eyes. 'Forget that. They're probably doing their best.'

Paget returned. 'C.P.O. Archer is coming right up, sir.'

'Good.' Lindsay settled down again on the chair. 'Now I'll have to think of something to tell him.'

'Yes, sir.' Paget looked completely lost.

A signalman shouted, 'Signal from escort, sir! *Merlin* has strong contact at zero-nine-zero. Closing!'

Paget stared at him, his mouth hanging open.

Lindsay snapped, 'Sound action stations!' He felt the sweat gathering under his cap. 'Well, jump to it, man!'

As bells shrilled through the ship he stood up and walked to the port wing where Maxwell was still looking at the ammunition ship.

'What's the matter, Guns? Didn't you hear that?'

Maxwell stared at him. 'Yessir. Sorry, sir.' He turned and ran for the control position as Hunter and the spotting team came pounding up the other ladder from the boat deck.

Ritchie was already here, brushing crumbs from his jacket and still chewing as he snatched his telescope and shouted, 'From commodore, sir. Alter course to two-five-zero!'

'Acknowledge.'

Lindsay gripped the screen, feeling the ship vibrating under his fingers as the voicepipes and telephones burst into life once again.

Ritchie's telescope squeaked as he readjusted it on the leading ships. 'Execute in succession, sir!'

Stannard was already at the gyro compass, his face expressionless while he studied the column wheeling slowly to starboard. The ship directly ahead was the convoy's remaining oil-tanker, a smart, newly built vessel which had already narrowly avoided a torpedo in the earlier attacks.

Ritchie said, '*Merlin*'s got 'er black pennant 'oisted, sir! She's goin' in for a kill!'

A messenger muttered, 'We *hope!*'

'Starboard ten.' Stannard's mouth twitched as a pattern of depth-charges exploded somewhere on the port quarter. The *Merlin* was moving at full speed and swinging in a wide arc while the sea erupted in her curving wake like some impossible waterspout.

'Midships.' Stannard twisted his head quickly to watch the straight black stem of the *Demodocus* following round in obedience to the signal. More explosions, and a second escort came tearing back down the column, racing for the great spreading area of churned water where the last charges had exploded.

As she ploughed through the white froth Lindsay saw the charges fly lazily from either beam, while two more rolled from her quarterdeck rack into her own wash. He could picture them falling through the untroubled depths, ten feet a second, and then. . . . Even though he was expecting it he flinched as the charges detonated and hurled their fury skyward. How long the columns of water seemed to hang there before subsiding into the growing area of foam and dead fish.

'*Madagascar*'s signallin', sir!' The man's voice was almost shrill. 'Torpedoes approachin' from starboard!'

Already the cruiser was turning her grey bulk towards the invisible torpedoes, while far away across the commodore's bows a destroyer was turning to race in to give additional cover.

'Must be two of the bastards, sir!' Stannard raised his glasses and added sharply, 'Watch the ship ahead, Cox'n. Follow her like a bloody sheepdog, no matter what happens!'

'Aye, aye, sir.' Jolliffe eased the spokes and kept his eyes fixed on the oil-tanker.

'Missed her anyway!' Dancy swung round as a double explosion rattled the bridge screen and brought down some flecks of paint on to his cap.

The freighter astern of the cruiser had been hit. The torpedoes must have passed between the two troopships in the starboard column, missed the cruiser, and struck the other vessel as she attempted to follow her leader in the turn.

She was already staggering to port, thick smoke billowing from her side, her bridge wing hanging towards the sea in a tangle of twisted metal and broken rigging.

A great flurry of froth rose around her counter and Stannard said, 'She's going astern. Her skipper must be trying to get the way off her to save the bulkhead.'

Lindsay held the glasses jammed against his eyes while the gratings jerked and vibrated to the thunder of depth-charges. He saw tiny figures running along the freighter's boat deck, while further aft there were others struggling to slip one of the heavy rafts over the side. There was a sudden internal explosion, so that the bridge superstructure appeared to lift and twist out of alignment, the funnel buckling and pitching into the smoke as if made of cardboard.

Whatever had caused the explosion must have killed everyone on the bridge, Lindsay thought. Or else the controls had been shattered by the blast. Whatever it was, the ship was still churning astern, her engine room probably too dazed or desperate to know what had happened on deck.

The freighter which had been following the torpedoed ship had at last understood the danger and her captain was reducing speed, his bow-wave dropping while the distance between him and the runaway freighter continued to diminish.

One of the lifeboats had reached the water, only to be upended by the reversed thrust, hurling its occupants overboard to vanish instantly in the churned wash from the propellers.

The other seamen had at last succeeded in releasing

the liferaft, but could only stand huddled by the guard-rails as their ship continued to forge astern. She was heeling very slightly and certainly sinking, but as the convoy fought to maintain formation she was still a very real menace.

'Commodore's signalled *Rios* to take evasive action, sir!'

The *Rios* was the one astern of the torpedoed freighter, and with something like a prayer Lindsay watched her turn unsteadily and head diagonally from the broken column.

'Torpedo to port, sir!' Dancy had the masthead tele-phone gripped in his fist so tightly his knuckles were white. 'Two cables!'

Lindsay lifted his glasses and saw the flurry of excite-ment on the ammunition ship's bridge. It must be run-ning straight for her.

A man screamed, 'If she goes up we'll go with her!'

'Silence on the bridge!' Jolliffe's voice was like a saw, but his eyes stayed on the ship ahead.

It was more of a sensation than a sound. Lindsay saw the other ship stagger, her foremast and derricks falling in tangled confusion even as the tell-tale column of water shot violently above her fore deck.

In those few seconds nobody spoke or moved. Even breathing seemed to have stopped. As the *Demodocus* started to slow down and fall past *Benbecula*'s port beam, to those who were able to watch her it felt as if there were just seconds left to live. The sea and sky, the depth-charges and fast-moving destroyers, none of them counted for anything now.

The torpedoed freighter, her screws still dragging astern, ploughed very slowly beneath the surface, her hull breaking up as she dived for the bottom. But it was doubtful if any man on *Benbecula*'s decks even saw her last moments or the few struggling figures caught in the last savage whirlpool above her grave.

Lindsay lowered his glasses and rubbed his eyes, the movement making Dancy jerk with alarm.

The old *Demodocus* was still there. There was plenty of smoke rising above the hidden wound, and as he held his breath he heard the discordant grinding of her port anchor cable running out. The explosion must have blasted away a capstan or sheered right through the forepart of the lower hull.

'They're callin' us up, sir.' Ritchie cradled the Aldis on his arm and watched a small winking light from the other ship's bridge.

'Have fire in forrard hold.' He took another breath. 'Am holed port side but pumps are coping.' He gasped and then shuttered an acknowledgement before saying thickly, 'An' 'e says that there *is* a God after all!'

A telephone had been buzzing for some seconds. Or minutes. Nobody seemed to understand anything any more.

Then a messenger said, 'W/T office reports that the escorts have sunk another U-boat, sir. Definite kill.'

Lindsay wiped his face with his hand. It was clammy.

'That will keep them quiet for a bit.' He felt unsteady on his feet. As if he was recovering from some terrible bout of fever.

'From commodore, sir.' Ritchie was very calm. "E's callin' up the ammo ship.' He smiled grimly. 'Can't never pronounce 'er name, sir. 'E's enquirin' about damage, sir.'

Lindsay walked out on to the port wing and looked at the other column. The cruiser, the *Rios*, which had narrowly avoided being rammed by the sinking freighter, and now, dropping still further astern, the ugly bulk of the ship whose name Ritchie could not pronounce.

Eleven left of the seventeen which had headed so bravely from Liverpool.

Ritchie said suddenly, 'She's tellin' the commodore she can only manage five knots till they've carried out repairs, sir. But the fire's almost under control. There was no ammo in *that* 'old, sir.' He watched the slow winking light. 'But the next 'old is filled to the brim with T.N.T.'

Lindsay looked at Stannard. 'Near thing. She may still have to abandon. Tell Number One to warn the boat crews and lowerers.'

A destroyer was edging past the *Demodocus*'s hidden side, her raked masts and funnel making a striking contrast to the bulbous hull and outdated upperworks of the ammunition ship. As she moved into full view Lindsay saw she was the *Merlin*.

Her loud-hailer squeaked and then boomed into life. 'I have a message for you, Captain!'

Lindsay trained his glasses on the slow moving destroyer. The open bridge with the officers and lookouts standing down from their last battle, their last kill.

Her captain's face swam into the lenses, reddened by sea and wind, but the same man he had seen in the office at Scapa. He, at least, had something to be proud of. He had sunk a U-boat and damaged at least one other.

Lindsay picked up the megaphone and shouted, 'Well done, *Merlin!*'

As he said the words he felt a new upsurge of resentment and despair. To this young destroyer officer *Benbecula* would not be seen as anything more than just another charge to be escorted and protected. A big, vulnerable liability.

The loud-hailer continued, 'From the commodore. You will stand by *Demodocus* and act as her escort. He feels the risk to the troopships is too great to slow down.' He added almost apologetically, 'The cruiser too is somewhat naked under these conditions.'

Behind him Lindsay heard Dancy whisper fiercely, 'What's he saying? No escort? We're being left behind?'

The destroyer was starting to gather speed again. The voice called, 'By dawn tomorrow you should be joined by other escorts. But I'm pretty sure there are no more

U-boats in the vicinity now. If there are, they'll keep after the convoy.'

Lindsay lifted one hand to him. 'Good luck!'

He watched the destroyer surging ahead. Good luck. That young man certainly had that, and more. But it was hard to hide the hurt, the knowledge that he could have been on that bridge. Being useful.

He turned his back on the other ships. 'Signal *Demodocus* to take station astern. Find out her exact speed and reduce revs accordingly.'

Stannard was still watching the oil-tanker. She was drawing away so fast it made it appear as if *Benbecula* was going astern. Lights were flashing and more signal flags were breaking from the commodore's yards. The escorts re-formed and the cruiser altered course to lead the single line of merchantmen like an armoured knight watching over his private possessions. In fifteen minutes the convoy was so far away that the ships which had been old friends had lost their meaning and personality. In an hour there was little to see at all. Just a smudge of smoke on the horizon, a single bright flash of sunlight on the bridge screen of an escort as she turned in another sweep for echoes from below.

Ritchie said quietly, 'Now *'ere's* a fine thing, Swain.'

Jolliffe darted a glance at the officers and nodded. 'I know. A D.S.O. for the commodore, D.S.C. for the escort commander, and medals all round, I shouldn't wonder.' He grinned. 'An' us? We'll be lucky if we *sees* the bloody dawn tomorrow, let alone a soddin' escort!'

Stannard said, 'Look at the damage, sir.'

Lindsay followed him on to the port wing and studied the ship astern. It was a great gash, as if another vessel had rammed her at full speed. Smoke was still billowing from the hole and the deck immediately above. But there was less of it, and he could see plenty of activity on the forecastle where men were working to clear away some of the debris from the fallen derricks. It must be like

standing on one gigantic floating bomb, he thought. And
if the fire got out of hand again or the next bulkhead
became overheated, that would be that.

He said, 'Fall out action stations.'

Stannard looked surprised.

'Well, Pilot, if there *is* a U-boat about we can't see it, and
we can't damn well hear it, so where's the point of
wearing everyone down for nothing.' He touched Stannard's arm. 'Anyway, if there *was* one of the commodore's
Huns about, I think he would have announced his presence by now.'

Stannard nodded. 'I guess so.'

'But double the lookouts and keep all short-range
weapons crews closed up.'

Stannard hurried away as Goss mounted the bridge
ladder and stood breathing heavily for several seconds.
Then he swivelled his head slowly from side to side as if
still unable to grasp that the convoy had vanished.

Ritchie called, 'Ammo ship 'as R/T contact now,
sir.'

Lindsay strode quickly to the W/T office where Hussey
and his telegraphists slumped wearily in their steel
chairs.

Hussey said, 'Here you are, sir.' He handed a microphone to Lindsay and added shortly, 'Permission to
smoke, sir? My lads are just about dead beat.'

Lindsay nodded and snapped down the button. '*Benbecula* to *Demodocus*. This is the captain speaking. How is it
going?'

The telegraphists looked up at the bulkhead speaker as
a tired voice replied, 'Thanks for staying with us. We're
not doing too bad. But the collision bulkhead is weeping a
bit and I've got the hands shoring it up as best they can.
There's still a fire in the forrard hold, and we've no
breathing apparatus. Nobody can work down there for
more'n minutes at a time.' They heard his sigh very loud
on the speaker. 'Can't make much more'n four knots. If

that bloody bulkhead collapses the hold will flood. With the weight of cargo forrard it'll damn near lift my arse out of the drink! Then he laughed. 'Still, better that way than how the Jerry intended, eh?'

Lindsay said, 'Keep a good lookout astern, Captain. I'm going to drop a boat and send some breathing gear and extra hands.'

'I'm obliged.' A pause. 'A doctor too if you can spare him. Mine was killed by the blast and I've twelve lads in a bad way.'

'Will do.' Lindsay saw Ritchie in the doorway. 'Tell the first lieutenant. Quick as you can.'

He hesitated and then spoke again into the microphone. 'At the first sign of trouble, Captain, bale out. I'll do what I can.'

The speaker went dead and he returned to the bridge wing.

Goss said, 'I've got things going, sir. Boat will be ready for lowering in five minutes. I'm sending Lieutenant Hunter to take charge. Doc's already on the boat deck.' He added, 'I'll go myself if you like.'

'No.' Lindsay watched the port motor boat swinging clear of its davits. 'I need you here.'

Goss shrugged. 'Won't make much difference anyway if another U-boat arrives.'

It took another half-hour to ferry the required men and equipment to the other ship and recover the motor boat. Groups of unemployed seamen and marines crowded the *Benbecula*'s poop to watch the activity as hoses were brought to bear on the burning hold and a winch came to life and started to haul some of the debris clear of the fore deck.

All afternoon the work continued while the two ships ploughed across the blue water at little more than a snail's pace.

Aboard *Benbecula* the atmosphere was unreal and strangely carefree. In close convoy, with U-boats reported in every direction, death had seemed very near. But like most men in war, it had to happen to others, never to you. Now, without escort or aid of any kind, the mood was entirely different. Men went about their duties with a kind of casual indifference. Like people Lindsay had seen in the London air-raids. They could *do* nothing, so what the hell, the mood seemed to suggest.

C.P.O. Archer and his men had checked the liferafts for instant lowering, and as the sun began to dip towards a hazy horizon most of the ship's company appeared to accept the inevitable.

The last dog watch had almost run its course when a signalman said sharply, 'There's someone callin' us up, sir!'

Ritchie had been squatting on a flag locker, legs outstretched as if asleep, but he was across to the open wing before Lindsay could move from his chair.

'I don't see nothin'!'

The signalman pointed. 'There. On the upper bridge, Yeo.'

Lindsay trained his glasses and saw one of the ammunition ship's officers dimly outlined against the outdated compass platform, his arms moving very slowly like a child's puppet.

Ritchie raised his telescope and muttered, 'Bleedin' semaphore! 'Ow the 'ell does 'e expect me to read that in this light?'

Lindsay steadied his feet on the gratings. There was a lazy swell and the breeze had dropped considerably. At such slow speed it was difficult to hold the glasses on the tiny dark figure.

Ritchie gasped and said, ''E says there's somethin' astern, sir. Five miles or thereabouts.' He looked quickly at Lindsay's set features. 'Could be a submarine.'

Lindsay lowered his glasses. The ammunition ship had become part of the scene. Familiar. Almost part of themselves. It seemed impossible that anything could happen now. Just like this.

He said, 'That captain is a very clever man, Yeoman.' He watched Ritchie's telescope wavering in the motion like a small cannon. 'Most men as tired and worried as he must be would have used a lamp, or even worse, the R/T.'

Goss came hurrying from the chart room. 'What's it doing?'

Lindsay said, 'Go aft, Yeoman, and keep contact with the bridge by the poop telephone.'

To Goss he added, 'Reduce to dead slow and close the gap. We *must* keep visual contact. Their lookouts may be able to see the U-boat, but if we try and turn they'll know we've spotted them.'

Stannard asked, 'Why doesn't the bastard fire, sir?'

Goss nodded. 'Christ knows we're moving slow enough. He could catch us up in no time.'

A messenger called, 'W/T office reports no signals, sir.'

Lindsay nodded slowly. It could just be possible the U-boat had been damaged in that last attack. Maybe she could not dive, or perhaps her torpedo tubes had been put out of action by depth-charges. But she was back there all the same. Limping along like a wounded wolf, and every bit as dangerous.

He glanced quickly at the masthead pendant. It was flicking out very gently towards the stern. The wind was still coming from the south-east.

He turned and stared unblinkingly at the dipping sun. It was too high. The slow-moving ships would stand out against the horizon as perfect targets for another half-hour, maybe longer.

'I think the U-boat is going to close and use his deck gun.'

Even as he spoke his thoughts aloud he knew he was committing himself. All of them.

Goss stared at him. 'But if they get one shell into that bloody ship——.' He could not go on.

Stannard said tersely, 'Shall I signal them to abandon, sir? We could drop all our boats and rafts and maybe come back for them later.'

Lindsay was still watching the ship astern. Big, solid and black. That U-boat commander would recognise her all right. Would probably know her lethal cargo down to the last bullet. It would make up for the way his own command had been mauled. The terror of his men as the charges had rained down from the hunters on the surface.

'Leave her, you mean?' He spoke very quietly. 'Run away?'

Goss said, 'It's not that. We've the ship to consider. Our own people.'

A signalman called, 'The yeoman says that the ammo ship can still see the U-boat, sir. On the surface. Full buoyancy.'

Lindsay thought briefly of the *Demodocus*'s master. A man he would dearly like to meet. Someone who, despite the hideous death which was so close to him and his men, could note the small but vital details. No U-boat would chase after its prey fully trimmed to the surface. It would be ballasted well down with just part of the casing and conning tower visible. It *must* be damaged. It was their only hope.

'Tell the yeoman to use his Aldis. It should be masked from the U-boat by the other ship. I want the *Demodocus* to start another fire. It'll be damn dangerous. But her captain will know the risks without my telling him. Oily rags, anything, but I want plenty of smoke.'

He pushed past the others and snatched up the engine room handset. 'Chief? This is the captain.'

Fraser chuckled. 'I thought you'd forgotten us.'

'Listen. I want you to make smoke, everything you can do to produce the biggest fog in creation! Just as soon as I give the word!'

'Aye, sir.' Lindsay heard him yelling to his assistant,

Dyke, above the roar of fans. Then he asked calmly, 'Might I be told the reason, sir?'

'Yes. We're going to engage a surfaced U-boat.'

He dropped the handset as Stannard said, 'They've got a fire going already. God, I'd have thought the worst if I'd not heard your order.'

Lindsay saw the pall rising rapidly astern. 'Sound action stations.' He grasped Goss's arm. 'I'm going to go hard astarboard in about ten minutes.' He saw Goss's anxious features and wondered if he was fearing for his life or that of the ship. 'The fact that the U-boat's made no W/T signals doesn't mean she won't very soon. Her radio may be damaged, but if they once get it going again we're done for.' He had to yell above the alarm bells. 'So go to damage control, and *pray!*'

Dancy called, 'Ship at action stations, sir.'

'Very good. Tell control to stand by. Maxwell will have to engage with the starboard battery.'

He looked at Stannard. 'Inform the chief. Make smoke now.'

He turned to watch the thick greasy cloud which started to gush over the funnel's lip almost before Stannard had replaced the telephone. He made himself wait a few more minutes, feeling the ship heaving uneasily beneath him, trying to estimate her turning circle under such desperate circumstances.

'Ready, Cox'n?'

Jolliffe nodded. 'Ready, sir.'

'Pilot?'

Stannard forced a grin. 'As I'll ever be, sir.'

Lindsay took out his pipe and thrust it between his teeth. 'Stop starboard. Full ahead port.' He counted more seconds, feeling the deck shuddering violently to the added thrust on one shaft. 'Hard astarboard!'

He glanced through a stern scuttle at the dense smoke. Already the angle was changing. 'Starboard engine full astern!'

He turned again to face the empty sea beyond the bows. Perhaps it could not be done. There was nothing in the book to say it should even be attempted. But there was little in any of those books about the war either, he thought.

'Midships! *Full ahead together!*'

14 Hitting back

Heeling steeply to the violent thrust of screws and rudder the *Benbecula* thrashed round until she was steering almost the reverse of her original course. Lindsay stood in the centre of the bridge, his glasses level with his chin as he waited for a first sight of the enemy. The fore deck was almost hidden in a thick, choking fog from the funnel, as caught by a sudden down-draught and aided by the change of direction the wind fanned Fraser's screen over the ship in a solid wall. Lindsay knew they must be passing the *Demodocus* somewhere to starboard, although her improvised smokescreen was so thick she could have been a mile away or fifty yards. Even with the doors closed Lindsay could taste the acrid stench, just as he could hear the lookouts on the upper bridge retching and gasping above the din of racing engines. He lowered his eyes a few inches to the gyro.

'Steer zero-one-zero!'

He heard Jolliffe's quick reply but kept his eyes fixed on the thinning pall of smoke across *Benbecula*'s line of advance. Soon now and he would know if he had been right. Justified.

The U-boat commander may have seen the two ships as stragglers from the convoy, which indeed they were, and was so confident that he considered it wasteful to use his remaining torpedoes.

Lindsay dashed a trickle of sweat from his eyes. If that was the case, and the U-boat was undamaged, one salvo from her bow tubes would be enough. With *Benbecula* working up to her maximum revolutions the effect would be too terrible to contemplate.

Maxwell's voice came over the bridge speaker, detached and toneless. 'Starboard battery stand by.'

Lindsay dropped his gaze to the fore deck and saw the two starboard guns moving their muzzles slightly, like blind things in the swirling smoke. Further aft de Chair's marines would have to remain inactive for the present. Their starboard gun could not bear on the target if Lindsay's calculations were correct. *If, if, if.* The word seemed to hammer in his brain as if someone had shouted it aloud.

Slivers of spray spurted over the bows, and he knew that Fraser's gauges were well into the danger mark now. The old ship was shaking and groaning to the whirling screws and the whole bridge seemed to be quaking under the strain.

Maxwell's voice cut above the other sounds, as if he had the handset right against his lips. 'Submarine on the surface at Green two-five! Range oh-eight-oh!'

Lindsay gritted his teeth, willing the smoke to clear so that he could see what Maxwell and his spotters had sighted from their precarious position above the bridge.

There was a brief flash beyond the smoke and seconds later the sound of a shellburst. For an instant longer he imagined the enemy had already anticipated his move, was even now slamming a shell towards *Benbecula* to make her sheer away and present a perfect target for torpedoes.

Through the smoke there was another flash, the sullen bang of an explosion.

Lindsay glanced at Stannard and said, 'He's shooting at the ammunition ship!'

When he turned his head again he saw the U-boat. Even at four miles range her austere silhouette was exactly as he had pictured it in his mind. The dying sunlight seemed very bright on the slim conning tower, so that it looked as if it was made of pure copper.

Then the bells rang below the bridge and both six-inch guns fired in unison.

It seemed an age before the shells reached the narrow target. Then as Lindsay jammed his glasses against his eyes he saw twin columns of bursting water astern of the U-boat, very white against the darkening horizon.

'Over. Down two hundred.' Maxwell could have been at a practice shoot. Lindsay had never heard him so cool.

He watched the sudden reaction on the U-boat's fore deck, holding his breath. She was turning, steering almost on a converging course now. But she was still high on the water, the bow-wave creaming along her rounded saddle tanks as she completed the slight turn.

The bells sounded once more and both guns lurched back on their springs, the shockwaves rattling the bridge screens like gale-force winds.

Lindsay bit his lip as both shells ploughed into the sea to the right of the target.

There was an answering flash from the U-boat's deck gun, and he felt the hull shudder as the shell ploughed alongside and exploded, hurling up a great column of water and smoke as splinters clanged over the bulwark.

Lindsay felt very calm. Whatever happened in the next few moments would decide the fate of his own ship and that of the damaged *Demodocus.* But one thing was certain. The German captain could not dive, nor could he use torpedoes. He would have done both by now if it was humanly possible. Lindsay could imagine the consternation on that conning tower as Maxwell's six-inch shells ripped down on them, getting closer with each agonising second. And it must have all looked so easy. Just two more stragglers from a convoy and not an escort within miles.

Smoke funnelled back from the bows, and Lindsay heard the screeching crash of a shell exploding between decks.

'Range oh-six-two.'

He banged the teak rail by the screen with his clenched

fist. The U-boat showed no sign of turning and her gun
was firing with even greater rapidity than before. Just
one good shot and *Benbecula* could be slowed or stopped
while the German manoeuvred to a more favourable
position. Right ahead of the bows where not a single gun
would bear.

A shell ripped past the bridge and exploded somewhere astern. It made a terrible sound, like tearing
canvas, and so close that a gyro repeater on the starboard
wing exploded like a small bomb, the fragments thud-
ding into the door and steel plates overhead.

Lindsay heard a man cry out and Maxwell snap, 'First
aid party on the double!'

Stannard yelled wildly, 'We've straddled the bastard!'
He was almost sobbing with excitement as two waterspouts bracketed the U-boat, burying her after casing
beneath tons of falling spray.

Two tiny figures pitched from the bandstand abaft her
conning tower, where a four-barrelled Vierling pointed
impotently at the sky, and vanished into the falling
deluge of water. One of the shells must have exploded
close enough to rake the stern with splinters.

Stannard said tightly, 'She's turning, sir!'

The bridge speaker intoned, 'Target has altered
course. Moving right. Number Three gun stand by to
engage!'

Lindsay said, 'I think his steering is damaged.'

The U-boat's forward gun flashed once more, and he
felt the deck jump beneath him as a shell exploded inside
the hull.

From the boat deck an Oerlikon opened fire, the tracer
drifting like lazy red balls towards the U-boat before
pitching down into the darkly shadowed troughs.

Maxwell sounded furious. 'Number Three Oerlikon
cease firing!'

Lindsay could imagine the lone Oerlikon gunner losing his self-control. Even the knowledge that his gun was

almost useless above a thousand yards, his training and Maxwell's discipline were not enough under such circumstances. Just to see the enemy. To watch him in the sights and be doing nothing about it was too much for any man.

He flinched as the two forward guns belched fire yet again. He had lost all idea of time and distance covered. His brain and hearing seemed lost in the crash of guns, the blasting returns from the U-boat.

A tall waterspout shot skyward beyond the German's hull and the other shell exploded directly against her side. It must have hit a saddle tank just beneath the surface, and for several seconds Lindsay imagined she had been blasted apart. As spray continued to fall he saw the black hull sliding clear, heard Stannard gasp, 'Oh, the bastards! They're still afloat!'

Lindsay steadied his glasses, waiting for some sort of reaction to take hold of him. He heard himself say, 'She's going over. Look, Pilot, the gun's crew are baling out.' Why was his voice so flat? So empty of excitement?

He moved his glasses very slightly to watch more dark shapes tumbling from the conning tower which was already tilting towards him. The way was off the hull and gigantic air bubbles were exploding on the surface alongside, like obscene glassy creatures from the depths.

'Reduce to half speed. Starboard ten.'

He swung around as the second gun on the well deck lurched inboard, the shell exploding alongside the U-boat's listing hull like a fireball.

Lindsay shouted, 'Cease firing!' He lowered his eye to the gyro. 'Midships. Steady. Steer zero-four-five.'

That last one had been more than enough. The U-boat's bows were lifting very slowly above the dotted heads in the water. Greedily the sea was already clawing along her buckled after casing, dragging a corpse with it as it advanced.

Lindsay watched without emotion. The Atlantic was

having another victory. It was as impartial as it was ruthless.

Dancy called, 'Damage control reports flooding in Number Three hold, sir. There's a fire on B deck, too.'

Lindsay kept his eyes fixed on the submarine. In the powerful lenses he could see the weed and slime on her exposed hull. She had probably been at sea for weeks, months. Maybe she would have been on her way home by now but for her commander's determination. The sight of two helpless, ungainly targets.

Almost distantly he asked, 'Is Number One coping?'

'Yessir.' Dancy's voice was shaking with emotion or barely suppressed excitement. 'But one man has been killed, sir. Twenty more wounded by splinters or burns.'

'Very well. Make a signal to *Demodocus* and request they send the doc to us as soon as possible.'

He turned and looked through a quarter scuttle. The black ammunition ship looked even darker now against the shadows. But she had stayed to watch the fight, even though she would have been blown to hell if *Benbecula*'s tactics had failed.

There was a yell, 'There she goes!' And from the upper deck Lindsay heard more shouts and then wild cheering as the submarine began to slide under the surface. For just a few more seconds she hung with her raked stem pointing straight at the sky, holding the last tip of sunlight from the horizon, as if burning from within. Then she vanished.

The cheering faltered and died, and Lindsay saw some of the seamen lining the guardrails to watch in silence as a patch of oil continued to spread across the water, making an even greater darkness, like the shadow of some solitary cloud. 'Slow ahead both engines.'

He let the glasses drop against his chest. He could almost feel what those men were thinking, their confusion and uncertainty. This was their first victory, probably one of the few occasions in which a ship built for peace had destroyed one created for war. Now it had happened, their emotions were lost in shock and disbelief.

Stannard said, 'Light's almost gone, sir.' He watched Lindsay's impassive face, waiting for a reaction.

Ritchie called, 'Motor boat from the ammo ship approachin', sir!'

'Very well. Pass the word to Number One's people to assist the doctor aboard.'

Lindsay walked slowly to the open door and stared at the shattered gyro repeater. There was a scorched black scar on the plating. The shell had been that near. Twenty feet and it would have exploded inside the wheelhouse. He thought of Stannard and Dancy, Ritchie and all the others who would have died with him.

Stannard joined him by the screen. 'Stop engines, sir?'

Lindsay watched the dark shape of a power boat chugging towards the side. 'Yes.' He knew Stannard was still there. Waiting. He added shortly, 'Put a party of our people in the boat and send it to pick up survivors. If there are any.'

He gripped the rail until the pain steadied him. He heard the telegraphs clang again, the sigh of water against the hull as the ship began to slow down. They had been made to steam past sinking ships. Men like themselves crying out and dying while they and other ships in convoy had obeyed the signal. Keep closed up. Don't look back.

Now there *was* time, and for a while anyway they were safe from further attack. So they would obey the code. Play out the game. Except that this time the survivors would be German and not their own.

Goss came up to the bridge and said, 'Fire's out, sir.' He sounded incredibly tired. Beaten. 'The pumps are holding the intake in the hold but the marines' messdeck has been destroyed. God, it looks like a pepperpot on the starboard side!'

Ritchie called from the wheelhouse, 'Ammo ship 'as just called us on R/T, sir. That one shell the Jerry slung at 'er seems to 'ave put 'er shaft out of line. 'Er chief says 'e don't reckon on bein' able to get even steerage way now.'

Lindsay removed his cap and turned to face the cool evening breeze. After all that, they would have to leave the other ship. Abandon her.

Aloud he said, 'If I'd known that before, I'd——'

Goss said, 'You'd have let those Jerries drown, sir?'

Lindsay looked at him, trying to control his aching mind. 'I think I would.'

Goss watched the motor boat as it started back for the *Benbecula*'s tall side. 'Not many of 'em left anyway.' He turned towards Lindsay. 'The *bastards!*'

Ritchie asked quietly, 'Any reply for the ammo ship, sir?'

Goss said, 'Could we stand by her till morning, sir?'

'Yes.' Lindsay replaced his cap. 'It would be safer than trying to transfer her crew in the dark.'

'I wasn't thinking of that.' Goss sounded strangely calm. 'We could take her in tow.'

Lindsay stared at him. 'Do you mean that?'

'I know we're not rigged for it. The old *Becky* was built for better things.' He spoke very quickly, as if he had made up his mind despite doubts and inner arguments. 'But with some good hands I could work all night an' lay out a towing cable. There's not much aft to help secure it, but I thought——'

'The twelve-pounder gun?'

'Yessir. It'll probably never fire again, but it'd make a damn fine towing bollard.'

Lindsay turned his face away. 'As far as I know it never *has* fired.'

There was so much to do. Plans to make and the damage to be inspected and contained. The wounded, too. And the men who had died.

But all he could think of now was Goss's voice and his

obvious conviction. It was even more than that. It was the first time since he had taken command that Goss had openly shared their mutual responsibility.

He nodded. 'Then we'll do it. At least we'll have a damn good try.' He beckoned to Stannard. 'Tell *Demodocus* we will stand by until first light. Explain what we are going to attempt.' He checked him. 'No, tell them what we are going to *do!*'

Goss shrugged his shoulders inside his heavy watch-coat. 'There may be fresh escorts coming for us tomorrow. But I expect they'll be sent from Freetown. Probably never find us anyway.' He tugged down the peak of his cap and stared at the promenade deck. 'Now I'll go and see what C.P.O. bloody Archer really knows about sea-manship!'

Lindsay stood on the gratings to watch the motor boat riding on the swell against the ship's rough plates.

'Number One.'

'Sir?' Goss paused, his foot in mid-air.

'Tell doc to make some arrangements for the German survivors. His sickbay must be getting rather crowded.'

'I'll lay it on.' He waited, knowing Lindsay had something more to say.

'And thanks, Number One.'

Goss swivelled around on the top of the ladder, squinting at Lindsay's silhouette dark against the sky. Then without another word he clattered down the ladder and vanished into the gathering darkness.

Lindsay took out his pipe and tapped it against the damp steel. Goss had his pride. It was unshakable, like his faith in this old ship. Just for a few seconds he had almost overcome it. But not quite.

He sighed and walked into the wheelhouse. 'Slow ahead both engines. Take the con, Pilot, until we can work out the drift. We don't want to ram the poor old *Demodocus* after getting this far.'

Stannard smiled gravely and walked to the compass.

He had heard most that had been said on the scorched starboard wing. He knew what it had cost Goss to make his suggestion about towing. He could have remained silent, and Lindsay would have abandoned the other ship. *God knows, he's done enough for all of us,* he thought, *without that.*

But Goss loved this ship more than life itself, and if he had to tow that bloody hulk with his bare hands to prove what his *Becky* could do, then Stannard had no doubt he would attempt that, too.

A telephone buzzed and the bosun's mate said, 'Sick-bay, sir. The doctor says there's one Jerry lieutenant amongst the survivors. 'E sends 'is thanks for us pickin' 'im up.' He waited. 'Any reply, sir?'

Stannard looked at Lindsay. 'Sir?'

'Just tell doc to do what he can for them.' He walked towards the chart room. 'But keep that bastard lieutenant off my bridge, *understood?*'

As the seaman spoke rapidly into the telephone Lindsay added from the doorway, 'What do they expect? A handshake? All pals again now that it's over for them?' His voice was quiet but in the sudden stillness it was like a whip. 'Well, not for me, Pilot. But if you happen to bump into this polite little German lieutenant on your rounds, you may tell him from me that I only picked them up for one reason. And that was to see what they *looked* like.'

'And now, sir?'

'Now?' He laughed bitterly. 'Now, I don't care. I don't give a damn.'

He seemed to realise they were all staring at him and added curtly, 'We will remain at action stations, but make sure the watchkeepers and lookouts are relieved as often as possible. Gun crews can sleep at their stations. And see what you can do about some hot food and have it sent around. There could be another U-boat about, although I doubt it.'

Stannard replied quietly, 'I'll do that, sir.' He watched Lindsay stagger against the open door, feeling for him, imagining what the strain was doing to him. He hesitated, 'And congratulations, sir. That was a bloody fine piece of work!'

Lindsay remained in the doorway, his face in shadow. 'You did well, Pilot.' He looked slowly around the darkened bridge. 'You all did.' Then he was gone.

Dancy moved to Stannard's side and said softly, 'I thought we'd had it.'

Stannard watched the pale arrowhead of foam riding back from the bows. 'Me, too. Now that we're still alive I don't really know if I'm on my arse or my elbow!'

Dancy nodded and ran his fingers along the smooth teak rail beside Lindsay's chair. It was impossible to understand. To grasp. In convoy he had been hard put to keep his fear from showing itself. Every minute had been an eternity. When on one occasion the ship's company had stood down from action stations he had been unable to go to his cabin, when moments earlier it had seemed the most important, the most vital goal in his existence. Sheer terror had prevented his going. He had found himself thinking of the brief Admiralty signals. Instead of six U-boats in the convoy's vicinity he had begun to think of the men inside them. Six submarines. That meant a total of some four hundred men. Four hundred Germans somewhere out there in the pitiless ocean, waiting, preparing to kill. To kill him. Even as he had crouched, sweating and wideawake below the bridge, he had imagined a torpedo already on its way. Silent and invisible, like those four hundred Germans.

The sudden action with the surfaced U-boat had changed all that, although he could not explain why or how. It was as if he had been pushed beyond some old protective barrier into another world. A no-man's-land. What was it the captain had called it? A killing ground. Sense, hope and reason were unimportant out here. Just the men near you. The ship around all of them. Nothing else counted.

Stannard said, 'Go and check around the messdecks, Sub. Make sure we're not showing any lights.'

Dancy replied, 'I could send someone.'

Stannard shook his head. 'You go. Walk about for a bit. It'll do more good than standing up here thinking. You can think too much.'

Jupp came into the wheelhouse. 'I've brought some sandwiches for the cap'n, sir.'

Stannard strode to the chart room and pulled open the door. Lindsay was sprawled across one of the lockers, one hand still reaching for a folio, his cap lying where it had fallen on the deck. He closed the door gently.

'Leave them, Jupp. I'll see he gets them later.'

Jupp nodded. 'Yessir.' Like Dancy, he did not seem to want to go.

Stannard said, 'Let him rest while he can. Christ knows, he's earned it.'

Steel scraped on steel and he heard Goss's resonant voice roaring along the promenade deck. He was at it already. Wires and strops, cable and jacks, it was something Goss had been doing all his life.

Stannard walked unsteadily across the gratings, massaging the ache in his limbs. He must have been standing as stiffly and rigid as one of de Chair's marines, he thought vaguely. *You did well, Pilot.* The words seemed to linger in his mind. Yet he could hardly remember moving throughout the action, giving an order, anything. Once he had thought of the girl in London, had tried to see her face.

He sighed. There was still a long, long way to go before they reached Trincomalee in Ceylon. And after that, where?

A signalman said, 'Ammo ship on the starboard bow, sir.'

Stannard shook his weariness away and hurried to the

screen. Time enough to worry about a future when this lot was finished.

'Port ten.' He rubbed his eyes. 'Midships.'

The watch continued, and in the dimly lit chart room Lindsay slept undisturbed either by dreams or memory, his outflung arm moving regularly to the motion of his ship.

At first light the next day the business of passing a towline was started. It took all morning and most of the forenoon, with motor boats plying back and forth between the ships to keep an eye on the proceedings. It took hours of backbreaking work and endless patience, and while Lindsay conned his ship as close as he dared to the drifting *Demodocus*, Goss strode about the poop yelling instructions until his voice was almost a whisper. Twice the tow parted even as *Benbecula*'s engines began to take the strain, and each time the whole affair had to be started from scratch.

The after well deck and poop were scarred and littered by wires and heavy cable, and the twelve-pounder gun mounting soon took on the appearance of something which had been squeezed in a giant vice.

But the third time it worked.

Ritchie said, 'Signal, sir. Tow secured.' He sounded doubtful.

'Slow ahead together.'

Once more the increasing vibration while very slowly the great length of towing cable accepted the strain.

Lindsay watched the other ship's massive bulk through his glasses, his eyes on an officer in her bows who was holding the bright flag above his head. Seconds, then minutes passed, with the *Demodocus* still apparently immobile in the shallow troughs, as if gauging the exact moment to break free again.

Quite suddenly her angle began to alter, and Lindsay saw the bright flag start to move above the officer's head in a small circle. Reluctantly the other vessel swung ponderously into the *Benbecula*'s small wake, her siren giving a loud toot as a mark of approval.

The tow did not part again, and when two destroyers found them on the following day both ships were still on course, the cable intact.

The senior destroyer made a complete circle around the two ships and then cruised closer to use a loud-hailer.

'Jolly glad we found you! It looks as if you've had a bad time!'

Lindsay raised his megaphone. 'Have you a tug on way?'

'Yes!' The other captain brought his ship even closer, and Lindsay saw the seamen lining her guardrails to look at the jagged splinter holes along *Benbecula*'s side. He added, 'You're damn lucky to be afloat! There was a report of a surfaced U-boat shadowing the convoy. But we'll take care of the bugger if she comes this way!'

Lindsay said quietly, 'Bring them on deck, Sub.'

He did not speak again until the German seamen and their lieutenant had been hurried on to the forecastle and lined up in the bright sunlight. He waited just a few more seconds and then called, 'We met up with her.' He saw their heads turn to stare at the small group on the forecastle. 'But thanks for the offer.'

Another day passed before a salvage tug appeared to take the crippled *Demodocus* in tow. They had made use of the time by ferrying ten badly wounded men to one of the destroyers. In Freetown they could get better attention, although it seemed to Lindsay as he watched them being lowered into the boats alongside that those who were conscious did not want to leave.

And when the tow was released he had that same feeling. He had still not met the ammunition ship's master and probably never would. But as she wallowed slowly abeam while the tug's massive hawser brought her under control Lindsay saw him standing on his bridge, his hand raised in salute. Along the upper deck his men waved and cheered or just watched the strange ship with a list to starboard and her dazzle paint pitted with splinter holes until she was lost in a sea haze.

Goss came on to the bridge, his hands filthy, his uniform covered in oil and rust. He shaded his eyes to watch the little procession as it turned eastward and then said gruffly, 'Well, *that* showed 'em.'

Stannard and Dancy were beside Lindsay, while the new lieutenant, Paget, was hovering nervously some feet away. But they all saw it. Even Jolliffe, who had been on the wheel with hardly a break, feeling the strain, nursing his helm against the tremendous weight of the tow.

Goss turned to face Lindsay and said, 'I don't reckon you could have done better, even if you'd been in the company.' Then he held out his hand. 'If you wouldn't mind, sir.'

Lindsay took it. He could see the faces around him, blurred and out of focus, just as he could feel the power of Goss's big fist. But he could not speak. Try as he might, nothing would come.

Goss added slowly, 'We've had differences, I'll not deny it. She should have been my ship by rights.' He stared up at the masthead pendant. 'But that was in peace. Now I reckon the old girl needs both of us.'

Lindsay looked away. 'Thank you for that.' He cleared his throat. 'Thank you very much.' Then he strode into the wheelhouse and they heard his feet on the ladder to his cabin below.

Goss was looking at his grimy fist, and then saw Paget staring at him with something like awe.

'What the bloody hell are you gaping at, *Mr* Paget?' He bustled towards the ladder muttering, 'Amateurs. No damn use the whole lot of 'em!'

Stannard looked at Dancy and then said quietly, 'They

always said there was *something* about this ship, in the company.' He glanced around him as if seeing her for the first time. 'Well, now I believe it. By God, I believe it!'

Then he looked forward and added, 'Now get those bloody Jerries below decks. I'd forgotten all about them!'

As Dancy hurried away he heard Stannard murmur, 'A will of her own, they used to say. And by God, I've just seen her use it!'

15 The dinner party

Lindsay stood on the gratings of the starboard bridge wing and watched the seething activity along the jetty below him. There seemed to be hundreds of coloured dockyard workers running in every direction at once, although from his high position Lindsay could see the purpose as well as the apparent chaos.

Heaving lines snaked ashore, seized by a dozen brown hands, all apparently indifferent to the hoarse cries from *Benbecula*'s petty officers, as very slowly the hull touched against the massive piles which protected it from the uneven stonework.

The lines were followed by heavy mooring wires, the eyes of which were cheerfully dropped on to huge bollards along the jetty, with no small relief from the officers on the forecastle and poop, as with tired dignity *Benbecula* nudged a few more feet before tautening springs halted her progress altogether.

A messenger called, 'Back spring secured, sir.' He was staring at the shimmering white building beyond the jetty and harbour sheds, handset pressed against his ear. 'Head spring secure, sir.'

Lindsay saw Goss waving from the forecastle, his bulk even more ungainly in white shirt and shorts.

'All secure fore an' aft, sir.'

'Very well.'

Lindsay leaned still further over the screen, feeling the sun across his neck as he watched the mooring wires slackening and tautening in the gentle swell.

'Out breast ropes. Then tell the buffer to rig the brow.'

He could see other white uniforms on the jetty amidst the busy workers, faces raised to watch as *Benbecula* handed over her safety to the land once again.

'Ring off main engines.'

He heard the telegraphs clang, the dials below swinging to *Finished with Engines,* where no doubt Fraser and his men would give a combined sigh of relief.

It had been a slow passage to the jetty. The whole of Trincomalee seemed to be packed with shipping of every description, so that even the two tugs which had been sent to assist had not found the last few cables very easy. Warships and supply vessels. Troopers, their rigging adorned with soldiers' washing like uneven khaki bunting, harbour craft and lighters, as well as an overwhelming mass of local vessels of every kind. Dhows and sampans, schooners and ancient coasters which looked as if they had been born in the first days of steam.

The gratings gave one last quiver and then lay still beneath him.

Ritchie said, 'One of the troopers is the *Cambrian,* sir.'

'Yes.'

Lindsay did not turn. Perhaps, like himself, the yeoman was thinking back to those first days out from Liverpool, with the commodore's ship leading the starboard line. Remembering the explosions and fires flickering across the dark water. The wasted effort, and the cost.

He heard Stannard speaking into a voicepipe and tried to imagine what he was thinking.

And at one time it had at last seemed that everything was going to be all right. A change of luck, if you could call it that.

After leaving the ammunition ship they had continued into a kinder climate, with something like a holiday atmosphere pervading the ship for the first time. Eighteen days out of Liverpool they had crossed the Equator

and all work had stopped for the usual boisterous ceremony of Crossing the Line. He could see it now. Jolliffe as
Neptune in a cardboard crown and carrying a deadly-
looking trident, his heavy jowls hidden in a realistic beard
made of spunyarn. His queen had been one of Boase's
S.B.A.'s, a girlish-looking youth whose sex, it had often
been said, was very much in doubt anyway.

Sunshine and blue skies, bodies already showing a
growing tan, and an extra tot of rum to complete the
ceremony. It had seemed a sure sign for the better.

They had paused in Simonstown to replenish the fuel
bunkers, and the ship's company had swarmed ashore to
see the sights and gather all the usual clutter of souvenirs
which would eventually find their way to mantelpieces
and shelves the length and breadth of Britain.

Barker had arranged for buses to take libertymen on to
Cape Town in a manner born. For just that one day he
had not been the supply officer to an armed merchant
cruiser. He was a ship's purser, and took as many pains to
make the short trips and tours successful as if every man
had been a first class passenger.

Then they were at sea again, and Lindsay could recall
exactly the moment Stannard had come to his cabin.
Benbecula had rounded the Cape and was steaming
north-east into the Indian Ocean for the last long haul of
her voyage.

All at once their own small world had been changed.
The outside events, the war, all that went with it had come
crowding in once more.

The Japanese had not been halted. That strip of water
between Singapore Island and the mainland was not an
English Channel as everyone had claimed it to be. The
enemy had crossed it and were already advancing into
the island itself. It was impossible but it was happening.

Stannard had stood in the sunlit cabin watching Lindsay as he had read the signal.

'What d'you think, sir? Will they pull our lads out?'

Looking back to that moment it was hard to remember what he had really believed. Not another retreat, surely? For this time there could be no Dunkirk with friendly white cliffs within reach of those brave or foolhardy enough to try for them. No sane man would write off the whole garrison. Not an army. It was inconceivable, just as now, standing on the sunlit bridge he could see it had been inevitable.

There had been a security clampdown on signals and little more was heard of that other war. *Benbecula* had continued across the Indian Ocean, enjoying perhaps the waters which had once been so familiar to her well-worn keel. They had passed several convoys heading in the opposite direction. Meat and grain from Australia and New Zealand, oil from the Gulf. The very stuff of survival for the people who waited in England for those ships to arrive.

The *Benbecula*'s people had watched them pass. Had waved and laughed at the usual exchange of crude or witty signals. Inwardly they had thought of that other ocean which still lay awaiting those convoys. Which they had endured and somehow survived to get this far.

Lindsay had watched Stannard going about his duties with growing concern. And he was not the only one with Singapore on his mind. Several men had brothers and friends there. Some even had fathers and uncles on the island, so great were the demands of war.

Then, just a week ago, while *Benbecula* had been passing within visual distance of the Seychelles, the news had broken. Singapore had fallen. The Gibraltar of the Far East, as it had been so often described by the press, had surrendered. And with it, every man who had been unable to escape on the few vessels left afloat by Japanese bombers.

Commodore Kemp's fast convoy, or the remains of it, still lay in Trincomalee with many other ships which had been expecting to go to Singapore's aid. Many a soldier would be thanking God right now that they had not arrived in time to be sacrificed for nothing.

Stannard came out to the wing and saluted. He was wearing sun-glasses and it was impossible to read his expression.

'All secure, sir. Permission to clear the bridge?'

'Carry on.' He hesitated and then said quietly, 'Look, Pilot, it may not mean your brother is still out there. He might have been one of the lucky ones.'

Stannard looked down at the milling figures which were struggling to assist Archer's seamen with securing the brow.

'I don't know whether I wish him dead or a prisoner. You've heard what the Japs have been doing to prisoners.' He added with sudden bitterness, 'And it seems to me the chance of our ever retaking Singapore, or any other bloody place for that matter, is pretty remote.'

'I know how you must feel.'

Stannard turned. 'Yes. I know how I feel, too. It's Jason I'm thinking about. Never been out of Aussie in his life. He's not like us. He's just a kid.' He saluted. 'I'll carry on then, sir.' Then he swung round and hurried into the wheelhouse.

Goss had appeared on the wing, his red face running with sweat. 'What's up with him then?'

'His brother.'

Goss nodded. 'Yes. I forgot.' He sighed. 'I reckon the dockyard people will be aboard to see about the damage, sir.' He glared at the crowded jetty below. 'We'll have to screw everything down to stop those bloody wogs from stealing it!'

'You deal with it.'

Lindsay watched him wearily. Goss had withdrawn into his old shell. Or partly. But there was a difference now. An unspoken understanding. One which had been sealed with a handshake. Lindsay knew he did not have to ask. It was unbreakable. Like the man.

'Aye.' Goss jerked his thumb vaguely. 'What'll they do with all these troopships and the squaddies?'

Lindsay watched some uniformed figures starting towards the brow. The first visitors. Questions and reports. Assessments and promises.

'Who knows? India maybe. South to Australia if the Japs look like getting that far.'

Goss scowled. 'It's all getting too big for me.' He too was watching the white figures at the brow.

'I'll go an' see 'em aboard, sir.' He showed his teeth. It was almost a grin. Then he pointed to the tall funnel where a grey submarine had been painted with a swastika below it. 'Reckon that'll take some of the starch out of their breeches!'

Maxwell climbed to the bridge and saluted. In his shorts and gleaming white shirt he looked as thin as a stick. A ramrod.

'I'm O.O.D., sir. The ambulances are arriving for our wounded. And an escort for the Jerries.'

'Good.'

Lindsay watched him march away. He had changed, too. He still made a lot of noise but was withdrawn and seemed to avoid the other officers whenever possible.

He had expected to hear of Maxwell's boasting about the accuracy of his guns and the sinking of a U-boat. Also that for once, the marines had been left out of it.

When he had congratulated Maxwell he had replied curtly, 'What I was trained for, sir. Given time, you can even teach a block of wood to shoot straight.' And that was all he had said.

Lindsay looked up at the painted U-boat and wondered why he had kept the prisoners aboard. He could have dropped them at Simonstown or passed them to the destroyers which had come to search for him and the *Demodocus*. He had seen them once or twice as they were exercised on the after well deck. A dozen in all, including the lieutenant who took his walks alone but for an escort.

He had even used his binoculars to study them without knowing why. What had he expected to see? Some sign of a master race? Superior beings which in captivity could still display their arrogance? For the most part they had looked very ordinary.

So perhaps he was getting like Goss and his submarine painted on the funnel. He wanted to show the Germans off like trophies. Heads taken in battle. Scalps.

He ran his hand over his neck and shuddered. The sun must be hotter than he had realised.

He glanced briefly at the wheelhouse, deserted now and strangely peaceful. Then he ran lightly down the bridge ladder and then another to A deck where an entry port had been opened to receive the heavy wooden brow from the jetty. He passed groups of ratings who had been dismissed from duty, already on their way below to prepare for shore leave. They seemed cheerful, even jubilant, and he could guess that they were still reliving their small victory. But once ashore they might find it even smaller, he thought. Other events had already outweighed and outreached one sunken U-boat, no matter what the circumstances had been.

Further aft some marines were busy polishing boots, apparently determined to retain their usual smartness in spite of having their messdeck blasted to blackened fragments.

He paused and looked at the smoke-grimed paintwork, the bright scars of deflected splinters, and was suddenly moved. After a destroyer, he had seen this ship as the end of the line. A limbo from which there was no return, and in which he could find no future.

Now he knew differently. And when the U-boat's last shell had shaken the bridge beneath his feet he had felt something more than anxiety. Affection, love, there was no proper word for it. But it was there all the same.

Maybe most of his officers had been appointed to her because they were not much use for anything better. The majority of the ratings had been untrained to the ways of war, so they too had been sent to make up the required numbers. His own appointment he understood well enough and had accepted it.

But somehow, back there over the hundreds of miles from the Arctic Circle to Ceylon, they had come together, and that was more than could be said for many ships.

Like Goss, *Benbecula* was all he had. Now, he needed her to go on living.

Goss was waiting by the entry port, an elegant lieutenant in white drill at his side.

The latter saluted smartly and announced, 'Commodore Kemp sends his compliments, sir, and would you join him at his residence for dinner?'

Lindsay nodded. 'Very well.'

'The admiral would like to see you too, of course, sir. But he sends his regrets and is unable to do so until tomorrow. You will be informed of the time, of course, sir.'

Of course. 'Thank you.'

The lieutenant gazed around at the nearby splinter holes. 'The wires were fairly humming about your U-boat, sir.' He sighed. 'But we are rather involved with this other unhappy affair at present.'

Boots clumped on the planking as the German prisoners marched towards the entry port, some military policemen bringing up the rear. Lastly, their lieutenant, who had miraculously retained his cap after jumping from the sinking submarine and being hauled into the motor boat, walked alone towards the sunlight.

Seeing Lindsay and the others he threw up a stiff salute which was returned with equal formality by Kemp's lieutenant.

The German made as if to speak but Lindsay turned away until he heard the footsteps recede down the brow.

He heard the lieutenant say testily, 'That man over

there! Don't you know you should stand to attention when an officer passes, enemy or not?'

That man there was unfortunately Fraser. Hatless, his boiler suit almost black from a recent inspection in the bilges, he was leaning against a ventilator shaft, his slight body bowed with fatigue. He stood up very slowly and stared at the angry lieutenant.

'*One,* I don't salute any bastard who's been trying to blow my backside off! And *two,* I don't take orders from some snotty-nosed little twit like you!'

Goss said gravely, 'This is Lieutenant-Commander Fraser. The chief engineer.'

The lieutenant blushed. 'I—I'm sorry, sir. I didn't understand.'

Fraser stared at him calmly. 'You wouldn't.'

The lieutenant turned desperately to Lindsay. 'I'll tell the commodore, sir.' He darted a frightened glance at Fraser. 'I have to go now.'

Goss looked down at Fraser and said, 'Amazing. I'm surprised he didn't recognise a real gentleman when he saw you like that.'

Fraser eyed him with equal gravity. 'In my book a gentleman is someone who gets out of his bath to have a pee.'

Goss turned to Lindsay. 'Now you see why we used to try and keep the engineers away from the passengers in the company, sir? Their *refinement* might have made some of them feel inferior.' Then he turned and walked slowly towards the bridge.

Fraser gaped after him. 'Well, I'll be damned! He made a joke! Not much of one maybe, but he *made* it!'

Lindsay smiled. 'And you asked for it, Chief. If you insult another up-and-coming admiral I may not be able to save you.'

Fraser shrugged. 'When the likes of that upstart are admirals I'll either be tending my garden at home or six feet under it.' He chuckled. 'But fancy old John Goss cracking a joke.' He was still chuckling as he walked towards his quarters.

Maxwell crossed the deck and saluted.

'I've assembled the dockyard people for you in the wardroom, sir.'

'Good idea. It never hurts to soften them up with a few drinks before asking their help.'

He paused by a screen door. 'Is there anything wrong, Guns? Any way I can help?'

Maxwell stiffened. 'Wrong, sir? Why should there be?' He stared at a point above Lindsay's shoulder. 'All the starboard watch and second part of port watch for liberty this afternoon, sir?'

Lindsay studied him thoughtfully. 'Yes. Have it piped.'

He would have to keep an eye on Maxwell. He was so tensed up he might well become another Aikman. He smiled bitterly. Or Lindsay.

He straightened his shoulders and pushed open the wardroom door.

'Now, gentlemen, about these repairs.'

Commodore Kemp's temporary residence was situated several miles from the naval base, and after the crowded, jostling streets, the seemingly endless numbers of servicemen, it gave an immediate impression of peaceful seclusion. A staff car, driven by a bearded Sikh corporal, had collected Lindsay at the jetty at the exact minute prescribed, and as it left him standing just inside the open gates Lindsay wondered how he had arrived without a fatal accident. The Sikh had driven with expressionless abandon, as if every street had been empty, using the car's horn as the sole form of survival.

It was a very attractive house, white-walled and fringed with palms. There was a colourful, well-tended garden, and he could imagine the number of servants required to keep it so.

A house-boy in white tunic and scarlet sash took his cap and ushered him into a cool, spacious room where the commodore was standing with his back to a large portrait. It depicted a bearded Victorian who was staring steadfastly into the distance, arms folded, and with one foot on a dead tiger.

Kemp waited for Lindsay to reach him and then offered his hand. 'Good to see you safe and well.' He snapped his fingers to the servant. 'You'll have a drink before dinner, I imagine.'

'Thank you, sir. Scotch.'

Kemp was smoking a cigar and gestured for Lindsay to sit in one of the tall gilt chairs.

'Nice place, eh? Belongs to a tea-planter. He stays up-country for most of the time. Just comes here to get away from it all.'

Lindsay tried to relax. The whisky was good. Very good. Kemp certainly appeared to be enjoying his new role. Relishing it, as if the house and all it entailed were his by right.

'I was damn glad to hear about your U-boat.' Kemp's eyes followed the cigar smoke until it was plucked into a nearby fan. '*Merlin*'s captain was pretty sure he'd done for that one, otherwise I'd never have left you without another escort, naturally.'

Lindsay thought of the convoy receding over the horizon. The sense of isolation and danger.

'But your ships got through all right, sir.'

Kemp shrugged. 'Lost the other freighter, I'm afraid. She had a bit of engine trouble. Her master signalled that some of our depth-charges had exploded too close for comfort.' He poured himself another drink without calling for the servant. His hand was shaking. 'But I *knew* there was no real risk of more U-boats attacking us, so I pressed on. The convoy was vital, as you know. Anyway, there were more escorts on way from Freetown, plus two destroyers from the inshore squadron.'

Lindsay watched him over his glass. 'You left him behind.'

Kemp looked uneasy. 'It should have been safe enough. But the destroyers could find no trace of the poor chap. Must have had an explosion aboard. Anyway, can't be helped. All water under the bridge, as they say.'

Lindsay swallowed his drink and held the glass out to the impassive servant. Kemp had abandoned the freighter. Just like *Benbecula* and the ammunition ship.

'Didn't she send any distress signals, sir?'

'No.' Kemp sounded too casual. 'Nothing.'

'That's strange.'

Kemp stood up and walked to one of the wide windows. 'Well, there's damn all we can do about it now.' He turned, his face set in a smile again. 'Now, about you. I gather you've had the repair yard hopping like mad all day. They'll do what they can, of course, but I can't promise too much. It'll have to be a patch up job. I've been informed that your damage is largely superficial where the hull is concerned.'

'We'll manage, sir.' He tried to hide his bitterness.

Kemp nodded. 'That's the spirit. Front-line ships are right at the top of the list, I'm afraid. But I don't have to tell you that.'

'I was wondering about the next assignment, sir.' He saw the decanter hovering above Kemp's glass.

'Well, we can't talk shop tonight, eh? This is a sort of celebration for you. A welcome back.' He became serious. 'Of course, with Singapore in the enemy's bag there's nothing for all these reinforcements we brought out from U.K. I've seen the admiral and his Chief of Staff, and I gather we'll be expected to help in another convoy.' He sounded vague. 'I daresay the troops will be a godsend elsewhere, anyway. Things have been getting a bit grim in North Africa to all accounts.'

Lindsay watched him as he took another drink. You don't care. Don't give a damn about anyone but yourself.

Ships left without help, men dying, none of it counted. It was outside, beyond Kemp's vision, and interest too for that matter.

Kemp seemed to realise Lindsay was studying him and said with forced cheerfulness, 'But you shouldn't complain.' He wagged his glass. 'I'll not be surprised if you get a decoration for saving the ammunition ship and sinking the U-boat. Promotion too, I wouldn't wonder. Now that you've overcome your, er, past problems, I see no reason why you should not be given something better.'

'There are several of my people I'd like to recommend for——'

Kemp frowned. 'Well, we must wait and see. Nothing definite, you understand. Everything's in turmoil here, and it sounds as if the whole naval structure is being changed. *Merlin*'s captain is being promoted and is to be given one of these new escort groups. Killer-groups, they're being called. Nice young chap. Should do well.' He stared vaguely at Lindsay's glass. 'But for your early setback I daresay you'd have been on the list for something of the sort, too.'

Lindsay replied calmly, 'I lost my ship, sir. I was blown up in another. Many have suffered the same fate.' His voice hardened. 'Many were less fortunate.'

Kemp seemed to have missed the point. He nodded gravely. 'I know, Lindsay. We who face death and live to fight again rarely realise how narrow the margin can be.'

Lindsay fixed his eyes on the portrait opposite his chair. His immediate anger at Kemp's words was already giving way to a new realisation. Not merely that Kemp was drunk but that he needed to be so. *We who face death.* Kemp had not been to sea in wartime before this last convoy. Had it really been the vital need of ships and men for Singapore which had made him drive them without letup? Or was it his own fear, his new understanding that he had been left behind by war, of a role he only vaguely recognised?

Another house-boy appeared in the doorway. 'Dinner served, sir.' He grinned from ear to ear.

Kemp lurched to his feet. 'Impudent lot. Still, they have their uses. Mean well, I suppose.'

He paused beside the table and added abruptly, 'When we meet the FOIC tomorrow, I'd be obliged if you'd not mention your ideas about commerce raiders and so forth. He's quite enough on his plate at the moment. He'll not thank you for wasting his time.'

'Even if it means saving ships and men, sir?'

Kemp seemed to have difficulty in holding him in focus. 'That last freighter sank by accident, Lindsay!' He was shouting. 'And that's all there is to it!'

Lindsay stood stockstill. He had not even been thinking about that unfortunate ship, except for the fact Kemp had left her unaided. But now it was out in the open and there was no avoiding the truth. Kemp actually *believed* what he had been telling him, yet was equally prepared to ignore it for his own survival. He needed things to stay as they were, like stopping the clock, just long enough for him to achieve some better appointment elsewhere.

As he followed Kemp's thickset figure across a marble floor to the dining room his mind was already working on this frightening possibility.

The terrible news about Singapore could be all it needed to make the Germans take full advantage of their ally's victory. For the next few months naval resources would be stretched far beyond safety limits as troops and supplies were re-deployed to meet the new dangers. The Japs might invade India and march on into the rich oil-fields of the Middle East. They could have it planned for months, even years with the Germans, so that an eventual link-up between their forces was made a brutal fact. One vast pair of steel pincers biting through Russia and the Middle East, to carve the world in halves.

Inside the tea-planter's cool house it all seemed so clear and starkly obvious he was almost unnerved. It must be just as plain to those in real authority. Unless. . . . He looked at Kemp's plump shoulders. In past wars it had always taken several years to rid authority of men like him. It was said that in the old battlefields of Flanders the ploughs were still churning up countless remains of the men thrown away by generals who had believed cavalry superior to machine-guns and barbed wire. And admirals who had scoffed at the trivial consequences of submarine warfare.

He was surprised to find he was not the only guest for dinner. A bearded surgeon-commander from the admiral's staff, the commodore's aide who had wilted before Fraser's verbal barrage and an elderly major of artillery were already standing around a well-laid table. Midshipman Kemp was also present, standing apart from the others, and there was a dried-up little woman acting as hostess, introduced as the surgeon-commander's wife.

In spite of the fans it was very hot, and the ample helpings of varied curries did little to help matters. Beyond the shuttered windows Lindsay could see the last rays of bronze sunlight, the palms very black against the sky.

There was a lot to drink. Too much. Lindsay was astonished at the way the commodore could put it away. Wine came and went with the soft-footed servants, while his voice grew louder and more slurred.

Beside Lindsay the midshipman ate his meal in silence, his eyes rarely leaving the table until his father suddenly said, 'By God, Julian, don't pick at your food! Try and *eat* like a man, if nothing else!'

Lindsay recalled the boy's face after the action. Tight-lipped but strangely determined. Stannard had told him how the midshipman had worked with his plotting team. How he had been sick several times but had somehow managed to keep going. And all that time he had prob-ably been picturing his father speeding to safety with the heavy escort. Leaving him alone, as he had always done.

Lindsay leaned back in his chair. He felt light-headed but no longer cared.

'Actually, sir, he did very well on this last trip.' He knew the boy was staring at him, that the surgeon's wife had paused in her apparently insatiable appetite with a fork poised in the air.

The aide said swiftly, 'Good show. I remember when I was at Dartmouth I——'

The commodore said flatly, 'Hold your noise!' To Lindsay he added, 'You don't know my son or you might think otherwise.'

He signalled for more wine, unaware of the sudden tension around the table.

'My *son* does not like the Service. He would rather sit on his backside listening to highbrow music than do anything useful. When I think of my father and what he taught me, I want to weep.'

The army major dabbed his chin with a napkin.

'Spare the rod, eh?' He laughed, the sound strangely hollow in the quiet room.

'I think he's old enough to know his own mind.' Lindsay could feel the anger returning. 'When the war's over he'll be able to make his choice.'

'Is that what you think?' The commodore leaned forward, his eyes red-rimmed in the overhead lights. 'Well, I'm telling you, Commander Lindsay, that I will decide what he will or will not do! No son of mine is going to bring disgrace on my family, do you hear?'

'Perfectly, sir.' He gripped his glass tightly to prevent his hand from shaking. 'But at present he is under my command, and I will assess his qualities accordingly.'

The commodore shifted in his chair and then snapped, 'We will take our port in the next room.'

Lindsay stood up. 'If you will excuse me, sir. I would like to be excused.'

The surgeon's wife said hastily, 'You must be worn out, Commander. If half of what they're saying about you is true, then I think you should get some rest.'

The commodore only succeeded in rising to his feet with the aid of a servant's arm.

'You *are* excused.' He faced Lindsay and added thickly, 'And as far as I'm concerned you can——' He turned and walked unsteadily to the door without finishing it.

Lindsay left the room and waited for a house-boy to fetch his cap. He heard footsteps and saw the young midshipman staring at him.

'I'm sorry, sir. I'd not have had this happen for anything.'

Lindsay forced a smile. 'Forget it. My fault entirely.'

'You don't understand, sir.' Kemp's face was tight with concern. 'I *know* him. He'll try and get his own back on you.' He dropped his eyes. 'He's not like you, sir. If he were, I'd never have needed to be told to enter the Navy.'

The boy's sincerity, his shame and humiliation, made him appear even more defenceless than usual.

Lindsay said quietly, 'That was a nice compliment. One which I happen to value very much.'

He took his cap and walked quickly into the garden.

Behind him the boy stood staring at the open door long after Lindsay had disappeared in the shadows.

A slow, lurching taxi carried Lindsay back to the base, his head lolling to the jerky motion, his throat parched in spite of the wine.

By the time he had found the jetty a moon had appeared, and in the pale light he could see the *Benbecula* resting against the piles, the dazzle paint strangely vivid and garish. A sentry paced back and forth on the gang-way, and in the glow of a blue police light he saw the quartermaster drooping over his desk, probably engrossed in a book or some old letter from home.

It was very still, and after lighting his pipe Lindsay walked the full length of his ship, from her towering straight stem to her outmoded poop where the ill-used twelve-pounder pointed at the moon like a rigid finger. Then with a sigh he walked up the steep brow, nodding to the startled quartermaster and then walking forward towards his quarters.

As he passed a door he heard the crash of breaking glass. It was Stannard's cabin, but as he made to reach for the clip he heard Dancy say, 'I'd leave him, sir.'

Dancy had been leaning against the rail, his body merging with the deep shadows.

He added quietly, 'There was a message sent aboard just after you left, sir. Pilot's brother is aboard one of the hospital ships.'

Lindsay watched him. 'He got away then?'

Dancy did not seem to hear. 'He went across right away. He's been in there drinking ever since.' Dancy rested his elbows on the rail and added, 'He saw him all right. But he'd got no arms!' His shoulders shook uncontrollably. 'And he can't see either, sir!'

Lindsay stared past him towards the distant buildings, so white in the moon's glare.

'You've been here all the time?'

Dancy nodded. 'Just in case, sir.'

Lindsay touched his arm. 'I'll not be turning in yet. Come and have a drink in my cabin when he's asleep.' He waited. 'If you feel like it.'

Dancy straightened his back. 'Thank you, sir.'

Lindsay walked on towards the bridge ladder. In just one evening he had learned a lot about his officers. And himself.

16 A miracle

For three more days no fresh instructions were sent to *Benbecula* or any intimation of what her next duty might be. Lindsay had still not had the expected interview with the admiral or even his chief of staff, but at first this omission had not troubled him. Indeed, when he thought about it at all, he was almost relieved. The local naval staff had enough work on hand as it was, and he was being kept more than busy with his ship's repairs.

But it was concerning *Benbecula*'s repairs and general replenishment which at last gave him a hint that something was happening outside his own knowledge. Small items for the most part, which added together grew into a definite pattern.

Lieutenant Hunter had called on him to complain of his inability to secure any six-inch shells to replace those fired, although he had been told that plenty were available.

When Lindsay had asked, 'Have you spoken to Guns about this?' Hunter had sounded guarded.

'Well, sir, he has been a bit preoccupied lately. Anyway, I can deal with it once I've got the authority.'

Maxwell had been acting even more strangely, that was certain. He had stayed ashore every night, although nobody had seen him or knew where he went.

Goss too had been perturbed by the apparent lack of attention which was being paid to his list of repairs by the dockyard staff. That was normal enough on its own. Goss saw every dockyard worker as a potential thief, layabout and someone bent on spoiling his ship's appearance and efficiency. But it was true that some of the work had been skimped rather than properly rectified.

Lieutenant Barker had much the same tale. Stores were difficult to obtain, and apart from the basic rations of food and clothing, very little seemed available for the *Benbecula.*

Added together, Lindsay felt it was more than mere coincidence.

The ship's company on the other hand accepted the situation with obvious delight. Trips ashore, strange sights of native women and rickshaws, elephants and snake charmers, all helped to make each day an event.

Stannard had been ashore very little. In fact, apart from occasional duties he hardly seemed to leave his cabin.

Lindsay had seen him alone after the night of the commodore's dinner party and had asked if he could do anything.

Stannard had replied, 'They've sent Jason to a hospital, sir. He's being sent up to another one at Karachi tomorrow. After that, they say it'll take time.' He had looked at Lindsay with sudden anguish. 'Just tell me how I'm to write to the old man, sir. Can you imagine what it will do to him?'

After that brief interview Lindsay had seen little of him. Even Dancy seemed unable to reach him or help ease his despair.

Perhaps when they got back to sea things might change. Lying alongside a jetty in the blazing heat was no help to anyone tortured with such thoughts as Stannard.

On the morning of the fourth day the summons to naval H.Q. was received, and with Jupp hovering around him like an anxious hen Lindsay changed into a white uniform which he had not worn since the outbreak of war.

Jupp remarked, 'A bit loose around the middle, if I may make so bold, sir. You should've let me get it fixed sooner.'

He handed Lindsay his dress sword, adding, 'Not been feedin' yourself enough, sir. Too much worry is bad for you.'

Lindsay looked at himself in the bulkhead mirror. Even in war the formalities had to be observed. To show there was no crack in the foundations.

He grinned. 'I shall eat better when I know what's going to happen.'

He waited, half expecting Jupp to supply a rumour or at least some reason for the sudden call to H.Q. But Jupp seemed concerned only with his appearance, the impression *Benbecula*'s captain would make when he got there.

At the gangway Goss had to shout above the rasping rattle of a rivet-gun.

'You won't forget about my paint, sir? We're getting very low, and I'm not happy about the port anchor cable.'

Lindsay smiled briefly. The side party stood in a neat line, the bosun's mates wetting their calls on their lips ready to pipe him over the side.

Lieutenant Paget, who was O.O.D., stood very erect, his eyes fixed on Lindsay with something like terror, as if he expected the brow to collapse or one of the side party to run amok in his presence.

He said, 'I'll do what I can. I've a few questions of my own, too.'

Then with one hand to the oak-leaved peak of his cap and the unfamiliar feel of his sword in the other, he hurried down the brow where a car was shimmering in heat-haze to carry him to the presence of the mighty.

But he was met by a harassed flag-lieutenant who hurried to explain that the admiral would not, after all, be able to see him. The F.O.I.C. had been whisked away to some important conference. It was one of those things. Unavoidable.

Lindsay spent a further twenty minutes in a small room
before the lieutenant reappeared to usher him into an
adjoining office. The Chief of Staff came round a big desk
and shook his hand.

'Sorry about this mix-up, Lindsay. Bad times. But I have
no doubt you've seen enough of admirals anyway.' He
smiled. 'As I have.'

Lindsay took a proffered chair and watched him as he
stared out of a window towards the harbour.

The other man said slowly, 'Also, we've been waiting for
instructions from Admiralty. Certain recommendations
have been made, and it's my duty to inform you of them.'
He turned and studied Lindsay thoughtfully.

'The war's speeding up. Increased submarine activity
and long-range aircraft have made previous ideas obsolete. Almost overnight, in a manner of speaking.'

Lindsay tensed. He had been expecting a hint of orders,
even acceptance of his own recommendations for some of
Benbecula's company. But something in the Chief of Staff's
tone, his attitude, seemed to act like a warning. He was
troubled. No, he was embarrassed.

'My staff are arranging your orders, Lindsay. But I
think it best all round if you know without any more
delay.' He sat down behind the desk and looked at his
hands.

'*Benbecula* will return to U.K. as soon as the dockyard say
she is seaworthy.'

Seaworthy. Not ready for action or patrol duty. She
merely had to be able to make the passage home.

Lindsay asked tightly, 'And then, sir?'

'Rosyth. I gather they want her as a sort of depot cum
accommodation ship for incoming drafts, replacement
personnel and so forth.' He flicked over some papers.
'Your first lieutenant will be promoted to commander
upon arrival there. He will also assume command from
that time.' He tried to smile. 'Bit of a rough diamond, I
gather, but he should be all right for the job.' He dropped

his eyes again. 'It seems very likely that your promotion is already on its way here. I'm glad for you. You've more than earned it.'

Lindsay felt as if the walls were moving inwards. Crushing the air from his lungs.

'And *my* appointment, sir?'

The Chief of Staff did not look up. 'The Navy's growing every day. Recruits are flooding the depots like ants. We're having to cut courses rather than lengthen them, and they need the very best help they can get.' He plucked at the litter of papers. 'I detest this job. I entered the Service to feel a ship around me. I know this work is important and I'm doing more good here than I would be on the bridge of some cruiser in Scapa Flow.' He shrugged. 'But I still find it hard to take.' His eyes lifted to Lindsay's face and he added quietly, 'As you will, at first.'

'Shore job?'

'They're putting the finishing touches to a new training depot on the east coast. Hasn't got a name yet, but I've no doubt their lordships will have dreamed up something grand by the time you take command.'

Lindsay was on his feet without noticing he had moved from the chair. East coast. Shore job. Probably a peacetime holiday camp or hotel converted for training purposes. A white ensign on a flag mast. A ship's bell by the main gate. A temporary illusion for temporary sailors.

He said, 'I thought I was going to get——'

The Chief of Staff watched him sadly. 'I know. You can appeal against the decision of course, but you know as well as I do what weight it will have.'

Lindsay crossed to the window and stared blindly at the courtyard below. He could see the new depot as if he had actually visited it already. Could almost hear voices saying, 'The new captain? Oh yes, came to us because he's a bit bomb happy.'

Most of the officers who commanded such establish-

ments were old, retired and brought back to the Navy to
help spread the load. Men like Commodore Kemp.

He heard himself ask, 'I take it this was Kemp's idea,
sir?'

'You know I cannot discuss confidential reports.' The
Chief of Staff added, 'But you may draw your own conclu-
sions.'

'I *will* appeal.' He turned away from the window and saw
the other man give a brief shake of the head.

'It is your privilege. However, as there is a war on, and on
the face of things you are being given a just promotion, I
think you should be warned against such a course of
action.'

A telephone rang impatiently and the Chief of Staff
snapped. 'No. *Wait.*' He slammed it back before adding
quietly, 'I do not know Kemp very well. I would go further.
I do not *wish* to know him very well. But from what I hear of
him I would say he is not the sort who would act without
apparent justification.'

Lindsay strode to the desk and leaned on it, his voice
almost pleading. 'But there must have been signals, sir?
Some hint of all this?'

'Again, they are confidential. But there was a full report
made to Admiralty.' He looked away. 'Including one from
the staff medical officer.'

Lindsay straightened his back, sickened. He recalled the
bearded surgeon with the wife who could not stop eating.
Kemp must have planned the whole thing. Must have
worked on his first dislike which their meeting at Scapa
had begun.

He remembered the midshipman's voice when he had
said, *He'll try and get his own back on you.*

Or maybe he had started it all himself when he had
defended the boy at the dinner table. Had walked into the
trap which he had sprung by his own carelessness.

In those dragging seconds he could even see the looming bulk of the *Benbecula* leaning against the piles in the

bright sunlight. Now even she was being taken. That real-isation most of all was more than he could bear.

'Look, Lindsay, try not to take this too badly. The war is not going to end next week. And who knows, you'll proba-bly find new orders in England which will make all this seem like a bad dream.'

A bad dream. It seemed to linger in his mind. Perhaps someone aboard his own ship had made the first move. Had listened to his ravings as he relived the nightmare. Had recorded every small action or mood in order to destroy him.

He thrust out his hand. 'I will leave now, sir.' He met the other man's troubled gaze. 'I would not have been in your shoes for this. Thank you for trying to spare my feelings.'

The Chief of Staff smiled. 'I have tried. But I feel like an executioner nonetheless. I only hope the men who pass through your hands appreciate what you will no doubt offer them.'

'And what is that, sir?'

'I am not going to indulge you with all the trite words of leadership and example. You'll get plenty of those later.' He sat down again, his eyes suddenly distant. 'Give them the same sense of value, of *belonging* as you have to the old *Benbecula*. That'll be more use than a room full of admirals.'

Lindsay picked up his cap and walked slowly to the door. It was over. For him and the ship.

He said, 'I will try to remember that. There will be plenty of time from now on.'

Outside, the flag-lieutenant handed him an envelope and said, 'Here's a brief rundown on appointments, sir. It will be all right to mention them to your people if you so wish.'

Lindsay walked through the building without another word. He got vague impressions of men at desks, the chatter of telephones and typewriters. A different sort of war. One he would soon be joining or watching from the sidelines.

He returned the salutes of two marine sentries and headed for the parked staff car.

He must hold on. Just long enough to reach his cabin. Hide, like Stannard and Maxwell. But he knew it was only a deception. For there was nowhere he could hide from himself.

―――――――――

Goss stood a few paces away from Lindsay's desk, his face hidden while he listened to the neatly typed instructions.

'So you will have the ship after all, Number One.' Even as he said it Lindsay thought this bare fact was the only shred of comfort which really affected him. 'And with promotion, you should be well placed after the war with another shipping company when you may be competing with younger men.'

He did not know what he had expected. Goss's silence was like something physical. He turned in his chair and asked, 'Aren't you pleased? I thought it was what you wanted?'

Goss opened his big hands and closed them again. 'I always wanted the *Becky*. Ever since I can remember.' His fingers clenched into tight fists. 'But not like this!'

'She'll be safe as a depot ship. No more convoys. No being left alone with nothing but a few First World War guns to hit back.'

Goss said quietly, 'A ship dies when she's inactive. I've seen a few good ones go like that during the depression.' He seemed to be struggling with his words. 'A ship should be at sea. She needs it. It's her life. Her purpose for being.' He turned slightly so that Lindsay saw the emotion on his heavy features. 'Like an old man who takes to his chair. He starts to die from then on. He can't help it.'

Lindsay tore his eyes away from Goss's despair. 'I'll leave it to you to tell the others. You can use this list. Stannard's to go on an advanced navigation course. He'll probably be appointed to a new destroyer. de Chair and his marines are to be sent to Eastney Barracks for re-allocation, and Maxwell's to get his half stripe. He'll be going to Whale Island for an instructor's course.'

He wondered how he could keep his voice so level when his whole being was screaming like a tortured instrument. Calm, even matter-of-fact. It had to be that way. The only way.

He recalled the time his mother had made her decision to leave for Canada. For good. He had wandered round the old house, watching the familiar things which he had always taken for granted, going under the auctioneer's impartial hammer. Things he had known all his young life. Things he had loved.

It was like that right now. Familiar faces being parted and sent to the winds.

'Young Dancy is going on a navigation course, too. His work with Stannard will stand him in good stead. The other young subs are being transferred to escort vessels when they return from home leave. Hunter is to be gunnery officer in one of the Western Approaches ships.'

Goss asked abruptly, 'What about Fraser?'

'The chief is transferring to a fleet repair ship.'

'I see.' Goss walked a few paces and stopped, as if uncertain where to go. 'Isn't *anyone* staying from the old company?'

'Dyke will take over the engine room, although being a depot ship his duties will be pretty limited.' He added, 'I thought you disliked Fraser?'

Goss said vaguely, 'Dyke can't do the job. It takes a proper chief engineer. She's old. She must have proper care.' He added with sudden fierceness, 'No, I've never liked him much. But he's a good chief. The best in the company, and no matter what he's told you, he bloody well cares about this ship right enough!'

'I know that, too.' Lindsay stared at the papers on his desk. They were blurred, like those on the Chief of Staff's desk. 'You're keeping Barker. He's getting a half stripe like Maxwell.'

Goss walked to the desk and stood looking down at Lindsay for several seconds.

'And *you're* on the beach, sir. I know a lot of people'll only see your extra stripe and envy you, most likely. But I know different. I'm not a clever man an' never was. I sweated blood to get where I am, and saw many a useless bastard get promoted over my head because I'm slow by nature. I'm slow, and I take my time. I've never been able to afford mistakes. There's not been a captain in the company I've not envied, nor one whose job I've told myself I couldn't do better given the chance.' He rested his hands on the desk. 'But I've not envied you, because I couldn't have done what you've had to do. No matter what I've kidded myself on that score, I know that, and nobody can tell me otherwise.'

Lindsay did not look up. 'Thank you.' He heard Goss moving restlessly to an open scuttle.

Goss added slowly, 'Christ, she can feel it already. Poor old girl, she can *feel* it.'

Lindsay lurched to his feet. 'For God's sake, Number One, we have to carry out orders. Nothing else *can* matter. Ships don't feel. They're steel and wood, pipes and machinery, and only as good as the men who control them.' Even as he said it he saw the other man shaking his head.

'It's no use talking to me like that, sir. You don't believe it either. She feels it all right.' He swung towards the scuttle, his eyes staring into the harsh sunlight as he shouted, 'Those toffy-nosed bastards who sit in their offices will never understand, not if they live a million bloody years! I don't know much but by the living Jesus I know ships! And above all I know this one.' When he spoke again he was very calm. 'Sorry about that. I should be used to kicks at my time of life.'

Somewhere a tannoy bellowed, 'Hands to dinner. Leave to port watch from 1400 to 2300. Chief and petty officers 0830 in the morning. Ordinary Seaman Jones muster at the quartermaster's lobby for mail.'

Goss moved to the door. 'Can you see her tied up to some stinking pier, full of gash ratings and layabouts, sir? With nothing to do, no use any more?' He waited, staring at Lindsay's lowered head. 'No, and no more can't I.'

As the door closed behind him Jupp entered the cabin and asked, 'Will you be wantin' your lunch now, sir?'

Lindsay shook his head. Goss had known. Must have known. One more minute and he would have broken down.

'Fetch some whisky, please.'

Jupp picked up the dress sword from a chair where Lindsay had thrown it and replied, 'If you'll pardon the liberty, sir, it's not fair.'

'Just the whisky.'

Jupp hurried away. For once in his long life he could think of nothing to say or do which would help him understand what was happening.

In his pantry a young steward said, 'What's up, Chiefy? The end of the world comin'?'

Jupp looked at him and saw the steward pale under his fierce stare. 'For once in your miserable life, I reckon you're right.' He picked up a clean glass and held it automatically to the light before putting it on his silver tray.

The steward stammered, 'I was only jokin', Chiefy!'

Jupp placed the decanter carefully on the tray and thought of Lindsay in the next cabin staring down at his desk.

Aloud he said, 'You don't joke, son, when someone's dyin'.'

But the steward had already gone.

———————

Lindsay could not remember how he had reached this particular restaurant. He seemed to have been walking for hours, his feet taking him down narrow streets and away from the main crush of people and tooting vehicles. It appeared to be quite a small building. The upper part was an hotel under the same ownership and bore a sign depicting a bejewelled elephant and the words 'English and French dishes. Only the best.'

It was evening and the sun already hidden beyond a towering white temple on the opposite side of a dusty square. He guessed the hotel would probably look very shabby in harsh sunlight.

But it was quiet and seemed almost deserted. No uniforms or familiar faces like those he had seen at the Naval Club where he had paused for a drink. He had recognised several people there. From the past. From other ships and forgotten places. They had meant well but always he seemed to see the questions in their eyes. Curiosity, sympathy? It was hard to tell. He had finished his drink and started walking again. He realised now that he was very tired, his shirt clinging to his back like a damp towel.

A board creaked beneath his feet as he thrust through some bead curtains and dropped into a chair at one of the small cane tables. There were fortunately only two other occupants and neither gave him more than a cursory glance. Their conversation seemed to consist entirely of the latest rubber prices. The cost of local labour. The general inefficiency of transport. He guessed they were both planters, so familiar to each other that neither appeared to listen to what the other was saying.

A smiling waiter bowed beside the table. 'Sair?'

Lindsay stared at the proffered menu, realising for the first time that he had been drinking heavily since noon. Since he had seen Goss. But the drink did not seem to have had any real effect, other than to make the thought of food impossible.

'Perhaps the commander would wish to order later?'

He looked up at the second figure who had appeared. Either the newcomer was cat-footed or Lindsay was more drunk than he imagined. It seemed impossible he could have missed seeing such a man. He was gross, his huge body impeccably covered in a cream linen suit, his girth encircled by a crimson sash to match a small fez which appeared minute on his round head. A chair groaned loudly as the man sank into it.

'A drink first, maybe?' He snapped his fingers. 'I have some gin.'

Lindsay eyed him dully. He wanted to leave right now. He did not wish to talk. There was nothing to say.

The man announced calmly, 'I am the owner.' He waved a plump hand, several rings glinting in the coloured lanterns overhead. 'And bid you welcome.'

The waiter was pouring out two glasses of neat gin. On the bottle he saw the words. *Duty Free. H.M. Ships only.*

'Thanks.' He took a glass, wondering what it would do to his stomach.

The owner sipped at the gin and smiled. 'My religion regards gin as an evil. However.' He took another sip. 'One must adapt to the country's ways, eh?' He watched Lindsay unblinkingly. He had very dark, liquid eyes, like those of a younger man encased in a grotesque mask.

He continued in the same gentle tone, 'I am Turkish. Once, although some may find it difficult to accept, I was in the Grand Cavalry. A Captain of Horse.' He chuckled, the sound rising from a great depth. 'Now it would take more than one beast to carry me, you are thinking?'

Lindsay smiled. 'I am sorry. I am bad company.'

'Only loneliness is bad, Commander.' He signalled to the waiter. 'I fought your people on the Dardanelles in that other war. I learned to respect their courage, even though their leadership was less inspiring. So when I had to flee my own country I decided to come here. Halfway between two ways of life. East and West. I will be happy to end my life here.'

Lindsay felt the gin scraping his throat like fire. 'I really must go.' He tried to smile. 'As I said, I am bad company.'

The man shook his head. 'Not yet. It is not time.'

'*Time?*'

The man smiled gently. 'Do not play with fate, Commander. You will have one more glass, and then, perhaps, it will be time.'

Lindsay stared at him. He must have misheard or had finally taken leave of his senses. He looked quickly around the room but it was quite empty. The two planters had vanished.

The man said quietly, 'It is all right, Commander. They were there. They have gone up to their rooms for an arrangement with some women.' He wrinkled his nose disdainfully. 'They drink a lot first and then their women begin to appear beautiful again!' It seemed to amuse him greatly.

Lindsay sighed and raised the glass to his lips. What would they be doing aboard the ship? Some might be celebrating their forthcoming promotions and appointments. Others would be ashore, making the most of the last few days in Ceylon. Back in England it would be cold and grey. Air-raids and ration queues. Tired faces and pathetic bravery. The memories of Ceylon would become precious to many of *Benbecula*'s company in the months or years ahead.

The massive Turk snapped his fingers and as if by magic the gin bottle disappeared.

'I must go to the temple and make amends, Commander.' He stood up and took a deep breath. 'I have enjoyed our little talk.' He held out one fat hand. 'Maybe you will come again. But I think not.'

Lindsay groped for his cap, thinking he should offer to pay for the drinks but knowing also that the man would resent it.

He heard him add quietly, 'Now, you may leave. Somehow, I feel that your hurt will be easier to carry.'

Lindsay thanked him and walked out into the purple gloom, his mind still dazed by the unexpected encounter. Perhaps the man was crazy. Why the hotel was so deserted.

He lurched against a shuttered shop front and gasped. But the gin was real enough.

At the end of the street he saw bright lights and the hurrying criss-cross of crowds. Perhaps he might find a taxi. He could not face fighting his way back to the base through those same cheerful throngs of people.

But there was no taxi available, so with tired determination he increased his pace, shutting his ears to the din of voices and music, car horns and rickshaw wheels, while he tried to concentrate on the gross Turk who had once been a Captain of Horse at the Dardanelles.

'Hey, mate, got a light?'

He stopped to face two Australian soldiers who were clinging to each other for support. He took out his matches and waited while one of them made several attempts to light their cigarettes. Their voices reminded him of Stannard.

The first soldier squinted at Lindsay's shoulder straps. 'Pommy sailor, eh?' He grinned. 'But never mind, mate. You got me an' my cobber out of Singapore.' He laughed as if it were one huge joke. 'Leastways, somebody did!' They staggered away, their bush hats strangely alien against the coloured lanterns and bazaars.

He took out his pipe and then realised the soldiers had left without returning the matches. He was still patting his pockets when a taxi scraped against one of the nearby stalls and sent a mountain of fruit cascading under the wheels. A

crowd gathered in seconds, prepared to be freely amused
by the fierce exchange between driver and merchant. He
tried to free himself from the growing crush but it was
impossible. Above those around him he saw two impassive
faced policemen forcing their way through the crowd
towards the taxi which was now completely hemmed in by
spectators.

He saw a dark doorway and decided to make for it. The
police would take several minutes to clear the crowd. He
might even find some matches. Two white figures were
already in the doorway, probably with the same idea as
himself. An eddy of figures pressed against him and he felt
himself being pushed slowly towards another shopfront.
He gave up. It was hopeless, and he was feeling worse.
Sick.

Yet even through the excited babble of shouts and jeers
he seemed to hear a voice. It was like part of a dream. A
nerve laid bare in his memory.

'Commander! Commander Lindsay!'

All at once he was fighting his way back through the
crowd, pushing with all his strength even though he knew
it was just one more crack in his reserve.

A policeman grabbed at his arm, yelling at him, but he
knocked him aside, his ears deaf to the roar of voices, his
eyes blind to everything but the doorway and the two
figures in white.

Against the darkness they seemed to hover like ghosts,
and in those last desperate moments he imagined he had at
last gone mad.

Gasping with exertion and almost sobbing he burst
from the crowd and threw himself into the opening. Then
he stood quite still. Afraid to blink or breathe, even though
it was just one more dream.

She said, 'I *knew* it was you!'

Very slowly he reached out and put his hands on her
shoulders. '*Eve.*' He felt her shiver under his grip. 'Eve. I
thought——' She was still staring up at him, her face

almost hidden in shadow. The other Wren had moved away and stood uncertainly by the shopfront. Then he pulled her to him. Holding her tightly as he murmured, 'Oh Eve. All this time.'

She said quietly, 'You're not well.' To the other girl, 'Tell that policeman to get us a taxi.' Then she pressed her face into his chest and whispered, 'It's a miracle. We were trying to get back to the base. Then this crowd, and I saw you. I had no idea you were here.' She trembled. 'I still can't believe it.' Then she looked up at him again, her eyes very large in her face. 'You didn't get my letter then?'

He stared at her, still fearful it would suddenly end. 'We've had no mail except local letters.'

'And you thought I was in Canada!' She laughed, her eyes shining with sudden tears. 'There was a last minute mix-up. My medical report got confused with another Wren's, and by the time it was sorted out the convoy had sailed without me. So they sent me here instead. I'll bet they're laughing like hell about it in Canada.'

She reached up to touch his face. 'You're like ice! Tell me, what happened?'

'The convoy.' He could feel his body trembling violently. 'It was attacked. The ship with the Wrens aboard was destroyed. I was there. I saw it.' He felt her hair with his fingers. 'Burning. I tried to find you.' He broke down and whispered, 'To bring you back.'

A policeman shouted, 'What's going on here?'

The other Wren replied just as loudly, 'Get a taxi and don't be a bloody fool!'

Lindsay heard all of it but was conscious only of the girl pressed against his body. He had to hold on to her. Otherwise. . .

She asked, 'Is the taxi coming, Marion? We must get him to his ship quickly. He's ill.' She touched his face again, her hand very gentle. 'It'll be all right now. My poor darling, I'm so sorry!'

'Here's the taxi!'

Lindsay remembered very little of the journey. There was some sort of argument at the dockyard gates, a pause while the other Wren hurried away to make a telephone call.

Then she said, 'We can't come any further. Regulations. We've been on four days leave. Should have been back hours ago.' She pulled his head down on to her shoulder, speaking very softly. 'Or else I would have known you were here. Would have seen your ship come in.'

The other girl came back and peered into the taxi. She said vehemently, 'I spoke to the Third Officer and explained. Silly cow!'

Eve whispered, 'You'd never believe her father was a lord, would you?' She was half laughing, half crying.

The other Wren added, 'Then I got the sentry to put me through to the ship. Just as you said. I wouldn't speak to anyone else but him.'

Feet scraped in the darkness and Jupp loomed above the girl's shoulder.

'Ah, there you are, sir!' He saw the girl and nodded gravely. 'I'm so glad for you, Miss. For you both.'

She said, 'Take good care of him.' As Lindsay tried to keep hold of her arm she added, 'It will be all right, darling. I shall see you tomorrow. I promise.'

'Come along, sir.'

Jupp helped him from the taxi, the driver of which was watching with fixed fascination until the Wren whose father was a lord snapped, 'Our quarters, and double quick!'

Lindsay realised they had reached the brow. At the far end of it he could see the same quartermaster. The same blue light.

Jupp said evenly, 'Just a few more paces.' He moved back. 'On your own, sir.' He followed Lindsay, his eyes fixed on his shoulders, willing him up the endless length of brow.

The quartermaster had been joined by the O.O.D. It

was Stannard. He saw Lindsay and Jupp's set face behind him and snapped, 'The captain's coming aboard!' Then he stepped between the quartermaster and the entry port and said quietly, 'Welcome back, sir.'

Jupp smiled but kept his eyes on Lindsay.

'I think some 'ot soup might do the trick, sir.'

Stannard watched them fade into the shadows. Paget had been O.O.D., but when Jupp had come to him to ask for his help he had sent the lieutenant away, although he could not recall what for. He had been in his cabin drinking with Dancy at the time. Not talking, just drinking in companionable silence.

He was touched in some strange way that Jupp had chosen him. Had trusted him to share his secret.

Paget came back breathing fast. 'I couldn't find it, Pilot.'

'What?'

'What you sent me for.' Paget stared at the gangway log. 'The captain's aboard then?'

'Yeh.'

'And I missed him.' Paget sounded cheated.

'Shame, isn't it?' Stannard walked towards his own quarters whistling quietly to himself.

Jupp had succeeded in getting Lindsay to his cabin without meeting anyone else.

He waited until he had dropped on to his bunk and then said, 'I'll fetch the soup, sir.'

Lindsay's eyes were closed. 'Don't bother. I'm all right.'

'I 'ad it ready. It's no bother.' He saw the reading-lamp shining directly across Lindsay's face. 'I'll switch it off.'

'No. Leave it.' He opened his eyes. '*You* saw her, didn't you?'

'Course I did, sir!' He grinned broadly. 'Don't you worry, light or no light, she'll see you tomorrow, if I 'ave to fetch 'er meself, an' that's a fact!'

Lindsay's eyes closed again. 'There was this Turk. He made me stay there. Said it wasn't time. Something about fate. I wanted to go and yet I couldn't move. Kept on about the time and the Dardanelles.'

Jupp waited as Lindsay's words grew quieter and his features became more relaxed.

'Was trying to find some matches. And then I heard her call my name.' His voice trailed away.

'That's right, sir.' Jupp watched him sadly. 'I don't understand a word of it but I'm sure you're right.' He snapped off the light and padded from the cabin.

In his pantry he sat down on a stool and stared at the soup which was simmering on a small heater. He'll not be wanting it now. He cocked his head to listen but heard nothing. Just the creak of steel, the muffled sounds of a sentry's regular footsteps.

Then he groped into a locker and took out a bottle of Drambuie. It was his one weakness for special occasions. He wiped a clean glass and held it to the light before pouring himself a generous measure.

For to Jupp it was a very special occasion indeed.

CR

17 The house by the sea

Petty Officer Ritchie waited until he heard Lindsay's voice and then stepped into the cabin.

'Good mornin', sir.' He placed his signal pad on the desk and then handed him a sealed envelope. 'Just arrived from H.Q., sir.'

As Lindsay slit open the envelope Ritchie darted a quick glance at Jupp. He had already heard about Lindsay's return on board. Jupp had awakened him just before dawn to tell him. He saw the untouched breakfast on the cabin table and Jupp's obvious anxiety.

Lindsay said, 'Orders. You'd better ask Number One to come and see me as soon as he's finished with Morning Colours.' He stared at the carefully worded instructions. Four days time. It was not long.

The bulkhead telephone buzzed and he made himself sit very still until Jupp announced, 'Just the O.O.D. About requestmen an' defaulters.'

'I see.'

He tried to hide the disappointment and to concentrate on his written orders. Work was to be completed before sailing time but leave for the ship's company could continue at the captain's discretion. Further information would be forthcoming etc. etc. etc.

Beyond the cabin a bugle blared the 'Alert' and on the tannoy system a voice bellowed, 'Attention on the upper deck. Face aft and salute!'

Lindsay stood up and walked slowly to an open scuttle,

feeling the morning sunlight on his face. As he listened to one of de Chair's marine buglers he could picture the ensign rising at the taffrail, while the Jack was hoisted in the bows. Once at sea the ensign would be replaced by one of the well-worn ones, tattered and stained, which Ritchie retained for harder use.

He had awakened in his bunk with Jupp touching his shoulder, a cup of black coffee poised and ready. For just a few seconds he had been gripped with something like terror until Jupp had grinned at him.

''S'all right, sir. It *'appened* just like you remembers!'

As he shaved and dressed and the ship had come alive around him for another day he had tried to piece it all together in his mind. Each small moment, so that he could hold it intact forever.

To think that mere seconds had saved them. Another moment and they might never have met. The letter which she had written had probably been lost or bogged down in some forgotten mail office. If he had not stayed in that strange restaurant. If, if, if. . . . It seemed unending.

Goss appeared in the doorway, 'You wanted me, sir?'

'Orders, Number One. Four days notice.'

'Not much. Still a lot of work undone. I suppose they don't care any more.'

'Well, do what you can. They might still cancel the orders.'

Goss shook his head doubtfully. 'I went ashore last night and met an old mate of mine. He says there's a big convoy being assembled. Any time now, it seems.'

It made sense. Every available escort would be required if the convoy was to be a large one.

He replied, 'Leave will be granted as before.'

Goss nodded. 'Good. Gives me room to get things sorted out with most of the jolly jacks ashore.'

The telephone buzzed again. Jupp's face was expressionless. 'It's the Signals Distribution Office, sir.'

He handed the phone to him and said breezily, 'Now, Mr Goss, what about a cuppa while you're 'ere?'

Her voice seemed right against his ear. 'Sorry about the deception, although this *is* the S.D.O.' Then she asked quickly, 'Are you all right?'

'Yes. Never better.' Goss, Jupp and the cabin had faded away. 'When can I see you?'

He heard a typewriter clattering in the background as she replied, 'Now, if you like. At the gates. I must see you as soon as possible.' She added very clearly, 'There isn't much time, is there?'

'No.' He glanced quickly at his watch. 'I'll be there right away.'

When he had replaced the handset he saw Goss watching him, a cup like a thimble in his large hand.

'I'm going ashore, Number One. Not for long.'

Goss nodded. 'I can cope, sir.' He studied Lindsay over the rim of the cup. So that was it. Well, bloody good luck to him.

Jupp asked, 'Nice coffee, Mr Goss?'

Goss stayed poker-faced. 'Very nice.' Surprisingly, he winked. 'Better for some though, eh?' Then he followed Lindsay from the cabin.

At the brow he stood beside Lindsay and looked at the busy jetty below.

'By the way, sir, if, and I say *if* you were thinking of taking a bit of leave yourself.' He waited until Lindsay was facing him. 'Then we can manage quite well.' He shrugged. 'After all, the sooner I get used to carrying the weight on my own the better, so to speak.'

'Yes. Thank you.' He turned to watch a column of soldiers marching along the next jetty, their bodies deformed by packs and weapons. 'I may hold you to that.' Then he saluted and ran quickly down the brow.

She was waiting just outside the gates, looking very young in her white uniform. But exactly as he remembered her.

She said, 'There's a little Chinese restaurant just up the road. It's quiet.' She shot him a quick glance. 'Not too bright either.'

As they hurried past the dock-bound vehicles and groups of saluting sailors she added breathlessly, 'I had to pinch myself this morning. Even now I'm afraid I'll wake up.'

The restaurant was just as she had described it. And at such an early hour quite empty.

They were ushered to a table and he said quietly, 'My God, you're even more beautiful than I remembered.'

'It must be darker in here than I thought!' Her voice was husky, and for a few moments neither of them spoke.

Then she removed her cap and shook out her hair. That too was like a touch against his heart.

'I'm working in the S.D.O.' She did not look at him. 'So I know about your orders. Four days.' She fell silent until a waiter had brought some tea. 'I will be going, too. Back to old England.' She faced him and reached out to grasp his hand. 'Maybe we'll be in the same convoy.' She squeezed it gently. 'Don't worry. It won't be like that other one. It can't be.'

'No. But why are you going back so soon?'

She wrinkled her nose. 'I was sent here with some others for the Singapore operation. We were to work here on communications. Now that's all over we're going home again. Maybe I'll even get my proper signals course now.' She dropped her eyes. 'I'm sorry. I was forgetting about those other Wrens. It must have been terrible.'

He started to speak but she tightened her grip on his hand.

'Just a minute. There's something I must tell you. I don't know what you'll say or think but I must say it.'

He waited, suddenly tense.

'You remember my friend Marion?'

'The one whose father is a lord?'

'Yes, that Marion. Her father's terribly rich. But she's very nice.' She seemed suddenly nervous. 'He has business out here. Her father. There's a place down the coast. We stayed there during the last leave.' Her hand trembled slightly. 'I can get leave again now that I'm on draft.' Then she turned and looked directly into his eyes. 'If you'd like that.'

'You know I would, Eve. If you're sure——'

She stared down at their hands on the table. 'I'm sure. It's just that I'm afraid of losing you again. This way we'll know.' She tried to laugh. 'I was also scared you'd think I was in the habit of taking all my commanders to a coastal villa!'

'When can you leave?'

She looked up again, her eyes very bright. 'Today. And you?'

He remembered Goss's words. Perhaps he knew about it, too. Maybe the whole ship did.

'This afternoon. How do we go?'

'I can get a car. Or rather Marion will. She can get anything.'

'I'm beginning to like her, too.'

She replied quietly, 'We'd better go now. There are things I must do.' She replaced her cap and added, 'At least you'll know you've got a good driver.' She faced him and he saw the colour on her cheeks. 'The best in Scapa, they used to say!'

'They were right.'

Outside the restaurant the sunlight was almost blinding.

He said, 'I'll phone your quarters.'

'Yes. Then I'll pick you up.' She grinned. 'That sounds bad.'

'Not to me.' He touched her bare arm. 'I love you.'

A working party of seamen marched along the road, and as they passed the petty officer bawled, 'Eyes left!'

When he turned again she saluted him too and said, 'And I you, *sir!*'

He watched her until she had disappeared into a nearby building and then hurried through the gates after the working party. Even when he reached the top of the brow he was still expecting something to go wrong. A change of orders. A staff conference. Some crisis which would hold him aboard like one last cruel trap.

Goss listened to his instructions and said, 'Where will you be staying, sir? In case I need to contact you.'

'I'll telephone the ship when I know the number where I can be reached.'

He saw Stripey, the ship's cat, sauntering up the brow after a brief visit to the dockyard.

Goss nodded. 'Then I suggest you get going, sir.'

In his cabin as he threw a few things into a case he kept one ear for the telephone.

Jupp helped him pack, and as he was about to leave said, 'Perhaps you'd take this too, sir.' He held out a tiny silver replica of the *Benbecula*. It was less than two inches long but perfect in scale and detail. He added awkwardly, 'It was made by the *Becky*'s boatswain many years back. Shouldn't be tellin' you this o'course, but 'e 'ad to melt down four silver teapots from the first class dinin' saloon to complete it.'

Lindsay stared at him. 'But you'll want to keep this!'

'I was savin' it, sir.' He shook his head. 'Maybe this is what for. Anyway, I reckon she'd appreciate it.'

Lindsay placed it inside the case. 'She will. As much as I do.'

Jupp shifted from foot to foot. 'Well, this won't get the work done. Chatterin' like this.' He hesitated. 'An' good luck, Cap'n.'

'I shall miss this sort of treatment when I go back to the real Navy.'

Jupp grinned. 'I'll probably take a pub after this lot's over, sir. You can come an' see me sometimes.'

'It's a promise.'

Jupp followed him to the ladder and watched as he hurried down to the promenade deck. It was strange to be parted from the little silver ship after all these years, he thought vaguely. But the girl for whom it had been intended had not waited for him. His lip curled with disgust. She had married a bloody bricklayer, and it served her right.

He heard the trill of pipes and gave a deep sigh of relief. Lindsay had got away all right. He loped into the cabin and picked up the telephone.

''S'all right, Bob. You can reconnect the phone now. All's well.'

Then humming cheerfully he went to his pantry to find the bottle of Drambuie.

———————

The car was a very old open M.G. but the engine sounded healthy, and when they had cleared the town limits the miles began to pass more quickly.

Once, as they swung around a wide curve above the sea she asked, 'Why are you staring at me? It's not fair. I have to watch the road.'

Lindsay rested his arm along the back of her seat, his fingers touching her hair as it ruffled in the wind. He had never seen her out of uniform before. At the dockyard gates he had almost walked past her. The dress was pale green and very simple. It was, she had explained, straight off a stall, and had proved it by removing a price tag which had been dangling from the hem.

'I'm enjoying it. So you drive and I'll stare, okay?'

Another time, while they waited for some cattle to wander aimlessly across the road, they held hands, oblivious to the heat and dust or the native driver who paused to study them.

Green hills with trees almost touching above the road

changed in seconds to long open stretches and only an
occasional building or bungalow to show any sign of life.
The dust poured back from the wheels in an unbroken
yellow bank, the car jerking violently across deep ruts
and loose stones with careless abandon. Climbing in low
gear then roaring down again, with quick flashes of dark
blue between the tall palms to show that the sea was never
far away.

Then another road, narrower than the main one, and
the girl had to reduce speed to take an increasing number
of bends.

She said, 'What you were saying about the ship. Is it
definite?'

He nodded. 'Yes.'

She reached out and grasped his hand, keeping her
eyes on the road. 'You feel bad about it, don't you?' She
hesitated. 'Maybe I can get transferred near this place
you'll be going.'

She must have been thinking about Canada again for
she added, 'I'm not jolly well going away from you again,
if I can help it!'

'You'd better have a word with Marion! She's bound to
know about these matters.'

She laughed, showing her even teeth, and shouted
above the engine, 'She did that already for another
girl. Told her to get herself pregnant to avoid going
overseas.'

'And did she?'

'Shouldn't think so. You should have seen her bloke.
Like a rhinoceros!'

The car stopped eventually on the crest of a small hill.
Below, Lindsay saw a crescent of beach, the sea making a
necklace of surf to the next headland. There was some
sort of building set amongst the palms. It looked as if it
had been there since time began.

'Is *that* it?'

She turned and studied him gravely. 'You are nutty.

That's an old temple.' She let the car move forward again and called, 'There, *see*!'

The house was inside a low wall, painted white and partly screened by a line of trees. It looked very cool and inviting.

Lindsay could see no sign of life, and even when the car halted outside the gates nothing moved.

She said, 'An old chap and his son look after things most of the time. When proper visitors come here they have more servants, of course.'

'It's marvellous.'

She jumped from the car and dragged at his arm. 'Brother, you ain't seen nothing yet!' She was laughing. Like a tanned child. Watching his face as she pulled him towards the house.

There was only one storey, and the whole house seemed to have been built of stone and marble. Even in the days of cheap labour it would have cost a small fortune.

She said, 'Ah, here he is.'

The head servant was grey-bearded and extremely wrinkled. He must be about eighty, Lindsay thought.

He said, 'Welcome back, Missy. I have sent my son for your luggage.'

The girl looked at Lindsay. 'You'll be wanting a telephone?' She gestured to a door. 'In there.' For an instant her face clouded over. 'Don't go back. No matter what. Even if the base is on fire!'

'What will you be doing?'

She ran her fingers through her hair. 'Ugh, the dust! I'm going to have a swim. Then we'll have something to eat.' She made a mock curtsy. 'Anything *sir* desires.'

Lindsay walked into a low-ceilinged room. There was little furniture but what there was looked old and hand-carved. An unlikely brass telephone stood beside the window, and he imagined someone in the past sitting there. Listening to a voice from the outside world. Who would ever want to leave such a place, he wondered?

The line was surprisingly clear, and after a short delay he was connected to the ship's telephone.

'This is the captain. O.O.D., please.' He waited, picturing the sudden bustle on the upper deck, and tried to control a pang of apprehension.

But it was not the O.O.D.

Goss sounded calm and matter-of-fact. 'Everything's all right this end, sir. Two marines just brought aboard drunk. And I'm about to kick the arse off a thieving coolie I found in the bosun's store.' He paused. 'A normal day, in other words.'

Lindsay looked at the number on the telephone and gave it to Goss. Then he said, 'Thanks for holding the fort.'

'No bother, sir.' There was a pause and the sound of someone else murmuring in the background. Then Goss said abruptly, 'Just heard where I can lay my hooks on some paint. Can't stop, sir. Might lose it!' The line went dead.

'I take it from your cat's smile that the base is *not* on fire?'

He swung round and saw her framed in the open doorway. She was wearing a black swimsuit which made her limbs appear even more tanned.

'You're staring again!'

He walked towards her. 'As I told you. You're very lovely. Especially today.'

She put her hands on her hips and tried to frown. 'My mouth is too wide, I'm covered in freckles and I've got a figure like a boy.' She watched him as he put his hands on her shoulders. 'And I love you, even if you are a liar.'

'I'm surprised they allowed you in the Wrens.' Her skin was very smooth. 'You must need glasses.'

She dropped her head against his chest. 'A nice liar.' Then she pushed him away. 'Get your pants, or whatever commanders wear for informal occasions, and join me on the beach.' She paused and looked back at him, her cheeks flushed. 'Old Mohammed will tell you where your gear is stowed.'

'Is that *really* his name?'

But she was already running out into the sunlight, her bare legs like gold against the nodding palm fronds.

The old man was waiting at the door of an end room, the swimming trunks in his hands.

He said impassively, 'The young missy is very much alive. It pleases me to see her so.'

Lindsay threw off his soiled shirt. 'Was she unhappy?'

'I think lonely. But that is gone now.' He picked up the shirt and added, 'I will have the women attend to this for you.'

Lindsay watched him walk slowly down the hallway. Old but very dignified. Another Jupp perhaps.

Then he turned and looked around the room. The green dress lay on a chair beside the bed. He touched it. It was still warm. Then he opened his case and took out the silver model. On a teak table was the girl's wristwatch. After a second's hesitation he put the little ship beside it. Four silver teapots, Jupp had said. It must have taken some explaining at the time.

With a smile he turned and ran down the hallway, the floor very cool under his bare feet.

He found her standing waist deep in the sea, her slim body being pushed from side to side in the deep swell.

'Come *on!*' She was squinting into the sunlight and he wished he had brought a camera. 'There you go! You're *doing* it again!' Then she laughed, the same sound he had heard that night at Scapa Flow, and plunged into the water.

When finally they emerged dripping and gasping from the sea the light was already fading. The tall line of trees was topped in the last of the sun's rays, their shadows like black bars across the house.

She threw him a towel and began to rub another one vigorously over her hair.

She said suddenly, 'I haven't asked yet.'

He turned but she had her back to him. 'What?'

'How long?'

'Two days.' He saw her shoulders stiffen, the skin still shining with droplets of spray.

Then she replied quietly, 'We'll make it last, won't we?'

Her shoulders were shaking now as if from a chill breeze, but when he put his arm around them she said, 'I'm not going to cry.' Then she twisted on his arm and looked up at him. 'I'm so happy. I can't tell you.'

He picked up his towel. 'By the way. The old man was quite upset when I called him Mohammed.'

She stared at him, appalled. 'You *didn't*!' Then she saw his face and exclaimed, 'You beast! I'm not speaking to you again, ever!' She chuckled. 'Although I suppose he *is* pretty old!'

Together they ran up the shelving beach and into the house. Several lights were already burning, and in the low-ceilinged room a table was laid and a bottle of wine stood chilling in a silver bucket beside it. They stood side by side in the doorway just staring at the table and the quiet room. Then he slipped his arm around her shoulders again, the damp skin almost cold under his touch.

He heard her say, 'It's quite marvellous. I didn't know things like this could happen.'

'Nor me. I have a feeling that your friend Marion has had a hand in it.'

'Yes. I was thinking the same thing.' She moved away, light on her feet, before he could reach her. 'I'm going to change. I shall try and look like a lady, just for you.' She paused. 'Then you can get into something. But not uniform. This once.'

'I wasn't going to.' He smiled. 'This once.'

'Help yourself to a drink over there. Not too much. I want to share everything.' She ran down in the hallway towards the bedroom. 'God, I feel wicked! I really do!'

The old servant appeared silently with a bath robe. 'I will call you when missy is ready, sir.'

'You've done a fine job here. Thanks very much.'

The man shrugged. 'It is nothing.' But there was a hint of a smile as he walked away as dignified as ever.

Lindsay was stooping at a drinks cabinet when she burst in on him again. She was still wearing the swimsuit and was holding the silver ship in her hands.

'This is a wonderful present, darling!' She ran to him and kissed him impulsively on the cheek. Her face was wet, but it was not spray this time.

'It was Jupp's. He wanted you to have it.'

'Bless him.' She stood back and studied him for several seconds. 'And you.' Then she walked away again, very slowly, holding the ship against her body like a talisman.

The dinner, like everything else, was perfect. While Lindsay had been changing into shirt and slacks, candles had appeared on the table, and while the old man and his son waited on them, he and the girl sat facing each other, aware of nothing but each other. In the distance an animal was howling in the darkness and insects maintained a steady buzzing attack on the screened windows. But beyond the circle of candlelight nothing was real or important.

She was wearing a dress of soft yellow which left her shoulders bare. In the candlelight her face was very clear, her expression changing to match their mood with each passing moment.

Only once did she touch on that other world.

'When is it all going to end? It might be years yet.'

'Don't think about it.' Their hands clasped across the table. 'Think about us.'

After that they said very little, and when the table was cleared, the coffee cups empty, Lindsay could sense yet another change in her mood.

She walked to the door and said, 'Don't look at me. I——I don't want to make a fool of myself.' She turned towards him, her voice very low. 'But it's so little time.' Her lip quivered. 'And I want you so badly.' When he made to speak she added quickly, 'Just give me a few minutes.' Again she tried to laugh. 'I'm a bit fluttery inside!'

Lindsay sat in the quiet room listening to the insects against the screens. The animal had stopped howling, so that the silence seemed all the more intense.

Then he blew out the candles and walked from the room. One light still burned in the hallway and beneath the bedroom door was another.

She was lying quite motionless in the bed but her eyes followed him as he moved into the lamplight and stood looking down at her.

A black nightgown lay across a chair and she said, 'It belongs to Marion.'

He sat down on the edge of the bed and touched her hair.

She added quietly, 'But I don't want anything belonging to anyone else. You don't think I'm silly?'

'No. Of course I don't.' He leaned over and kissed her forehead. 'I think you're very special.'

'I just want you to be happy with me.' She dropped her eyes to his hand as he pulled the sheet gently from beneath her chin. 'I don't want to spoil *anything*.'

Then she closed her eyes and lay still as he dragged the sheet away and sat looking at her, his hand moving gently across her body. She did not move until he had slipped out of his clothes and lay down beside her, an arm beneath her head, his other hand around one of her breasts. Then she opened her eyes and watched him, her breath warm against his face.

'Two days and three nights.'

He felt her body go rigid as he moved his hand across the gentle curve of her stomach, and when he lowered his head to her breast he could feel the heart beating like a small trapped animal. Beating to match his own.

Her arms came up and around his head, her fingers gripping his shoulders with sudden urgency as she whispered, 'Oh, God! I do love you!'

The fingers seemed to be biting into his flesh as he moved his hand still more, feeling her come alive to his touch, the need and the desire breaking down their reserves like an unspoken word.

As he rose above her she threw open her arms and stared up into his face, her mouth moist in the lamplight.

Then he was falling, feeling her arch to receive him, holding him, dragging him down and down, until the fierceness of their love left them entwined in the soft glare like statuary.

The next thing Lindsay realised was that he was awake, his head cradled against the girl's hip while she ran her fingers gently through his hair. The lamp was out and through the shutters he could see the faint gleam of dawn.

She whispered, 'You cried out, my darling. Just once, and then you were still again.'

He kissed her hip and felt a tremor run through her. Was the nightmare gone at last? Had it found the one, unmatchable strength and left him in peace?

He kissed her again and said, 'I want you.'

She pulled his head across her stomach, moaning softly as he postponed the moment a while longer.

Later, as they lay and watched the first yellow sunlight through the shutters, she said simply, 'I don't feel like me at all. Strange, isn't it?'

'Whoever you are, I think you're wonderful.'

He thought he heard footsteps in the hallway. The clatter of cups. He almost expected to see Jupp peering around the door.

He dragged the sheet over their bodies and said,

'Cover yourself, you shameless creature.' He kissed her hard on the mouth. 'Or we may be asked to leave.'

She took the mood, swinging her legs over the bed and seizing her robe from a chair.

'Lay another finger on me and I'll——' She ran back to him and held him against her. 'I'll probably let you do anything you like with me.'

And that was how it continued for the next two days and nights. Moments of peace and intimate silence. Swift, exploring passion which left them both breathless and limp like young animals. The sun and blue sea, the isolation and the sheer perfection of it all was like a backcloth to their own happiness.

When they climbed into the old car again Lindsay said quietly, 'I will never forget this place.' He squeezed her hand. 'One day I'll remind you of it. When you start getting fed up with me.'

She looked at the house. The old man and his son had made their farewells as if to allow the moment of departure a certain privacy.

'They'll put a plaque up there one day.' She shook the hair from her eyes. 'To Wren Eve Collins, who fell here.'

They smiled at each other and he said, 'Time to move.'

The car jolted up the hill past the ruins which they had not found time to visit.

They hardly spoke during the return journey, and once when he had seen a tear on her cheek she had reached out for his hand, saying, 'I'm all right. Don't worry, my darling.' She had placed his hand on her thigh and continued to drive along the dusty road above the sea. 'It's just me. I'm selfish, pig-headed and silly.'

He gripped her leg, knowing she felt as he did. 'And perfect.'

The first buildings of the town swung into view as she said, 'I'll drop you at the gates.'

He nodded. 'Right. I'll ring you as soon as I know what's happening.' The car stopped, the bodywork glittering in the harsh sunlight. She kept both hands on the wheel.

'You're not sorry?'

'Grateful.' He watched her turn to look at him. 'And happy.'

She revved the engine. 'Me too, as it happens.'

The car moved away into the traffic and Lindsay walked towards the gates.

He returned the sentry's salute. 'Good morning.'

The marine watched him from the corner of his eye. 'Good for some,' he said.

18 Passage home

Goss's private information proved to be very true. Within twelve hours of the libertymen returning aboard, the last few missing ones being found and delivered by shore patrols, *Benbecula* was steaming out of harbour.

The day prior to sailing Lindsay had attended a conference at the H.Q. building, and from it had gleaned some importance of the ships being allotted to the convoy. Troops, munitions, oil and food, it was to be organised like some vast relay race. The first leg across the Indian Ocean was more or less straightforward, as Japanese submarines had so far made little or no impression there. Once around the Cape more escorts would be joining and leaving the convoy, like guards changing on a valuable treasure, and a powerful cruiser squadron would be at sea the whole time, never too far away to give support against heavy enemy units.

Off Gibraltar the convoy would be reorganised. Some ships would slip under the Rock's own defences with supplies for the fleet and the desert army. Others would be joining with another convoy to head westward to America. The bulk of the ships would press on for the last and most hazardous part, to run a gauntlet between U-boats and German long-range bombers.

The fact that so much care was being shown for the final part of the voyage was proof of the importance given to it. It was hinted that an aircraft carrier and her escorts would be available to provide vital round-the-clock air cover, something almost unheard of.

Once at sea, *Benbecula* joined with other naval vessels in sorting out and organising the ships into three columns. There were twenty-four to be escorted in all. Lindsay had been in far larger convoys but somehow this one seemed so much bigger. Perhaps the size and majesty of individual ships made up for actual numbers. The four troopers, for instance, were ocean liners of repute before the war. Large, well-powered and new. The other ships were as varied as their flags, but unlike most other convoys Lindsay had seen, were fairly modern vessels, well able to keep up a good pace under almost every circumstance.

As they had gathered, from Colombo and Bombay, from Kuwait and as far away as New Zealand and Australia, he had been conscious of the variation. Almost every flag seemed to represent a country occupied by an enemy. French and Dutch, Danish and Norwegian, there seemed unending colours on hulls and flags. There were several British ones and two Americans, and Lindsay wondered what it must feel like to be at sea, depending on your own resources but free, while your homeland was under the enemy's heel.

Goss's special information had omitted one fact, however. Because of the convoy's changing shape and size it would be necessary to retain one naval officer in sole charge, in a ship which would be employed for the whole of the journey. *Benbecula* was that ship. Commodore Kemp was to be senior officer.

Maybe Kemp was still unsure of Lindsay's reaction, or perhaps he was at last aware of his own unpopularity with higher authority. Either way, he appeared content to stay at a distance, keeping his contact with Lindsay to a bare, cool minimum.

When he had first come aboard he had said, 'You command the ship. I will control the overall pattern of events.'

Now, four days out, and steaming south-west across

the blinding blue glare of the Indian Ocean, Lindsay wondered what the commodore had been offered as his next appointment. A lot would no doubt depend on the success of the convoy, although with such a well planned series of escorts it was hard to see how things could go wrong.

He walked to the extent of the port wing and stared astern at the great panorama of ships. *Benbecula* was leading the starboard line, while one of the big troopers led the centre. The port column was headed by a dazzle-painted cruiser. He let his eyes move along each ship, and wondered how many would survive the whole war. Oil-tankers and freighters, grain ships and ore carriers, while in the centre the four stately liners carried the most precious cargo of all. Even without binoculars it was possible to see the packed masses of men on their decks, like pale khaki lines over every foot of open space. The second troopship was partly hidden by the leader, and he wondered where Eve was at this moment. Peering at the *Benbecula*? Resting in her cabin or chatting to the irrepressible Marion? He could not see the ship without seeing her face in his mind.

Because of the convoy conferences, the planning and last minute organisation he had only been able to meet her twice, and then briefly.

As he strained his eyes towards the ship he thought of all the coincidences which had brought and held them together. Even the mistake at Liverpool which had sent a girl to her death and kept Eve safe seemed like part of some uncanny plan.

Through the open wheelhouse door he heard Stannard's voice as he handed over his watch.

'Course still two-two-zero. One-one-zero revs.'

He heard Hunter's muffled reply.

Stannard walked on to the wing and stared at the ships. 'Quite a sight, sir.'

Lindsay glanced at him. He looked strained and

sounded as much. He had not spoken of his brother again and made an obvious effort to be his old self. But the signs were only too clear. Perhaps when he got involved with the new navigation course and his next ship he might be too busy to brood.

'How does it feel, sir?'

Lindsay saw the Australian's eyes move to his shoulder straps. The fourth gold stripe was very bright and new against the others.

The unexpected promotion had been one of the first things which Goss had mentioned when he had returned from the two days leave. You never really knew a man like Goss. If he was deadly serious or trying to hold on to a secret joke.

He had said, 'Two bits of news, sir. One good. One not so good.'

The good news had been Lindsay's advancement to captain. The bad had been Commodore Kemp's arrival on board.

He smiled. 'I don't feel any different.'

It was true. Once, years back, he would have imagined that reaching the coveted rank was all a young officer could wish for. He had changed. Everything seemed and felt different now.

Stannard seemed surprised. 'It's just that I've never seen you looking so well, sir. I guess I'll never know the strain of command. Not sure I want to.'

Lindsay looked at the ships. 'I am getting married when we reach the U.K.'

Stannard gasped. 'Well, Jeez, that is, I'm very glad, sir.' He held out his hand. 'Hell, that's good news.'

'You're the first to know.' He wondered why he had told Stannard. Just like that. Seeing his obvious pleasure made him glad he had.

'Certainly sudden, sir.'

A signalman called, 'From the *John P. Ashton*, sir. Permission to reduce speed. Engine failure.'

Lindsay nodded. 'Affirmative. Better now than when we run into trouble.'

The ship in question was an American destroyer, and apart from *Benbecula* the oldest in the convoy. They had been launched the same year, and Lindsay could sympathise with her captain's problems. She was one of the old four-pipers, now on way to be handed over on loan to the Royal Navy for anti-submarine duty. She was not the first to change flags by this arrangement, but unlike the others she had been on picket duty at Singapore when the Japanese had struck. Now, rolling unsteadily above her own image, she was falling away on the convoy's flank, her captain no doubt praying that the fault was nothing fatal.

Ahead of the convoy two other destroyers were barely visible in sea haze, but Lindsay knew one to be the *Merlin*. Her captain would be thinking, too. Of his next command. Not one ship but a group. A positive job. Something which really mattered.

For the first time since rejoining the ship he felt the return of resentment and bitterness. Ashore, he had tried to hide his feelings from Eve, guessing she was probably grateful for his new appointment. You could not get drowned or burned alive in a training depot. Unless you were born unlucky.

But now, as he watched the escorting cruiser, the wink of signal lamps, he knew the same feeling.

He saw de Chair standing on the forward deck watching some of his marines exercising with Bren guns. In their shorts and boots, their bodies tanned from Ceylon's swimming and sunlight, they looked like strangers.

'From *John P. Ashton*, sir. Am under way again.' The man paused. 'This chicken is ready for the pot.'

Stannard said, 'What a helluva name for a ship. I wonder who he was.'

Lindsay grinned. 'Old or not, she'll be very welcome. Just about anything afloat is wanted now.'

Stannard looked up at the masthead and said quietly, 'Except the *Becky*. They don't want her any more.'

Lindsay looked away. 'I know how you feel.' What he had said once before to Stannard. 'But there's nothing we can do about it.'

Stannard sighed. 'Well, I think I'll get my head down, sir. Plenty to do later, I guess.'

Lindsay waited until he had left the bridge and then raised his glasses to study the second ship of the centre column. It was just possible he might catch a glimpse of her.

Eighteen days out of Ceylon the convoy was off the Cape of Good Hope and heading north-west into the Atlantic. Each day was much like the preceding one. Drills and general routine, with the weather still warm and friendly. The leading destroyers had been relieved by another pair from Cape Town, and the Royal Indian Navy sloop which followed them this far had returned to her own country. The cruiser was still with them, and surprisingly, so was the *John P. Ashton*. She had had two minor breakdowns but always she seemed to manage to be there when a new dawn broke.

As the forenoon watch took stations around the ship, Lindsay climbed up to the bridge and found Commodore Kemp sitting in his chair staring at the open sea across the bows. Goss had the watch but was on the starboard wing, apparently staying as far as possible from his superior. The latter had hardly shown himself throughout the voyage so far. He had a large cabin aft, formerly an extended stateroom for very important passengers, which was still retained for much the same reason, although Lindsay suspected Goss's sentiment had a good deal to do with it.

Kemp turned as Lindsay saluted formally. 'I was going to send for you.' He turned to stare forward again. 'I've just had a top secret signal from Admiralty.' He sounded hoarse, and Lindsay wondered if he was drinking heavily in his private quarters. 'Been a spot of bother off the Cape Verde Islands. A freighter has been sunk. Believed to have been shelled by a surface ship.' He shifted his shoulders beneath the spotless drill jacket. 'Not our problem, naturally, but it's as well to know these things.'

Lindsay watched him narrowly. 'Was that all, sir?'

'Admiralty appears to think there may be some connection with another report. A cruiser was badly damaged by a mine. Too far out in the Atlantic for a drifting one from a field. Dropped with some others apparently, on the off chance of hitting any stray ship in the area.'

Lindsay clenched his fists to steady himself. 'It must be that raider again. Has to be.'

Kemp replied evasively, 'We don't know that for certain. Nobody does. Anyway, if the two attacks *are* connected, the Hun is in for a shock. This convoy is on the top secret list and so is our additional cruiser screen. If the enemy tries to tangle with us, I can whistle up enough heavy guns to cut him into little shreds!' He swivelled in the chair and glared at him. 'Satisfied?'

Lindsay caught the smell of brandy. 'Not entirely.' He walked to the teak rail and ran his hands along it. 'Was there any other information from the freighter before she was silenced?'

Kemp swallowed. 'She was a Greek. Said she was going to the assistance of a Spanish merchantman which was in difficulties.'

Lindsay bit his lip. How long would it take for people to realise and see through this simple trick? Without effort he could visualise the savage gunflashes against the drifting ice, the burning hull and the Wren who was blind.

Kemp was right about one thing. If the raider came upon this convoy, even the one cruiser in company should be more than a match. But with the distant screen as well she would not stand an earthly, even of getting in range.

Kemp appeared to think his silence was an acceptance and added curtly, 'In another week we'll be meeting with a heavy additional escort from Freetown.' The thought seemed to give him new confidence. 'Like a clock, that's how I like things.'

The rear door slid back and Midshipman Kemp walked into the wheelhouse.

The commodore watched him make a few notations in the bridge log and said, 'Ah, Jeremy. There you are. Wondered what you were doing.' He gave a careful smile. 'Been hiding from me, eh?'

The boy looked at him. 'Sir?'

The commodore spread his hands. 'I shouldn't be at all surprised if you have a pleasant surprise waiting for you in England. I'm not promising anything, of course, but if I put a word in the right direction, I believe you may get something to your advantage.' He beamed around the quiet wheelhouse. The impassive quartermaster, the signalman, a bosun's mate who was looking anywhere but at him.

The midshipman asked flatly, 'Is that all you wanted, sir?'

The commodore swung away. 'Yes. Carry on.' As the door slid shut he snapped, 'Bloody ungrateful little tyke!'

Jupp came from the port wing carrying a tray covered with a napkin. He saw Lindsay and showed his teeth.

'Coffee and a sandwich, sir.'

Kemp said coldly, 'What about me?'

'Sir?' Jupp placed the tray carefully on a vibrating flag locker. 'I will inform your steward that you wish 'im to fetch somethin' for you.' He looked at the man's angry face. 'Sir.'

The commodore thrust his thickset body from the chair and stalked to the door. As he disappeared down the ladder Lindsay seemed to feel the men around him come to life, saw the quartermaster give a quick wink at the signalman.

He said, 'It won't do, Jupp.' He smiled gravely. 'And it won't help either.'

Jupp folded the napkin into four quarters. 'I'm not with you, sir? Did I do anythin'?'

Lindsay grinned. 'Get back to your pantry while you're still alive!'

Goss re-entered the wheelhouse and yawned hugely. 'God, it smells better in here!'

Lindsay turned away. They were all at it. Even Goss. For the ship and for him. It was the only way they knew of showing their true feelings.

Jupp was still hovering by the flag locker. 'Beggin' yer pardon, sir, but I 'ave to report some missin' gear from the wardroom.'

Goss interrupted calmly, 'Not to worry. I expect some bloody coolie lifted it. Or maybe it went down a gash chute by accident.'

Lindsay did not know how to face them. 'Silver teapots?'

Jupp sounded surprised. 'Well, as a matter of fact, yes, sir.'

Goss sighed. 'One of those things.' He walked to the wing again, his face devoid of expression.

Lindsay began to see more and more of the commodore in the days which followed. He said little and contented himself with examining incoming signals or just sitting in silence on the bridge chair.

That he was growing increasingly worried became obvious as news was received from the Admiralty signals of a new and changing pattern in enemy activity. It seemed there was no longer any doubt that all the incidents were linked. A German raider was at large, and more to the point, was the same one which Lindsay had last seen off Greenland.

Her captain was a man who appeared to care little for his own safety. Several times he had barely missed the searching cruisers and the net was closing in on him rapidly. The last sinking had been three hundred miles north-east of Trinidad, and because of it some small convoys had been held up for fear of another attack. There were too few escorts available on the opposite side of the Atlantic, and the U-boat menace further north made the hope of any quick transfer of forces unlikely. Badly needed convoys were made to stay at anchor or in port while the cruisers increased their efforts to hunt the German down once and for all.

Two days before the anticipated meeting with the Freetown escorts Kemp sent for Lindsay in his quarters. He was sitting in a deep sofa, the deck around his feet covered with signals and written instructions. He seemed to have aged in the past week, and there were deep furrows around his eyes and mouth. He did not ask Lindsay to sit down.

'Another sinking report.'

Lindsay nodded. He had seen it for himself. A Danish tanker sailing in ballast without escort had been shelled and sunk barely a hundred miles from the previous sinking. This time the Danish captain had managed to get off more than a cry for help. There was now no doubt the raider was the same ship.

He replied, 'The German's working south, sir. Trying to catch the Americas trade as much as possible.' He added, 'He'll sink a few more poor devils before he's run to earth.' He did not try to hide the bitterness.

Kemp picked up a signal and then dropped it again. 'I know he can't get at us.' He looked up, his eyes blazing. 'They've ordered our cruiser screen westward. Taken it away from my support!'

Lindsay watched him coldly. 'Yes, sir. I heard.'

'Didn't even consider what I might think about it.'

'They've no choice. If the raider continues to move south or south-east the cruisers will have him in the bag. He can't run forever.'

'This is a valuable convoy. Perhaps vital.' He seemed to be speaking his thoughts aloud. 'It's wrong to expect me to take all the responsibility.'

Lindsay said, 'Was that all you wanted, sir?'

The commodore watched him with sudden anger. 'I know what you're hoping! That I'll make some mistake so that you can crow about it!'

'Then you don't know me at all.' Lindsay kept his voice level. 'When you are in charge of any convoy there is always the risk of change and sudden alteration in planning. It doesn't necessarily go like a *clock*.'

There was a tap at the door and Stannard stepped into the cabin.

Kemp glared at him. 'Well?'

'Another signal from Admiralty, sir. Request you detach the cruiser *Canopus* and destroyer escort immediately.' He looked at Lindsay. 'They are to leave with all speed and join in the search.' He shrugged. 'It seems that the net is tightening.'

Kemp nodded. 'Execute.' As the door closed he muttered, 'Now there's just this ship until the Freetown escorts arrive.' He looked up. 'When will that be?'

'Forty-eight hours, sir. We crossed the twentieth parallel at noon today.'

Lindsay left him with his thoughts and returned to the bridge. The cruiser was already moving swiftly clear of her column, and far ahead of the convoy he could see the two destroyers gathering speed to take station on her.

'Signal the freighter *Brittany* to take lead ship in the port column.' He raised his glasses and watched the lamp winking from the other vessel's bridge.

He said, 'It seems we're in charge of things, Yeo.'

Ritchie, who was keeping an eye on his signalman,

nodded. ''Cept for the Yank, sir.' He jerked his thumb over his shoulder. '*She's* still with us, more or less.'

Lindsay smiled. There was no real danger but it was strange that in a matter of hours their hidden strength had melted away to leave the two oldest ships as a sole protection.

'Signal the *John P. Ashton* to assume station ahead of the convoy.'

Ritchie said, 'She'll blow 'er boilers, sir.'

'Her captain will know he's the only one now with submarine detection gear. He won't have to be told what to do.'

Later, as the elderly destroyer thrashed past the other ships he saw her light blinking rapidly and heard Ritchie say, 'Signal, sir. This must be Veterans Day.' He shook his head. 'He ain't kiddin' either.'

When darkness fell over the three columns the American four-piper had retained her position well ahead of the convoy. Lindsay hoped she did not break down overnight. She stood a good chance of being rammed by several of the big ships if she did. With that in mind, her engineers would no doubt be doubly careful.

He was lolling in his chair, half sleeping, half listening to the engines' steady beat, when Stannard roused him again. He was actually asleep when the watch had changed and had heard nothing at all. He had been dreaming of a sunlit beach. The girl, wet with spray and warm in his arms. Laughing.

He straightened himself in the chair. 'Yes?'

Stannard had his back to the shaded compass light and Lindsay could not see his face.

'Just decoded an urgent signal, sir. Admiralty. If you come into the chart room you can read it.'

'Just tell me.' He waited, almost knowing what he would say.

'R.A.F. reconnaissance have reported a large German unit at sea. Out of Brest, sir.'

Lindsay stared at him. 'When was this?'

'That's just it. They don't know. Weather has been very bad for aerial photography and the flak has been extra thick around Brest lately. The Jerries have been using all sorts of camouflage, nets and so forth. All they do know for sure is that one large unit is not there any more.'

'When was the last check made?'

'Two weeks back, sir.' Stannard sounded apprehensive. 'Won't affect us, will it? I mean, this is a top secret convoy.'

Lindsay slid from the chair. 'Nothing's that secret. How can you hide twenty-four ships and God knows how many people?' He added sharply, 'Send someone to rouse the commodore. He'll want to know.'

As Stannard hurried to a telephone Lindsay walked out on to the port wing. He could see the nearest troop-ship quite clearly in the moonlight, her boat deck and twin funnels standing out against the stars like parts of a fortress.

A mistake? It was possible. The Germans were always trying to move their heavy units to avoid bombing raids. They had to keep them afloat and to all appearances ready for sea. Just by being there they were a constant threat. Enough to tie down the Home Fleet's big ships at Scapa and others further south. Having the whole French seaboard as well as their own, the enemy were more than able to extend the menace.

He gripped the screen and tried to clear his mind of the nagging doubt. Just suppose it was part of a plan? That the raider's attacks on *Loch Glendhu* and the other convoy had been a working-up for all this? At best, it would mean the Germans had been right in assuming that a single raider could tie down a far greater mass of ships than her worth really suggested. At worst . . . he gripped the screen even tighter. Then it would mean that every available cruiser had been withdrawn from this convoy to search for a red-herring. The raider would be caught and sunk. He stared fixedly at the troopship. But in exchange for their sacrifice, the Germans might hope for the greatest prize of all. A whole convoy. Men, supplies, vital materials and. . . .

He swung round as a man called, 'Commodore's comin' up, sir.'

Stannard joined him by the screen. 'What shall we do, sir?'

'Wait, Pilot.' He did not look at him. 'And hope.'

The following morning was another fine clear one. Even during the last part of the morning watch the sun gave a hint of the power to come and the horizon was hidden in low haze, like steam.

Maxwell was officer of the watch, and as Lieutenant Hunter started the daily check on the columns and bearing of the various ships nearby, Maxwell stayed by the screen, staring at the tiny shape of the American destroyer directly ahead. The haze was playing tricks with her upperworks and spindly funnels. As if she had been cut in halves, with the upper pieces replaced at the wrong angle.

He glanced at Lindsay but he was still asleep in his chair, one arm hanging down beside it like that of a corpse. He returned to his thoughts, unconsciously clasping his hands behind him as if on parade.

Soon now he would be getting his half stripe. Without effort he could see himself at the gunnery school on Whale Island. The toiling ranks of marching officers and men. The bark of commands and snap of weapons. It would be like picking up the threads all over again. With luck, further advancement would follow automatically, and people would forget the one mistake which had cost him so much time.

Maxwell had been young and newly-married to Decia

when it had happened. Her family had been against the marriage from the start but had put a brave face on things when it had come about.

As gunnery officer in a destroyer he had been in charge of a practice shoot, a normal, routine exercise. His assistant had been a sub-lieutenant, a spoiled, stupid man whom he should never have trusted. Perhaps he had been thinking about his new bride. The excitement and sudden prosperity the marriage had brought him. He was a proud man and had at first disliked the idea of having a rich wife while he lived on a lieutenant's meagre pay.

Whatever he had been thinking about, it had not been the shoot. The sub-lieutenant had made a serious mistake with deflection, and instead of hitting the towed target, the shell had ploughed into the tug and killed seven men.

The sub-lieutenant had been dismissed the Service with dishonour. But he had been inexperienced, a nervous breakdown following the accident had more than proved the point to the court's satisfaction. So if Maxwell had not directly pressed the trigger, he was certainly recognised as the true culprit. Only his excellent record had saved him from the same fate. To be required to resign was a lesser punishment in the court's eyes, but to Maxwell it spelled disaster.

Returning to the Navy because of the war, he had half expected that his past would be buried. Another chance. One more fair opportunity. He had been wrong. One empty job after another, until finally he had been appointed to *Benbecula.* The bottom rung of the ladder.

He swayed back on his heels. But when he reached Whale Island again no one would sneer or cut him dead. *He* would be the man who had sunk a U-boat and made history. Ancient six-inch weapons with half-witted conscripts behind them against the cream of the German Navy. And it had been his eye and brain which had done it.

Then he thought of Decia. The nightmare vision of the
bedroom and the man on his knees pleading with him. It
would all be too late. He would not have her. Not see the
admiration and envy on the faces of brother officers
when he entered a room with her on his arm.

The telephone by his elbow made him start. 'Officer of
the watch?' His eye moved to the pod on the foremast as
he formed a mental picture of the lookout.

'Aircraft, sir. Green four-five.'

Lindsay was awake. 'What was that?'

Maxwell kept his eyes on the foremast. 'Say again.'

'I'm sure it was an aircraft, sir.'

Maxwell covered the mouthpiece and looked at Lindsay. 'Bloody fool says there's an aircraft on the starboard
bow, sir.' He frowned. 'Fifteen hundred miles from the
nearest land and he sees an aircraft! Must be the bloody
heat!'

Lindsay moved from the chair and took the handset.
'Captain here. What exactly can you see?'

The seaman sounded flustered. 'Can't see nothin' now,
sir.' Then more stubbornly, 'But it was there, sir. Like a
bit of glass flashin' in the sun. Very low down. Above the
'aze.'

'Keep looking.' To Maxwell he added, 'It's disappeared.'

Maxwell sniffed. 'Naturally.'

Hunter came out of the sunlight, folding his shipping
lists. 'Could be a *small* plane, sir.' He smiled awkwardly as
they looked at him. 'But I was forgetting. There are no
carriers hereabouts.'

The phone rang again.

Lindsay took it quickly. 'Captain.'

'Just saw it on about the same bearin', sir. Just one flash.
Very small, but no doubt about it.'

Lindsay handed the telephone to Hunter. 'Inform the
commodore that I would be grateful of his presence
here.' He waited for Maxwell to pass his message. 'Very

well, Guns.' He glanced towards the nearest troopship.
'Now you can sound off action stations.'

For a moment longer nobody moved. Then Maxwell
asked, 'But, sir, *why?*'

'It may give us,' he paused, recalling the deserted
restaurant, the gross Turk at his table, 'it may give us
time.'

Maxwell shrugged. Without another word he pressed
his thumb hard on the red button.

———————

Dancy rubbed his forehead with a handkerchief. In
spite of the bridge air ducts it was stifling.

He asked quietly, 'Do you reckon anything will
happen?'

Stannard glanced at the commodore's bulky shape in
the chair, at Lindsay who was standing just outside the
starboard door.

'I dunno. This waiting makes me sweat a bit.'

The ship had been at action for two hours, although it
seemed much longer.

Without warning the commodore heaved himself from
the chair and snapped, 'Chart room.' He waited until
Lindsay had followed him and added, 'You, too, Pilot.'

In the chart room it was even hotter with every scuttle
and deadlight clamped shut.

The commodore said, 'Nothing.'

Stannard looked at Lindsay. He seemed very com-
posed, even calm.

'The lookout was certain about the plane, sir.' Lindsay
watched him across the table. 'He is an experienced
rating.'

'I see.' The commodore's hands fluttered vaguely and
then came to rest on the chart. 'What do you suggest?'

Lindsay relaxed slightly. 'If I'm right, sir, it would be
inviting disaster to make a radio signal for assistance.
One, we know the Freetown ships will not make contact

before tomorrow at the earliest. Two, if there is an enemy ship out there, it might be in total ignorance of our position.'

'Well?'

'I suggest you should alter course to the east'rd, sir. Or turn one hundred and eighty degrees and *then* call for assistance. Increase to maximum speed. It would give us time and room to manoeuvre.'

'Do you know what you are asking?' Kemp's voice trembled. 'For me to run away from a shadow! You must be out of your mind!'

Lindsay said patiently, 'That aircraft was probably catapulted from its parent ship. If so, you can expect the worst.' He added with sudden sharpness, 'What is the alternative? Head on into destruction?' He spoke faster as if to prevent interruption. Stannard saw his hands clenched into fists against his sides, could almost feel the effort he was making to break Kemp's resistance. 'Think, sir, of the effect it will have if we allow this convoy to be decimated. Quite apart from damage to morale on top of the Singapore disaster, the actual losses would be terrible. These troops are vital for the next few months, and for all we know, so too are the supplies and equipment.'

Kemp took a few paces to the bulkhead and turned his back on them. 'Can't do it. It's too big.' He added hesitantly, 'We have to take the risk.'

'There have already been too many of those, sir.' Lindsay spoke very quietly. 'Admiral Phillips took a risk with *Repulse* and *Prince of Wales* but they were both sunk, and Singapore fell just the same. We took risks by sending an army to help the Greeks when anyone but a fool should have seen it was impossible to stop the rot there. Result, we lost more men and plenty of good ships trying to get them away at Crete.'

'You're accusing me of risking this convoy. Is that it?' Kemp still did not turn.

'I do not see you have any choice but to take evading

action *now,* sir.' When the commodore said nothing he persisted, 'If you wait, it will be useless trying to scatter the convoy. We have a whole day of clear visibility——'

Kemp faced him abruptly. 'Leave me to think.'

Stannard asked, 'What about my plotting team, sir?'

Kemp shouted, 'Let them wait until I am ready! Now for God's sake *leave me alone!*'

Stannard followed Lindsay into the passageway and thrust past the waiting midshipman and his yeoman. Under his breath he muttered, 'Stupid bastard!' Then he slammed the door behind him, making one of the messengers jump with alarm.

Above the bridge in his armoured control position Maxwell heard the door slam. His shirt was wringing with sweat, and the backs of his spotting team and Lieutenant Hunter immediately below his steel chair looked as if they had just emerged from the sea. In the Denmark Strait they had somehow kept going with thick clothing and the small electric heaters. In this glare there was no defence at all against the sun.

Hunter twisted round and looked at him. 'No more aircraft. No bloody anything. So why can't we fall out action stations?'

Because that stupid commodore can't make up his mind, that's why. But aloud Maxwell replied sharply, 'For God's sake, don't you start!'

Hunter shrugged and reached out to open a small observation slit on the port side. It made a very small breeze, but the sight of the nearest troopship was somehow reassuring. The same view, day after day, after bloody day. He felt Maxwell stirring behind him and smiled. Whale Island. Maxwell would love that. All mouth and trousers, like the rest of his breed.

For a split second he imagined an aircraft had dived from the sky, although it was impossible. The screaming roar seemed to press down on him, until his mind was a complete blank. Then came the explosions, and as he stared incredulously at the troopship he saw the towering waterspouts rising beyond her, higher and higher, until they shone like white silk in the sunlight.

As the tall columns began to subside he saw the tell-tale pall of black smoke, growing and rising against the clear sky like a filthy stain. A ship on the port column had been hit. But with what? It had all been just a matter of seconds. Seconds in which everything and each man around him seemed suspended in time and space.

Then Maxwell yelled, 'Don't gape at me! Start track-ing!' He punched the shoulder of the nearest seaman. 'Come on, *jump* to it!'

He pressed his eyes to his powerful sights as the control position turned slightly on its mounting. He blinked in the harsh light and rubbed his forehead with his wrist. Nothing. The horizon was still hazy but not that much. You should be able to see something. He felt a chill run down his spine as he picked up the handset and reported, 'Captain, sir. Those shells came from below the horizon.' He heard Hunter gasp. 'No target, sir.'

Lindsay heard his flat voice and then ran to the wheelhouse door. The ship which had been straddled by three or more heavy shells was falling out of line, her upper deck burning fiercely beneath the towering smoke pall.

He snapped, 'Make the signal.' He scribbled a brief addition before Ritchie dashed to the W/T office. 'At least someone will know what's happening.'

He heard the commodore pushing through the bridge watchkeepers, his voice shaking as he called, 'What was it? Where is the enemy?'

Again that screaming roar, and Lindsay tensed, imagining the projectiles hurtling down from their high arc of fire. He had been right. Three columns of water shot above the far line of ships.

He shouted, 'I've reported we are under attack!' He did not take his eyes from the burning freighter.

'Yes, yes.' Kemp seemed unable to think clearly. He was also peering at the ship, at the smoke and flames which had now engulfed the whole of her poop.

Lindsay said, 'Spotting plane. It was just a freak hit.' He glanced at the other man's stricken face. 'But I'm afraid we can't rely on luck any more.'

Then he left the commodore on the gratings and entered the wheelhouse. It was too late to turn the convoy now. At any second the other ship would show herself. But to shoot this far and with such accuracy she must be big. Too big.

He saw the faces of the men around him, watching, waiting for his decision.

He said quietly, 'As soon as we know the enemy's bearing we will make a signal to the convoy. To scatter.'

Kemp's shadow filled the doorway. 'I did not order that!' He was tugging at his collar. 'I demand to be informed!'

'Then I am informing you now, sir. Do you have any objections?'

Kemp dropped his eyes. 'I suppose some will get away. There's nothing we can do.'

Lindsay eyed him calmly. Christ, how could he feel so remote?

He said, 'As you told me when you came aboard, sir. This is my ship. When the convoy scatters, *your* control will be at an end.'

Kemp stared at him, his eyes watering with fixed concentration. 'There's still the American destroyer!'

For once Lindsay did not bother to hide his contempt. 'You'd send *her*, would you?' He turned his back. 'She'll be needed anyway, to shadow the enemy when it's all over.'

As if to mark the finality of his words, the tannoy speaker intoned, 'Control to bridge. Enemy in sight!'

19 'They made it safe...'

The burning freighter had dropped a mile astern of the convoy when the port column of ships wheeled away in response to Lindsay's signal, their rising wash giving evidence of increasing speed.

'From *John P. Ashton,* sir.' Ritchie steadied his telescope. *'Request permission to engage the enemy.'*

The bridge shivered as another salvo came screaming out of the sky. The shells exploded in an overlapping line of spray and dirty smoke, a mere cable from the leading troopship.

'Negative.' A near miss from one of those shells would sink the elderly destroyer. 'Make to the second column to scatter *now.*'

Stannard muttered fiercely, 'They can't get far. Christ, those bastards are shooting well.'

Another sullen roar enveloped the bridge and he saw the shells explode where the big liner might have been but for the change of course.

Lindsay slid open a shutter on the starboard side and raised his glasses. At first he saw only haze and the clear blue sea below the horizon. Behind him he heard Hunter's voice on the speaker.

'Green three-oh. Range one-eight-oh.'

Then quite suddenly he saw the enemy ship. She was a darker blur in the horizon haze, but as he watched he saw the ripple of orange flashes which momentarily laid bare her superstructure in the powerful lenses. He tried not to swallow, although his throat was like a kiln. He knew those nearby were watching him. Trying to gauge his reactions.

A cruiser at least. He heard the screaming whine of shells as they tore down over the scattering ships, the tell-tale shiver as they exploded harmlessly in open water.

'Make the signal to our column. Tell them to be as quick as possible.'

The enemy fired again, and the rearmost ship in the column was straddled by three shells. As she steamed stubbornly through the falling torrents of spray he saw she had been badly mauled. Her boat deck looked as if it had been crushed by an avalanche of rock.

'All acknowledged, sir.' Ritchie scribbled automatically on his pad. Not much point. Nobody would ever read it.

There was a sudden silence in the wheelhouse as Lindsay said, 'Give me the mike.' He took it from Dancy, seeing in his mind the men throughout his command.

'This is the captain speaking. We are under attack by a heavy enemy warship which is now about nine miles off our starboard bow. She is big and therefore fast. With bad visibility or darkness the convoy might have been saved by scattering.'

He paused as the sea erupted far away on the port quarter, smothering another ship with those deadly waterspouts. Across the distance he heard the jolting metallic cracks, like a woodsman using an axe on a clear day. The sounds of jagged splinters biting into her hull.

He continued, 'To have even a hope of escaping, these ships must be given *time*.'

Lindsay snapped down the button and looked at Ritchie. 'Very well, Yeoman. Hoist battle ensigns.'

The commodore, who had been staring at the freighter with the smashed boat deck, swung round and shouted, '*Stop!* I order you to——.'

Lindsay interrupted harshly, 'I intend to give the convoy as much of a chance as possible. With or without your help, sir.'

Ritchie pushed between them and grasped the wrist of

a young signalman. 'Come on, boy! Somethin' to tell yer kids!'

Lindsay stooped over the gyro. 'Starboard ten. Midships. Steady.'

'Steady, sir. Course three-four-zero.'

'Full ahead both engines.'

Stannard listened to the urgent telegraphs. 'Shall I call up the chief, sir?'

'No. He knows what's happening up here.' Lindsay felt the gratings shaking and rattling under his feet. 'He *knows* all right.'

As the ship heeled slightly on to her new course Lindsay saw a dark shadow fall briefly across the screen. He looked up at the great ensign climbing the foremast and at some of the gun crews turning to watch it.

He heard Ritchie remark, 'Funny, really. Bin in the Andrew all these years an' never seen 'em 'oisted before.'

When he turned again Lindsay saw that the sea astern seemed full of ships moving away on differing bearings and angles. Once more the air cringed to the ripping passage of shells, and again they exploded close to a careering tanker.

'Aircraft, sir. Dead ahead.'

He watched the sliver of silver above the horizon as it moved calmly in the sunlight. The enemy's eye, unreachable and deadly. Reporting each fall of shot. Standing by to pursue and guide the cruiser like a pilot fish with a shark.

Too fast for Maxwell's ponderous guns. Out of range for the automatic weapons.

But as yet nobody aboard the enemy ship appeared to have noticed the *Benbecula*'s challenge. Maybe they imagined she was out of control or trying to escape in the wrong direction.

Stannard said tightly, 'Maxwell's guns will never even mark the bastard at this range.'

Lindsay did not look at him. He picked up a handset,

feeling it shaking violently as the bridge structure hummed and vibrated to Fraser's engines.

'Guns? Captain. Commence firing with the starboard battery.' He waited, shutting out Maxwell's protest. 'I know the marines can't get their guns to bear. But we *must* draw the enemy's fire from those ships. I will try to close the range as quickly as possible.'

He replaced the handset and heard the fire gong's tinny call, the immediate crash of guns as One and Three lurched inboard together.

'Short.'

He lifted his glasses in time to see the thin feathers of spray falling in direct line with the enemy's hazy outline. But she was much clearer now. Bridge upon bridge, her turrets already swinging as if to seek out this sudden impudence.

Dancy watched transfixed as the sea writhed like surf across a reef before bursting skyward on the starboard beam. He imagined he could feel the heat, taste the foul stench of those great shells.

He realised that Stannard's fingers were around his wrist, his voice intense as he whispered, 'Take this letter. Keep it for me.' He looked him in the eyes. 'Just in case, eh, chum?'

Dancy made to reply and then felt himself falling as the whole bridge shook to one terrible explosion. He felt Stannard and a signalman entangled around his legs, and even when the deafening explosion had stopped it seemed to linger in his ears like pressure under water.

He saw shocked faces, mouths calling silent orders, and the starboard door pitted with bright stars of sunlight. He pulled himself upright as his hearing returned and saw that the stars were splinter holes, and then almost vomited as he stared aghast at the bloody shape beneath them.

Lieutenant Paget had been sent to assist on the bridge and had been almost cut in half by the explosion. Yet as his hands worked like claws across his torn body his screams grew louder and louder, like those of some tortured woman.

'Starboard twenty!' Lindsay locked his arm around the voicepipes as the helm went over. 'Stand by, the port battery!' He wiped paint dust from the gyro with his elbow.

'Midships. *Steady.*'

'Steady, sir. Course zero-three-zero.'

Jolliffe had to grit his teeth as a signalman wrapped a bandage around his arm. A small splinter had laid it open after passing cleanly through the screaming lieutenant a few feet away.

The port guns hurled themselves back on their springs, their muzzles angled towards the sky in their efforts to hit the enemy.

Lindsay made himself ignore the cries and screams until they became fainter and suddenly stopped. He knew that a stretcher party had entered the bridge but did not turn his head as he concentrated every fibre of his mind on the other ship.

'Range now one-six-oh.'

He moved his glasses carefully. Eight miles separated the armoured cruiser and the garishly painted ship with the list to starboard. The enemy had got the message now all right. She had turned towards *Benbecula* using her two forward turrets alternately. The six guns fired with regular precision so that her bridge seemed to dance in the flashes as if ablaze.

When at last he glanced over his shoulder he saw that Paget's corpse had been removed. Just a brush-stroke of scarlet to show where he had been torn down.

As the gunfire mounted Lindsay changed course at irregular intervals, their progress marked by the curves in their seething wake. Starboard battery and then port. Two by two against the German's six.

Maxwell remarked over the speaker, 'She's the *Minden*.

Eight-inch guns, twelve torpedo tubes.' A brief sigh. 'Estimated speed thirty-three knots.'

Lindsay bit his lip to hide his despair. A miniature battle-cruiser as far as *Benbecula* was concerned.

A telephone buzzed, the sound muffled by explosions, the roar of fans.

'W/T have received a signal about that other raider, sir!'

Lindsay blinked as the sea beyond the bows vanished behind a towering wall of spray. He felt the hull buck to the shockwave as if she had been struck by a bomb.

'Read it!'

The man tore his eyes from an observation slit and crouched over his telephone.

'*Raider sunk. All available assistance on way to help you.*' And a few seconds later. 'Cruiser *Canopus* calling us, sir. *What is your position?*'

Lindsay saw the sea erupt again. Much closer this time. 'Tell her our position is *grim!*'

Stannard touched the man's arm. 'Here. I'll give it to W/T.'

Lindsay called, 'How are the ships, Sub?'

Dancy ran aft and peered through the *Benbecula*'s drooping plume of funnel smoke. In those seconds he saw it all. The scattered ships, so very small beneath the great ensign on the mainmast. The twisting white wake, the sea, everything.

'Troopships out of range, sir. The rest well scattered.'

'Good.'

'Range now one-five-oh.'

All four guns were firing and reloading as fast as they could move, with Maxwell's spotters yelling down bearings and deflexions with each veering change of course.

In the engine room Fraser clung to the jerking platform and watched his men swarming around the pounding machinery like filthy insects. In damage control Goss sat unmoving in his chair, facing the panel, hands folded across his stomach. Throughout the ship, above and below decks, behind watertight doors or on exposed gun platforms, every man waited for the inevitable. Meeting it in his own way.

Far astern, and spread fanlike towards the horizon, the once proud convoy had long since lost its shape and formation. The first ship to be hit had sunk, but the others which had received near misses still managed to maintain their escape, some leaving smoke-trails like scars across the sky.

Aboard the second troopship the decks and emergency stations were crammed with silent figures, mis-shapen in lifejackets as they stood in swaying lines, as they had been since the attack had begun.

A deck officer at his boat station said suddenly, 'God, look at the old girl! I'd never have believed it!' In spite of the watching soldiers he took off his cap and waved it above his head. But his voice was just a whisper as he called, 'Good luck, old lady!'

The small party of Wrens packed at the after end of the boat deck huddled even closer as the distant ship was again straddled by waterspouts.

The one named Marion slipped her arm around her friend's shoulders and said, 'Don't cry, Eve.'

She shook her head. 'I know I'm crying.' She strained her eyes to try and see the ship with the stubborn list and outdated stern. 'But I feel like cheering!'

Something like a sigh transmitted itself through the watching soldiers.

A voice called, 'She's hit!'

When the sound finally reached the scattered ships it was like a roll of thunder. Even the officers with binoculars could hardly distinguish one part of *Benbecula* from the next because of the dense smoke.

Marion tightened her grip. 'But they're still firing. How can they do it?'

The Wren called Eve did not answer. She was seeing

the little villa, the table in candlelight. And him sitting on the bed. Looking at her. Holding her.

Another set of explosions rumbled across the sea's face. More muffled now as the distance steadily mounted between them.

A man said, 'Direct hit that time. Must be.'

'Would you like to go below?' Marion stared sadly at the great spreading smokestain far astern. 'It's safe now. They made it safe.'

'No.' She shook her head. 'He'll know I'm here. I'm sure of it.'

'So am I.' Together they stayed by the rail in silence.

'Shoot!'

Maxwell was hoarse from yelling into his mouthpiece. The compartment seemed full of smoke and the din was unbearable as time and time again the ship rocked to the enemy's salvos.

'Why can't we *hit* her?' Hunter shouted through the tendrils of smoke below Maxwell's chair. 'We're down to six miles range, for Christ's sake!'

The starboard guns crashed out again and Maxwell cursed as his shells exploded into the haze.

'Up two hundred!'

He was still speaking when the next salvo straddled the ship in a vice of steel. He saw Hunter lurch in his chair to stare up at him, his expression one of horror even as the blood gushed from his mouth and his eyes lost their understanding forever.

Two of the seamen were also down, and the third was crawling up the side of Maxwell's chair holding his hip and sobbing with agony.

'First aid party to Control!' Maxwell sighed. The line had gone dead. He stood up and hung his microphone on the chair, then giving the wounded seaman a vague pat on the head climbed out into the sunlight.

Figures blundered past him in the smoke and a man yelled, 'Up forrard! Starboard side!'

Number One gun was still firing when Maxwell arrived, and he found Baldock, his elderly warrant officer, giving local orders to its crew. The other gun was in fragments, hurled inboard above a deep crater around which human remains lay scattered in bloody gruel.

Baldock shouted, 'Both quarters officers are done for on this side!'

Maxwell nodded, feeling very detached. 'You carry on here then.'

He strode to the opposite side where he found the young sub-lieutenant in charge sitting on a shell locker, an arm across his face like a man in the sun.

'All right, Cordeaux?'

The officer stared at him. 'Yes, sir.' Then he saw a spreadeagled corpse at the opposite gun. Headless, it still wore a jacket. Like his own, with a single wavy stripe.

A shell whimpered close overhead but Maxwell did not flinch. 'Luck of the draw, my boy.' He adjusted his cap. 'I'm going aft to see the bootnecks. Keep at it, eh?'

The youth watched him leave and then groped for his helmet. In front of him the gunlayer and trainer, the gloved seamen who worked the breech were all waiting as before. They were going to die. All of them. Like his friend who now lay headless and without pain.

The gunlayer said thickly, 'We're turnin' again, sir!'

Cordeaux heard himself say, 'Stand by, Number Two.' Then with the others he watched the bows start to swing to starboard.

———————

'Midships!' Lindsay had to yell to make himself heard. The enemy gunners were shooting rapidly and he knew that *Benbecula* had been badly mauled. But the noise was too great, too vast to recognise or distinguish. Time no longer meant anything, and as he conned the vibrating ship, swinging her drunkenly from bow to bow, he was conscious only of the distance which still separated the ill-matched enemies.

'Wheel's amidships, sir!' Jolliffe was clinging to the wheel, his face ashen from loss of blood.

Ritchie climbed up beside him and said, 'We'll go together, eh, mate?'

The coxswain peered at him glassily. 'Cheerful bastard!'

Ritchie looked away. Christ Almighty. The poor old sod still thinks we're going to survive!

Lindsay swung round as sunlight lanced through the smoke and he saw the spotter plane flashing down the starboard side less than half a mile distant. The little seaplane looked near and remote from the crash and scream of gunfire. Like a child's toy, her approach made soundless by the din. As it tilted slightly he saw the black cross on one stubby wing, and imagined he could see a helmeted head in the cockpit. Watching with the patient indifference of a cruising gull.

Somewhere aft an Oerlikon came to life, the bright tracer licking out through the smoke, making the seaplane veer away, startled, disturbed. Too far away for good shooting, but Lindsay could understand the Oerlikon gunner's gesture. Strapped in his harness, vulnerable and helpless as the ship came apart around him.

Stannard shouted in his ear, 'The ships'll be safe now!' It was more like a question.

Lindsay looked at him. 'There's still too much daylight left.'

He watched the seaplane turning for another run. But for the plane the ships would have been beyond reach by now. But once *Benbecula* had been destroyed the German captain would be in pursuit again. What had Maxwell said? It was hard to think. To remember. *Thirty-two knots.*

The deck canted violently and a wall of flame shot skyward from the forecastle.

Telephones buzzed and he heard men yelling over the remaining voicepipes.

'Bad fire forrard, sir! Number One gun knocked out. Mr Baldock has been killed.'

Lindsay dragged himself across the littered gratings. 'Who's still down there?'

Stannard called, 'Young Cordeaux, sir.'

Lindsay wiped his face with his hand. Just a boy. And Baldock was gone. He should have been at home with his grandchildren.

A savage explosion tore down the ship's side, filling the air with splinters and heavier fragments. Cabins and compartments, machinery and bulkheads felt it as the scything onslaught expended itself through the hull. The funnel was streaming tendrils of smoke and steam from countless holes, and Lindsay saw that the mainmast had gone completely.

Not long now. Something splashed across the nearest telegraph which still pointed to *Full Ahead,* and glancing up he saw blood dripping through a split in the deckhead. Probably Hunter's, he thought wearily.

When he dropped his eyes he saw that the chair was empty. For an instant he imagined the commodore had been cut down by a splinter.

Stannard called harshly, 'He ran below, sir! Puking like a bloody kid!'

Lindsay shrugged. It did not seem important now.

He raised his glasses again. There was so much smoke that it was hard to see beyond the bows. Smoke from guns and bursting shells. From the ship herself as she defied the efforts of hoses and inrushing water to quench the creeping fires.

The range was less than six miles. It was impossible to know how many times they had managed to hit the enemy. If at all. The cruiser was still coming for them, moving diagonally across the bow, her turrets tracking *Benbecula*'s approach with the cool efficiency of a hunter awaiting a wounded beast to be flushed from cover.

A pencil rolled across the counter beneath the screen and for a brief second he stared at it. The list which had defied owners and shipyards for years had gone at last. Goss had probably flooded the magazines nearest the fires, the weight of water bringing the old ship upright with kind of stubborn dignity. How would she appear to the enemy and the German gunnery officer? This battered, half-crippled ship, limping towards destruction but refusing to die. What would they feel? Admiration, or anger at being delayed?

He clenched his jaw again as more explosions made the hull quake. Not *delay*. The German must be held off until help arrived.

'Where's *Canopus* now?'

Stannard glanced at him. 'W/T office is badly hit, sir. Can't be sure of what's happening.'

Lindsay opened his mouth to speak and then found himself face down on the gratings with someone kicking and struggling across his spine. There was smoke and dust everywhere. He could hardly breathe and felt as if the air was being sucked out of him. Near his face small things stood out with stark clarity. Rivets, and pieces of his watch which had been torn from his wrist to shatter against the steel plates. A man's fist, and when he turned his head he saw it belonged to Jolliffe. The coxswain had been blasted from the wheel and lay with his skull crushed against the binnacle.

Lindsay lurched to his feet, spitting out dust and blown grit, searching for the remains of the bridge party. He saw Stannard on his back, blood running between his legs, and Dancy kneeling over him.

Ritchie was already dragging himself to the wheel and managed to croak, 'Got 'er, sir! Steady as she goes!' He grinned. 'To 'ell!'

Stannard opened his eyes and stared at Dancy. 'Easy,

mate. I'm all right. Christ, I can't feel much of anything!'

Two more figures entered the smoke-filled compartment, slipping on blood and broken panels, groping for handholds. Midshipman Kemp and Squire, the navigator's yeoman.

Lindsay said, 'Man those voicepipes!'

Kemp nodded wildly. 'I've sent for the first aid party, sir!'

Dancy crouched over the Australian, holding him as the deck jerked to another shellburst.

'You'll be fine. You see. We can be in England together and——'

Stannard looked past him at Lindsay and grimaced. 'The letter. See she gets it, will you? Don't want her to think I've forgotten——'

His head lolled to one side and Lindsay said, 'Leave him, Sub. He's gone.'

Dancy stood up, shaking badly. Then he said, 'I'm okay, sir.' He tried not to look at his friend on the gratings. 'Later on I'll——' He did not finish it.

The rear door rattled across the splintered gratings, and Boase with two stretcher bearers ran into the wheelhouse. Boase looked deathly pale, his steel helmet awry as he peered round at the chaos and death. A signalman had been pulped against the rear bulkhead, a messenger lay dead by his feet but totally unmarked.

In an unexplained lull of gunfire Kemp shouted wildly, 'Go on, Doc, show us what you can do!' He shook Squire's restraining hand from his arm and continued in the same broken voice, 'You're bloody good at offering advice to others!'

Boase stood with his arms at his side, his helmet jerking to the relentless vibration.

Lindsay snapped, 'Get a grip on yourselves!'

Kemp's face seemed to crumple. 'He was helping my father and that surgeon to ruin you, sir. Was giving a bad report so that you'd be finished.' Some of the fury came

back to his face as he yelled at the stricken doctor, 'You
rotten, cowardly bastard! You're like my father, so why
don't you run down and hide with him?'

Squire took Boase's wrist and pushed him towards the
grim-faced stretcher bearers. 'Get him away, chum.' He
turned his face to the screen as Boase allowed himself to
be pulled from the door. A long thread of spittle was
hanging from his chin.

A bosun's mate said, 'First lieutenant on the phone,
sir.'

Lindsay took it. 'Captain.'

Goss sounded far away. 'Forrard bulkhead is badly
cracked. If it's not properly shored the whole thing will
go.' He coughed harshly and added, 'There's a bad fire
here, too. No room for any bloody thing.'

Lindsay forced his brain to react to Goss's brief sum-
mary. It must be bad to have got him out of damage
control in person.

'You want me to reduce speed?'

Goss waited a few seconds. 'Yes. At full revs she'll go
straight to the bottom if this lot caves in.' Another pause.
'We'll need fifteen minutes. No more just yet.'

Fifteen minutes. He could as easily have asked for a
week.

Dancy was watching him, another telephone in his fist.
'It's the chief, sir. Two pumps out of action. Engine
room is flooding.'

Lindsay jumped as a shell exploded somewhere aft. He
heard heavy equipment falling between decks, the tearing scrape of splinters ricocheting from the ravaged hull.

'Yes, Chief.'

Fraser seemed very calm. 'I can still give you full speed,
sir. But I'm warning you that things could get dicey down
here.'

'Yes.' Even the one word seemed an effort. 'Get all your
spare hands out right away and put them in damage
control. It may not be long now.'

again he might want to do it. To wipe out the insult of this delay to a set plan.

Goss muttered, 'There's no time to get the lads off, sir.'

He watched the bows labouring very slowly to starboard as the port screw continued to forge ahead. He had guessed Lindsay's intention almost as soon as he had seen his face. Knew what he would do even in the face of death. He was surprised to find he could understand and meet the inevitable. Just as he had accepted the ruin of his cabin. He had been chasing after his damage control parties, plugging holes, dragging the sobbing wounded out of mangled steel, repairing obsolete pumps and trying to stay alive in a prison of screaming splinters and echoing explosions. The cabin had been torn apart by splinters, his pictures and relics just so much rubbish. Anger, despair, resentment; for those few moments he had known them all. It was like seeing his life lying there amidst the wreckage. Carefully he had unpinned the company flag from the bulkhead, and with it across one arm had crunched out of the cabin. His foot had trodden on the picture of himself and the old company chairman.

Aloud he had murmured, 'Chief was right. You *were* a mean old bastard!' Then without looking back he had got on with his work.

Goss had seen the commodore crouching on a broken locker pleading with a young S.B.A. to treat his wound. The S.B.A. had been more than occupied with other injured men and had retorted shrilly, 'You're not wounded! For God's sake leave me alone!'

No wonder the midshipman was the way he was. With a father like that it was a marvel he was still sane.

And now the noise and din were all but over. Already the sky was showing through the drifting pall of smoke, and the water between the ships was no longer churned by the racing screws. In fact, Goss decided, it looked very cool and inviting. With narrowed eyes he watched the little seaplane etched against the cruiser's side, imagining some officer giving the orders to hoist it inboard, maybe under the eyes of the captain. Like Lindsay.

Goss shook his head angrily. No, not like him.

Then he heard himself say, 'I'm ready to have a go if you are.'

Lindsay met his gaze and said quietly, 'It's only a faint chance.'

'Better'n sitting here waiting to be chopped.' Goss walked aft. 'I'll tell de Chair. Maxwell, too, if he's still in one piece.'

Lindsay touched the screen. It was warm. From sun or fires it was impossible to say.

'Stop port.'

Before the last clang of the telegraph he had the telephone against his ear.

'Chief? Listen.' Through the open shutter he saw the seaplane rising up against the grey steel. A toy.

Dancy stood by the voicepipes listening to Lindsay's even voice. Knowing he should understand as Goss had done. But the quiet, the painful heaviness of the ship beneath him, the stifling smell of death seemed to be muffling his mind like some great sodden blanket.

Lindsay joined him by the voicepipes and groped for his pipe. But it was broken, and he said, 'Disregard the telegraphs. Hold this phone, and when I give you the signal just tell the chief to let her rip.'

Before Dancy could speak he added to Ritchie, 'Just keep her head towards the enemy's quarter. I'm going to give the after guns a chance. Only one of them will bear. But if we miss I'm going to turn and try again.' He smiled grimly. *There'll be no second go. By that time we'll be heading straight down.*

Somewhere below a man cried out in agony and feet crashed through the wreckage to search for him.

Aft on the well deck Goss found Maxwell squatting on the side of a gun mounting, his cap over his eyes as he stared at the glittering water. Between the two guns the wounded lay in ragged lines, moaning or drugged in silence. A few exhausted stokers and seamen waited in little groups, and some marines were looking down at de Chair in the shadow of a shattered winch. His face was enveloped in dressings, through which the blood was already making its mark.

His hands moved slightly as Goss said, 'You are to engage with Number Six gun. Captain's orders.'

Two men carried a corpse and laid it by the rail. It was Jupp. Even with his face covered Goss would have known him anywhere. He sighed.

The marine sergeant said, 'Right, sir.'

But as he made to move Maxwell bounded over the coaming and threw himself against the big six-inch gun.

'*No!*' He thrust the gunlayer aside and crouched in his seat as he added petulantly, 'Check your sights!'

A young marine bugler at Goss's side said shakily, 'Anythin' I can do, sir?'

Goss tore his eyes from Maxwell's frenzied movements, his hands as they darted across his sighting wheels. *Gone off his head.* 'Yes. Why not.' Carefully he unfolded the company flag and added, 'Bend this on to that radio antenna. We've no ensigns and no bloody masts.' He forced a grin. 'I guess the old *Becky* would rather end her days under her right colours anyway!'

Another marine had found a telephone which was still connected with the bridge and stood outlined against the sky like an old military memorial. Only his eyes moved as he watched the little bugler clamber up to the boat deck and seconds later the big flag billow out from its improvised staff.

The sergeant rubbed his chin. 'The Jerries'll think we've gone nuts!'

Goss eyed him impassively. 'It's what I think that counts.' Then he strode forward towards the bridge.

He found Lindsay just as he had left him. 'Ready, sir.'

Lindsay nodded. 'Chief says the engine room is flooding faster. Without those two pumps——' He broke off and stiffened as the seaplane rose out of the cruiser's shadow and swung high above the rail.

He turned and looked at Squire. 'When I drop my hand.'

Squire swallowed hard and glanced quickly at Kemp. 'All right, sir?'

The boy stared at him, his stained face like a mask. But he jerked his head violently and replied, 'Fine. Thank you. Fine.'

Lindsay concentrated on the distant warship. He saw some of the *Benbecula*'s rafts drifting haphazardly in the current. They might help. The German captain would probably imagine that some of the survivors were trying to escape.

Gently. Gently. How slowly the seaplane was moving on its hoist.

He held his breath and then brought his hand down in a sharp chop.

Squire gasped, '*Now!*'

Along the remaining telephone wire and into the ear of the motionless marine. Across the littered deck and pitiful wounded, past Jupp's still body and the blinded marine lieutenant to where Maxwell was poised over his sight like an athlete awaiting the starter's pistol.

Just one more agonising split second while the cruiser's upper deck swam in the crosswires like something seen through a rain-washed window. Maxwell had to drag his mind from the others around the gun, the trainer on the opposite side, the men waiting with the next shell and the one to follow it. This was the moment. *His moment.*

'*Shoot!*'

He felt the sight-pad crash against his eye, the staggering lurch of the gun recoiling inboard, and was almost deafened by the explosion. He had forgotten his ear plugs, but ignored the stabbing pain as he watched the shell explode directly on target.

There was one blinding flash, and where the seaplane had been hanging above its mounting there was a swirling plume of brown smoke. It was followed instantly by another, darker glare, the flames spreading and dancing even as the breech was jerked open and the next shell rammed home.

On the bridge Lindsay had to hold down the sudden surge of excitement. The seaplane had been blasted to fragments and the whole section below it was ablaze with aero fuel.

He shouted, 'Now, Sub!'

The gun crashed out again and drowned Dancy's voice, but far below them Fraser had heard, and as he threw himself on his throttles the screws came alive, churning the sea into a great welter of spray, pushing the old ship forward again, shaking her until it seemed she would come apart.

The sudden fire on the cruiser's deck had done its work. The torpedo crews were being driven back while their comrades with hoses and extinguishers rushed into the attack.

Maxwell's next shell was short, the explosion hurling the spray high above the enemy's side, the flames dancing through the glittering curtain like bright gems.

Lindsay pounded the screen with his fist. The revolutions were speeding up, and already the cruiser had dropped away on the port bow. But not fast enough, and already he could see her forward turret turning in a violent angle to try and find the hulk which had returned to life.

On his steel seat beside the one remaining gun which would bear, Maxwell took a deep breath. He ignored the bright flashes as the enemy fired, did not even see where the shells went as he concentrated on the column of smoke just forward of the cruiser's mainmast. Just the one set of tubes would do. Six torpedoes in a neat row, all set and ready to deal *Benbecula* a death blow. Except that

now they were unmanned, abandoned because of his first
shot. In spite of the tension he could feel the grin spreading right across his face. If Decia could see him now. If
only——

　'Shoot!'

The two ships fired almost together, the shockwaves
rolling and intermingling until the noise was beyond
endurance.

Maxwell did not see what happened next. His gun, the
crew and most of the marines at the opposite mounting
were blasted to oblivion by the explosion. In seconds the
well deck and poop were ablaze from end to end, the
scorching heat starting other outbreaks below and as
high as the lifeboats.

Lindsay felt the shock like a blow to his own body,
knew that the ship had done her best and could fight no
more. So great was the onslaught of metal that he was
totally unprepared for the wall of fire which shot skywards above the billowing smoke. Then as a down-eddy
parted the huge pall he saw the cruiser's raked stem
moving steadily into the sunlight, the forward turret still
trained towards him, her grey side reflecting the bright
wash of her bow wave.

The first cries of despair gave way to a lingering sigh as
the cruiser emerged fully from the smoke. Her bow wave
was already dropping, and as the smoke swept clear of
the upper deck Lindsay saw that her stern was awash.
The torpedoes must have blasted her wide open with
greater effect than if they had been fired into the hull. It
was impossible.

Lindsay felt Dancy gripping his shoulders and Ritchie
croaking in either joy or disbelief. Throughout the battered hull men were cheering and embracing each other,
and even some of the wounded shouted up at the sky,
crazed by the din but aware that despite all they had
endured they were still alive.

The cruiser was slewing round, her bilge rising to blot

out the chaos and torment on her decks as she started to roll over. More explosions echoed across the water, and even at such a distance Lindsay heard heavy machinery and weapons tearing adrift to add to the horror below decks.

There was no hope of saving any lives. *Benbecula* was devoid of boats, and most of her rafts were either lost or destroyed in the savage battle.

Steam rose high above the cruiser's bows as very slowly they lifted from the water, a black arrowhead against the horizon and clear sky. Then she dived, the turbulence and spreading oil-slick marking her last moment of life.

Dancy asked thickly, 'Shall I get our people off, sir?' He seemed stunned. 'We could build rafts.'

Fraser, without orders, had already cut the speed to dead slow, and Lindsay guessed that many of his men would have thought their end had come when Maxwell's gun had been smashed, to say nothing of the German's violent ending.

'Yes.' He touched his arm. 'And thank you.'

But Dancy did not move. He looked as if he was doubting his own reason. 'Sir! Listen!'

Feebly at first. Little more than a murmur above the hiss of flames, the occasional crackle of bursting ammunition, Lindsay heard the sounds of Fraser's pumps.

He took the handset. 'Chief?'

Fraser was chuckling. 'The old cow! I told you, didn't I?' He sounded near to tears. 'Bloody old cow judged it right to the last bloody moment——' His voice broke completely.

Lindsay said quietly, 'If we can get these fires out and hold the intake we might keep her afloat.' He lowered the handset very gently.

Then he walked out on to the remaining wing and gripped the screen with both hands. Slowly he looked down and along his command. The death and the terrible damage, even the leaping fires on the well deck could not disguise the old ship's familiar outline. Hoses which had been lying smouldering came to life again, and more men emerged like rats from their holes to control them. He saw a stoker, his head bandaged, carrying the ship's cat and standing it down by a cup full of water. Then he stood back to watch the cat's reactions, as if witnessing the greatest miracle in the world.

Three hours later, as the ship struggled forward at a dead slow speed, her hull cloaked in smoke and escaping steam, a lookout reported another vessel on the horizon. It was the *Canopus,* hurrying back in the vain hope of saving some of the convoy.

The sight of the riddled, fire-blackened ship with some unfamiliar flag still flapping jauntily above the destruction made her captain believe the worst had happened.

Ritchie lowered his telescope and reported, ''E wants to know, sir. *What ship are you?*'

Goss, bare-headed and black with filth from top to toe, was sipping tea at the rear of the bridge. He looked at Lindsay's tired face and winked.

Then he said to Ritchie, 'Make to *Canopus. This is H.M.S.* Benbecula.' He turned away in case Lindsay should see his eyes. *'The finest ship in the company.'*